THE EDGE OF THE
SHADOWS

ELIZABETH GEORGE

THE EDGE OF THE SHADOWS

VIKING

An Imprint of Penguin Group (USA)

VIKING
Published by the Penguin Group
Penguin Group (USA) LLC
375 Hudson Street
New York, New York 10014

USA * Canada * UK * Ireland * Australia
New Zealand * India * South Africa * China

penguin.com
A Penguin Random House Company

First published in the United States of America by Viking,
an imprint of Penguin Group (USA) LLC, 2015

LIBRARY OF CONGRESS CATALOGING-IN-PUBLICATION DATA
George, Elizabeth, date.
The edge of the shadows / by Elizabeth George.
pages cm
Summary: Someone is setting fires on Whidbey Island and Becca King
and her friends may know who the arsonist is.
ISBN 978-0-670-01298-5 (hardcover)
[1. Arson—Fiction. 2. Psychic ability—Fiction. 3. Secrets—Fiction.
4. Abandoned children—Fiction. 5. Whidbey Island (Wash.)—Fiction.] I. Title.
PZ7.G29315Ef 2015
[Fic]—dc23
2014009139

Printed in USA

10 9 8 7 6 5 4 3 2 1

In memory of Iver Olson,
island man through and through

What seest thou else
In the dark backward and abysm of time?

—WILLIAM SHAKESPEARE,
THE TEMPEST

THE EDGE OF THE
SHADOWS

PART I

Island County Fairgrounds

ONE

The third fire happened at Island County Fairgrounds in August, and it was the first one to get serious attention. The other two weren't big enough. One was set in a trash container outside the convenience store at a forested place called Bailey's Corner, which was more or less in the middle of nowhere, so no one thought much about it. Some dumb practical joke with a sparkler after the Fourth of July, right? Then, when the second flamed up along the main highway, right at the edge of a struggling little farmers' market, pretty much everyone decided that *that* one took off because an idiot had thrown a lit cigarette from his car window right in the middle of the driest season of the year.

But the third fire was different. Not only because it happened at the fairgrounds, which were just yards away from the middle school and less than a quarter mile from the village of Langley, but also because the flames began during the county fair when hundreds of people were milling around a midway.

A girl called Becca King was among them, along with her boyfriend and her best girl friend: Derric Mathieson and Jenn McDaniels. The three were a study in contrasts, with Becca light-haired, trim from months of bicycle riding, and wearing heavy-rimmed glasses and enough makeup to suggest she was auditioning for membership in the reincarnation of the rock band Kiss; Derric tall, well-built, shaven-headed, African, and gorgeous; and Jenn all sinew and attitude, hair cut like a boy's and tan from a summer of intense soccer practice. These three were sitting in the bleachers set back from an outdoor stage upon which a group called the Time Benders was about to begin performing.

It was Saturday night, the night that drew the most people to the fairgrounds because it was also the night when the entertainment was, as Jenn put it, "marginally less suicide-inducing than the other days." Those other days the entertainment consisted of tap dancers, yodelers, magicians, fiddlers, and a one-man band. On Saturday night an Elvis impersonator and the Time Benders comprised what went for the highlight of the fair.

For Becca King, with a lifetime spent in San Diego and just short of one year in the Puget Sound area, the fair was like everything else she'd discovered on Whidbey Island: something in miniature. The barn-red buildings were standard stuff, but their size was minuscule compared to the vast buildings she was used to at the Del Mar racetrack where the San Diego County Fair took place. This held true for the stables for horses, sheep, cattle, alpacas, and goats. It was doubly true for the performance ring where the dogs were shown and the horses were ridden. The food, however, was the same as it was at county fairs everywhere, and as the Time Benders readied themselves to take the stage after Elvis's final bow during which he nearly lost his wig, Becca and Derric and Jenn were chowing down on funnel cake and kettle corn.

The crowd, who turned up to watch the Time Benders every single year, was gearing up its excitement level for the performance. It didn't matter that the act would be the same as last August and the August before that and the one before that. The Time Benders were a real crowd pleaser in a place where the nearest mall was a ferry ride away and first-run movies were virtually unheard of. So a singing group who performed rock 'n' roll through the ages by altering their wigs and their costumes and re-enacting the greatest hits of the 1950s onwards was akin to a mystical appearance by Kurt Cobain, especially if you had any imagination.

Jenn was grousing. Watching the Time Benders was bad enough, she was saying. Watching the Time Benders at the same time as being a third wheel on "the Derric-and-Becca looove bike" was even worse.

Becca smiled and ignored her. Jenn loved to grouse. She said, "So who are these guys, anyway?" in reference to the Time Benders as she dipped into the kettle corn and leaned comfortably against Derric's arm.

"God. Who d'you *think*?" was Jenn's unhelpful reply. "Y'know how other county fairs have shows where has-been performers give their last gasp before they finally hang it up and retire? Well, what we got is *unknown* performers re-enacting the performances of has-been performers. Welcome to Whidbey. And would you *stop* feeling her up, Derric?" she said to their companion.

"Holding her hand isn't feeling her up," was the boy's easy reply. "Now if you want to see some serious feeling up . . . ?" He leered at Becca. She laughed and gave him a playful shove.

"I *hate* this, you know," Jenn told her friend. She was returning to the previous third-wheel-on-the-looove-bike topic. "I shoulda stayed home."

"Lots of things come in threes," Becca said.

"Like what?"

"Well . . . Tricycle wheels."

"Triplets," Derric said.

"Those three-wheel baby buggies for joggers who need to take their kids with them," Becca added.

"Birds have three toes," Derric pointed out. Then, "Don't they?" he said to Becca.

"Great." Jenn reached for more funnel cake and jammed it into her mouth. "I'm a bird toe. Lemme send that out on Twitter."

Which would, of course, be the last thing Jenn McDaniels could have done, since among them Derric was the only one who possessed anything remotely close to technological. Jenn had neither computer nor iPhone nor iPad nor laptop, because her family was too poor for anything more than a third-hand color television the size of a Jeep, practically given away by the thrift store in town. As for Becca . . . Well, there were a lot of reasons why Becca remained at a distance from technology and all of them had to do with keeping a profile so low that it was invisible.

The Time Benders came forth at this point, climbing onto the stage past amplifiers that looked like bank vaults. Their wigs, pegged pants, white socks, and poodle skirts indicated that—

just like last year—they'd be starting with the fifties. The Time Benders *never* worked in reverse.

The crowd cheered as the show began, lit by the rest of the midway with its games of chance and its creaking thrill rides. The best of the fifties blasted forth at maximum volume. Over the noise, Jenn shouted at Becca, "Hey, you probably won't need that thing."

That thing was a hearing device that looked like an iPod in possession of a single ear bud. It was called an AUD box and, despite what Jenn thought, Becca didn't use it to help with her hearing. At least not in the way Jenn thought she used it. Jenn and everyone else believed that the AUD box helped Becca understand what was being said to her by blocking out nearby noises that her brain wouldn't automatically block: like the noise from other tables that you might hear in a restaurant but normally be able to ignore when someone was talking to you. That was what Becca let people believe about the AUD box because it did, actually, block out *some* noise. Only, the noise it blocked was the noise inside the heads of the people who surrounded her. Without the AUD box she was bombarded by everyone's thoughts, and while hearing people's thoughts *could* have its benefits, most of the time Becca couldn't tell who was thinking what. So since childhood, the AUD box was what she wore to deal with her "auditory processing problem," as her mom had taught her to call it. Thankfully, no one questioned why the AUD box's loud static helped her in understanding who was speaking. More important, no one knew that without it, she was one step away from reading their minds.

Becca said, "Yeah, I'll turn it down," and she pretended to do so. Up on the stage, the Time Benders were rocking and rolling through "Rock Around the Clock" while on either side of the stage, some of the older audience members had begun to dance in keeping with the music's era.

That was when the first gust of smoke belched across the heads of the crowd. At first, it seemed logical that the smoke would be coming from the line of food booths, all doing brisk sales of everything from buffalo burgers to curly fries. Because of this, the Time Benders audience didn't take much note. But when there was a pause in the music and the Time Benders were getting ready for the sixties with a change of costumes and wigs, the sirens hooting from the road just beyond the fairgrounds' perimeter indicated something serious was going on.

The smell of smoke got heavier. People started to move. A murmur became a cry and then a shout. Just at the moment that panic was about to set in, the regular MC for the show took the stage and announced that "a small fire" had broken out on the far side of the fairgrounds, but there was nothing to worry about as the fire department was there and "as far as we know, all animals are safe."

The last part was a serious mistake. "All animals" meant everything from ducks to the 4-H steer lovingly brought up by hand and worth a significant amount of money to the child who would sell it at the end of the fair. In between ducks and steers were fancy chickens, fiber-producing alpacas, award-winning cats, sheep worth their weight in wool, and an entire stable filled with horses. Among the audience for the Time Benders were the owners of these animals, and they began pushing their way in the direction of the buildings in which all the animals were housed.

In short order, a melee ensued. Derric grabbed Becca and Becca grabbed Jenn, and they clung to each other as the crowd surged out of the midway and past the barn where the crafts were displayed. They burst out behind it into an open area that looked onto the show ring and to the buildings beyond.

At the far side of the show ring, the stables were safe. The fire, everyone saw at once, was opposite them on the side of the show ring that was nearer the road into town. But this was where the dogs, cats, chickens, ducks, and rabbits had been snoozing in three ramshackle sheds that flaked old white paint onto very dry hay. The farthest of these sheds was up in flames. Fire licked up the walls and engulfed the roof.

The fact that the fire department was directly across the street from the fairgrounds had the effect of getting manpower to the flames in fairly short order. But the building was old, the weather had been bone dry for nine weeks—almost unheard of in the Pacific Northwest—and there were hay bales along the north side of the structure. So the best efforts of the fire department were directed toward keeping the fire away from the *other* buildings while letting the one that was burning burn to the ground.

This wasn't a popular move. There were chickens and rabbits inside. There were dozens of 4-Hers who wanted to save those animals, and the news that someone had apparently released them at some time during the fire only made the onlookers crazed to get to them before they all got trampled. Soon enough there were too many fire chiefs and too few onlookers and enough chaos to make Derric, Jenn, and Becca head for the safety of the stables some distance away.

"Someone's going to get hurt," Becca said.

"It ain't going to be one of us," Derric told her. "Come on, over here." He took her hand and Jenn's, and together they made their way beyond the stables to where a woods grew up the side of a hill to a neighborhood tucked back into the trees. From this spot they could watch the action and listen to the chaos, and while they did this, Becca removed the ear bud from her ear and wiped her hot face.

As always, she heard the thoughts of her companions, Jenn's profane as usual, Derric's mild. But among Jenn's colorful cursing and Derric's wondering about the safety of the little kids whose parents were trying to keep them away from the fire, Becca heard quite clearly, *Come on, come on . . . get it why don't you?* as if it was spoken right next to her.

She swung around, but it was dark on all sides, with the great fir trees looming above them and the cedars leaning heavy branches down toward the ground. At her movement, Derric looked at her and said, "What?" and then shifted his gaze into the trees as well.

"Is someone there?" Jenn asked them both.

"Becca?" Derric said.

Out of here before those kids . . . was enough to give Becca the answer to those questions.

TWO

Hayley Cartwright looked around for her sister Brooke, who'd claimed that she was leaving the family's booth at Bayview Farmers' Market just long enough to do her business in the rest room. Total lie. She'd been gone thirty minutes, leaving Hayley and her mom to run the booth all by themselves when it was, minimally, a three-person job. Brooke did the bagging and the weighing of veggies, Hayley wrapped the flowers and boxed the jewelry, and their mom took the money and made change. But with Brooke gone, Hayley was left dancing from one side of the booth to the other and trying to keep her eye on everything but especially upon the jewelry, which was fashioned from sea glass, difficult to make, and her main source of personal income.

Not that people actually shoplifted from the Cartwrights, at least not people who knew them. Taking even a dime from the Cartwrights was close to the same as emptying the family's pitiful bank account, and everyone on the south end of Whidbey Island who knew the family also knew that. So most of the time people lined up patiently to pay for the flowers and veggies that the Cartwrights grew at Smugglers Cove Farm and Flowers. They chatted to each other in the warm early September sun, petted the myriad dogs who accompanied the market-goers among the colorful stalls, and listened to the music weekly supplied by one or another of the local marimba bands.

This day, though, a girl unknown to Hayley had been pawing through her necklaces, bracelets, earrings, and hair pieces for at least ten minutes. She'd also been trying them on. She was very pretty, with a swimmer's broad shoulders and shapely arms and legs that were on full display beneath her tank top and shorts. She wore her hair in an odd Cleopatra style—if Cleopatra had been extremely blonde—and her bangs dipped almost into her eyes, which were so cornflower blue that only colored contact lenses could have achieved the hue.

She saw Hayley watching her as she was putting a third necklace around her ivory-skinned throat. She'd already donned four of the bracelets, and she was reaching for one of the more complicated pairs of earrings quite as if there was nothing strange about decking herself out like a jewelry tree.

Seeing Hayley observing her, she said, "I c'n *never* decide a single thing when I'm by myself. It's absolute murder if I'm trying on clothes. My grandam is here somewhere"—here she looked around the crowded market distractedly—"and I guess I could ask her, but she's got the most *wretched* taste, which you'd more or less have to expect from someone who carves up trees for a living. *Not* that there's anything wrong with carving up trees, mind you. I'm Isis Martin, by the way. Egyptian. I mean the *name* is, not me. Isis was the goddess of something. I can *never* remember what but I truly hope she was the goddess of hot desire because

I've got a seriously delicious boyfriend back home. *Any*way, what're these made of and which do you think looks best on me?" During all this, she'd put on a fourth necklace, odd because she was already wearing her own, a gold chain with elongated links that disappeared into her tank top and must have cost a fortune. She was peering into the stand-up mirror that Hayley provided, and she paused in her inspection of Hayley's necklaces to put on lipstick that she excavated from a basket-weave purse.

Hayley liked the purse but was afraid to say this, for fear of setting the girl off again. So she said, "It's sea glass. I make them. I mean, I make all the jewelry."

"*Sea* glass?" Isis said. "You mean 'sea' like from the ocean? So do you get it from . . . like . . . I mean, are you a diver? I tried to learn to dive. My boyfriend before my current boyfriend? He and his family were into diving in a major way and they took me to the tip of Baja for spring vacation one time? They tried to help me learn to dive, which was a total joke because I am so, like, totally claustrophobic."

"I find it on the beach," Hayley told her when Isis took a breath. She looked over the other girl's head to see if Brooke was anywhere in view. No such luck, which meant she had to get back to bagging and weighing. She glanced over her shoulder. The line of patient shoppers was extending and her mom was beginning to bag and weigh. She looked harried. She cast Hayley a supplicating glance.

"On the beach? Way cool," Isis said. She reached for a fifth necklace. "I love the beach. Maybe I could go with you sometime? I've got a car. Well, my parents had to give me *something* to come up here, after all. I wouldn't be any good at looking for sea glass, though. I'm blind as a whatever without my contacts and I generally don't wear them at the beach because of the sand and how it can blow into your eyes if you know what I mean."

"It's over past Port Townsend," Hayley told her. "The time to find it is winter, after a storm, more or less."

"What's past Port Townsend?" Isis peered at her reflection, then laughed. "Oh, I bet you mean the beach where you get the glass. God, I'm a flake. I c'n never remember what I'm talking about. Where's Port Townsend? Should I go there? D'they have any decent shops?" She handed Hayley a sixth necklace, one that she hadn't tried on. She picked one of the bracelets already on her arm along with a pair of earrings she'd not inspected and a barrette that matched nothing at all. "I think this'll do it. Did you tell me your name? I can't remember. I am *such* a ditz."

She began disentangling the rest of the necklaces she'd donned as Hayley said that her name was Hayley Cartwright and, yes, Port Townsend had some really cool shops, if you could afford them. Hayley herself couldn't, but she didn't add that. She just wrote up the sale of the necklace, bracelet, earrings, and barrette, and she helped the other girl remove from herself everything else she'd donned. She told Isis the price, and the girl dug a thick wallet out of her woven purse. It was crammed with all sorts of things: newspaper clippings, folded notes with scribbles all over them, coffee reward cards, pictures, and cash. A great deal of cash. Isis pulled out a wad of it and distractedly handed it over.

She said, "Could you . . . ? Just take what you need." Then she laughed. "I mean take what I owe you!" And she fixed the new necklace around her neck and scooped up some of her hair behind the barrette. She did this latter action with a lot of skill. She might be bird-brained, Hayley thought, but when it came to her appearance, she knew what she was doing.

Hayley counted out the appropriate amount of money and handed the rest back. Isis was admiring the barrette in her hair. The sea glass around her neck, as it turned out, was an inspired choice. It exactly matched the color of her eyes.

Isis took the rest of the money and crammed it into her wallet. She had a section of pictures inside this that was three fingers thick. She said, "Oh, you've *got* to look at him," and flipped open to the first. "*Is* he totally hot or what?" She showed Hayley a picture of a boy whose hair stood out from his head in a way that made him look like a cartoon character recently electrocuted.

"Uh . . . he's . . . ?" Absolutely nothing came into Hayley's mind.

Isis laughed in delight. "He doesn't really *look* like this. He just did that to piss his parents off." She shoved the wallet back into her purse. "Hey, d'you want to get a lump-whatever? I can't remember what it's called but there's a lady over there selling them and they look totally like something I shouldn't be eating in a million years. Which, of course, is why I fully intend to buy two or three. *What* are they called?"

Hayley laughed in spite of herself. There was something beguiling about Isis Martin. She said, "Lumpia?"

"That's it. I can tell I need you to help me navigate these

mysterious island waters. I've been here since June. Did I tell you that? Me and my brother . . ." She rolled her eyes expressively, and at first Hayley thought this was in reference to her brother until Isis made the correction with, "My brother and *I*. Grandam goes berserk when I say 'me' as the subject of a sentence, so sometimes I do it on purpose. She thinks I don't know it should be *I*. Well, I'm a congenital idiot, but I *do* know *me* is an objective case pronoun, for heaven's sake. So d'you want a lumpia or two or six?"

Hayley said, "Sorry. I can't leave . . ." She waved around her. "The booth, you know. My sister's supposed to be here, but she's disappeared."

"Siblings. What a trial. Well, maybe another time?"

"You go on, Hayley." It was Hayley's mom speaking. She'd been on the edge of the conversation all along. "I can handle things here. Brooke'll be back."

"It's okay. I don't—"

"You go, sweetheart," her mom said firmly.

Hayley knew what that meant. Here was an opportunity to be "just a kid," and her mom wanted her to have that opportunity.

BROOKE FINALLY SHOWED up when they were disassembling their booth and getting ready to drop the unsold veggies at the nearby food bank, a feature of the island that most visitors to Whidbey didn't know about. Tourists to the island came to soak up the atmosphere: the razor-edged bluffs rising up from beaches studded with sea shells and jumbled with driftwood, the pristine waters where a crab pot brought up fifteen

Dungeness within two hours, the deep forests with shadowy hiking trails, the picturesque villages with their clapboard, seaside charm. As to the homeless population and the needy families . . . To visitors, they remained unseen. But people who lived on the island didn't have to look far to find people in need, because many of them were neighbors, and when Brooke groused about how "totally dumb it is to be giving our food away when we should be selling it somewhere and making some money," their mom cast a look into the rearview mirror and said to her, "There are actually people worse off than we are, sweetheart."

Brooke's response of "Yeah? *Name* 'em," was out of character. But a lot of her remarks had been out of character lately. Their mom called this a stage that Brooke was going through. "The middle school years. You remember," she said to Hayley as if Hayley had also been a Mouth with Attitude when she'd been thirteen. Hayley, on the other hand, pretty much believed that Brooke's attitude had nothing to do with middle school at all. It had, instead, everything to do with the Big Topic that no one in their family would ever discuss.

Their dad, Bill Cartwright, was falling apart. It was a slow process that had begun in his ankles and had now worked its way up his legs so that they didn't do what his brain asked them to do any longer. Time was when their dad would have been with them at the farmers' market, working the booth. Time was when he would have shared the labor at Smugglers Cove Farm and Flowers, too. Hayley's mom would have been raising the horses that she no longer raised and growing the flowers while he raised goats and worked in the huge vegetable beds as the girls took care of the chickens. But that time had passed, and now what went on at the farm was whatever the women could manage, minus the littlest Cartwright woman, Cassidy, who was only competent at collecting eggs. What couldn't be managed by the women simply no longer occurred on the farm, but no one mentioned anything about this or anything about doing *something* that might help them out. It was, Hayley thought, an extremely dishonest way to live.

They were heading north on the highway on the route home, when Julie Cartwright asked Hayley about "the chatty girl who bought the jewelry." Who was she? A day-tripper from over town? A vacationer? Someone from school? A new girl friend, perhaps? She didn't look familiar.

Hayley heard the hopefulness in her mom's voice. It had two prongs. The first was to change the topic of conversation in order to alter Brooke's mood. The second was to direct Hayley toward getting a normal life. She told her mom that the girl was Isis Martin—

"What kind of weirdo name is that?" Brooke demanded.

—and she'd been on the island since June. She lived with her grandmother and her brother and . . . Hayley realized that despite all of Isis's chatting, those were actually the only two facts she knew aside from her having a boyfriend. Isis had bought four lumpias and, cleverly, had decided that she could only eat two of the pastry-like stuffed delicacies. She'd handed the other two over to Hayley, saying, "Do me a fave and snarf these, okay." It had been breezily done. Hayley had found herself liking the girl for doing it.

After eating and when Hayley had said she needed to get back to the market stall, Isis had scribbled down her smart phone number and handed it over. She'd said, "Hey, maybe me and you c'n be friends. Call me. Or text me. Or I'll call you. We can hang. I mean, if you c'n put up with me." She'd excavated in her straw purse for an enormous pair of sunglasses with rhinestones along the ear pieces, saying, "Aren't these the trippiest ever? I got them in Portland. Hey, give me *your* number, too. I mean, if I haven't totally put you off with my babbling. It's ADD. If I take my meds, I'm more or less focused, but when I forget . . . ? I'm a verbal shotgun."

Hayley had given the other girl her phone number, although her cell phone was as basic as they got, so there would be no texting. She also told her the family phone number to which Isis had said, "Wow, a land line!" as if having this was akin to having kerosene lamps.

"Anyway," Hayley said to her mother, "she was sort of ditzy, but in a good way."

"How lovely," Julie Cartwright said.

THREE

When they arrived at Smugglers Cove Farm and Flowers and trundled up the long driveway toward the collection of barn-red buildings, they found Hayley's dad on the front porch along with Cassidy. They were on the swing looking out at the farmyard. Cassidy had a death grip on one of the barn kittens. Bill Cartwright had a similar grip on the chain from which the swing did its swinging.

He struggled to his feet, and everyone did their usual thing of pretending not to notice. This was becoming progressively more difficult since he had begun using a walker. He worked his way to the edge of the porch as his women clambered out of the car. He called out, "Hayley, would you get that young man out of the vegetables? He wouldn't take no for an answer," which made Hayley look in the direction of the vegetable beds stretching out gloriously with the beginning of the autumn harvest.

She saw Seth Darrow's 1965 VW before she saw him. The restored bug was parked to one side of the barn. Seth himself was crouched at the near end of the sweet potatoes. He had to be dealing with the watering system, she decided. They'd been having trouble with it all summer and he must have stopped by the farm, had a conversation with her dad during which the watering system had come up. It would be just like Seth to set off to deal with it.

"I tried to tell him I'd be getting to it tomorrow," Hayley's dad said.

"Oh, you know Seth," her mom said airily. "Brooke, go ask him if he'd like a tuna sandwich please."

"No way. *I* want a tuna sandwich." Brooke tramped up the front walk, blasted across the porch, said, "You know, you're going to kill that stupid cat," to Cassidy, and entered the house with a bang of the screened door.

Julie Cartwright said with a sigh, "I thought if she saw the dog, it might distract her." *Away from food* was what she didn't add. Brooke was putting on weight—far more than was natural—but it was another subject they didn't talk about.

The dog in question was Seth's golden Lab, Gus. He was snuffling around the squash.

"I'll go," Hayley said.

"Tell Seth I'll have a sandwich ready for him," her mom told her, which was code for "let him finish what he's doing." This surprised Hayley. They generally didn't accept help from outsiders and, despite Seth being her former boyfriend, he wasn't a member of the family.

Deep into his repair of the watering system, Seth hadn't heard the rest of the Cartwright family arrive. He didn't even look up till Gus came loping along the pathway between the beds once

Hayley entered through the tall gate in the fence that protected the area from the island's marauding deer and rabbits.

He was dressed for work, Hayley saw. Instead of his usual garb of baggy jeans, sandals, socks, T-shirt, and black fedora, he wore his carpenter's overalls, heavy work boots, and a baseball cap from which his long hair pony-tailed out of the one-size-fits-all opening at the back. Had he not been garbed like this, Hayley would have known he'd just come from work anyway, for his ear gauges were flecked with sawdust and his hands were newly nicked from construction.

He said, "Hey," and paused to raise the baseball cap slightly. "Came by to give you some news and your dad said . . ." He nodded to the work he was doing.

She said, "Thanks, Seth. Mom's making you a sandwich for afterwards." She bent to pet Gus, who was bumping around her legs to get her attention.

"Coolness," he replied. Then, "Gus, cut that out."

"It's okay," Hayley said. "And . . . thanks, Seth. He can't really get out here. I mean, he *can* but not to do anything hard."

"Yeah. I could tell." He squinted up at her, seemed to evaluate what might happen if he said what he wanted to say next, then said it anyway. "I wish you guys could catch a break, Hayl."

"You and me both." She watched him for a minute. He was working with wrenches, pliers, and wires, and she had no clue what he was doing. She said, "So why'd you stop by? You said you had news?"

"I passed the GED."

She felt her face brighten. "That's *great*, Seth."

"My tutor's totally relieved, let me tell you. The whole math thing was touch-and-go. And she still thinks I can't read worth beans, which is more or less true. But my mom'll be doing a naked celebration dance in the moonlight. I'm gonna sell tickets. That's not the best part, though."

"No?" It seemed to Hayley that there couldn't be better news. Seth had dropped out of school in his junior year, had avoided studying for the GED throughout what would have been his senior year. Only in the last six months had he pulled himself together. The fact that he'd surmounted both his fear of failure and his catalogue of learning disabilities to take the equivalency test and pass would be a very big deal to his entire family.

Seth said, "Triple Threat is playing at Djangofest this year." He was trying to sound casual about it, but Triple Threat was his gypsy jazz trio, Djangofest was a five-day international festival celebrating the intricate music of French guitarist Django Reinhardt, and to be invited to play at one of the many venues around the village of Langley during the festival had long been one of Seth Darrow's dreams.

Hayley said, "Oh my God! Seth, that's amazing! Have you told your parents? Your grandpa? Where're you going to be playing?"

"My mom and dad know but that's all. Aside from the guys in the trio, 'course. We didn't score a good time—Wednesday afternoon at five at the high school and who's gonna show up then but—"

"*I'm* showing up. And so's your family. And so's Becca and Jenn and—"

"Well, yeah. S'pose." He sounded indifferent, but Hayley could tell he was pleased. He said, "Anyways . . . This is looking pretty good now." He was referring to the repair he'd made. He heaved himself to his feet and brushed off his hands. This put him eye-to-eye with Hayley, as well as closer than she was comfortable with. They were friends now, not what they'd once been. It had to be this way, and while she knew that he knew it, she sometimes felt from him a longing for more.

She took a step back. She covered this by looking toward the house where her dad was at the edge of the porch watching them. She frowned at his posture, at how he had to cling to the walker to stay upright now, at how he heaved one leg and then another just to move a few feet.

Seth seemed to read what she was thinking. He said, "Not good, huh?"

"How can I?"

"What?"

She gestured to the farm around them: the huge fields, the paddocks empty of horses and goats, the long low chicken barn down by the road. "You know," she told him.

He followed her arm's semicircle, gazing at the sights and considering what they actually meant. He said, "You decide where you're applying yet, Hayley?"

Hayley knew where he was heading. But she had no intention of applying for universities. No one in her family knew about this. Neither did Seth. She wanted to keep things that way until it was too late to do anything about it.

She said, "I'm pretty close," which was a total lie.

"Where's it gonna be?"

"Don't know. Like I said, I'm close but not there yet."

But Seth was no fool. He heard something in her voice and he said, "Don't play that game, Hayl. You got the smarts. So use 'em."

She looked at him. "It's not as easy as that and you know it, Seth Darrow."

FOUR

Seth ended up going to his grandfather's house for two reasons, only one of them having to do with his good news. The other one was inspired by eating the tuna sandwich he'd been promised by Mrs. Cartwright. He devoured it while sitting at the family's kitchen table. There, he'd caught sight of the local newspaper discarded on a chair.

He never read the *South Whidbey Record*, because his reading skills were the pits. He wouldn't have thought to read the paper then in the kitchen except for the fact that a picture on the front page attracted his attention. It wasn't the most recent copy of the *Record*, he saw, because the story was about the fire at the fairgrounds. The fire had happened in the middle of August, and since it was now the beginning of September, he had to wonder why the paper was still lying around. As he was attempting to answer that question, he saw the picture.

Becca King was in it. So were Derric Mathieson and Jenn McDaniels. They weren't especially close to the camera, but they were completely visible in the crowd because they were moving *away* from the fire and everyone else was moving toward it.

Becca was especially visible. Wondering if she knew about this was what took Seth to his grandfather's place.

Becca had lived there since the previous November. First she'd been hiding out in a sturdy, snug tree house built by Seth far back in Ralph Darrow's forest. Now she was in Ralph's house itself, trading housework and cooking for a room. She was also charged with keeping an eye on Ralph Darrow's diet, which veered in the direction of Whidbey Island vanilla ice cream topped with whipped cream, nuts, and chocolate sauce for dinner if someone didn't pull the plug on that one.

Seth's grandfather lived on a huge spread of land off a road called Newman. You rumbled up a hill to get to it. Then you parked in an open space just below the crest, followed a path around the hilltop itself, and finally descended a trail toward a meadow. It was in front of you, then: a huge garden featuring rhododendrons the size of military tanks along with various dogwoods and a collection of specimen trees. The shingled house sat on one edge of this garden, with Ralph Darrow's forest backing up to it.

At this time of year, like everyone else who had a garden, Ralph was in his. As Seth followed Gus down the trail that led to it, Ralph paused in his raking of the long-spent rhododendron blooms, pushed his wide-brimmed hat to the back of his head, and massaged the small of his back. He was seventy-three and when he looked around the property, Seth could see from his expression exactly what he'd seen from Hayley's expression when she looked around her family's farm. *How the heck am I going to keep up with this place?* The only difference was that Hayley didn't need to keep up with her family's place. She only believed she did.

Ralph caught sight of Seth's dog first and then he saw Seth. He said, "Seth James Darrow. What brings you here this fine afternoon, favorite male grandson? And keep that damn dog out of my herbaceous border before I go after him with a shovel."

Seth said, "Gus, *no.* Here, boy," and he went to the porch where, inside a wooden chest, Ralph kept a supply of beef bones for the Lab. He rooted one out and Gus was happy to gnaw it. This left Seth free to talk to his grandfather.

Becca King, he discovered, was not at home. She'd gone off with Derric that morning and they'd not returned. She'd been charged with buying vegetables, eggs, cheese, late peaches suitable for jam making, and bread at the farmers' market, Ralph told him. From there . . . who knew? Derric had been making cow eyes at her and she'd been doing much the same to him, so they could be anywhere at this point. "Such," Ralph concluded, "are the ways of deep and abiding adolescent love."

"Hey, you met Gram when you were fifteen," Seth pointed out.

"I b'lieve that makes me an authority." His grandfather nodded at a second rake that leaned next to the handrail of the porch steps. "Join me, grandson. What d'you want with Miss Becca?"

Seth couldn't tell Ralph about the picture in the *Record* because of where it would lead if he gave his grandfather the information. So instead he said, "Wanted to tell her something. You, too." He went on to share his good news: the GED and the invitation to play at Djangofest.

His grandfather smiled and tossed down his rake. "We are due," he said, "for a celebration."

Knowing that this would involve Whidbey Island vanilla and the trimmings, Seth sought a way to head his grandfather in another direction. That proved unnecessary as it happened because a shout of hello from the top of the hill and a "You! Ralph Darrow!" announced a visitor.

SETH LOOKED IN that direction to see they were being joined by a woman in overalls with disarranged gray hair somewhat tamed by a sagging French beret. Behind her trudged a boy. He looked either bored or ticked off but it was hard to tell which. His hair was dyed black, and his face bore bizarre mutton chop sideburns like something out of another century. He was tall and gangly with shoes the size of hockey stick blades and jeans so baggy the crotch was nearly at his knees. He wore all black. He was carrying a skateboard under his arm and gazing around as if to say there sure as heck wasn't going to be a place to ride it *here.*

Seth didn't know either one of these people, but he figured his grandfather did. Ralph Darrow knew everyone on the south end of the island, especially old-timers, and this lady looked like an ancient hippie who'd come to Whidbey sometime in the late 1960s, probably wearing what she wore now: sandals, a tie-dyed T-shirt, jeans, and obviously handmade socks. When she reached them, she smiled, and said, "There you are, Ralph Darrow." Seth saw that some of her teeth were missing.

She was, he discovered, one Nancy Howard, and the boy with

her was her grandson Aidan Martin. He'd been on the island for a while, he'd moved up here from Palo Alto, California, with his sister, he'd done "jack-darn-all to meet anyone and I mean even at the high school and don't lie about that, young man," so his grandmother Nancy had "hogtied him into the passenger seat of the camper" in order to do something about that. She'd heard Ralph Darrow had a young thing boarding with him, and Aidan here was going to meet that person. Nancy glanced at Seth expectantly, as if he were the young person in mind. She looked pretty doubtful about that. Seth was too old for high school and he looked it.

"That's Becca King," he told her.

"She's out and about," Ralph said to Nancy Howard. He extended his hand to the boy and said to him, "Ralph Darrow, Mr. Aidan Martin. This young man is my grandson Seth: builder, carpenter, and first-rate musician."

Aidan looked largely indifferent to the introduction, but this wasn't something to deter his grandmother. She said, "You boys go get to know each other. Shoo, now. I want to ask Ralph about his rhodies." She turned her back to do this, drawing Ralph over to his prized New Zealand specimen.

That left Seth to deal with Aidan. He called to Gus and said to the boy, "Show you the pond if you want to see it." Aidan shrugged. He shifted his skateboard to a spot beneath his other arm, and he shuffled along in Seth's wake as Gus came loping from the porch, with the bone in his jaws like a duck he'd retrieved.

The pond was old but not a natural feature of the land. Ralph had backhoed it into existence at about the time he'd also constructed the house. It lay immensely in a dip of the land, with lawn growing up to its edge on its near side and a deep green conifer forest leaping up on its far side. Trails led off into this forest, one of them to Seth's tree house, others making long loops elsewhere. Gus headed for the tree house trail, but Seth called him back by means of a ball. Next to gnawing bones, Gus loved chasing balls. It was something to do, Seth figured, while he showed the kid the pond.

Aidan, he saw, was not impressed. He stared at the pond with dull eyes and said, "Yeah. Cool." That was the limit, a real conversation ender.

Seth said, "You a boarder, huh?" in reference to the skateboard. "Snowboard, too?"

"Hell yeah," Aidan said. "You board around here? Does anyone?" He asked the question like a kid who thought Whidbey Islanders were living in a period prior to the existence of skateboards. He didn't seem to expect an answer, either. He dug deep in the pocket of his jeans and brought out a pack of Camels. He said, "You got a match?" which Seth didn't. When Seth told him this, the other boy swore and shoved the cigarettes back where he'd found them. He set his skateboard on the ground and sat on it, staring moodily at the surface of the pond. He said, "Christ, what a pit. How d'you stand living here? She doesn't even have *Internet*. You got Internet?"

Seth joined him on the ground. Gus ran over with the ball in his mouth. Seth kept throwing it to keep the dog entertained.

He said, "Here?" and gestured around the place. "Nope. Grand doesn't believe in the Internet."

"So how the hell d'you . . . I dunno . . . How do you talk to your friends?"

"I don't live here," he said. "I got Internet where I live. They got it in the Commons, if you need it. South Whidbey Commons. In Langley. You been there? It's where kids hang out."

Aidan scoffed. "She wants to handpick who I meet," he said. "So if it's kids in general and she don't know them or at least know *about* them . . . ? No way. I might get in 'trouble.'" He sketched quotation marks in the air. He snorted. "She makes me run to the beach and back twice a day," he went on. "Isis goes, too, because she's my frigging guard, you know? She rides a bike so I can't ditch her." He smiled to himself. "I ditch her anyway. Into the forest and what's she gonna do? Ride after me? Not hardly. She might break a fingernail. She doesn't want to tail me anyway. She hates it here as much as I do."

"Who's Isis?" Seth asked, as there wasn't much else Aidan was giving him to go on conversation-wise, aside from a general air of unpleasantness that Seth decided it was best to ignore.

"Sister," he said. "Prison guard. Whatever." He looked around, his expression indifferent. "What do people freaking *do* around here?"

Seth thought about telling him that the island was pretty much like everywhere else. Whatever you wanted, you could find if you looked hard enough as long as it wasn't a fast-food chain, of which there were none except a single Dairy Queen on the highway coming up from the ferry dock. But he figured Aidan would work things out for himself.

A question gave Seth the information that the boy was enrolled at South Whidbey High School, so Seth knew that all Aidan had to do was ask around for what he wanted. The school was small, but it was like any other high school in the country: There were your dopers, your athletes, your heavy scholars, your techies, your various kinds of artists, your losers, your dweebs. There was booze aplenty. There were drugs of all kinds. There were also parties that featured both. Since the kid didn't look like a narc and he didn't act like one, he'd do okay if he lost the attitude.

Seth said, "Kids do regular stuff, I guess," to which Aidan replied with a guffaw, "I bet."

Seth felt himself bristle at this implied judgment of a place he'd lived all his life. He started to say something but Aidan interrupted.

"Sorry, man," he said quickly as if he realized how he'd been acting. "I c'n be a real asshole sometimes."

FIVE

Becca and Derric shared a long kiss. His hands in her hair, she lost the ear piece of the AUD box and caught *not much longer really want . . .* from him. This matched what she was thinking, so she wasn't surprised. But she also wasn't ready.

It was simple for her. When she gave herself to someone, it was going to be Derric. But she wasn't going to do it in the back of a car, on someone's sofa, out in the woods, or half-freezing to death at night on a Whidbey beach. She wanted . . . well, what *did* she want? She hadn't yet worked that one out. All she knew was that the time wasn't right.

They'd done the shopping at the farmers' market. They'd gone from there deep into the woods to a place called Mukilteo Coffee, where roasting beans filled the air with the scent of burnt toast and where a few dollars bought them a lunch to share, out on the back deck looking into the forest. Now they were sitting inside Derric's Forester, in Ralph Darrow's parking area. Two other vehicles were next to them: Seth's restored Bug and a completely un-restored, rusty, rickety-looking VW camper van. The presence of these vehicles was what put the brakes on their make-out session. Getting caught with Derric's hand up her T-shirt . . . That would be too embarrassing.

Becca said, "Got to go," against Derric's mouth and she caressed his perfect, shaven skull.

"See you tomorrow, then?"

"Only if you're up for homework."

"You're killing me," he told her, but he said it with his high-wattage smile.

A final long kiss and she scooped up the shopping bags from the back seat. She watched until his car disappeared back down the hill. Then she turned and headed for Ralph Darrow's house.

She saw the driver of the VW camper straight off when she peaked the hill. An older lady stood in the garden below, talking to Ralph, and when Ralph saw Becca, he gave a yell for Seth. She saw Seth then, a few moments later. He came from the pond with Gus bounding around him, in the company of a strange-looking boy. It was the sight of this boy that encouraged Becca to leave the AUD box's ear piece out of her ear. He was projecting an attitude that made a chill run down her spine.

She got nothing in the way of thoughts from anyone as she descended. It wasn't until she was closer that the first of the scattered mental murmurings filtered through the air. And then it was *damn not what I thought*, which she assumed had to come from the older woman, because she was openly assessing Becca, like someone who's looking at a horse to buy. After that came *saved by the Becca bell . . . could be something good for the boy but God knows that nothing's helped to make him . . . I can't forget*

to tell her about the picture . . . she keeps her wits about her with
that young man . . . would have been way cool . . . what's with
the face paint . . . some half-Goth skank . . . what you'd expect . . .
frigging dumb idiot sometimes . . . besides making him run to the
damn beach.

It was a lot to deal with all at once, but the length of the frac-
tured thoughts pleased Becca mightily. What floated to her was
still broken up by what other people would have called static,
but to Becca it marked the progress she'd made in hearing more
and more of what she'd learned to think of as whispers. In her
earliest years the thoughts of others had come to her only as
simple words. Then they'd advanced to phrases whose ownership she couldn't identify. Now she was beginning to snatch full
sentences out of the air. She wasn't always sure who was thinking
what, but often the context was enough to tell her.

She hadn't got far in blocking out the whispers without aid
of the AUD box, though. That was the ultimate goal: to hear the
complete thoughts of whoever was nearby, but *only* when she
wanted to hear them.

Ralph called out, "Meet our guests, Miss Becca," and gestured
to her to join them. He introduced her and added, "They're your
fellow Californians. Least, Aidan here is."

Becca said hi and indicated the bags she was carrying. "Want
to come inside?" she said to Aidan. "Got to put these away and
find a recipe that disguises brown rice, or Mr. Whidbey Vanilla
here won't eat it."

"We c'n eat the ice cream for him," Seth told her, taking two of
the shopping bags from her.

"Break your arm first," was Ralph's reply to this. But he walked Nancy Howard to the far side of the garden, where they continued their discussion about his plants.

More time for them to get to know each other put Becca in the picture of what she was intended to do. She shot Aidan a smile, but he didn't return it. Whatever, she thought, and she led the way to the house.

Aidan asked her where she was from as soon as they got inside. She stalled on answering because where *he* was from was pretty crucial. The story she'd been telling for a year was that she was from San Luis Obispo, California, and if he was from anywhere near that town, she would be in trouble when it came to questions of "Hey, do you know . . . ?" which she wouldn't be able to answer. So she put away veggies and fruit and eggs and she pretended she didn't hear him long enough to hear Seth ask him where *he* was from. Palo Alto, it turned out. She had about two hundred miles to play with, then.

She turned from the counter. Aidan was at the table. A candle sat at its center and he was playing with it. He lit it from a book of matches that lay nearby. He stared at the flame.

"San Luis Obispo," she told him.

"Cow town," he said. "I went there once. What a dump."

Becca and Seth exchanged a look. "Oh well," she said.

Aidan seemed with it enough to catch her tone because he said immediately, "Sorry," and looked around the kitchen as if seeking inspiration for what to say next. He settled on, "So what d'you guys do around here?" *Out of here on the next ferry* indicated his own wishes in the matter.

"Aside from school?" Becca said. "Football games. Dances. Parties. Hanging out. Kids go over to the mall in Lynnwood. What else?" She asked this of Seth.

"Biking, hiking, kayaking, camping, hunting, clamming, fishing, crabbing."

Aidan looked back at the burning candle and said, "Fab," as if what he meant was "Shoot me first." Then he said, "What's the dope scene?"

"What you want is here. I guess," Becca said.

"Like . . . where?"

"Don't know."

"Don't *know*?" His question was backed by *Everyone knows so she's holding back Goth skanks always put it out there so what's with—*

Becca wanted to tell him she wasn't a Goth, heavy makeup or not. Instead she said pleasantly, "Nope. Don't know. I don't do drugs."

"Oh yeah right. Bet you get 'good grades' in school, too." He made sarcastic air quotes on the *good grades* part. *Hate straight skanks what a freaking poser* went with this.

Seth said a little hotly, "You know, Becca is a—"

"S'okay, Seth," Becca interrupted. "I like good grades. Don't you?"

"Good grades don't like me," was Aidan's reply. He turned the candle, using his palms as if this would warm them. "I get distracted too easy. That's why I'm here. To get *un*-distracted."

Seth joined him at the table once he'd helped Becca put away her shopping. She went for a recipe book, brought it to the table, and started leafing through it. She said, "You been at school this year? I don't think I've seen you. You a junior? Senior?"

It turned out he was both of the above and neither of the above. He was taking classes and waiting for his credits to arrive from his previous school so South Whidbey could decide what the heck he was. His sister was a senior and he should be the same, but who the hell knew what was going to count up here.

"You got a twin?" Seth asked.

"Irish," Aidan said. "I'm the mistake."

"Huh?"

Aidan flipped the book of matches in his fingers. "It's a lame expression for having two kids within a year of each other. My sister's only ten months older'n me."

"Wow. Fast work," was Seth's remark.

"Bad work." Aidan leaned back in his chair, yawned, and scrubbed his hands in his too-black hair. His hands, Becca saw, both bore tattoos: a devil on one and an angel on the other. His fingernails were painted black. It came to her that Aidan Martin looked like someone in disguise. Just like her, he was running from something. She couldn't help wondering what it was.

SIX

After Aidan and his grandmother departed, Becca set about dinner, which Seth shared with them. He didn't seem to want to leave, but he also seemed to want Ralph to go to bed or go *somewhere*, which wasn't like him. She figured something was up.

When he showed Becca the front page of the *Record* that he'd scored from the Cartwrights' kitchen, she understood why he'd waited till Ralph took himself upstairs to bed. There she was, clearly in focus in a photograph, and Becca King clearly in focus on the front page of a paper was not a good thing. Seth was the only person who knew this. She was on the run. Her mom was on the run. The person they were running from had turned up once on Whidbey Island in a failed search for them both.

At the time Jeff Corrie had been looking for his wife and step-daughter: Laurel Armstrong and her fatso kid called Hannah. But Laurel was now in hiding in British Columbia and Hannah Armstrong had long ago morphed into Becca King, who hadn't been remotely fat in a year. Only the fake glasses, heavy eye makeup, dark lipstick, and black clothing remained of the girl she'd become on the run from Jeff Corrie.

Still, Becca logged on to the Internet at least once a week to see if her stepfather was making any progress in trying to find her. He wanted her back because he wanted her talent; he wanted to use that talent for his money schemes. But he had serious problems of his own now: Not only had his wife and stepdaughter disappeared, but so had his investment firm partner, Connor, and the investigation into these disappearances had been going on for a good six months. That would be keeping him occupied in San Diego. But it wouldn't necessarily be keeping him away from the Internet, where googling Whidbey Island could lead to the *Record* could lead to looking at the *Record* could lead to Jeff Corrie laying his eyes on the *Record*'s front page. Where this could lead was to Jeff Corrie showing up again, only this time with a picture of Becca King and questions for the sheriff's department.

That couldn't happen, and Becca knew it. So did Seth.

Becca breathed out two words. "Oh no."

Seth said, "I figured you needed to know. Lookit the caption, Beck."

She read it. The photographer hadn't asked their names. Because so few people lived on the south end of the island, most people knew everyone. So when she saw, "Derric Mathieson, Becca King, and Jennifer McDaniels show good sense in running away from the fire," she assumed someone at the paper had supplied their identities. Derric's would be simple, mostly because, born in Uganda and adopted into an island family, he was the only African boy at South Whidbey High School. As for Becca and Jenn, Becca was Derric's girlfriend and Jenn's family had been on the island for generations. It wasn't rocket science to work out who they were. She studied the picture to see if she resembled her old self in any way.

She didn't think so. But she couldn't be sure. She needed an old photo of herself to compare.

BECCA WENT TO South Whidbey Commons after school. It sat on Second Street in the center of Langley, a community of some one thousand inhabitants whose colorful cottages were built high above the waters of Saratoga Passage. Some of these cottages had gone through conversions, becoming everything from boutiques to the local museum. One of the conversions was the Commons, painted mustard yellow with a late summer garden still blooming out front and a bookstore, art gallery, and coffee house within. At the very back was a room used for games and general hanging out. The computers were here. When Becca arrived, Seth was there too.

For some reason, so was Aidan Martin, along with about a dozen other kids and the other two members of Seth's trio, Triple Threat. The musicians were playing an uplifting piece of gypsy jazz on mandolin, bass, and guitar. Their listeners had their gazes fixed on the amazing dexterity of the musicians' fingers.

This didn't apply to Aidan Martin. His skateboard was lying upside down across his lap and his fingers were spinning its wheels. He looked sardonically amused by everything around him. Midway through the piece, he set his skateboard on the

floor and reached for a deck of cards on a nearby table. He manu-
factured an exaggerated yawn and began to shuffle.

What a dolt, Becca thought.

With everyone focused on Triple Threat, the computers
were free. Becca logged on. She made short work of googling
Jeff Corrie's name. He wasn't in the papers as often as he'd been
initially, when Becca and her mom had taken flight from him.
Then, he'd been dealing with multiple investigations. His plate
crammed full of legal troubles, he'd done the smart thing. He'd
lawyered up. From that point on, his lawyer had done the talking
for him. But what the lawyer said was what the paper pointed
out: There was no evidence of foul play associated with the disappearances of these people. There was only a trail of money that
filtered to Connor and Jeff instead of to their investors and even
that, the lawyer said, had been orchestrated by Connor to make
Mr. Corrie look guilty. So why wasn't the investigation centered
on *him*? San Diego was a stone's throw from the Mexican border and maybe the cops should be calling their cohorts there
because it made a lot more sense to figure Connor West had
slipped across that border than to believe Jeff Corrie had somehow done away with him without leaving a scrap of evidence,
didn't it?

Jeff was playing it smart, Becca concluded. Unless they found
Connor's body or she herself stepped up and explained how she
helped the two men get money by listening to the investors'
thoughts to pinpoint their weaknesses, Jeff would stay a very free
man. He'd also stay a man who was looking for her, and Becca's

blood went to ice cubes when she followed a link to an edito-
rial in the San Diego paper and her gaze fell on the two words
Whidbey Island.

"Corrie has said from the first that his wife's cell phone
was found on Whidbey Island," she read, "and since the sheriff's department in Coupeville, Washington, confirms this, one
has to ask whether the man's claims of persecution constitute
yet another example of how things tend to go wrong in the San
Diego police department."

God, Becca thought, he was getting the newspaper on his
side! Soon enough he'd be back up here searching for her.

She went back in time on the Web. She needed the first serious
mention of the disappearance of Laurel and Hannah Armstrong.
That was the one that featured their photos, her own being her
fifth grade school picture.

When she found it, she took the front page of the *Record* from
her backpack. She glanced around the room, satisfied to see that
everyone was enthralled with Seth's music. Quickly, then, she
unfolded the page and compared herself now at nearly sixteen
to the person she'd been in San Diego at the time of the picture:
eleven years old and forty pounds overweight.

That much excess weight on a frame of less than five feet four
inches made a lot of difference, and she could see that difference
in the picture. Then, she'd had chipmunk cheeks and a gruesome
double chin, and if the picture had been full length, she'd have
been also looking at thunder thighs and a butt the size of West
Virginia. She'd had long hair, bangs, and braces. All that was

gone now, most especially the weight. When she held the newspaper picture up to the screen to compare it to the other photo, it didn't seem to her that there was any resemblance.

Or maybe that was wishful thinking, she decided. What she really needed was to have Seth look at it because—

"What're you doing?"

She swung around to see that Aidan Martin had come to the computers. He was standing directly to her left with a very fine view of the monitor. He was looking at it and looking at the front page of the paper and Becca knew that her only choice was to knock the ear bud of the AUD box away from her ear in the hope that she could pick up something from him.

Could not go for a guy with ear gauges no way . . . very hot . . . in tune because if it is I can join them . . . not about me at least thank God . . . sweet looking butt on that babe . . . don't study for that physics quiz I am in such trouble . . . totally hot . . . not pregnant I swear . . . I hate her guts to the max she is such a liar . . . oh right she's so not cheerleading material . . . dinner tonight because it is not my turn and I'm not going to make it no matter what she . . .

Useless, Becca thought. There were too many people. It was the curse of not being able to control *anything*, not the thoughts of others and not her life. She forced a laugh, said, "Whoops," and put the ear bud back in. She said, "Helps me hear. It's a brain thing. Sorry. What did you say?"

He pulled out the chair next to hers. "Just asked what you were doing." He nodded again at the computer. He looked friendly enough but there was something weird about the way he watched her, with his upper lip jerking in a spasmodic tic.

She said, "An assignment. Art class. Facial structures. I'm hopeless." She went back to the main Google page, folded the newspaper paper, shoved this into her backpack, and said, "The only thing I'm worse at is math. What about you?"

"I suck at everything." He spun the back wheels of his skateboard, and added, "'Cept this and a snowboard." He watched the wheels spin. Becca gave a little sigh of relief at the change of subject, but just when she thought she was safe, Aidan said abruptly, "So what about facial structures?"

"Like I said. Just an assignment."

His blue eyes fixed on her disconcertingly. "What kind of assignment?"

"Some kid in class asked . . ." She thought furiously. She didn't even take an art class. What the heck had she been *thinking* with this whole lie? She laughed self-consciously. "I can't even remember *what* he asked. I was probably doodling or something. Anyway, we ended with this lame assignment about using a picture of ourselves and finding a picture of someone else and what*ever.*"

"Cripes. How can you stand school?" The question seemed casual, but he was still entirely focused on her, zeroing in, as if he had laser eyes into her brain.

She said, "I might as well like it since I'm stuck with it."

He didn't reply to this. Instead, he looked away from her, back at the musicians, and he nodded at Seth. He said, "I heard he dropped out," and he made it sound like an idea that he himself wanted to grab onto.

"He took the GED," Becca told him. "He works for a contrac-
tor now. He's an amazing carpenter. *And* he's got his music,
which he writes, and—"

"You sound worried," Aidan said, turning back to her. "What's
that about?"

Becca halted abruptly and felt herself getting hot from her
neck to the top of her head.

He said, "Oh. Are you and him . . . ?" with a tilt of his head in
Seth's direction.

"No!" But her protest was way too loud. He was throwing her
off. He was like someone in a boxing ring, jumping all around
her and confusing her with punches. She said in a completely
lame fashion, "I have a boyfriend."

Aidan smirked. "Did you think I was coming on to you or
something?"

"No! I mean . . . You said me and Seth . . ." *God*, she thought,
what was going on?

As if on cue, Seth fingered expertly into a solo, and they
turned to listen appreciatively. It was part of the performance
of gypsy jazz. One musician at a time took a solo turn. At the
end of Seth's the audience applauded. But before the mandolin
player launched into his solo, a young man rose from the audience and raised a fiddle to his shoulder. He began to play as if
he'd rehearsed with the trio a thousand times.

Becca had never seen the young man before, but she knew
that the musicians for the upcoming gypsy jazz festival were
arriving in Langley, and this was probably one of them. Unlike
Seth and the others, he completely looked the part of gypsy jazz

musician. He had mounds of black hair tied back with a leather cord, he was swarthy-skinned, his eyes were so dark they were practically the color of coal, and he had gold earrings in his ears and four wedding bands on a chain around his neck. And he played the fiddle like someone who'd been doing it from the crib.

Best of all, he took Aidan's attention away from Becca. He demanded everyone's gaze, but especially the girls'. He radiated health, vitality, and sex. And when he smiled at the applause that followed his solo, Becca figured it was swoon-time for every girl in the room.

For her, it was time to disappear before Aidan Martin wanted to ask her any more questions. She waited long enough to hear Seth yelling, "Get over here, man!" to the fiddler, who moved through the people in order to join the trio. At that, she faded out of the room.

It was only when she was outside the Commons that she remembered she hadn't shut down the computer.

SEVEN

Hayley Cartwright got called into the office of Tatiana Primavera just before lunch. Tatiana Primavera was the former Sharon Prochaska, who had changed her name long ago in the fashion of others newly born to the more offbeat aspects of island life. She was also the A through L counselor at South Whidbey High School, and one of her responsibilities was shepherding the A through L seniors through the process of applying to colleges and universities. Hayley was not on track with this. She wasn't even exploring the possibilities.

That she didn't intend to apply for higher education was what she was trying to make clear to Ms. Primavera when the lunch bell rang. Luckily that bell saved Hayley from a full-blown argument with the counselor. When Ms. Primavera dismissed her with "We're not finished talking about this, young lady," and "I'll see you later," Hayley made a swift escape to the New Commons, where the student body of the high school ate together.

The New Commons was sparsely populated on this day. Since the weather was still good, most everyone was eating outside. The lowlifes and the dopers were thus not represented at any of the tables. Neither were the athletes and their hangers-on, who were out in the sun, engaged in flexing their muscles and having their muscles admired.

Hayley was about to join her regular tablemates when someone locked onto her arm. "God," Isis Martin said. "Why aren't you in my French class? Where are we eating?" She didn't wait for an answer as Hayley led her to the table she generally shared with her friends. They were already there, but Isis didn't stop talking long enough to be introduced. "It was just the worst," she said to Hayley. "You know Mr. Longhorn, right? Except, of course, we have to call him *Monsieur*, although if *anyone* could possibly look less like a *monsieur*, I don't know who it is. So he's ragging on me after class. Why? Well, excuse me but I got my period. And pardon me, but he wants me to explain why I missed the tardy bell? *And* I'm supposed to explain in *French*? Anyway, he's all, 'Mademoiselle, *vous êtes* whatever,' and I'm *trying* to explain and he apparently decides he's humiliated me enough for one day and he lets me go. Or at least I think he's letting me go 'cause I start to walk off and he yells *arretez*, which I totally think he's yelling at someone else. So I say, '*What* for God's sake?' and he writes me up for my attitude. Do you believe that?"

At last, Isis took a breath and a bite of her sandwich. Hayley heard Jenn McDaniels snicker. Jenn and Becca King were at the table with them, and Becca's eyes—fixed on Isis—had become the size of silver dollars. As Hayley looked in her direction, she saw Becca remove the ear bud of her hearing thingy. Jenn said to Becca meaningfully, "I'd turn it *up*, not off," and Hayley shot her a look to say *Hey, cool it*. So Isis was a talker, Hayley thought. She's my *friend* and you accept your friends for who they are.

Becca's gaze shifted to Hayley. Her lips curved in a small smile. It wasn't a mean smile, though. Instead, it looked encouraging. Or encouraged. Or *something* because Hayley didn't know for sure. And Isis was winding up again. She'd swallowed her bite of sandwich, taken a gulp of non-fat milk, and was about to say something when Derric Mathieson dropped onto one of the two empty chairs at their table.

He said, "Hey. Happenin'?" to all of them, but aside from Isis, everyone knew he was talking to Becca.

Isis looked stunned into silence. It had to do with Derric, Hayley figured. He was tall, dark, and exotic. He wore a T-shirt that showed he was seriously built: pecs, lats, biceps, triceps, whatever, and Isis's pretty face said *yum-yum-yum*. Clarification as to Derric's status was going to have to be made clear.

In any other situation, the girlfriend of the Spectacular Male Specimen would have done the clarifying. But Becca, Hayley had discovered, wasn't the kind of girl who went out of her way to tell anyone anything.

As things turned out, Derric did the clarifying, although not directly. He helped himself to a bite of Becca's sandwich, said, "PBJ *again*? Babe, when're you going to di-ver-si-fy?" and then went on with, "I blew it with the ride thing. I've got a Big Brother deal with Josh after school, which I totally forgot. I *could* call his grandma and say something came up, but I hate to do that." He wove his fingers with hers as he spoke.

Hayley saw Isis take this in with a glance from Derric to Becca. She also saw Jenn McDaniels hide her smile. Isis said brightly, "I got a car. I c'n drive someone somewhere if anyone needs a ride."

Derric looked at Isis. His slight frown said that he didn't know who she was. Isis seemed to understand his expression. She extended her hand across the table. "Sorry. Isis Martin," she said. "From Palo Alto? Down by Stanford University? Me and my brother live with Nancy Howard. The chain-saw artist? She's our grandam. My brother . . ." Isis half stood and gazed around the New Commons. She seemed to find the person she was looking for because she pointed, "He's over there. God, *why* is Aidan sitting by himself? Hey, will you guys excuse me?" And off she went, weaving her way through the tables to the far side of the commons and then along the wall to a spot near the door. There, at the farthest possible corner, a boy sat hunched over a table with his back to the rest of the kids.

"Whoa." Derric was the one to speak.

"She's new." Hayley realized how lame that sounded. "I met her at Bayview. At the Saturday market. We got to talking and—"

"'*We* got to talking'?" Jenn cut in. "Don't you mean '*she* got to talking'? 'Cause, does she actually *listen* once in a while?"

"Don't sugarcoat things, Jenn," Derric said with a smile.

"I think she's just nervous," Hayley said. "You know: meeting a whole bunch of new people? Having to move to a new school in your senior year? I sort of get the impression she had a lot of stuff going on in her old school."

"Like what?" Jenn said with a laugh. "I mean, besides her mouth."

"A great boyfriend. I think she misses him a lot. They text and stuff all the time. She told me they Skype every morning. But it's not really the same and I think—"

"Hayley, you are way too nice," Jenn interrupted.

Becca said quietly, "She's just scared." She gazed toward Isis and her brother. Isis had pulled her brother to his feet and was leading him toward the doors.

AS IT HAPPENED, while Hayley was saved by the lunch bell, it was a brief salvation. Ms. Primavera caught her on her way to class. The counselor was coming down the stairs with a cardboard box in her arms, and Hayley was heading up to class. Ms. Primavera said, "Hold it right there, Hayley Cartwright," and Hayley figured she was in for more lecturing. But instead, Tatiana Primavera lowered her box to a stair step and began shifting around its contents.

They were college catalogues, Hayley saw. The counselor pulled out one for Reed. "In Portland," she told Hayley. "Not too far, not too close. Not too big, not too small. It's private but there're scholarships and grants available. They've also got work study and their science department is just what you're looking for. Now, you take this and we'll talk next week. Meantime, target nine other schools. By the beginning of November you're going to be applying."

Hayley reasoned that there was no point to arguing at the moment. So she took the book about Reed and then another that Ms. Primavera was inspired to hand over. This one was for Brown University. Rhode Island? Hayley thought. Uh . . . right.

She went on her way to class and found Isis waiting for her just outside the door. Her face was deadly stricken. For a moment Hayley thought something terrible had happened.

Isis took her arm. "I'm hopeless. I'm sorry about how I went on at lunch." She looked around the corridor. It was emptying quickly. Class was about to begin. "I wish I could tell you more, Hayley. It's just that my family's had a bunch of troubles and I get all anxious about it and really that's all I c'n say. I *know* you have to get to class and so do I and I just want to say thank you for being my friend. Please say I didn't totally blow it forever at lunch."

Hayley couldn't help smiling at the other girl's sincerity. "No way did you blow it," she told her.

EIGHT

Becca was at her locker at the end of the school day when Hayley Cartwright offered her a ride. Hayley could drop her off anywhere she wanted to go, she said, and she added mentally *Because I want to know if what she said means something*, which was startling in its clarity. Becca had removed the AUD box's ear bud as she often did at the end of the day, in order to practice "those mental on/off buttons, sweet girl," as her grandmother would have said. The point was to allow the whispers to fade, to make them white noise the way the wind outside your house is white noise. Most of the time, Becca was a total failure at this, and the sounds of everyone's whispers swarmed her.

But through those whispers, Hayley's thoughts had come at Becca so clearly that she knew her face registered her surprise. Hayley said in response, "What?"

Becca said, "It's only that I was just thinking about how I was going to get where I'm going and it's like you read my mind."

"I wish," Hayley said. "So. You want a ride?"

"Sure. Yeah." Becca found the books she needed for her homework, and she went on to say that she'd appreciate the ride because she hadn't brought her bike with her as she normally did when Derric had something going on. So, yeah, she was basically stuck.

They were on their way to the Cartwrights' pickup when they were waylaid by Isis Martin. She wasn't alone but rather had her brother with her. She called out, "Here he is, you guys. I want you to meet Aidan."

Becca hadn't talked to the boy since she'd run into him at South Whidbey Commons. They shared no classes, and at lunch he avoided everyone, always sitting alone in the corner, either at a table or on the floor. Now, his sister was pulling him across the parking lot. His face was expressionless. He looked like someone who was wearing a mask.

Less than pathetic appeared to come from one of the two Martins. *Dyed hair how weird* seemed to come from Hayley, as did *hoping to replace Derric . . . no way . . .* which was the limit of what Becca caught since Isis went into conversation full steam ahead.

She said, "*Here* he is," as they all met near Hayley's truck. "This is Aidan. We're heading up to that hardware place. What's the name, Aidan? I have a list somewhere. Oh, here it is. It was in my statistics book. God, I hate statistics. So we're going to the hardware store and I've got a slew of things Nancy wants. She's our grandam. Nancy Howard. I mentioned her before, right? She hates being called Grandma so we have to call her by her first name. Lord, Aidan, *say* something. Don't be so clueless."

That San Diego Internet story . . . because if she's looking made skeleton fingers dance down Becca's spine. Her gaze went to Aidan as if dragged there by a magnetic force. He was watching her with enigmatic eyes. How, she wondered, had he managed to perfect having no expression? She strained to hear something more from his whispers but Isis's thought nonsense was fracturing the inside of Becca's skull. *Please she's got to . . . the only way . . . being friends oh right like that's possible . . . should never have even thought about . . . he liked it and loves me and even now there's no one who can make him . . . I was always there . . . more important than anything* and on and on it went. Becca fumbled for her ear bud, turned up the AUD box volume, and felt soothed by the resulting blast of static.

She said, "Your grandma introduced us."

"She *did*? Nancy? When? Oh my God! Were *you* the girl he met when he met Seth Darrow? Weird! 'Cause he said . . . well, it doesn't matter. But Aidan, why didn't you tell me you already knew Becca?"

"You didn't give me a chance." When Aidan finally spoke, it was something of a surprise. There was a weariness underlying the boredom in his voice. He said, "Let's go," and without a glance in Hayley's direction, he turned and went off the way they'd come.

Isis said, "God, he's *so* rude."

Then she was gone, off across the parking lot again. Hayley looked at Becca and shrugged. But even with the AUD box plugged in to block the whispers, Becca could tell something was going on with Hayley. She wondered if it was the mention of

Seth, Hayley's former boyfriend. Hayley clarified matters when they got into the old pickup with SMUGGLERS COVE FARM AND FLOWERS fading on the doors.

They were on the curving road that would take them from the high school into Langley village. The woods grew right to the edges of this road, and Hayley was taking care to watch for deer. She said to Becca without looking in her direction, "It's got to be Aidan. I was wondering about it, but it's got to be."

"What?"

"You know how you said she was scared?"

"I did?"

"Yeah. You said Isis was scared. *Is* scared. You said that at lunch."

Becca looked down at her backpack on the floor of the pickup. She said cautiously, "Oh. I forgot," and prepared herself to keep from revealing any of the whispers she'd sorted through as Isis was babbling away in the New Commons.

"I wanted to ask you about why you said it. At first I thought, Well, Isis wants us to like her and she's scared that we won't," Hayley said. "Only, even at lunch it seemed like something more. And I was going to ask you if you thought the same thing. Like . . . if you thought something going on with her because of what you said. Only . . . now I think it's Aidan."

Becca glanced at Hayley. She drove with hands at two o'clock and ten o'clock, and she never took her eyes off the road, which made Becca feel safe with her. But she didn't trust "safe with her." She couldn't afford to. So she drew from her own experience and said, "Coming here to the island when you're not, say, a baby? It's way hard. Everyone's known everyone else from pre-school. It's a freak-out having to try to make friends because people all seem to be already in fixed groups."

Hayley glanced at her, then. "You did okay. You're doing okay."

"On the outside, maybe. On the inside? Not so much."

"You've got Derric and Seth. You've got Jenn. You know me, not as good as you know them, but you still know me and here we are in the truck together and it's not like I'm freaking you out, am I?"

Becca smiled. The last thing Hayley Cartwright would be able to do was freak anyone out. She was way too nice. And Becca, too, felt something flowing from Isis Martin. It *seemed* to be fear but she didn't know of what. She said, "Why Aidan?"

"What? Oh. You mean why do I think whatever's going on with Isis has to do with Aidan? I didn't at first. But at lunch today . . . how she tried to get him out of the New Commons? And then just now? I mean, wow, are they completely different from each other or what? And here's something else: Where're their parents? She talks and talks but so far she hasn't said word one about her mom and dad."

Becca didn't want to go near that subject since the last thing she ever wanted to do was to talk about her own parents. But the thought of her own unwillingness to speak of her mom and stepfather prompted her to consider Hayley's words in a way she might not have done otherwise. Even the whispers that came at her from Isis and her brother had nothing to do with parents, which was odd.

She said, "I dunno, Hayley. She'll probably tell you what's going on eventually. When you talk about your family, she'll probably talk about hers, too. And if something's going on with her family that's making her act sort of strange . . ." Becca's voice faded as she saw the immediate change in Hayley. She'd said something to affect the other girl. But she didn't know what it was. She loosened the ear bud casually so that it dropped onto her shoulder, away from Hayley's view. Immediately she heard *after the walker . . . the worse it gets and when there's a wheelchair . . . got to deal with that because no way can Mom . . . and now with Brooke being such a pill . . . I don't care I don't care only don't lie Hayley because you do and you know it . . . shut up shut up shut up.*

Becca was startled with the ferocity of Hayley's thoughts, all of them running beneath the pleasant exterior of the girl. Slowly, she returned the ear bud to her ear.

What she knew at the end of their conversation was pretty simple, as things turned out. If something was going on with Isis and Aidan Martin, something was going on with Hayley Cartwright, too.

NINE

Derric and his Little Brother came out of the Cliff Motel just as Becca left Hayley's pickup. The Little Brother lived at the Cliff, not in one of the motel's rooms but in the apartment behind and above the office. His dad was in prison, his mother was long gone to meth addiction, and Josh and his little sister, Chloe, were being raised by their grandmother, who owned the place.

Both of the children knew Becca, as did their grandmother. For along with her grandkids, she'd taken in Becca as well when she'd first ridden her bike into Langley, wondering what she was going to do when her mom's plans for her fell apart in an instant.

Josh yelled, "Hey! Hi, Becca! Me 'n' Derric's going for a hike. He's takin me to th' institute. *Whidbey* Institute. Up in th' woods. You ever been there?"

At this, Derric saw Becca as well. He gave her a grin and strolled over to her. Josh accompanied him, darting around at his side. He punched the air and scuffed his feet and said, "There's *tons* of trails, Derric said. *An'* he said we can't get lost 'cause he's got a map only we've got compasses, too, so we're not using the map at *all*. We have it just in case."

Derric said, "Think we should invite Becca, Josh?"

"Becca? No way. She's a girl. Bleagh. This's for *guys*. Anyways, she c'n play Barbies with Chloe."

"Way cool," Becca said. "I *love* Barbies." She exchanged a look with Derric and added, "Among other things," and stepped up to kiss him. Derric's arms went around her, and he made the kiss last.

"Yuck!" Josh shouted. "Gross! Stop it! Come *on*, you guys. We got to *go*."

"That's telling them, Josh," a man's voice said from the other side of the street. "Break it up, you two. Come up for air. You're out in public."

The tone was jovial. It was also highly recognizable. While they were kissing, Derric's dad had pulled his sheriff's car into the front parking lot of the arts center. He'd got out and he stood there at the edge of the lot. He was watching them, his arms folded across his chest and his head shaking in one of those kids-will-be-kids kinds of movements.

It was odd that Dave Mathieson would be in Langley. As the undersheriff of the county, he had his office twenty-eight miles to the north in the county seat, which was the old Victorian town of Coupeville. Langley had its own tiny police department to handle the routine problems in the village, so if he'd come to town, it was an indication that something was going on.

"Whatcha doing here, Dad?" Derric asked his father.

Dave crossed the street to join them. He gave Becca an arm-around-the-shoulders hug. He made much of shaking Josh's little hand. He said, "Djangofest."

As an answer, it was totally inadequate, but then the fire chief's SUV pulled into the parking lot and stopped right next to the sheriff's car. The fire chief called out, "See you inside?" to Dave Mathieson, which put the upcoming music festival and fire together.

"Might be a firebug around," the undersheriff clarified. "Those early fires could've been carelessness. But after the fairgrounds fire, we're looking at how to protect all of the Djangofest venues. Setting a fire in the middle of a concert? That'd be a real thrill for a firebug if that's what we've got going here." He looked down at Josh, who was listening, wide-eyed. He said, "You don't mess with matches, do you, kiddo?"

Josh shook his head solemnly. "Grammer would smack me a good one."

At that point, Dave Mathieson should have gone off to his meeting, but he didn't. Instead, he asked the boys what they were going to do together on this fine day and when Derric mentioned the hike, he told them to skedaddle while the light in the forest around Whidbey Institute was still good. Then he gave Becca a glance that seemed rich with meaning. She decided to stay where she was in case he wanted to tell her what was up.

Derric and Josh drove off with a wave. Derric yelled, "Call you tonight, babe," at Becca and then they were gone.

Dave said, "He thinks the world of you."

Becca said in return, "Feeling's totally mutual."

Dave Mathieson was silent at that, as if tossing this around in his mind. Becca wondered if he was worried about Derric and her the way parents worried when their kids got involved with each other. It was pretty much a universal worry: boys, girls, hormones, and sex.

She wanted to pull the ear bud from her ear in order to catch what was on Dave's mind. She managed to do this surreptitiously. What she heard made the breath catch in her chest.

A single word only. *Rejoice.* This was followed at once by *wonder if she knows . . . betraying . . . finding out could mean all the difference . . .*

Becca wanted to jump in and say *something* to get Dave Mathieson to reveal everything that was coursing through his mind. But she couldn't think of a single thing to say to effect this, so she forced a smile and referred to the subject that Dave himself had brought up. "He's the greatest guy, Sheriff Mathieson. But c'n I say something?"

Dave seemed to rouse himself. "Sure," he told her.

"You got nothing to worry about with me and Derric. You know."

He gazed at her, as if evaluating this. Then he said the unthinkable. "Becca, let me ask you this. Has Derric ever mentioned someone called Rejoice?"

BECCA WAS COMPLETELY unready for a frontal assault. She bought time with, "Rejoice? Is that really someone's name?" to which Dave Mathieson said, "It's a girl from Uganda. From the same orphanage where my wife met Derric. He's . . ." Dave looked off in the direction that Derric had taken in his Forester. He frowned as if considering how much to say. *Don't want to mess up what the boy has going* suggested to Becca that Dave's hesitation had a lot to do with her own relationship with Derric. This pleased her since it indicated that he didn't want to cause a problem between them, especially a problem having to do with another girl. "He's been writing to her since he first came here, letters that he's never sent. It feels like . . ." *In confidence now . . . from the past like a crush so it doesn't mean . . . and yet unfinished business . . .*

Becca tried to sound thoughtful. "Could it be . . . like, a journal or something? Like there's no real person at all? 'Cause it's sort of odd, isn't it? First of all, the name's kind of a non-name. And then writing letters but not sending them? If she was real, wouldn't he just've asked you to mail 'em?"

Dave considered this. "There's that," he admitted. "But . . . well . . ." *Always holds back . . . if there's a way for a break-through . . . dad and son trust and he can trust me I swear it . . .*

Becca furrowed her brow. She *thought* she got it and what she got was that Derric wasn't hiding the truth about Rejoice nearly as well as he thought he was. She said, "He's never said anything to me about a Rejoice, Sheriff Mathieson. And . . . well . . . I kind of think he would."

Still he gazed at her steadily. That he was trying to read her for truth or lie was something Becca could tell even without his whispers. He wouldn't be able to read the truth from her, though. She'd been on Whidbey Island for just a year, and her biggest accomplishment so far had been perfecting her ability to lie with an innocent expression on her face.

He said with a sigh that sounded relieved but could have meant anything, "Okay, then. Can we keep it between us that I asked you about her?"

"About Rejoice? Sure," Becca said.

THE TRUTH WAS that Becca knew all about Rejoice. The truth was that Rejoice was Derric's sister. The truth was that he'd never told anyone at the Ugandan orphanage that among the children with him whom they'd picked up off the street in Kampala was a two-year-old girl who didn't remember that the boy sharing the cardboard cartons in the alley in which they'd been discovered was her older brother. That Becca knew all this was purest chance. For she was the person who'd found the letters that Derric had written to his sister and hidden from the world, along with his shame at having kept their very relationship his most closely guarded secret.

Becca could have told Derric's father all of this. But aside from wishing not ever to betray Derric, she also believed that the story of Rejoice had to come from Derric and not from her. He wasn't ready to do that. That was how the situation had to stay for now.

Or so it seemed until she caught sight of an older woman in a baseball cap walking an elegant standard black poodle along Cascade Street in her direction. This was Diana Kinsale, the first adult Becca had met on Whidbey and the only person whose whispers Becca had never been able to hear, unless Diana *wanted* them heard.

Becca set off to meet her. The woman and the poodle were taking their time, with lots of stops so that Diana could admire the Cascade Mountains, the jagged range clearly visible from the top of the bluff along which the street ran. They rose far in the distance across the water and beyond the city of Everett, whose port buildings caught the sunlight of the late afternoon.

As Becca approached the woman and dog, Diana went to one of the benches along the bluff and sank down onto it. She bent to caress Oscar's floppy ears. The poodle leaned into her in his usual fashion. Diana pressed her head to the top of his. This, too, he accepted without stirring from her knees. It came to Becca that something wasn't quite right.

She called out, "Where's the rest of the pack?" referring to Diana's other four dogs.

Diana turned. She tilted her baseball cap back and exposed her face. Becca felt a shiver. Diana looked unwell.

"Becca," the older woman said in greeting. She patted the bench. "Join me. Oscar's had his teeth cleaned today, and I'm giving him a bit of exercise before home. Well, I *was* until the view got my attention. How are you? We haven't seen you in ages."

By *we* she meant herself and her dogs. When Becca had lived in the Cliff Motel and even when she'd lived in the tree house in Ralph Darrow's woods, she'd been a regular visitor to Diana's house outside of Langley.

Becca sat beside her. She'd always taken great comfort from being in Diana's presence, and today was no different. Diana put her arm around Becca's shoulders in a hug that stayed just where it was, and what Becca felt was what she always felt from Diana. An incredible sense of peace and warmth came over her.

"How's school?" Diana asked her. "How's life at Ralph's? How's Derric?"

"Fine, fine, and fine," Becca said simply. Then she caught Diana inspecting her. Diana read things in people and this reading, Becca believed, came from touch. So did the comfort that she was able to provide them. Allow Diana to touch you and your troubles weren't gone, but how you felt about those troubles was altered forever. Becca said, "Really, Mrs. Kinsale."

"As to Derric . . . ?"

"It's nothing. Just something his dad asked me."

"*About* Derric?"

God, she got to the meat of things fast. Becca bent to pet Oscar. He accepted the affection. Since he was a poodle, he wasn't inclined to do much more than blink at her and move his tail languidly to indicate his willingness to allow her a further show of devotion. Like his mistress, he gazed at the view. A few gulls flew over them. Two majestic bald eagles sailed by on the lookout for food. Far out in the water, a ripple suggested the presence of a seal.

"Wow," Becca said in reaction to all of this.

"Heavenly, isn't it?" Diana replied. And then she said, "Are you avoiding it?"

Becca knew exactly what she meant. Diana had picked up

on her indecision. She meant was Becca avoiding the subject of Derric and his father? The answer was yes.

She said to Diana, "It's a loyalty thing."

"Loyalty to Derric?"

"I know something. His dad asked me about it."

"I take it you said nothing."

"That's about it. It's not illegal or anything. It's just something private."

"Between you and Derric?"

"Yeah."

"Ah. Parents worry, you know."

Becca felt herself getting hot. "It's not *that*. Just something personal about Derric that his dad wants to know and it didn't feel right for me to tell him."

"Because of what he might do?"

"Because of how he might feel."

Diana shot her a look. "Are you thinking you can control how people feel?"

"I'm thinking how Derric feels is more important to me than how his dad feels. What I also think is he should tell his dad and tell his mom but he doesn't want to, so it's not up to me to do the telling for him. I didn't like lying to the sheriff, though."

Diana turned from reading her face. She said, "Trust."

"What?"

"I think trust is the next step for you." And then Diana added meditatively, "Could be it's the next step for everyone."

"Next step where?"

"Next step on life's journey."

Becca scowled. "You're doing that Yoda thing again, Mrs. Kinsale," she told her in warning. "Next you'll start sounding like a fortune cookie."

Diana laughed. "There are worse things," she told her. "I quite like fortune cookies."

TEN

The fiddler who'd joined Seth and his group during their rehearsal at South Whidbey Commons turned out to be in town for Djangofest. His name was Parker Natalia, he was from Canada, and he'd been a longtime member of a Canadian group called BC Django 21.

"Till they kicked me out for someone they figured was better," the young man had said with a shrug. But Seth could tell that the shrug hid heartache, and if anyone on earth knew about heartache, Seth was that guy. So he kept asking Parker to jam with Triple Threat whenever he was in South Whidbey Commons while the trio was practicing. Admittedly, it was partly to cheer Parker up that Seth asked him to play his fiddle, but it was also partly because he was so damn good. Seth couldn't believe that anyone with ears and a brain would ever kick Parker Natalia out of a group.

Ultimately, Seth talked the members of Triple Threat into inviting Parker to join them during *all* their rehearsals, with an eye toward having him play with them during their appearance at Djangofest. It was high time to bring a fiddler into Triple Threat to broaden their musical offerings, he pointed out, which was critical if they were ever going to do more than just play as background music for local fund raisers. More important, though, Parker Natalia had the potential to provide what Seth referred to as the heartthrob factor for females in the audience. And growing their audience was just as critical as growing their music.

The reason Seth decided to take Parker to meet his grandfather had to do with housing. One of the quirky things about Djangofest was that the local citizenry opened up their homes to house the performing musicians. The problem here was that Parker wasn't one of the musicians scheduled to play. While his former band BC Django 21 was on the schedule and thus happily ensconced in someone's house, he was not.

Seth discovered that Parker was sleeping in his car in a hidden corner of the fairgrounds. With limited funds, he didn't want to spend money on a motel room. What money he had with him had to last until he left Whidbey Island to return home, so he was making do with a sleeping bag in the back of his Ford Taurus and using the facilities—when they were open—at the fairgrounds.

Seth had a better idea. It wasn't a motel room, but it was definitely a step up from a Taurus. And a bathroom with a shower was available if Parker didn't mind a bit of a hike. It would, of course, all depend on Ralph Darrow's approval.

When they got to Ralph's property, Seth let Gus out of the VW and watched the Labrador lope in the direction of the house. He and Parker ambled along after the dog, and they found Seth's grandfather at work in front of the woodshed, along with Becca King, Derric Mathieson, and a mound of fire wood. Three cords of it had just been delivered and needed to be stacked. Ralph was doing this. So were Becca and Derric. Gus was bounding around them, barking and waiting to be noticed.

"Get that dog one of those bones before I clobber him," was Ralph's greeting to Seth.

Becca hurried to the box on the porch. Gus followed, knowing exactly what was in the offing.

Seth nodded hi to Derric and introduced Parker both to his grandfather and to the other boy. When Becca returned to the woodpile, he did the same for her. She said with a smile, "You're the fiddler at South Whidbey Commons. I was there when you jammed with Seth. It was totally amazing."

Parker shot Becca a smile, and said, "Thanks," as he shook hands with Ralph Darrow and Derric.

He and Seth joined in with the wood stacking, and Seth's grandfather stood back and let the younger people take on the job. He wiped his hands with one of his cowboy handkerchiefs and commented, "Tom Sawyer couldn't've managed this better. How're the rehearsals coming along, favorite male grandson?"

"Excellent," Seth replied. "Parker's joining us."

"Is he indeed?" Ralph looked Parker over.

Perhaps it was something in Ralph's speculative tone that sounded less than convinced this was a good idea because Parker said quickly, "Not permanently. Just for a few numbers at Djangofest."

Seth added that Parker had come to Whidbey Island as part of the contingent of gypsy jazz lovers who showed up yearly to attend the performances of musicians from around the world. "He used to be part of a group from Canada," Seth said, "BC Django 21."

"British Columbia," Parker added helpfully. "That's the B and the C."

"Anyways," Seth said, "you know how the musicians all get put up during the festival by people around Langley? Well, see, I was sort of wondering . . ."

"Ah," Ralph said.

Becca smiled. She knew where this was heading. She also knew that Seth had learned his lesson when it came to making decisions about his grandfather's personal property and his land. Seth wanted to put Parker up in a tree house that Seth had built deep in the woods. But since he'd stowed Becca there without his grandfather's knowledge the previous winter and spring, he wasn't about to make that mistake another time.

"British Columbia is it?" Ralph said affably. "Whereabouts?"

"In the Kootenay Mountains," Parker replied. "Town called Nelson."

SETH SAW BECCA freeze when Parker said this, but he didn't know what it meant. Derric saw her freeze, too, and his glance went from Becca to Parker to Becca again, as if some message had passed between them that was unreadable to everyone else. For Ralph's part, he seemed to notice nothing. He merely said, "Not familiar with the place," to which Parker replied, "It's north of Spokane."

Quickly and perhaps to cover for whatever she'd felt when she'd heard the place name Nelson, Becca went back to work. So did Derric. Seth could see, though, that she was listening intently. In her haste to put the firewood where it belonged, however, she'd lost the ear bud to the AUD box.

"Anyways," Seth said, hoping for his grandfather's agreement to the plan, "Parker's been sleeping in his car, and I was thinking the tree house might be better. He could maybe use your downstairs shower if Becca doesn't care. It wouldn't be for that long. Just till after Djangofest. More or less."

Ralph shot him a look at the *more or less* part of it. He said, "I expect that's up to Miss Becca, Seth. It's her bathroom."

Becca said, "Fine by me long's Parker knows it's a hike from the tree house."

"I'll show him the place," Seth said. And then, a little anxiously, "'S okay, Grand?"

Ralph waved him in the general direction of the woodland trails beyond the pond. He said, "Have at it," and Becca added, "I'll go, too, Seth," and gave no one—and specifically Derric—any chance to quash her intention.

ELEVEN

Becca's ear bud had kept becoming dislodged as she was stacking the wood, and she'd finally removed it altogether. This hadn't been a problem. She needed the practice tuning out whispers, and those coming from Ralph and from Derric had been easy enough to "un-hear," as she was starting to call it. Ralph's whispers had been about *enough wood for winter* and *can't remember if there was snow last year* and *Sarah's question's got to be answered* while Derric's had been concerned with his dad, her butt, her boobs—he was *such* a guy—and a coming test in Sports Medicine.

But when Seth and Parker arrived, things changed and the air became thick with thoughts that Becca didn't want to try to un-hear. So she replaced the ear bud and went on working, listening idly to Seth's plans for his new friend Parker . . . until Parker had said he came from Nelson.

It was an oh-my-God moment, and Becca thanked her stars that she didn't blurt out a single word. She did pull the ear bud out of her ear at that point, though, because if Parker Natalia knew *anything* about Nelson that he didn't want to say aloud, she needed to delve through all the whispers to learn what it was.

Unfortunately, mostly what she picked up on was Derric. He'd seen her reaction to hearing Nelson mentioned, and he was worried. He'd assumed her reaction had to do with Parker, who looked like a cross between a male model for Jockey shorts and a movie star.

Derric was ten times the *only* guy for her, and Becca wanted to tell him that. He didn't need to worry, and he would never need to worry. But she couldn't say this to him without revealing to him that she'd heard his thoughts.

When she said she'd tag along into the woods with Seth and Parker, she half expected Derric to protest. But he said nothing and as for what he thought, it was jumbled up with what everyone else was thinking. And she didn't have time to sort through that because Seth and Parker were heading across the lawn to descend to the pond. She hurried after them.

The tree house was an excellent excuse since she'd hidden out there for months. She followed Seth, Parker, and Gus along the trail that wound into the woods, and for the next ten minutes they crunched along a path strewn with alder leaves and the disintegrating pine cones from Douglas firs. Ferns and salal and wild huckleberry bushes grew to the edges of this path along with Oregon grape, elderberry, various creepers, wild grasses, holly, and invasive ivy. The air was sharp with the musty scent of decomposing vegetation.

When they reached the tree house, they paused at the clearing that held it in the interlocking branches of two towering hemlocks. Parker muttered, "Holy hell. Who built this thing," and Becca was happy to announce that every board of it had been put in place by Seth.

It wasn't a tree house in the tradition of a kids' platform fixed into the trees. Rather it was a tiny house, with a deck in the front, a secure roof over it to keep out the rain, double-paned windows to hold in the heat, and a woodstove inside to provide the necessary warmth. To this had been added a cot for sleeping, a camping stove for cooking, a lantern, and shelf for books.

Becca had to wait while Parker made much of the building and its contents and while Seth schooled him in the use of the stove. She put in two cents about banking the fire at night although they all agreed he wouldn't need to use the stove much for warmth as the weather hadn't turned bad yet and probably wouldn't till late in October.

Becca looked for an opening. She tried to read significance into the whispers she heard. There was nothing there, though. Just stuff about the tree house and music and gratitude and *I'll show them I swear to God*, which seemed to come from Parker.

She knew she might have to wait forever for something to be said that related to Nelson, and she couldn't wait. So she went for it. "Hey, what's Nelson like?" she asked when there was a break in the conversation. There was going to be no way to ease into it. The direct approach seemed best although Seth glanced at her strangely when she asked the question.

Parker smiled, showing straight white teeth. "I dunno," was his totally unsatisfactory answer. "Just a town, I guess. I grew up there." He squatted to examine the interior of the stove. It was filled with ashes from Becca's winter stay. It would need to be cleaned to be useful. "It's on a lake," he added. "It's huge."

Becca's spirits sank at this. A huge town meant—

"The lake, I mean," Parker said, closing the stove's door and rising. "Lake Kootenay. It's huge. Nelson itself's pretty small. I mean, it's bigger than Langley, but . . . well, pretty much every place is probably bigger than Langley."

Seth said, "Yeah. We're putting in for another stop sign, but we'll never make it to a traffic light. Grand says there was a time you could lay down in the middle of First Street at one in the afternoon right in front of the movie theater and not have to worry about anyone coming along to run you over."

Parker laughed. "We got traffic lights. And maybe ten thousand people. And you lay down in the middle of the street, a logging truck'd probably run over you."

"Way bigger than here," Becca acknowledged.

"It's all relative," Parker said. And then to Seth, "This place'll be great." And to Becca, "Thanks for sharing the bathroom. I'll stay out of your way much as I can." And back to Seth, "I totally appreciate it, man. And Triple Threat too."

Because they will see they all will see and if they don't . . . the girls're gonna go bananas but a permanent fiddler's got to be told Becca that they were close to being finished entirely with the topic of Nelson, which she couldn't let happen.

"Around here everyone pretty much knows everyone, don't they, Seth?" Becca said.

Seth shot her a look that said "Huh?" as well as if he'd said it aloud.

Becca added, "Is that how it is in Nelson?" to Parker.

"S'pose," Parker said. He went over to the cot and tested it. He looked out of the window and worked its crank to open and close it. He said, "Amazing," to Seth. "You got some major talent."

"I c'n build and play the guitar is all. When it comes to—"

"I got a cousin up there," Becca said desperately. "Maybe you know her?"

"Maybe," Parker said. "My family's got a restaurant downtown. It's been there pretty much forever and there're slews of regulars. What's her name?"

"Laurel Armstrong." Becca knew it was an incredible risk, but she had to take it. Nelson was where her mom had been heading when she'd dropped Becca at the Mukilteo ferry for the ride over to Whidbey Island. But it was long past the time that her mom should have returned to claim her and to whisk her to her new life in British Columbia. Becca added, "Well, she's my mom's cousin really, so she's a lot older than me, like in her forties?"

Parker smiled his dazzling smile. "Then I wouldn't know her 'cause mostly I go for the younger feministas. What's her name again?"

Becca said, "Laurel Armstrong," although the truth of the matter was that, for all she knew, her mom had adopted another name.

"Never heard of her. Is she—"

Becca cut in. She couldn't let a big deal be made of this. She said and tried to sound cheerful about it, "Oh. I just wondered, is all. Hey, want me to show you where the bathroom is? I mean, in the house. It's next to my bedroom."

Parker offered that smile again and said, "Sure."

Becca tried to ignore the look Seth cast in her direction.

BUT SHE COULDN'T ignore his whispers on the way back to the house. He was throwing a ball for Gus to seem like someone occupied with his dog but all the time his mind was asking *what's the deal* and *maybe this was a* ve-ry *bad idea* and *I already made my peace with that dude and if Beck hooks up* and on and on. Becca gritted her teeth. Soon enough they were back where they'd started, she'd shown Parker where the downstairs bathroom was, she'd said that she bet Seth's grandpa wouldn't mind if he brought some food inside to keep in the old fridge, and they were all back outside where Derric was still stacking firewood.

She could tell Seth was eager to get Parker out of there. She could tell that Derric was beginning to feel much the same. For his part Ralph Darrow seemed to be taking the temperature of things and finding it not quite what it should be. None of that seemed to matter at the moment, though. Becca was feeling pretty black about the Nelson conversation.

Perhaps Parker saw this. He was saying his goodbyes and talking about getting his stuff and bringing it to the tree house and setting the time for his return when he looked at her and added, "I check in with my parents pretty often. Next time I talk to them I'll ask about your cousin. Laurel Armstrong, right?"

Becca didn't look at anyone except Parker as she said, "That's the name," as quietly as possible.

But it wasn't good enough. Derric looked her way. So did Ralph Darrow. One of them thought *cousin* and the other *what the hell* and it pretty much didn't matter which was which.

TWELVE

While she'd been at the tree house, Derric and Ralph had made tons of progress, especially since Derric appeared to be working off a head of steam. He was stacking split logs like a reincarnated Abraham Lincoln.

His mind was running. *When's she going to start telling me . . . not now not now* declared that he was arguing with himself. But the strength of his wanting a full story from her told Becca that they were both just postponing an inevitable Q&A. Ralph Darrow seemed to reach this same conclusion because he said, "I've had enough for today. So've you two. Let's finish this later. Next week, next month, next year. Derric, a soda?"

Derric said, "No, thanks. I'm good, Mr. Darrow."

Ralph said, "Well, I'm having me a rest," and he strode back to the house. Generally in fine weather he took his rests on the porch. Today, however, he went inside.

Derric waited only a beat before asking, "So d'you want to tell me what's going on?" His whispers continued. He knew it was irrational to be feeling what he was feeling, which was insecurity, but that was what he was feeling and *like, why does she have to tell him and probably Seth . . . it's all uneven and out of control. . . .*

Becca grabbed the ear bud to put in her ear. He and she needed a level playing field, at least. She said, "Nothing's going on."

"So what was the deal with the tree house? Seth could have shown him. No way did you need to."

"I wanted to tell him about the stove. I showed him how it works but—"

"Like Seth couldn't do that?"

"*But* I forgot that there's a tricky thing with the door. And you got to be careful how you bank it or it goes out by the morning. That's what I wanted to show him."

He stared at her. "You must think I'm an idiot." He'd earlier removed a long-sleeved T-shirt he'd been wearing, and he went for this now and jerked it over his head.

"What's *wrong*?" she said.

"What's with this cousin of yours that you never once ever mentioned to me?"

"Why would I mention her?"

"Why wouldn't you? Is she some kind of secret?"

"Derric, this is stupid. It's not like *you* do any mentioning of relatives."

His face altered. He read a threat in her words. She hadn't intended it that way, but the truth was that she knew his deepest secret while all the time she hid hers from him. He said, "Nice, Becca."

He began to walk off. He started for the hill and its upward path that would take him to where he'd left the Forester. She went after him.

"Look," she said. "You've got a bigger worry right now than whether I have some deep, dark secret cousin, okay?"

He stopped. "That's supposed to mean what?"

"Rejoice."

He looked around. It was a frantic look that told her once again he thought she was threatening him.

She put her hand on his arm and didn't let him pull away. She said, "Derric, your dad asked me about her. When he was going to that meeting at the arts center with the fire chief, remember? He asked me if you'd told me about someone in your life called Rejoice because you'd been writing letters to her that you never mailed."

His lips appeared dry. His mouth probably was, too. "What'd you tell him?"

"I said that I didn't know, that maybe she was just a pretend person you'd been writing to if you hadn't mailed the letters. But he looked like he believed *that* just the way he'd believe me if I told him you'd been using a Ouija board to do your homework."

"And that was all?" He sounded formal and stiff and not like her Derric whom she loved beyond reason.

"Of course that was all. Look, this is eating you up. *And* it's part of why you and I argue. You *have* to tell them the truth, Derric. You have to do it so you can be whole."

At this, his face became so hard that it looked carved but Becca knew that beneath was a perfect soul and she wanted him to *see* this about himself and to understand it as well. He'd done something to someone that was inconceivable. But he wasn't evil. He was just a kid.

"And what d'you suggest I tell them?" His voice was cold and as hard as his face. "That I left my baby sister in Africa? That I didn't tell anyone she *was* my sister. That I let *her* forget it because she was too young to remember anyway and there were people who maybe wanted to adopt me and get me out of there and I wanted that, boy I *really* wanted that, Becca, and that I don't know where Rejoice even is now or if she's alive or dead because she could be dead, just like our parents she could be dead. AIDS or TB or a hundred other diseases. And d'you *think* I want to know if she is? Because . . ." He swung away from her. He started for the path.

Becca dashed after him and flung her arms around his waist, holding him in place, her head pressed to his back. She felt his broken breathing and the cry that tore through his throat.

"Let it *go*," he said to her.

"I can't," she murmured. "Because neither can you."

"Then let *me* go. We both know that I'm worthless."

"You aren't and I won't. I won't do that either."

THIRTEEN

When Hayley Cartwright saw Tatiana Primavera at the farmers' market on the following Saturday, she knew that trouble could be in the offing. For Tatiana saw her inside the family's booth and waved gaily, calling out, "Stay there. I'll be right back." In her floppy hat and platform sandals, she headed toward the marimba band at the far end of the market. The music was lively, and it would probably keep the counselor occupied for a while. But she would be back soon or later, and Hayley knew she needed to use the time to get out of there.

As if sent by heaven, Isis Martin showed up in need of advice. She called Hayley over to the side of the Cartwrights' booth and brought forth a silver ring with a turquoise stone planted on it.

She said, "I can't decide. I *think* this is right for him, but is it, like, manly?"

Hayley looked at the ring. She knew the designer, an offbeat woman with magenta hair and very serious gold eye shadow. She was a Whidbey Island antique, but she knew her silver.

"Wow," Hayley said when she took the ring in her hand. "Nice, Isis."

"It's a present," she said. "I wasn't sure about it. I mean, it *looks* guy-ish, don't you think?"

"Sure. Is it Aidan's birthday or something?"

"Aidan!" Isis laughed. "Not hardly. It's for Brady. My boyfriend. God, Aidan's made my life one enormous, hellacious disaster. The last thing I'd do is get a present for him. Like thank you for making us end up here in the middle of nowhere without even a Starbucks. As if." And in a typical move that Hayley was becoming used to, Isis covered her mouth with her hand and said, "God! I'm sorry. Whidbey Island's great. *I'm* an airhead. I just blah blah blah and in goes my foot. Anyway, I've got Brady's ring—well, it's not really his, because they don't do rings at our school—and I wanted to send him something in return. Here, look." She pulled a heavy gold chain from her neck, the same chain Hayley had admired the day they had met. Hayley hadn't seen anything upon it earlier as the chain was long, and it left whatever pendant might be on it dangling within whatever top Isis happened to be wearing. But now she drew the chain out and on it like a pendant was a man's large ring. It was white gold with a deep blue stone. "It's his dad's university ring, but he doesn't wear it. So Brady figured he wouldn't mind. Anyway, like I said, I want to get him a ring in return and I saw this one. What do you think?"

Hayley said it looked perfect to her. Isis stuffed the other ring back into her top. She said, "D'you know the time? C'n I look at your watch because . . . Damn damn damn. I'm s'posed to pick up Aidan! Hey, do you want to come? I got to bike with him to Maxwelton Beach. Grandam makes him run there from her house and back two times a day. Do *not* ask me why because she is just so weird. Only she doesn't believe he'll really do it, so I have to trail him on a bike to make sure. Can you come with me? I c'n take you home after. Hey, Mrs. Cartwright! Hi! Hi! C'n Hayley come with me for a while? The market's almost over, isn't it?"

Truth was that the market had two hours to go and although Brooke was there, helping out for once, she immediately began saying, "No fair! I don't want to do this stupid work all alone! Come *on*, Mom. Hayley can't go. And I'm *hungry*."

But Julie Cartwright looked from Isis to Hayley and perhaps it was the possibility of a budding friendship and its benefits that she saw because she smiled and said, "You two go on. Brookie and I c'n handle things here."

When Brooke cried out, "That is so *totally*—" the girls' mom added, "But just today, Hayley. Okay?" She also said to Isis, "We can't have this as a permanent arrangement."

To which Isis replied, "Absolutely. You are a peach, Mrs. Cartwright."

Hayley heard Brooke's continued protests as she hurried out of the market in Isis Martin's wake. It was a blessed escape, mostly from Tatiana Primavera.

IT TURNED OUT that Aidan Martin was skateboarding at South Whidbey Community Park. This was situated directly behind the high school, and it comprised acres of playing fields, a sweeping forest, and trails. In the midst of it a children's playground had been built, a castle-and-fort structure with bridges and swings and walkways for inventive games. Just to the north of this was the concrete skateboard area, complete with ramps and bowls and ridges.

Aidan was, Hayley thought, the best boarder she'd ever seen. She didn't know the names of what he was doing, but they weren't anything like she'd ever witnessed on the island. She said to Isis, "He's really good."

"Yeah, he got good in the last two years," Isis replied. "Well, he had to do something. Aidan! We gotta get back to Grandam before she produces a cow."

Oddly, Aidan stopped his boarding at once. He slapped hands with the four other boys—"Boy, they look like losers," Isis muttered—and he came to his sister. He said, "You're late, so you better be the one to explain."

Isis said, "She's probably, you know, *occupied*." She said the last word with sly emphasis, adding, "Linda was s'posed to be coming over," and told Hayley frankly, "That's the grandam's lesbian lover."

They trooped to the car. Aidan climbed into the back, where he lit a cigarette. His sister said, "Aidan! Where the hell did you get—" and he said, "What?" like someone for whom this was business as usual. He added, "You want a hit or something?" and he laughed strangely, a high sound like a caught animal.

Isis glanced at Hayley and rolled her eyes. "Siblings." She sighed.

"I hear you," Hayley told her.

FOURTEEN

Nancy Howard's place was on the same road as the high school and the community park, but many miles away: across the highway and on the far west side of Whidbey Island. To get there they coursed through Midvale Corner with its rich farmland. This altered soon enough to the spacious vistas of Maxwelton Valley and then to forest and a winding road, which ultimately opened up on the south end of an enormous body of water whose extreme low tide had given it its name: Useless Bay. Before reaching this water, Isis turned right off the road and took them up a narrow driveway. This bore a sign reading MAXWELTON ART, which was wood carved to depict hand-painted soaring bald eagles, breeching orcas, swimming salmon, and grazing deer.

"Grandam's," Isis said of the sign. And as they got out of the car in a half-moon area that was thick with wood chippings, the roar of a motor came from behind the house.

Hayley trailed Isis up stairs that appeared to be built along the side of a garage. They followed the roar of the motor. This took them along a balcony and around the corner of the building, where a deck overlooked a working area so littered with debris that Hayley had to wonder how anyone moved among the logs, blocks of wood, half-finished sculptures, discarded lumber, assorted chain saws, awls, hammers, handsaws, nails, screws, bolts, and buckets of paint. In the midst of this, the Martins' grandmother was applying a very large shrieking chain saw to an enormous upright block of wood. She wore major earphones to protect her ears, overalls and a long sleeved T-shirt to protect her body. She had goggles on her eyes and a hard hat on her head.

Hayley had to smile. Palo Alto, she figured, had malls and at least one Starbucks if not half a dozen. But she'd bet her life there was no one within a hundred miles of the place remotely like Isis Martin's grandmother.

When Nancy Howard paused for a moment, switched off the chain saw, and stepped back from her work, Isis yelled, "Hey, Nance!"

Her grandmother looked up. She removed her earphones. "Where in God's creation've you been?" she demanded. "Where's your brother?"

"Getting ready to run. We were at the market. This is Hayley Cartwright."

"Bill's daughter," Nancy Howard said. "You look just like his mom."

"Whatcha doing?" Isis asked her grandmother.

"Now that is one hell of a stupid question. What does it look like I'm doing? This's that Sills Road project I was telling you about. God knows why they want a bear—nothing stupider, you ask me—but if that's what they want and they got the *dinero* to pay for it, a bear it is." She used her teeth to pull the sleeve of her T-shirt back and she looked at a man's watch on her wrist. She said to Isis, "Two hours. There's clean-up work to be done down here and I want you and Aidan back to do it. Got it?"

Isis said to Hayley, "Servitude. How much happier can that possibly make me?" And then to her grandmother, "Aye aye, Captain Howard, sir."

"And keep your eyes on Aidan," Nancy added.

Isis muttered something that Hayley couldn't hear. She waved gaily, however, called out, "Will do," and led the way back to the front of the building. Hayley saw that the house itself was on the opposite side of the property. It was afflicted with the same amount of debris that appeared to be everywhere else, but there were finished wood carvings nearby, attempting to decorate something that looked like a garden in extremis.

Aidan came out of the house. He'd put on running shoes, but that was the extent of his changing his clothes for a run. While he came toward them, Isis led Hayley into the open garage where two bikes were leaning against a wooden trailer. She said to Hayley, "Grab one of these. We ride, he runs." And to Aidan, "Go on, then. We'll catch up."

He shrugged and jogged off down the driveway as Isis rolled her bike out of the garage. It was an ancient thing with wheels like doughnuts, and Hayley's bike turned out to be the same. These belonged to Nancy and Linda-the-lesbian-lover, Isis told her. They possessed only one gear, but they were the only things on offer.

The two girls set off, and they soon caught up to Aidan, who was cooperatively jogging along the side of the road. But within two hundred yards of Nancy Howard's driveway, Aidan leaped off the road and disappeared along a trail into the forest. Isis saw him go but made no protest. She merely continued heading toward the beach, as if nothing unusual had occurred.

Hayley came up alongside her. "Shouldn't we follow him or something?"

Isis cast a look over her shoulder in the direction her brother had taken. "No way is he about to put up with that. And anyway, he'll just go in there and smoke if he managed to steal some matches from Grandam. We'll meet up with him on the road later. Far as Grandam knows, we'll be glued to him like a second skin. Come on. Race you to the beach, okay?"

The girls made quick work of getting down to Maxwelton Beach, a community comprising the large homes of people made wealthy by the Northwest's tech industry and old beach cottages that had long been the summer places of generations of families from over town who came to the island only when the weather was fair. A ball park and tiny playground gave the community a place to gather, and a boat launch offered them the opportunity to set a course into Useless Bay if the tide was high enough.

It was to this boat launch that Isis rode with Hayley following. There at its edge, she dropped her bike to the ground. She waited for Hayley to do likewise, and together they walked onto the beach.

It was mostly very wet sand, some driftwood, a lot of mud, and half a dozen tidepools. Here, there were walkers with dogs, moving along the vast expanse of Useless Bay, which horseshoed from tree-rich Indian Point in the south all the way north to Double Bluff Light. This was marked by the great tan bluffs of sandy earth that gave that spot its name.

Isis said to Hayley, "I want to show you something. I got the best idea . . ." and she set off down the beach in the direction of Indian Point. Not one hundred yards along, however, a large sign told potential beach walkers that the property beyond it was private and they were to keep off.

Hayley pointed this out to Isis. Isis pooh-poohed the warning, continuing on her way. She said, "No beach c'n be private. No *way* does that happen in California. You c'n be a movie star or something and you can't keep people off a beach in front of your place in Malibu."

"Isis!"

The other girl stopped walking. She said, "What?"

Hayley stumbled for words. "It's . . . Things're different here. The beach is private."

"That sucks. I want to *show* you something."

"Someone's going to come out and yell and—"

"Good grief. Like we're scared to get yelled at?" Isis continued on her way. "Let 'em call the cops if they don't like it. We'll be out of here before the cops show up."

"But if it's private property . . ."

Isis stamped her feet. "Hayley! Cowgirl *up*, for God's sake."

Hayley looked to her left, feeling furtive. The closest houses appeared uninhabited. More of them would become so as autumn deepened. And anyway, they were separated from the beach by a canal of wetland, so what was the big deal, truly, if she and Isis merely walked by them? It wasn't like they were burglars. They were just two girls strolling along the beach in the sun. So she followed Isis.

Some way along, the canal of wetland ended. At that point, Hayley and Isis came to a vacant lot, then to a tiny beach cottage listing to the right, then to another vacant lot with a chain across it. Isis stopped walking at a final house that was larger than all the rest. To Hayley's horror, the other girl walked right up to this place. It had a low wall separating a small yard from the beach and she climbed over it. She said to Hayley, "No big deal. I've been coming since June. The place's for sale. It's empty. Come *on*."

At least, Hayley thought, as she followed Isis, the other girl didn't proceed through some open window or push in a sliding glass door. What she wanted Hayley to see was a fire pit and its accompanying seating area along with a covered in-ground spa and the kind of outdoor kitchen one saw featured in magazines.

"Isn't this the coolest ever?" Isis asked. "This is exactly what I'm going to have when Brady and I are married. Course that's not happening for *years* because he's got to do medical school and all that, but when he starts making piles of money, it'll be the beach for us." There was a stack of beach chairs abutting the house, and Isis went for one of these as she talked.

Hayley watched her, incredulous, as Isis brought a chair over to the fire pit, went for another, sat down, and gestured Hayley to do the same. She put her feet up on the river stones of the fire pit's edge and continued chatting. "Course, I wouldn't tell Brady any of this. You won't say anything, will you? He's gonna come up if Aidan 'n' me are still here at Christmas." Isis was digging in her purse as she spoke and she seemed finally to notice that Hayley hadn't joined her. She said, "I'm just babbling. It's 'cause I'm nervous. How are *you*? You look so nice today. That color is perfect for your complexion, which is *also* perfect and I know perfect 'cause my mom's a dermatologist. And *anyway* . . . " She finally found what she was looking for and she brought out a slim chrome box from which she took out a cigarette.

Isis caught Hayley's look of surprise and said, "I used to smoke. This's electronic. You ever see one? Watch."

It took no lighting at all but when she sucked on it, the tip of it glowed and what it emitted looked like smoke but was instead vapor that bore no scent. It gave her a hit of nicotine, Isis said. Unfortunately, she was still addicted. This was how she dealt with the addiction. It had been her mom's idea.

"My parents know everything about me," she confided to Hayley. "Sex with Brady and two other guys before him, smoking, diet pills till I got caught, weed *also* till I got caught. Oxycontin once. *Just* once. We talk about it all 'cause the one thing they don't need is more than one kid who likes to keep secrets."

WHEN THEY RETURNED to the spot on the road where Aidan had disappeared into the trees, the boy himself was waiting for them. He joined them wordlessly and they trooped back to Nancy Howard's house. There, Nancy's partner, Linda, had arrived. Isis declared that she didn't know Linda's last name and didn't want to know it but what she *did* want to know was why Linda didn't at least remove that mustache of hers. Then she bundled Hayley into the car while Aidan silently made for the house and his bedroom, where Isis said he had "a cache of *Hustler* magazines under the bed."

True to her word, Isis drove Hayley home. The drive to Smugglers Cove Farm and Flowers was a long one from Maxwelton Beach, but Isis kept up her chatter all the way. When they got to the farm, Hayley told her friend just to drop her at the end of the driveway, but Isis said that no way was she going to do that, and she turned right in.

She said, "Is *all* of this your family's? I get it now. You didn't want me to know you're rich. Wow, what kind of barn is that?"

"It's for chickens."

"Chickens? In a barn that size? Who would've thought. My mom *never* told me there were places like this up here. It's just like *Little House on the Prairie*."

As she was talking, they were bumping along the road toward the house. In the distance, Hayley could see that her dad had come out of the big barn where the tractor was kept. He was dragging himself across the farmyard, demanding that his legs work as they used to work while the walker helped keep him upright. Seeing his struggle, she felt a pain in her chest.

"Mom never says one nice thing about Whidbey Island," Isis was continuing. "What my grandam says when Mom starts going on about Whidbey is, 'You never knew when you had it good, Lisa Ann.' Lisa Ann's my mom. Are you aware of how many Lisas there are in her generation? Only like a billion. It's why she named me Isis. Like, how many Isises are you gonna run into in one lifetime? I tell her if she hates her name she should have changed it to Chloe or something 'cause there aren't any Chloes her age. Or Beulah." Isis laughed. "It's not like there's *ever* going to be a run on Beulah."

Hayley watched her dad. He'd reached the big sycamore tree that shaded part of the house. He paused there and took note of the car's approach. He lifted a hand to wave and Hayley held her breath. But he didn't fall.

Isis stopped the car and said, "*Any*way thanks, Hayl. You're the best. I hope I didn't talk too much. Like I said, it's just nerves. Thanks for putting up with me."

Hayley's dad stumbled. Hayley bit her lip. She grabbed the door handle and said, "Got to go. See you in school, okay?"

Then she was out of the car and over to her father. Behind her she heard the sound of Isis reversing the car, turning, and steaming off happily down the driveway.

HAYLEY KNEW BETTER than to offer her father help. But she walked with him and told him about her day as they inched toward the back door. There were two steps to be negotiated and Hayley took her dad's arm. He said, "I'm not an old fart, Hayley," and shook her off. Thankfully, the door opened and Hayley's mom came outside.

She wouldn't take "leave me be" from her husband. She said, "Don't be silly, Bill. I'm not intending to let you fall and break a leg." He relented and they got him inside. But from there, he worked his way through the kitchen to the back of the house, where the downstairs bathroom was.

This, apparently, was what Hayley's mom had been waiting for because once the bathroom door closed, she said to Hayley, "Sit yourself at that table because you and I are going to talk."

Hayley did so. She saw that on the table lay the catalogues from Reed College and from Brown University, so Hayley knew that not only had Tatiana Primavera spoken to her mom but her mom had also gone into her bedroom and rooted through her things.

"Exactly what is going on?" Julie Cartwright demanded of her daughter.

Hayley went for dumb. "Huh? I got those at school. Miss Primavera—"

"I know all about Miss Primavera and her recommendation that you apply to either Reed or Brown. As far as I'm concerned, it's a fine idea because there're scholarships available and you have the grades and there's also work-study and low-interest loans and financial aid but *none* of that"—she slapped her hand on the table when she said *none*—"is going to make the slightest bit of difference if you don't get your butt in gear. So you better have a very good story about why you haven't even begun your senior essay."

"I've begun it."

"Have you indeed. And when did you intend to let Ms. Primavera have a look at it?"

"It's too complicated, so far."

"I'm supposed to believe that?" Julie demanded. "Let me see. A string of perfect grades in every English class you've ever taken since seventh grade and suddenly an essay to accompany your college applications is too complicated? Do you actually want me to believe—"

"Mom," Hayley said.

"Do not 'mom' me. The last thing I need is for you to become one more thing I get to worry about."

Hayley heard the tremor in her mother's voice and as if to underscore this, the toilet in the downstairs bathroom flushed, the water ran, the door opened, and her father's walker scraped the jamb. He swore in a low voice, but it carried to the kitchen. Both Hayley and her mom looked in his direction.

"I have," Julie Cartwright said quietly, "quite enough to handle."

"I'm not going to college."

"What kind of game is this? Is this Seth's idea to keep you on the island?"

"Seth has nothing to do with anything."

"You think that's so? He'd love it if you stayed right here on this farm and never gave a thought to going anywhere, to college or even to the mall."

"Hayley's not going to college?" Brooke had slithered into the room from beyond the dining room, where the living room lay. In there, Cassidy was watching something on television. It was too loud, as usual.

"Your sister and I are discussing something," Julie Cartwright said to her middle child. "This is private. And you're supposed to be spending time with Cassie."

"She won't turn it down," was Brooke's reply, "and it's Hayley's turn to watch her anyway."

"Brooke, I told you—"

Fiercely, Brooke pulled a chair out from the table. "And *I'm* telling *you* that I'm sick of watching her and I'm sick of doing stuff Hayley's supposed to be doing like helping at the market and I'm sick of cleaning chicken shit out of the—"

"Brooke Jeannette, another demonstration of that kind of language and you know what happens."

"What?" Brooke demanded. "Shit shit shit. What're you going to do? Wash my mouth out?" That said, she flung herself out of the room. She stormed down the hall toward the back of the house. Hayley and her mother both heard the crash as she ran into her father.

Bill Cartwright cried out. Brooke shrieked, "I'm *sorry!*"

Hayley said to her mom as she hurried from the kitchen, "I can't go off island and I won't go off island."

PART II

*South Whidbey High School
Djangofest*

FIFTEEN

Only three rehearsals were necessary to bring Parker Natalia up to speed on what Triple Threat would be performing at Djangofest. So when the first day of the festival rolled around, the young Canadian was ready. He was also eager to show up the members of BC Django 21.

Seth couldn't blame him. He and Parker had heard that group jamming beneath the bandshell at Useless Bay Coffee House, a trendy coffee and bean-roasting establishment on Second Street in Langley. The sound carried over to the front garden of South Whidbey Commons across the street where Triple Threat was going over their program, so every one of the Triple Threat members had an earful of how good those guys were.

BC Django 21 had replaced Parker with a girl. Seth saw Parker's shoulders slump when he got a look at her and a listen to her music. Loyally, he said to Parker, "You're just as good, man," but Parker didn't buy it. He wandered off, looking completely bummed. Well, Seth thought, Triple Threat would give him plenty of opportunity to show his stuff.

The slot of 5:00 at the high school was reserved for groups

who weren't going to bring in a crowd, but the organizers had reckoned without the vast Darrow clan. There were five original Darrow brothers among the immediate family of Seth's grandfather, and all of them had remained on the island and had produced large families. These families had also remained on the island, marrying into other island families until the Darrow connections were so numerous that people had stopped trying to keep track of them. One thing was certain, though. Every individual with a drop of Darrow blood in his veins showed up at the concert, along with Seth's employer, his fellow builders, and his friends.

The performance was held in the school auditorium. Aside from his family, Seth was happy to see from backstage that Hayley had come. So had Becca and Derric. Jenn McDaniels was with them. The kid he'd met at his grandfather's place—Aidan Martin—was hanging with those others, too. So was a girl Seth didn't recognize, but he got introduced to her at intermission when he took Parker over to meet anyone he hadn't yet met.

The girl was Isis Martin, Aidan's sister, and it turned out she was tight with Hayley. She was a serious babe, and Seth gave a glance at Parker to see if he'd registered this. But he found the young Canadian man eying Hayley, who was also eying him. She was even blushing. Seth heard Jenn McDaniels mutter to Becca, "Whoa, trigger that Romeo and Juliet music," which told him he wasn't imagining things about some sort of instant attraction between Hayley and Parker.

People were talking all around him, but he was listening to Hayley tell Parker that she was a senior at the high school, that she was an old friend of Seth's, and that she lived up island a ways on a farm called Smugglers Cove Farm and Flowers. Then someone started talking directly to him so Seth couldn't catch the rest but he was relieved when Parker said he was going outside to have a smoke to steady his nerves for their performance. He was quickly *unrelieved*, however, when Parker added, "See you later?" to Hayley.

Parker worked his way out of the auditorium. Derric said, "Nice score, Hayley." Isis Martin said, "That guy? He's, like, totally gay. You c'n tell by looking." Her eyes were speculatively on Parker as she spoke. He was digging a package of cigarettes from his shirt's breast pocket. She said something about the way the dude moved his hips. Then she added, "I need a hit, too," and she followed him out of the auditorium.

Jenn said sardonically, "Uh right. He's *extremely* gay. You better hope he gets back in time for your set, Seth, 'cause I betcha what Isis has in mind is going to take a while."

Hayley spoke. "Jenn! That's not fair."

Jenn rolled her eyes. "Come on. Am I the *only* one who's noticed that whenever she's around—" She seemed to realize that everything she was saying was in front of Isis's brother as well. She turned to him with a "Sorry, Aidan," but he had already left them.

"He's a smoker, too," Hayley told them as if in explanation.

"He's a weirdo," Jenn said. "He probably wants to watch."

Becca said something that Seth didn't catch because for his part, he was fixed on Hayley. He knew he couldn't do a thing about her and her feelings, but in spite of this knowledge there were times when he *still* wanted to change how it was between them. She caught him looking at her. She offered him a smile and the words, "Good luck up there," and that was it.

At that point, he became more concerned about when Parker intended to come back inside. Time was ticking away and the MC had just taken the stage to tell everyone the concert was about to go on. Someone opened a door and yelled this information to those who'd left the auditorium, and soon enough Parker Natalia returned. Behind him came Isis Martin. It looked, Seth thought, like Jenn was right. Isis was smiling knowingly. She rejoined the others and the last thing Seth heard her say as he walked away was, "Uh . . . maybe he's *not* gay after all."

After that, Triple Threat took the stage with their instruments. A murmur went around the auditorium. This was directed, Seth figured, at Parker. The Canadian was providing the *ahhh* factor for the ladies. When it came time for his solo, though, the *ahhh* factor turned into the *oh-my-God* factor. He was one hell of a fiddler.

After their performance, it was time for the final group of the evening to come onto the stage. But they only got as far as taking up their instruments when the first of the sirens split the evening in two, and an alarm went off.

THE FIRE WASN'T at the school. But the alarm and the proximity of the sirens put the crowd on its feet and sent them toward the doors. Some people went outside to the front of the school; others went through the New Commons and out to the back. From there, they could see the fire engine on the sweep of hill that led up to South Whidbey Park. It flashed red and yellow lights into the night sky while some distance from this, a group of fire fighters hosed a blaze that was eating up an old shed on the side of one of the baseball diamonds within the park.

A sheriff's car was there, too. Seth heard Derric say to Becca, "Looks like the plan didn't work."

For a crazy second, Seth thought the guy was talking about *his* plan to burn down a shed in the middle of his concert. But they told him that the sheriff's department and the fire chief had planned security at every Djangofest venue just in case the summer's firebug showed up for the thrill of setting another blaze in close proximity to a crowd.

"They thought he'd set a fire right *at* the event," Becca said to Seth.

"Looks close enough to me," Seth said. Then he looked around, although he couldn't have said what he was seeking in the crowd.

What he found, though, was Hayley and Parker with Parker's arm around Hayley protectively as if he intended to prove to her that he'd be just the guy to save her if they had to make a run for safety.

SIXTEEN

Jenn McDaniels was the one who brought up Isis. She did it in her usual Jenn way, without putting any icing on the subject. They were at the lunch table and the first thing Jenn noted was that Isis Martin had not graced them with her presence. She was, instead, sitting with her brother across the New Commons where Aidan generally sat alone. Becca wished they were closer so that she could pick up their whispers because their conversation looked intense. As it was, Becca could only get the whispers of her immediate companions, Jenn's having to do with loathing Isis, Hayley's having to do with wondering when Jenn was going to *come out and admit it because no one really cares*, and Derric's having to do with *never knew there was an album and now what am I supposed to*, which caused her to look at him and wonder what was going on.

She used the ear bud so that she could focus on what was being *said* at their table instead of hearing what people were thinking. What was being said was Jenn declaring, "There were *no* fires till that chick showed up."

Hayley said, "That's not something you should even hint at without having proof, Jenn."

"I'm not hinting. I'm *saying*. There's something way seriously wrong with that space case: how she never shuts up, how
it's all about her, her, her, how she pretends to be friends and
then . . . like, hey, look at how she followed that dude Parker when
he left the Commons the other night when *everyone* could see he
was hot for you."

"Here she comes," Derric said quietly.

Isis, Becca thought, looked a little pinched around the eyes.
On the other side of the Commons, her brother slouched out of
the room. Isis thumped down into an extra chair at the table and
said, "He has a bad day and the world's the problem." She wasn't
speaking to anyone in particular, but Hayley was the one who
asked, "Is something wrong?"

Jenn mouthed at Becca, Here we go, and next to her Becca
heard Derric chuckle. She couldn't blame either of them because
the simple question from Hayley was all it took.

Isis said, "He's all upset about American Lit. I mean, it was a
quiz, that's all, but the teacher had *said* there would be one and
he forgot. *And* he didn't read what he was supposed to read in
whatever-it-was, a chapter in *Moby-Dick* or whatever, and now
it's the end of the world to him. Brothers. You're lucky you have
a sister, Hayl."

"Jenn has brothers," Becca offered. "She c'n relate."

Isis looked at her, her eyes rather vague and unfocused as if
Becca were on the other side of the room. She said, "Jenn? Oh,
Jenn. You do?"

"Two," Becca said because she knew very well that no way on
earth was Jenn going to talk to the girl.

Isis said, "I had two. Only one now but . . . wish I had a sister. Hayley, c'n I talk to you? In private?" And then to the others, "No offense, you guys, but this is personal." She got to her feet and said, "Hayl? I mean, if you don't mind. You're the only one I can . . . you know."

Hayley got to her feet. She shoved the rest of her lunch into its paper sack and said, "Oh gosh. Sure," and followed Isis. They went out of the New Commons in the direction of the stairs to the classrooms above.

"I'm telling you, there is something r-o-n-g with that chick," Jenn declared.

"You forgot the *w*," Derric told her.

W OR NOT, Becca wondered about Jenn's aversion toward Isis Martin. Jenn always had a chip on her shoulder and it was especially large if she figured someone came from a privileged background. From Isis's chatter, all of them had learned about her life in Palo Alto, about her boyfriend, Brady, and about her parents who were both doctors and, in Jenn's eyes, consequently rolling in cash. Isis had a car, an iPhone, an iPad, and a wardrobe that had not been purchased at the local thrift store. Those facts alone would have made Jenn hate her on principle. But the truth was that Isis Martin hadn't been the only person newly come to the island and in the vicinity since the time of the first fire. Her brother also was new to Whidbey. But so was someone else.

She went to the library to check on this last person: Parker

Natalia. For if Isis and Aidan had both ducked out of the high school auditorium prior to the latest fire, so had Parker. And now Parker was staying in the forest at Ralph Darrow's place at the end of a very dry summer.

She left Derric with Jenn. They'd just been joined by Jenn's old friend Squat Cooper, whose "Whassup, you guys?" had to be answered at length with an invitation to enter an argument about who was more inclined to set fires, boys or girls. Squat was more than willing to join in, so it was easy enough for Becca to take off alone with just, "Library," to Derric, to which she added, "Later?" He nodded.

Inside the library, there was one computer free. She logged on and thought about where to begin. Checking out his story seemed the logical place. He'd said he was from Nelson, he'd said his family had a restaurant there, it was called Natalia and had been there for years . . . If all this was true, it would be somewhere on the Net because everything was if you knew where to look.

This was the case for Natalia, an Italian restaurant that specialized in Sicilian food. Turned out that it had been reviewed by newspapers from as far away as Calgary and Vancouver. So it was real enough, and right where Parker said it would be. As to Parker himself—

"So why'd you lie?"

Becca swung around.

Aidan Martin stood there. He read the computer's screen over her shoulder.

At the entire idea of lying, Becca knew she had to get more off the boy than merely his spoken words. She flicked the ear bud out of her ear and said, "What're you talking about?"

Some kind of secret . . . didn't give her a lot to work with. What was it to him anyway if she had secrets? It was starting to look like she wasn't the only one.

He said, "You said you were doing an assignment for art class."

"What're you talking about?"

"Drawing faces? Comparing faces? That day over at South Whidbey Commons? Only you don't take art, so I guess you were lying. Why?" *All the people to look at in the entire frigging world so what would it really take for her* made Becca's palms start to sweat, especially in combination with the idea of an art class.

She said, "And you know this how?"

"That you aren't taking art? Because I *am* taking art and you ain't in the class."

"Uh . . . right, Aidan. But there's more than one art class in this school, you know."

"Sure. But you aren't in any of them."

"And you know *this* how?"

"Because I checked your schedule." *Something not right all the way around . . . if her and me get talking . . . boyfriend but if I know Isis . . .*

Becca felt the alarm bells jangling through her nerves. His whispers were heading in more than one direction and she didn't like any of them. She said, "What's it to you? And, by the way, there're other art classes on this island besides the ones taught at school, okay?"

He sat down next to her, pulling a chair over to do so. He looked at the monitor, where the screen still showed its references to Natalia's Restaurant in Nelson, B.C. He said, "That's the last name of that fiddler dude, right? Natalia. You hot for him?" *Because that black dude would . . .*

"I have a cousin in the same town," Becca said, going back to the story she'd used with Parker. "She never mentioned the restaurant Parker's family owns, and I wanted to check it out. D'you want to tell me why this is *any* of your business?"

"Hey, chill."

"I'm not gonna chill. You looked up my schedule, you want to know why I'm reading about a restaurant in Canada, you accuse me of lying, and I'm not going—"

"'S happening?" It was Derric's voice. Becca hadn't heard him or seen him come into the library. And now there he was and the look on his face told her he was there to make sure that she wasn't harassed by anyone.

AIDAN GOT TO his feet. He said, "Hey, man," and he thought *trouble that I don't need.*

"Hey," Derric said in turn. But that was all. Obviously, he was waiting for an answer.

Becca logged off the Internet site because the only worse thing than having Derric wonder why Aidan Martin was bugging her was having Derric wonder why she was looking up anything having to do with Nelson, B.C.

She said to him, "Hey. You finished up fast."

"Finished what?"

"Lunch."

"Bell's in five minutes. I was planning to walk you to class."

Like she'd get lost or something was what Aidan was thinking but at least he didn't say it. What he did say with a lazy slow smile was, "Saved by the bell, then," to Becca. And "See you guys later," to both of them.

Derric said to him, "Too bad about American Lit," although he didn't sound particularly sympathetic.

Aidan frowned. "What about American Lit?"

"Quiz, test, whatever it was," Derric said. "Your sister told us—"

Aidan gave a high-pitched laugh. The PTA mom who ran the library at lunchtime hissed at them all to be silent or leave. Aidan said, "*That's* what she said?" and then he was gone, shouldering his backpack of books and shoving open the door.

SEVENTEEN

D erric was silent as they walked to Becca's next class, which was Health. She could tell they were thinking the same thing, though. His whispers were claiming *keep him in my sights* and while she wanted to tell him that he didn't exactly need to be her knight-in-armor when it came to Aidan, the truth was that the kid made her uneasy every time she ran into him.

When they got to her classroom, she said, "D'you think Isis lied?"

"About that American Lit thing?" And when Becca nodded, "Maybe Aidan's trying to make it look like she did. Or maybe Jenn's right."

"That Isis is setting those fires?" He studied her for a moment during which the final bell rang, telling them both that they were late for class. He said, "I don't know. But I have a feeling . . . Could be a good idea to give both of them a lot of space, Becca."

She *could* do that, she thought. But her reality was that the last person she wanted getting close to her secrets was someone like Aidan Martin.

AFTER SCHOOL, SHE realized that there was a good way that she could deal with part of her worries. She rode the free island bus from the school into Langley, and when it dropped her close to the Cliff Motel, she was practically at her destination's door step. This wasn't one of the days that Derric acted the part of Big Brother to Josh Grieder, so the coast was clear. But it wasn't as clear as she'd have liked it to be. A familiar pickup truck was parked in the lot.

Just as Becca was considering the option of coming back later, Chloe Grieder came out of the motel's office. The little girl saw her, and shouted, "Becca! You got to see! Grammer made a cake shaped 'xactly like a punkin. It's for Halloween. For the church bazaar. I mean not *yet* 'cause it's not Halloween and she's just practicing. Only we get to eat it tonight. You got to *see*, okay?"

Becca smiled. Only when you were seven years old could a pumpkin-shaped cake inspire such joy. She walked over and gave Chloe a hug. She said, "A punkin cake?"

"For church." She pointed across the street from the motel where the Christian Missionary Alliance had its church. There, on Halloween night, the church's multipurpose room morphed into bazaar, haunted house, and everything else imaginable to keep small children entertained.

Becca followed Chloe into the motel's office, which gave way to the apartment's living room with its family clutter. From there a kitchen opened up. Chloe's grandmother was seated at the old Formica-topped table, and she and Diana Kinsale were evaluating the pumpkin cake Chloe had been crowing about.

"Hey, darlin'," was Debbie Grieder's habitual greeting to Becca. "What d'you think? The color's not right. Too much orange, I say."

"Let's eat it!" Unbidden, Chloe climbed up onto Diana Kinsale's lap.

Diana had turned in her chair and was smiling fondly at Becca, but Becca didn't smile back at once. Diana looked so tired. And where was Oscar? Diana went nowhere without that poodle.

Diana extended her hand to Becca. Becca took it and Diana said, "Ah." Something flowed between them as it always did.

Debbie said to her, "So? The color. What d'you think?"

Becca gazed at the cake. Debbie had got the pumpkin shape. She'd got the green of the stem, too. But she was right. The color was too orange, and that's what she said, adding, "All the better to eat it right now."

"Yippee!" Chloe cried.

Diana stirred at this and said it was time for her to leave. She clasped Debbie's arm in her Diana way and said, "Be well, friend," and then to Becca, "Walk with me to the truck, Becca. I've been carrying something around for you."

Becca followed Diana out to her truck, where she rooted through her glove compartment and brought forth a small, beaten-up book. It was very old and the title on its cover had long since become unreadable. Becca asked what it was as she opened it. She saw the title within: *Seeing Beyond Sight.*

"What's it mean?" she asked.

"You'll have to read it to find out." Diana reached out in that way she had and smoothed her hand along Becca's hair. She—Diana—had been responsible for its alteration to sun-streaked fair from the disgusting muddy dark brown she'd dyed it when fleeing San Diego. Diana was also responsible for its style, which capped her head. She'd called it Becca's pick-me-up. For Becca it had meant a partial return to the human race.

Diana said, "You look troubled. Derric?"

"No. He's good. But there's this kid at school and I'm a little freaked out by him." And then, of course, there was Rejoice, but she wasn't about to tell Diana Kinsale a thing about her. She added, "We got into it a couple of times, and I don't know what to make of him. Neither does Derric. We're both sort of concerned."

Diana observed her in that questioning way of hers. "And that's all?"

"Pretty much," Becca lied. She'd told the truth as far as she could. There was more, but she didn't know what it was yet.

"Ah." Diana said nothing more for a moment. Becca felt her gaze and turned her head back to meet Diana's compassionate eyes. "Well, in my experience without struggle there is no growth and without growth there is no life."

Becca clenched her fists. "You're doing that Yoda thing again."

Diana laughed. "Then let me say it this way. We're here to learn, but every person we meet has a different lesson for us. What complicates matters is that our lessons keep colliding into other people's lessons. Is that less Yoda-like for you?"

"I guess," Becca said. "I'll think about it."

"That's all anyone can ask." Diana gestured at the small gift she'd given Becca. "Enjoy the book. And come to see me. The dogs are missing you."

AIDAN MARTIN'S CURIOSITY about Becca could have meant anything. But the fact that he was curious about her in the first place needed to be dealt with. One way to do this seemed to be by affirming the original story that Becca and Debbie had concocted to get her into South Whidbey High School. They hadn't used it again aside from passing it along to the sheriff at one point, but it was crucial that Debbie still be willing to make the same claim about her relationship to Becca.

They were straightening the kitchen from Debbie's baking of the pumpkin cake when Becca brought it up. She said to Debbie, "I got to ask you something, but I'm not sure how to do it."

Debbie was drying her hands on a tattered tea towel printed with chickens and chicks. "Going straight at it is probably best. You need to move back here, darlin? You're always welcome."

"No. Things're real good with Mr. Darrow."

"Then . . . ?" Debbie reached for a pack of cigarettes, lit up, inhaled, coughed way too much, then picked a piece of tobacco from her tongue.

Becca took her ear bud out because she was going to need Debbie's whispers in order to know how to guide the conversation. She said, "I was wondering . . . If anyone asks, c'n you still say you're my aunt like you did last year?"

Debbie observed her from behind the smoke from her cigarette. "Who's gonna ask?" she asked shrewdly. "You in some kind of trouble?"

Debbie had got her into school by saying that Becca was her niece. Then she'd covered for her the previous November when Jeff Corrie had shown up after receiving the sheriff's call that told him a cell phone purchased by his missing wife had been found in the parking lot of Saratoga Woods, just outside of a town called Langley. Jeff had come armed with a picture of Laurel but he hadn't brought one of Becca. Logically, he'd thought that where he found the mother, he'd find the child, because the last thing he would ever consider as a possibility was the truth: that Laurel had split away from her daughter.

Debbie knew nothing about a Laurel Armstrong and she told Jeff so. She also knew nothing about a mother and daughter newly come to town. What she did know was that in room four-four-four of her motel was living a girl called Becca King who was supposedly waiting for her mom to return for her, but since this stranger wasn't asking about a Becca King and since he wasn't asking about a girl waiting for her mother, Debbie said not a word to him about Becca. She'd just studied the picture he showed her and then she'd said nope, she hadn't seen this woman at all.

That had been it. Becca knew that Debbie had her suspicions about Laurel Armstrong and her relationship to Becca King and to the mom Becca was waiting for, but Becca had never brought Debbie into the picture and she was hoping that she wouldn't have to. Now, though, Debbie had asked her directly: Who's gonna ask any questions about you? And her whispers were telling Becca that at some point she was going to have to reveal more than she wanted to reveal to anyone. *Something's going on here* was right at the front of Debbie's mind. So was *If she is a runaway what kind of trouble is this going to make for me?*

Becca would have been thrilled to hear how well she was picking up Debbie's whispers had they not been verging so close to the truth. She said, "I dunno who'll ask. Except there's this boy at school . . . his name's Aidan Martin . . . and—"

It's really about Derric.

Well, that was true. Most things for Becca *were* about Derric one way or another, but not this time. She said, "It's just that this kid—Aidan—he keeps trying to trip me up about things. I don't know why. So I wouldn't be surprised if he showed up here and asked you about me. If you could say I'm your niece like you did before . . ."

"Sure, darlin," Debbie agreed. "Your story and mine? They're still the same till you tell me otherwise, no matter who asks."

EIGHTEEN

Hayley had just had an argument with her mom when Isis showed up at her house that night. Julie Cartwright had demanded that Hayley make an appointment for them both to meet with Tatiana Primavera to discuss "the sabotaging of her life." When Hayley refused, her mom burst into tears. Hayley's dad worked his way into the kitchen. Brooke followed him and said, "Nice *going*, Hayley," and their mom had shouted, "Keep *out* of this." At that, Brooke angrily claimed she was only trying to *help*, for God's sake. At which point, Hayley's dad asked what in hell was going on, and the last thing anyone wanted to do was actually to tell him, so Hayley's mom lied and Brooke then said, "Oh yeah, let's all just keep *pretending*," and crashed out of the room.

That was when the doorbell rang and there was Isis. Brooke answered with a hostile, "So I guess you want *Hayley*," and left Isis standing there. She'd shouted, "It's your *friend*, Hayley," making it sound like, "It's a pool of vomit, Hayley," and Hayley felt ashamed that Isis had to see her family like this. She hastened the other girl up to her room.

Isis started talking on the way up the stairs. "I needed to talk to you. I can't *believe* how you acted."

Hayley stopped and turned. Below her on the stairs, Isis's face was pinched. She had a shoulder bag that she was carrying and her fist was tight on its strap.

"Why did you treat me like that at lunch today?" Isis demanded.

"Like . . . Huh? What?"

"D'you think I *wanted* to have lunch with Aidan? Why didn't you come over to our table? I *know* you saw me there."

Hayley stared at her. She couldn't come up with a reply because she couldn't believe that someone else was actually about to rag on her.

Isis said, "You could have come over. You could have asked how things're going. You could have acted like you noticed that something was wrong. But you didn't and I have to ask myself why and I think I know."

Hayley went up the rest of the stairs and into her room. Isis followed. "I've been here for you," Isis told her. "I've been your friend. I've asked you to eat with me and come places with me and we've been to the beach and I've bought your jewelry and do you know how *much* it cost me to buy that dumb jewelry and what have *you* done for me in return? Just ignored me. Like it was perfectly okay with you that there I was trying to deal with Aidan, who happens to be the *only* reason I have to live in this hellhole."

Hayley felt pummeled, but there was something so crazy in what Isis was saying. . . . "What?" she demanded and her voice grew louder as she felt the anger bubbling in her. "*What* do you want, Isis? My mom's on my case and my dad is really *sick* in case you haven't noticed and not everything in life is all about *you*."

Isis gasped. Her eyes flooded with tears. "You can say . . . ? You're my *friend*. You're the only one I even trust. And now with what's happened . . ." She stumbled to Hayley's bed, sat down on the edge, and doubled over. "I'm sorry," she said, weeping. "I'm going crazy. I just attacked you, and it isn't fair, and I *know* it and now you hate me."

Tentatively, Hayley sat down next to her. She touched her shoulder and said more quietly, "What's going on?"

"It's Brady." Isis began sobbing. "He says he wants to 'take a break.' He says we can't keep Skyping each other and I'm texting him too much and he can't keep answering and his grades are slipping. I *know* that I need to ease up and I can't because this is about Madison Ridgeway, who was, like, just *waiting* for her chance to hook up with Brady. I want to *die*."

"Oh gosh, Isis," Hayley said. "I'm so sorry about Brady."

Isis raised her face, her melting mascara making raccoon rings around her eyes. "*Sorry?* Oh he c'n just wait for what I'm going to do to him." She wiped her nose on the back of her hand. Hayley got up and got tissues from her dresser, and Isis took about ten and crumped them into her fist. "I'm gonna make him so jealous. I'm gonna make him *have* to think about getting back with me. I'm gonna hook up with someone here and plaster it all over my Facebook page . . . Only with who? I *got* to hook up with someone but the pickings are so shitty except for that Parker dude but how can I . . . I could get to him through Seth, right? Or maybe I could hook up with Seth. He's not too bright and he probably wouldn't even think—"

Hayley felt herself getting hot all over again. "Seth," she said, "happens to be my friend."

"I didn't mean to—"

"He was her boyfriend," Brooke's voice said.

The girls both swung around and Brooke was in the doorway. God only knew how long she'd been standing there, a small and knowing smile on her face. "He's her ex-boyfriend now," Brooke said, "but he doesn't exactly like it that way."

"Oh my God!" Isis said. "I didn't mean . . . No *wonder* you hate me. I just say anything. It's like I can't help it. I keep blowing it and you're my best friend here and I didn't *mean* anything, Hayley, with what I said about Seth. I just mean that he's not my type. He's really so nice but if I posted him and me on my Facebook page, no one would ever believe—"

"Does she ever shut up?" Brooke cut in. "What's *wrong* with you, Hayley? Whatever happened to having *real* friends?"

ISIS WORKED ON quelling Hayley's concerns about her. She apologized at school the following day, and this time it wasn't a histrionic apology accompanied by tears and anguish and self-loathing. It was instead a "C'n I talk to you, Hayley?" said quietly in the morning before the final bell rang when Hayley was stowing her lunch in her locker. Hayley said sure, and Isis led her to a sheltered corner near the stairs.

She said, "My mom calls what I do throwing dog poop. Only she doesn't say *poop* if you know what I mean."

Hayley didn't reply because she was no longer sure what to make of Isis. The girl was totally altered now: calm like the waters of Saratoga Passage on a windless day.

Isis went on. "I get wound up, and I say stuff. I'm loud and I cry and I say the first thing that comes into my head. But I don't mean any of it. I'm so totally sorry you had to see that part of me because you didn't deserve it."

Hayley licked her lips. "Look, Isis . . . there's a ton of stuff going on at my house right now and—"

"Your dad. I know. I saw him that time I drove you home. I didn't want to say anything 'cause you hadn't ever told me something was wrong with him. What I figured was if you hadn't ever said anything maybe I wasn't s'posed to say anything either. I'm sorry you thought that I didn't care. I *do* care. I c'n be a decent friend to you if you'll let me."

Hayley nodded. There was real truth in what Isis was saying, especially when it came to Hayley's father. She *didn't* talk about him or his condition, so how could she expect other people to forge ahead and talk about him when it was so obvious that ignoring what was in front of them for as long as possible was the Cartwright way of life?

She said to Isis, "I'm sorry too. I could've been better at noticing. That day with Aidan and how upset you were at lunch? I know how it is to have a little brother or sister." Hayley quirked her mouth. "Brooke," she added. "She's really at a bad age."

"Poor thing," Isis said.

"I try to remember that."

"No," Isis told her. "I meant you. I get all over you because you're not noticing me when I should be noticing *you*. That's going to change if we c'n still be friends. I hope we can."

Hayley nodded.

ISIS CAME UP with the idea of the party on Maxwelton Beach. She wanted to do something nice for Hayley, and wouldn't it be fun while the weather was good to have a party? It would be a cookout and they could invite the "regular lunch table crowd" as Isis put it, along with anyone else that Hayley and she could think of. As if to make up for anything negative she'd said about him, Isis mentioned Seth as well. She said, "Hey, if he brought his band, then we could have music, too. And I bet those guys could supply us with beer 'cause they're old enough, aren't they? Weed, too. They c'n get us some weed."

Hayley told her that Seth Darrow didn't smoke weed, and at this Isis laughed. "Musicians *always* smoke weed."

"Not Seth. He's got a bunch of learning disabilities so he doesn't do drugs. He'll drink a beer but not more than one."

Isis said, "Wow," and she sounded admiring. "I wish Aidan would take a page out of *that* book. Well, whatever. Should we invite Seth and his group? What about that guy Parker?"

Before she got any further, Hayley knew she had to break the bad news to Isis. "We can't have a cookout on the beach," she told her. "We can't even be there at all."

Isis's face went slack. "But *part* of it's for the public, isn't it?

See, I figure me and Aidan can take a whole bunch of Grandam's discarded wood down there in advance. We can build a bonfire. We can take blankets and food and when it's—"

"Someone'll call the cops," Hayley told her. "No fires on the beach."

"But no one even *lives* there full-time. When you and I were there and we saw that one house, you *said* no one lives there full-time."

"In *that* house," Hayley said, "and in some of the others. But not all of them are summer homes or vacation rentals. There's people who've lived there for years. And anyway, there're certain hours when you can't even be on the beach."

"That is *so* stupid. I swear, this whole Washington beach thing is crazy." Isis thought about this, her mouth downturned till an idea apparently struck her and she said, "Okay, then. We'll use that fire pit we saw."

"What fire pit?"

"No one's living in that house. I told you it's for sale, right? And on either side, there's not *even* a house so we could use that fire pit in their yard and have our party and no one will know. Remember, there's chairs outside and a couple of driftwood benches and oh my God there's that hot tub, too! And the outdoor kitchen!"

"We can't—"

"I'll go down there and scout around. I'll check to see how close any of the other houses are. I mean houses where people are actually living. I'll report back and *if* no one's living nearby right now, let's do it. It'll be secret and fun and maybe an opportunity to put a serious lip lock on some total stud. I wouldn't mind that, would you? Like that dude Parker. He's seriously yummy. Have you seen him since Djangofest?"

Hayley shook her head.

"*Well* then . . . I'll just go down and check things out."

Hayley thought about it. It wouldn't hurt just to check things out, she decided.

NINETEEN

At first Becca thought that the book Diana Kinsale had given her, *Seeing Beyond Sight*, was going to be about having visions, and it was in a way. But the visions weren't premonitions about the future or seeing dead people and receiving messages from them. Instead, the visions had to do with people in everyday life and what their memory pictures were. They had to do with entering people's minds and *seeing* the pictures that defined their memories and thoughts, and this brought Diana Kinsale perilously close to declaring to Becca that she knew perfectly well that Becca could hear what was going in people's heads. This also brought Diana perilously close to saying, "Here's your next step, my dear."

What made it scary for Becca was that she'd already *had* these visions that were talked about in *Seeing Beyond Sight*. She'd had them three times. Twice she'd seen someone's picture memories through establishing a connection to that person with Diana Kinsale as the conduit, like a chain of three links formed with Diana in the middle. Once she'd had the vision by making a connection with someone on her own. Diana knew something about these visions, but what she didn't know was how clear they'd been.

Yet she seemed to be telling Becca that what she could become was someone able to see, hear, and somehow know many things that were unavailable to other people. The very idea terrified her. So she set the book aside on a shelf in her bedroom at Ralph Darrow's house and she gazed at it nightly next to her childhood copy of *Anne of Green Gables*. But she didn't pick it up again to read.

There were other things to concern her. Foremost was Derric. He'd been brooding about something for several days, and he'd not wanted to talk about it. When she finally allowed herself to invade his whispers, *album* was the only word she heard.

She resolved to say nothing to Derric till he said something to her. This he finally did after school on his third day of brooding.

She was at his house. In his bedroom together, they were working on homework when Derric shoved his notebook to one side and said, "I need to show you something." He pulled open a dresser drawer. Here was the album that had been in his thoughts, Becca saw, a picture album. He nodded at the bed and she sat down. He sat next to her and handed it over with *now she's gonna see* in his mind.

Inside the album, was a pictorial history of Derric's adoption into the Mathieson family. It began with the orphanage in Kampala, and it ended with the Mathieson clan here in this house welcoming him to his new home. It wasn't a large album, but it was a detailed one, complete with written explanations of how everything had begun with Rhonda's first trip to the Ugandan orphanage along with their church group. On this trip and on subsequent trips as the Mathiesons waited for Derric's adoption to go through, she'd taken dozens of pictures.

"This is great," Becca murmured as she turned the pages,

which were beautifully decorated with cutouts and maps and journal entries.

Derric said nothing in return, so she looked at him. His face was stormy. *It's what they want to know* said that he believed there was a hidden message in the pages of the album. She frowned and said, "Don't you like it? What's wrong?"

"She had us all sit together and look at it." There was an edge of anxiety to his voice.

"That makes sense, doesn't it?"

God's sake, Becca! came from him. Becca frowned. She put the ear bud back into her ear, the better to hear his words rather than thoughts that indicated his mood. "They wanted me to *name* the kids," he said. "In the pictures where there's a bunch of us doing something. 'Do you remember this boy?' they were asking. 'What about this little girl? She's a real cutie.'"

Becca saw where this was heading. She said, "Rejoice is in the pictures, isn't she?" and she looked down to seek his sister's face. She'd only seen one photo of the little girl, in a picture taken of the orphanage's small brass band. Derric had been a member of that band, a grinning boy with an overlarge saxophone in his hands, and Rejoice had been one of the listening children when the picture was taken, a laughing little elf of a girl in the midst of clapping her hands. Becca looked through the pictures to find that same face, and there she was, here and there among the other children but never photographed only with Derric.

Becca looked up. "What did you do?"

"What *could* I do? I named the kids, at least the ones I said I remembered. I told them I didn't remember all of them 'cause it had been a while, and I hadn't known them all that good, especially the littlest ones. I said whatever frigging thing came into my head. But that didn't stop her. Like anything would?"

"Rejoice." Becca said the name on a breath.

"My dad must've told her about those letters, and you *know* my mom. 'F she thinks anything is wrong in what's supposed to be my perfect life—saved from an African orphanage and all that—then she's not gonna give up till she finds out what it is and fixes it for me."

"So did she ask directly about Rejoice?"

"*Course* she did. 'Dad told me you had a special friend in Kampala. Is Rejoice in the pictures?' And believe me, I do *not* know why she needed to see her except she *always* wants inside my head and she *never* lets go of anything so she sure as hell isn't going to let go of the fact that I wrote letters to some babe called Rejoice and never mailed them and even felt I had to hide them away. At *least* she doesn't know I hid them in the woods because believe me if she knew that, I'd be signed up for counseling so fast I'd feel like the skids were greased to get me there."

"What'd you tell her?"

"I sure as hell didn't tell the truth."

"Derric, it was your *chance*. They gave you an opening."

He surged up from the bed and paced over to the window, then to the desk, then to stand in front of her. "*Think* about it, okay? I tell them I spent eight years writing to a frigging five-year-old and what're they going to think?"

"She's not five now."

He blew out an impatient breath. "So I started when she was five and I wrote them till she was thirteen or whatever and don't you think they'll figure that's a *little* weird? Like I'm a . . . a child molester or something? What eight-year-old kid writes letters to a five-year-old? I couldn't tell them who she really was so I pointed out the best-looking babe I could find and I told them *she* was Rejoice."

He pointed to the album and Becca saw that his choice was a girl taller than he'd been and older as well, fully developed with breasts and curves. She was very pretty, and Becca had to admit that Derric's selection made a lot of sense. But it *only* made sense if he had decided to keep lying to his parents about the existence of his sister.

Becca closed the album and looked at Derric. She loved him, but she couldn't understand him, not when it came to this. She said, "You're gonna have to tell them sometime. Seems to me that this album's your chance to do it."

"Oh great. After I told them someone *else* is Rejoice? Now I walk in and tell them I was lying?" He didn't wait for an answer. He walked to his desk and threw himself in his chair. He said, "I'm sick of it."

"What?"

"Her."

"*Rejoice?*"

"I don't frigging mean Rejoice. I mean my mom." He dropped his head into his hands.

Becca got to her feet and went to his chair. She knelt in front of it and said quietly, "I get that no one's life is perfect. I get that it bugs you that your mom somehow thinks yours should be and that would make me crazy too. But here's the deal. Part of what's not perfect in your life has to do with Rejoice—"

"I'm *not*—"

"Just listen for a second. Maybe the real reason you're going crazy is because you don't know what happened to her. Maybe that's been eating you up for what . . . nine years and counting?"

"Don't tell me to—"

"Derric, I'm not. You're gonna do what you're gonna do. I get that. But you need at *least* to find out for yourself how she is and where she is because if you don't, you're going to . . . I don't know . . . get sick or something or flunk out of school or wreck your whole life or whatever."

"And how am I s'posed to find out what happened to her?"

Becca considered this. It seemed to her that if Derric had been adopted, so might his little sister have been adopted. Derric had a Facebook page. So might Rejoice. It was better than nothing and worth a try, so she suggested that was where they should begin.

The problem, of course, was that all they knew was Rejoice's original name: Rejoice Nyombe, which hadn't been hers at the orphanage anyway since no one there had known that she was Derric's sister. It wasn't likely that anyone had assigned her that name, and they found out easily enough that no one had. Googling Rejoice didn't bring up anything either. Nor did any other approach they took. Their project to find out what had happened to her was, unfortunately, over before it had begun. They were back to the beginning: If Derric wanted to ease his mind, Derric needed to talk to his parents.

Becca stared at the laptop's screen. It had moved to screen-saver and she watched colorful bubbles floating around. Truth was, she thought, not everyone put themselves onto Web sites. Not everyone was into advertising to the world who they were and what they did. She certainly wasn't. She couldn't afford to be. And what she'd had on Facebook prior to making a run from Jeff Corrie, she and her mom had taken down permanently.

The whole idea of taking something down permanently prompted an idea in her head. She said, "Could I . . . ?" and indicated the computer. Derric shrugged. She typed in Aidan Martin's name. She said to Derric, "Aidan Martin looked up my schedule for some reason. There's something going on with that kid. He keeps turning up like he's following me."

"He's into you."

"Nope."

"Then what?"

"Don't know." But she did, of course, know very well. Aidan Martin was suspicious. He'd seen her looking at the story on the Internet about the disappearance of Laurel Armstrong and her daughter, Hannah. He'd heard her excuse about looking for a face for her art class. He'd not bought into her tale and he'd done a little investigating on her. She didn't know why he felt compelled to do that, but two could play that game, and she was going to do a little investigating on him.

But just like Rejoice, absolutely nothing came up for Aidan Martin, no matter how many different sites she tried. So she typed in Isis Martin instead, and what popped onto the screen was a virtual pictorial history of Isis's life in Palo Alto, most particularly her life with her boyfriend, Brady. There were pictures of them everywhere, from skiing in the mountains to surfing at the beach. There were also pictures of Isis and her scores of friends. Additionally, there were family pictures. Aidan was there and so were their parents.

Derric joined her in looking over the page. He murmured, "Does anyone even care about all this?" But he continued to look along with Becca, and he was the one to say, "Kinda strange that it's only Aidan."

Becca looked up at him.

"She said she had two brothers," he told her. "That day at lunch."

"She did?"

"You told her Jenn has two brothers and she said she did too. Only she said *had*, so she's only got one brother now and if the other one died or something . . ." He let his voice drift off.

"Maybe she doesn't like to remember."

"Or maybe she's not telling the truth in the first place."

"That's definitely what Jenn would say." Becca logged off the computer and swung around to Derric. She thought about truth versus lie as it applied to him and then as it applied to her. She knew one thing for sure when it came to people who bent the truth to fit what they needed other people to believe about them: If someone was lying, there was usually a reason.

TWENTY

Becca would have pursued the Isis and Aidan Martin conundrum had her world not undergone a shift two days later. The person who brought about this shift was Derric's father. The undersheriff of Island County, Dave Mathieson had a project that needed doing, and he figured that Derric and Becca might be just the two people who could do it.

Derric told her about this over the phone. His dad had some flyers that needed to be posted all over the island. They needed to go into tourist shops, fashion boutiques, antiques stores, grocery stores . . . everywhere. His dad had already got kids from the high schools up in Oak Harbor and in Coupeville to post the flyers in those two towns. He needed someone to do the same in all the small communities on the south end of the island. He was offering to pay, and he needed to rely on the kids to do the job fast and to do it right. Derric said that he hadn't seen the flyers, but he figured the sheriff's department was looking for someone on the run.

Since Becca hated to spend any of the money her mom had given her and since the job she'd had in the spring had come to an end, she signed on without hesitation. Her responsibilities at Ralph's didn't eat up all of her time, and she could spare a few hours after school and additional time on weekends. So Derric and she set off from South Whidbey High School in the afternoon.

They drove to Clinton to begin. On the south end of the island, this small enclave was where the ferry from the mainland docked. Derric drove them to the first of the businesses that defined the place. These were strung along the highway rising steeply from the rough waters of Possession Sound, and he parked just outside a nail salon advertising in stuttering neon that walk-ins were welcome.

The flyers were in the back of the Forester. Derric opened it, suggesting that he make a dash across the highway for the businesses there, while Becca saw to the shops on this side as well as Cozy's bar, the bank, and the used car dealership. Becca was fine with this and said so. She was still fine with it as Derric took out a thick sheaf of the flyers and handed them over. Then in a rush, she ceased being fine.

Have You Seen This Woman formed huge black letters in two lines at the top of the flyer. Beneath them was a very clear photograph of Becca's mother. *Laurel Armstrong* was printed beneath it, along with her age, and the information that she'd been last seen in San Diego the previous year in September. Beneath this was the phone number of the sheriff's department. Beneath that was the word *Reward*.

Becca felt as if the ground was tilting. Her chest got so tight that she thought she might be having a heart attack. She'd dodged the Laurel bullet once before on Whidbey Island, when she'd left in the information shelter at Saratoga Woods a cell phone purchased by her mom. When the undersheriff had got his hands on it, he'd looked for Laurel but he hadn't found her. That *should* have been the end of it. But obviously, something new had occurred.

Derric said, "Be right back," and headed to the highway before she could stop him. He dashed across.

Becca stood for a moment, staring down at the picture of her mother. She felt a stab of missing Laurel so much that for a few seconds she couldn't move. What she thought was, Where are you? Why haven't you come back? Please don't say you've forgotten about me.

She *hadn't*, of course. Laurel was merely waiting till enough time had passed to be sure there was no possible connection between one Becca King and a woman who had dropped off a teenaged girl at the Mukilteo ferry before herself driving off on the route to British Columbia and a town in the mountains where she would establish a hideaway for them both. But the thought of that town in the mountains led Becca inexorably to Nelson itself and the additional thought of Parker Natalia, who might now see this poster, recognize Laurel by face as someone who'd come into his family's restaurant, and then logically speak to the sheriff about it.

Her only option was to get rid of the posters. But if she did that, the sheriff would wonder why they weren't in every shop and restaurant and boutique and *wherever.* He would ask and what would she say? And what was she actually supposed to do anyway: run all over Whidbey Island and take the posters down wherever they'd been placed?

Becca tried to get calm. She tried to think of anything positive that could come out of this. While there was nothing at all that she could see, what did finally come to her was an aphorism her grandmother used to say: Thank God for small favors. It was her way of looking for the good in the bad, and in this case the good was that at least there was no picture of Becca herself on the flyer, announcing her identity to one and all as Hannah Armstrong, daughter of the missing Laurel.

The bad, however, seemed to outweigh the good. For it seemed to her that if Dave Mathieson was looking for Laurel and if there was a reward involved, Jeff Corrie had to be involved as well. Which meant something had changed in San Diego.

DAVE MATHIESON TOLD her what it was when she and Derric reported back to him on how far they'd gotten with the flyers: all of Clinton and a hugely unattractive strip mall on the route into Langley. "Truth is I don't know how much good it's going to do—this whole thing with the posters—but the San Diego PD *and* the county sheriff down there put in the request and they're paying for it, so we'll give it a go."

The words *San Diego PD and the county sheriff* made Becca's palms begin to sweat. She said, "Is the lady a criminal?"

"She's just missing, far as I know," Dave told her. Becca and Derric had run into him outside of the city hall, which housed Langley's small police department. He'd been there about Laurel, as things turned out, putting the local cops into the picture about the flyers that Becca and Derric were posting. Now the three of them were at the village pizzeria on First Street. They were sitting in the outside eating area sipping Cokes and waiting for their olive-and-mushroom extra large to be delivered to them. The eating area was a garden that overlooked Saratoga Passage, and while the sun was still shining in the Pacific Northwest in advance of the coming winter, plenty of people were taking advantage of it. There were a number of families hanging out at the wrought-iron tables, with little kids running around and dogs begging for food.

Dave went on. "Odd thing is, this Laurel Armstrong's *also* a woman I was looking for last year."

Becca said nothing. Her stomach felt frozen. Derric said only, "When last year?"

"You wouldn't remember," his dad told him. "You were out of it then." He knocked Derric fondly on the skull as a reminder of the time he'd spent coma-bound in a hospital bed. "Someone called nine one one the day you fell in the woods. The call was made from a cell phone, and we traced the phone to this Laurel Armstrong. It was a credit card purchase in San Diego. At the time, I figured she was a kid because the voice on the nine-one-one tape didn't sound like an adult. So we made a search for her but came up cold. No one knew her. I guess now we know why."

The logical question came from Derric since all Becca wanted to do was to avoid the subject forever if she could.

"Why?" he asked.

"You ask me, the husband got rid of her down there and then came up here to lay a false trail with that phone. He could've handed it off to any kid who then made that call and then just left the phone where someone would find it. Which is exactly what happened: It got turned in, I had it traced to the point of purchase, we got the number that went with the credit card that bought it, we called the number, and there the husband was: saying he knew nothing about a cell phone at all. No one up here thought to check him out with regard to this Laurel Armstrong because up here all we were concerned with was what had happened to you. Down there, though, the cops're thinking she was planning to leave him and it turned into the same old story: If I can't have you, no one can."

"I don't get the point of the flyers if that's what the cops think," Derric said. They had a slew of the flyers still with them, and he fingered these, picking up one and studying it. Becca looked away, out at the water. What she did *not* need was Derric starting to think that, hey, his girlfriend sort of resembled this woman, didn't she? "Why don't the San Diego cops just arrest him?"

"No evidence. He *looks* suspicious, sure. This guy didn't report the wife missing for months last year, and what's that mean, huh? He was already under investigation for some sort of squirrelly business he was running, so the cops along with the FBI were talking to him about that. And his business partner's missing too, the cops tell me, so he's got himself a shitload of trouble. Pardon my French."

"Sounds like he's been up to something," Derric commented.

"Sounds like. When a wife goes missing, the husband is generally behind it."

The pizza arrived and they took some moments scoring a piece each before Dave Mathieson went on. "He'd been cooperating, more or less, with this deal about his business partner, but the day the cops came to talk to him about the wife . . . ? He lawyered up. Some neighbor had called and said she hadn't seen the wife and daughter in a while and at that point—"

Stepdaughter, Becca wanted to say. Jeff Corrie is not my dad. I never knew my dad. Is Mom with my dad? Is he in Nelson? Where are you where are you where are you, Mom, because—

Dave's words terminated her anguished thoughts. He was saying, "—the cops started looking into things down there. But everything stalled out."

"Lucky for them you traced that cell phone," Derric said.

Becca *had* to say something. It looked too strange that she was practically making a biological study of the top of her pizza. She chose, "I don't get it. Why would a guy from San Diego lay a trail to Whidbey Island?"

"Couldn't tell you but you can bet the cops're are checking into that. One thing we've discovered is he was up here late autumn last year, a few months *after* we put our hands on that cell phone. Now, he admits that freely. Fact is, he's the person who told the cops down there that there has to be a Whidbey connection. You can argue that makes him look innocent, but you can also argue it just makes him look wily. He knew we'd found the phone, he wanted to look concerned, he comes up and pokes around and asks after his wife and daughter—"

Stepdaughter, stepdaughter, stepdaughter, Becca thought.

"—and he figures everyone'll think he's squeaky clean when it comes to their disappearance."

"How come she's not on the poster, then?" Derric asked. "The daughter?"

Dave shook his head. "Don't know," he told them. "Could be another picture's coming. Could also be they're thinking that where Laurel Armstrong is, there'll be her daughter."

It was again, Becca thought, a moment to thank God for small blessings. But she had a feeling it wouldn't last for long.

IT DIDN'T.

The *South Whidbey Record* was a twice-a-week affair, Wednesdays and Saturdays. The Wednesday paper was the one with the story, something Becca discovered in fairly short order since Seth brought it to her as he'd done earlier.

Seth was the only person on Whidbey Island who knew the danger she was in. She'd told him early on because she'd had to tell him. She'd needed help. She'd needed someone's friendship. From the first, Seth Darrow had been the person on hand to supply her with both. So when he saw the story in the *Record* with Laurel Armstrong's name and picture right on the front page, he grabbed the copy from his mom's kitchen table and that was what he had when he showed up Wednesday night after dinner at Ralph Darrow's house.

Parker Natalia was with him. Becca thought at first that Seth had brought Parker over from his tree house for some reason, but it turned out that the two guys had met up on Ralph's front porch. Parker was there for a quick shower prior to "going out with one hot feminista," he said, and Seth was there supposedly to check up on Ralph, his diet—and particularly his blood pressure—at the request of his dad. Or so he said, because Becca could see that something was off with Seth, so she took her ear bud from her ear and picked up on *get him out of the way long enough to tell her,* which seemed to indicate more was going on than his family's growing concern about Ralph's high cholesterol.

"Dad wants you to start using this," he told his grandfather and brought out a blood pressure reader.

An argument ensued. Ralph Darrow wasn't about to let his children dictate to him the terms of his well-being, especially his own son Ralph Junior, "who need I remind you, favorite male grandson, is at this precise moment not only twenty-five pounds overweight but also probably having his fifth beer of the evening while watching the Seahawks game."

"There's no Seahawks game on a Wednesday, Grand," didn't get Seth very far. Ralph wasn't going to have his blood pressure taken, and to make sure Seth understood this, he stomped up the stairs.

With Parker in the shower and Seth's grandfather fuming up

above them, Becca said to her friend, "What's going on?" and he handed over the newspaper.

"Oh no," was really all she could say when she saw the picture of Laurel, her name, and the same information that was on the flyer that she and Derric were still posting everywhere. An article accompanied the picture. She was about to read it, when Seth said, "It's worse 'n you think."

She saw why when she made the jump to page eight where the story continued because there was a picture of her as well. It was an old one, but that was hardly the point. For it was the very same picture that she'd been looking at on the Internet when Aidan Martin had come upon her.

PART III

Maxwelton Beach

TWENTY-ONE

Seth found out about the party at Maxwelton Beach through Parker Natalia. He'd been invited by "the two hotties giving it," as Parker put it, and when he revealed that one of the two hotties was Hayley, Seth decided to go. Parker's feminista date on Wednesday night had turned out to be with Isis Martin, and Seth figured that if Parker was interested in Isis, that left Hayley open and available.

Yeah, yeah, he knew he was being dumb. He and Hayley were still at let's-just-be-friends. But just because Hayley wanted things that way, it didn't mean he was meant to stop hoping they could return to being more than friends.

The party at Maxwelton was after dark, out of doors, and in back of one of the big beach houses. Seth figured this was where Isis Martin and her brother lived with their grandmother, but that wasn't how it was. It *also* wasn't a small party with people sitting around, having a few beers, smoking a little weed, and playing music. The word had gone out around the high school that something big was going on, and by the time Seth arrived, at least forty-five kids were already there and more kids were coming.

The house in question was at the far end of Maxwelton Road, where it dead-ended at a point about one quarter mile beyond a sign saying PRIVATE. This indicated a neighborhood that didn't encourage non-residents to wander in, and up above the PRIVATE sign, someone had posted a hand-lettered SHHHHH! on thick poster board, a message that appeared to be for everyone heading to the party. A FOR SALE sign hung outside the party site: a big, green-shingled and many-gabled getaway house that no doubt belonged to a dotcom millionaire with a permanent home on Lake Washington. When Seth saw the FOR SALE sign and also saw the pitch darkness inside the place, he had his first qualm about the party. But he was already there and there were others behind him coming along the road stealthily. There seemed to be safety in numbers.

He went around to the water side of the house. The yard in which he found himself gave directly onto the driftwood piles distinctive to beaches in the Pacific Northwest. From these piles kids had gathered smaller pieces of wood which were set to burning in the huge stone fire pit that was a feature of the house's well-landscaped exterior. Next to this fire pit a lot of scrap wood lay, waiting to go up in smoke as well.

There were kids everywhere, but they were doing a good job of keeping the noise down. The nearest houses were a long-abandoned fishing shack to the south—a building that the private road didn't even reach—and, some fifty yards to the north and past an empty lot, a summer cottage that was vacant. Across the street on the land side of things, there was only a steep slope of alders that rose to a thick forest of evergreens and then to a road. As long as they stayed relatively quiet, they could party without bothering a soul.

Seth looked around for friends. He heard his name called, and saw that Becca and Derric were there, sitting on a low stone wall that marked the property boundary from the empty lot next door. Jenn McDaniels was with them, and so was Jenn's long-time pal Squat Cooper. Seth didn't see Hayley, but he did see Isis Martin, who was arms-around-the-waist with Parker Natalia as someone took a picture of them with a smart phone. Parker gave a wave to Seth and Seth jerked his head in hello and continued looking for Hayley as he made his way over to Becca and the others.

"Happenin'?" he said to them.

They all had beers. This surprised him a little because he couldn't remember ever seeing Becca drink. She wasn't generally a partier, and neither was Derric. But now seven beer cans lay empty at their feet. He raised his eyebrows when he saw this and he figured they'd been at it for a while.

"I've never been drunk before," Becca said. "I decided to try it." She wasn't slurring her words but she didn't look altogether there. "I dunno . . . I hope I don't throw up."

"Who's driving you guys home?"

Derric raised a lazy hand. "When I c'n see straight. 'F I can't, we'll sleep on the beach. You okay with that, babe? Me 'n' you under the stars or whatever?"

Becca giggled, leaned against him, and yawned.

"Hell," Seth said, "you guys need to be careful."

"We need to get blitzed," Jenn told him. "The Squat man here came that way and the rest 'f us are trying to catch up." She nuzzled Squat's neck playfully and then said to Seth, "He had, like, a half gallon or something of Jack Daniel's that he stole from his mom. Where'd you put it, Studboy?" This last she directed to Squat.

Squat didn't answer. He was totally ruddy in the face, even in the darkness, and his eyes looked like embers. He finally managed, "Dunno. It was here and it's gone," and he waved aimlessly in the direction of some kids who were in the deep shadows at the edge of the water. Seth looked that way and could see a bottle being passed among them. He wondered if anyone in this crowd was going to stay sober enough to drive.

"Anyone know whose house this is?" he asked. He heard a shout and turned around to see flames and sparks flying high up from the fire pit as someone threw an armload of very summer-dry kindling on it. It looked like old blow-down that had been gathered from the woods, and the kids who'd done the gathering were dumping more of it next to the fire pit and stoking the blaze. Hayley was with them. So was Aidan Martin. For a second Seth thought they might be a couple because Hayley leaped back when the flames shot up, and she gripped onto Aidan's arm.

Someone shouted, "Holy shit! What're you guys doing?"

Aidan shouted back, "Thought you wanted a fire!" He grabbed up a burning piece of blow-down and used it like a sword, flashing fire in the sky.

Music came from somewhere, and Seth saw that one of the kids had found an outdoor electrical outlet. Into this, he'd plugged a set of speakers for an iPod. They were small but they did the job. Loud rap began.

A boy that Seth recognized from the high school football team came around the side of the house at that point, with a small metal beer keg on his shoulder. He was followed by three other guys, a slew of good-looking girls, and two guys somewhere in their twenties. They were both carrying grocery bags and the bags turned out to be filled with bottles. They started to unpack these on a circular table on the terrace outside the house's back door. A cheer went up from the kids who saw vodka, gin, rum . . . There were mixers, too, and a couple of bags of ice and plastic glasses.

"Come 'n' get it," one of these guys yelled.

Kids stormed the table from all directions. There was laughter. There was shoving. There was good-natured joking. And someone hurled another enormous armful of dry wood into the fire so that the flames leapt upward, looking like a beacon against the night sky. Sparks shot everywhere. Embers flew. A bottle fell from the table and broke and a girl got down on her hands and knees and began lapping up the booze that pooled on the terrace. A boy sat on her back and tried to ride her.

Now, Seth liked parties as much as the next guy, but this looked like one that was getting seriously out of control. There might have been no one inside the house and no one on either side of the house, but the noise was growing. There was no way someone from the neighborhood *wasn't* going to come investigate what was going on.

He made his way through the crowd over to Hayley. She was standing back from the fire, holding on to Aidan Martin's arm again. This time, though, she seemed to be trying to keep him from flinging his burning piece of blow-down onto the roof of the house. He was laughing and yelling, "Lemme *do* it, bitch." Hayley saw Seth coming toward her and mouthed "Help!" at him.

Or she might have been shouting it, for all he knew. The noise level was way too high at that point.

Seth said, "Hey, man," to Aidan, and he managed to get the burning wood away from him. He tossed it onto the fire. "Better watch it with that or this whole place'll go up in smoke."

Aidan said, "Hey, Seth, gotcher guitar? This music sucks."

"I totally agree."

"Well, I'm gonna do something 'bout that," Aidan said, and stumbled in the direction of the iPod, which was, unfortunately, also in the direction of the booze. Seth watched him grab a bottle of whatever the heck it was and lurch off with it. Then he turned to Hayley and said, "We better get out of here. This is, like, way out of control."

"I don't know how people found out," Hayley told him. "It was just going to be Isis and me and a couple of others and all of a sudden . . ." She looked around. "I didn't tell anyone."

"You had anything to drink?"

"Part of a beer. I set it down and . . . I don't know. I think someone took it." She pushed her glasses up on her nose. They were smudged and her right cheek had a smear of ashes on it.

"You ask me, we need to get away. And someone's gotta get Derric and Becca out of here because, I swear, the sheriff's going to show up. If he sees Derric, that'll—"

"Hey, you two." It was Isis. Parker Natalia was with her. She was hanging back as if she wanted to take him somewhere else and he was trying to come forward as if *he* wanted to talk to Seth. He was smiling, and his gold earrings flashed in the light.

"Take our picture!" Isis cried. She tossed her iPhone at Seth, put her arms around Parker, locked a leg around one of his, and dropped her hands to his butt. They began kissing long, hard, and obviously with a lot of tongue. Seth took the picture. She wanted another, with Parker standing behind her with his arms around her waist. "Kiss my neck," she commanded. He cooperated, laughing. Then he unlocked himself from her and came over to Seth and Hayley.

"This scene reminds me of high school in Nelson," Parker said to Seth.

"What, having some blitzed chick go for you?"

"I am *not* blitzed." Isis was linking her arm to Parker's and saying, "And I don't *need* to be blitzed to go for this guy's tongue."

"Some party," Parker said, this time to Hayley. "I didn't see you when I got here."

"That's 'cause she was in the woods," Isis said. She winked at Hayley. "How'd it go? Hook up with anyone?"

Hayley looked flustered. "We just got some wood. But, you know, it's so dry that I'm thinking—"

"Your brother was playing around with it," Seth said. "If he throws it up on the roof of this place—"

"Where is he?" Isis looked around for Aidan.

"Who the hell knows? Where'd all these people come from and who're those guys with the booze?"

"No clue," Isis said. "But it's totally rad that they showed up. Come on," this last to Parker, "we need a refill."

She led him off. He called out to Hayley and Seth, "Talk to you guys later."

Hayley called back, "Whatever," but it sounded more to herself than to him.

Seth said to her, "You got the farm truck here?"

"No. Isis picked me up. Why?"

"'Cause me and you are getting out of here, Hayl. But we need to score Derric's keys first. He was talking about driving. Seriously bad idea. You c'n drive his car and take him and Becca to Grand's so he c'n sober up. I'll follow you with Jenn and Squat and—"

"It'll be okay, Seth."

"Like hell. Someone's gonna call the cops. Come *on*, Hayley."

"Hey. You're not—"

"Your boyfriend. Right. But I'm still your friend, and friends don't let friends stay at parties that're going to be broken up by the cops so that their parents end up getting called to come fish their kids out of wherever their kids get taken."

It was the parents part that got to her as he figured it would. She said, "I'll get his keys," and she headed through the crowd to where Derric and Becca were sitting. They were making out like about twenty other couples, and next to them Jenn and Squat were sharing a bottle of something. Were they going to be sick in the morning or *what*? Seth thought.

He watched Hayley talking to Derric. He looked around. Some

girl had climbed up on the wall. She'd taken off her sweater. She started swinging it around her head. Some guys were yelling "Take it all off!" and as if further prompting was going to be needed, suddenly a spotlight hit her. The atmosphere of the party changed instantly.

A deputy from the sheriff's department strode forward with a powerful Maglite held above his head. Another deputy had a bull horn at his mouth and he shouted into this: "All of you, get up on the terrace. Now." Another deputy came around the far side of the house and behind him was the undersheriff of the county, Derric's dad.

Some of the kids obeyed at once. But a crowd of them began to flee in every direction, with about fifteen of them heading north up the beach in an attempt to get to their cars.

But the cops had already thought this one through. Reinforcements emerged from the side of a house about thirty yards to the north. To make sure everyone understood the situation, Derric's dad grabbed the bull horn and shouted, "No one's going anywhere. The road is blocked. Get back here and show some common sense."

Which, Seth saw, was just about the time Dave Mathieson saw his own son, Derric, throwing a beer can into the driftwood behind the wall on which he drunkenly sat.

TWENTY-TWO

In the ensuing chaos, Becca lost the ear bud that blocked people's whispers. She couldn't find it anywhere and was too dizzy to be able to figure out what might have happened to it since it was supposed to be connected to the AUD box, which was clipped to her waist.

To her horror, the first thing she did when she jumped to her feet was to throw up over the side of the stone wall. When she was able to stagger away from the vomit, she turned and saw that Dave Mathieson was coming toward them in a fury. Meanwhile, one of the deputies was making it clear that no one was going anywhere via car and everyone was going to be marching up Maxwelton Road to an old church standing at an intersection. There, inside that place, every last one of them was going to give their names and the names of their parents, who were going to be called and told to come and pick up their offspring. Anyone over twenty-one was in bigger trouble: not only trespassing on private property, but also contributing to the delinquency of minors. Now let's get moving, the deputy yelled. One of the other deputies came forward and used a garden hose to put out the fire.

Hit the fan now was what Becca heard and it could have come from Derric. But then so could have *when my mom finds out* and *just what I need* and *this is going to look great on my record*. Meantime, everyone else was bombarding the air with *their* whispers, most of which were swear words and scattered plans about how to escape the march up to the church. The problem for most of them, though, was that the first thing the cops did was to relieve every single kid of identification and car keys, so escaping via a vehicle wasn't going to be in the plan.

"Just what the hell were you thinking?" was what she heard from Dave Mathieson to Derric. "Are you drunk? Never mind, I can see for myself. And did you intend to drive this way?"

"I was getting his keys, Sheriff Mathieson." Hayley Cartwright spoke quickly. "Seth and I were taking all these guys home." She indicated Derric, Becca, Jenn, and Squat. Squat was on his back on the top of the wall, smiling loonily up at the night sky.

"Don't try to cover for them," Dave told her.

"I'm not covering."

"It's the truth," Seth told him. "Hayley and I haven't been drinking."

"'S all right," Derric said, with a tired wave. "My bad, Seth."

"You have *that* right," Dave Mathieson told him. "I thought you had more sense. Give me your damn keys," and when he had them, he walked away.

It was like a military POW march after that. The kids were herded to the front of the house and then lined up single file. Noise from the woods indicated that some of the kids were hoping to escape by climbing the slope up to Swede Hill Road. Maybe they'd make it, Becca thought, but the cops looked intent upon finding every last person who'd been at the party. In the world of throwing the book at people, the book was going to be thrown.

BECCA GOT SEPARATED from everyone except Derric when the kids were lined up along the road. They weren't sobering up quickly, but the mood among them had changed.

As they started their march, Derric stumbled and she caught his arm. He looked at her, said, "Thanks," and added, "This wasn't one of my better ideas. Have I screwed up my whole life or what?"

Becca didn't need to hear his whispers to know he wasn't talking about merely getting drunk at a party. Nor when he added, "My mom's going to be all over me," did she think Rhonda Mathieson's concern was going to be solely about the party either.

At least, she thought, a kids' party on private property broken up by the cops wasn't going to make the front page of the paper. And even if the story itself made the paper, there was no photographer there taking pictures to attract Jeff Corrie's attention if he was scanning the Whidbey paper online to see if her face or Laurel's face showed up in a crowd somewhere. So thank God for that. And thank God also that no one had broken into the house and nothing truly bad had happened except some kids—like her, for instance—throwing up on someone's property. They'd used the fire pit and that was bad and guys had probably peed in the vacant lot next door and, okay, they'd been drinking but it could have been a whole lot worse and there were definitely parents all over the place who were going to be happy that it hadn't been.

This was indeed how things remained till the march of partiers got halfway to the church. At that point flashing lights came in their direction and five seconds later a fire engine stormed past them as they scurried to one side of the road.

SOME KIDS TRIED to escape in the confusion. What Becca wondered was where those kids were going to go since no one had car keys. She couldn't see anything on fire back the way they'd come, and she herself had seen the cop turn a hose on the fire pit.

They didn't find out anything more till they were in the church. They had their orders from the deputy with the bull horn, "Keep marching, you guys," and so those who didn't try to fade into the fields and then into the forest along the road did pretty much what they were told.

The old church was waiting for them, a dull brown building surrounded by fir trees. All the lights were on, and the first of the parents were already there. Among these Becca recognized Nancy Howard, who lived on Maxwelton Road, as it turned out. She'd only had to come a half mile, but she didn't look happy. The other adults Becca didn't recognize, except for Rhonda Mathieson. She swarmed over Derric and Becca like ten thousand bees following the flight of their queen.

What have I done wrong when I keep trying so hard produced two feelings in Becca. A thrill of pleasure burst upon her at the complete clarity of the whisper and her immediate knowledge of its source, which was Rhonda. But a cold bucket of guilt doused that pleasure soon enough because Derric's mom was so incredibly upset.

The only good part was that Rhonda's hovering around them produced the ear bud of the AUD box, which was dangling from its connection to the box at Becca's waist. She hadn't felt it hitting against her knees through her jeans as she walked, and she was seriously grateful that nothing had happened to it. She reestablished it in her ear. She looked around for the rest of her friends.

She saw Jenn, and with her was Squat, totally wasted. She saw Seth arguing with a deputy, and she figured he was telling the guy that he'd just arrived, that he'd tried to get Hayley Cartwright out of there, that at least they could give him a breath test or whatever so he could prove he was stone cold sober and completely able to drive Hayley home. She saw Isis Martin being strong-armed by her grandmother. She saw Parker Natalia trying to ease over to the door. He didn't get far. A cop standing guard at the door directed him back into the church.

"This isn't *like* you. What on earth is *happening* to you?" It was Rhonda talking to Derric. He looked sullen and sick to his stomach simultaneously. His reply of "Jesus. Lay *off*, Mom," didn't go down well. Rhonda turned to Becca. "What were you two thinking?"

Becca said, "Sorry. We were dumb."

"And lay off Becca, too," Derric snapped. "Let's just go the hell home."

"Do you actually think it's going to be that easy?" Rhonda demanded. "There's a fire down there and no one's going *anywhere* till that's taken care of."

"They put out the fire," Becca told her. "I saw the guy take a hose and—"

"Evidently, you didn't see what you thought you saw because it doesn't take the fire department to douse a fire on the beach."

"We weren't on the beach," Derric said. Unnecessarily, Becca thought. "An' the fire was in a legal pit."

"Illegally lit by a bunch of drunk kids on someone's private property," Rhonda countered.

"Give it a frigging rest," Derric said.

Rhonda's eyes filled with tears. She walked off, allowing Derric and Becca to be herded into one of the pews along with everyone else. Becca felt bad for her, but she felt bad for Derric, too, because she knew this was going to be yet another issue between him and his mom.

THEY WAITED NINETY minutes. By that time all the parents of all the kids had arrived and were milling around outside. Becca could see them when the doors opened, and she could hear them shouting questions when Dave Mathieson entered. The partiers were either sobering up or they were asleep. Five of them had been sick on the floor and were cleaning up their own mess as directed by a completely unsympathetic deputy. Dave went over to talk to Derric's mom, and they spent a couple of minutes in earnest conversation. Then Rhonda walked over to where Becca and Derric were leaning against each other at the far end of a pew.

She said to Becca, "You'll have to wait. He says no one leaves without an adult who'll take responsibility for them tonight. I'm sorry," and then to Derric, "Let's go home," and she turned and walked off.

At that point, Dave Mathieson strode to the front of the church and the set of his jaw made him look even angrier than he'd been when he'd confronted Becca and Derric at the party. He planted himself on a riser and said in a loud voice, "Listen up, all of you smart-asses, so you have a clear picture of just how serious this situation is. Your little party spread its wings. The building next door went up in flames from the fire you guys were all enjoying—"

Moans, shouts, angry retorts, and cries constituted the general reaction and it came immediately, breaking into the sheriff's words.

He said, "Yeah. That's right. So you've got one hell of a problem. Those of you who're legal age . . . ? You'll be taking a ride up to Coupeville. The rest of you are released to your parents as soon as they get here if they're not here already. *But*"—he increased the volume as kids started to move—"you'll be hearing from the appropriate authorities as soon as damages are assessed."

A few kids protested. They'd been on the beach, they'd not

even gone near that stupid fire pit, they'd been leaving when they saw the party was getting out of hand. But the undersheriff wasn't interested in this. He was finished speaking and he nodded to the deputy by the door. He opened it and allowed the parents to enter one by one to claim their offspring.

Derric said to Becca, "This is such bullshit. At least he could let us drive you home. I'm gonna go tell him—".

"'S'okay," Becca said hastily. There was no point in provoking anything else between Derric and either one of his parents. "I c'n call Mrs. Kinsale. It's better than Mr. Darrow." What she meant was that she couldn't risk her living situation with Ralph Darrow. She was sobering up pretty quickly at this point, but she knew she smelled like beer and vomit. Ralph Darrow would not appreciate having to be exposed to her scent.

Derric said, "Bullshit, Becca. What's the point of my dad being the undersheriff if he won't even give us a break?"

"That's the whole point. He can't. *Because* he's the undersheriff."

"I don't want you . . . Crap. I'm so frigging sorry."

"Hey, I'll be okay. Both of us blew it. You didn't exactly force me to go to the party and no way did you force me to chug a bunch of beers."

"We shouldn't've gone. When we saw it was at that empty house . . ." He put a fist to his forehead and gave it a tap. "I am totally losing it."

"Just go home with your mom. It'll be okay."

"I don't think so." He hugged her hard and swung around to go to his mother.

That was when the fire chief came into the room at such a pace that he nearly knocked over two sets of parents in his haste to get to the undersheriff. He spoke to him tersely. Dave Mathieson announced, "Everyone, stay where you are."

Then along with the fire chief, he rushed out of the place as protests rose around them and two deputies took up positions at the church's front doors.

TWENTY-THREE

No one was happy about being trapped inside the church, and the only alteration in their circumstances was that the parents were now trapped inside with them. For an hour no one knew what was going on. Everyone remained in ignorance until through the window someone saw an ambulance pass by, heading in the direction of the beach.

At first, Becca assumed that a fire fighter had been injured at the blaze next door to where the party had been. Or, perhaps, one of the kids who'd attempted an escape through the woods and up the slope had slipped and fallen and broken something. But finally Dave Mathieson arrived back at the church, and Derric's mom went to talk to him. Her expression of horror told the tale of something being very wrong. A minute later, the undersheriff made the grave announcement. A body had been found inside the building that had gone up in flames.

Dozens of cries of shock rose. Dave Mathieson silenced them by holding up his hand. He said, sounding totally wiped out, "Everyone with a parent can go. But we'll be in touch, and you can expect to be questioned about what went on down there at that house tonight."

More than this Becca learned in dribs and drabs as people filtered out of the church and as she herself waited for Diana Kinsale. The facts were sketchy but they made a partial picture of a tumbledown wreck of a fishing shack at the farthest end of Maxwelton Beach almost to the spear tip of land that turned the place into heavily wooded Indian Point. Long uninhabited, the shack had been taken over by someone homeless, and there he'd been camping and cooking over an open fire for God only knew how long. He came and went by night, it seemed, since no one on the road leading up to the shack had ever seen him. The fire investigators were set to examine the scene in the morning, and perhaps they'd know then exactly what had happened.

There was some relief found in the belief that the kids involved in the illegal party were not also involved in causing a nearby fishing shack to go up in flames. So the situation was bad but it could have been worse. Because of all this, it was a subdued crowd that began to drive off in the night.

Diana Kinsale showed up along with the final group of parents who'd had to return to the island from as far away as Seattle, where they'd gone for the evening prior to being summoned back to cart their miscreants home. In Diana's case, she'd come from over town, the mall in Lynnwood where she'd gone to see a film with a friend.

"No matter," she said to Becca's abject apology at having dragged her out of the film. "I'm embarrassed to tell you that I was so bored, I'd fallen asleep. Movies aren't what they used to be since Paul Newman died. Coming to get you turned out to be a welcome diversion." They were in Diana's truck and she cast a glance in Becca's direction. "Although," she added, "I don't expect you see it the same way. What on earth were you thinking?"

"I wasn't," Becca said. "It seemed sorta harmless."

"Which part?"

"The sitting around a beach fire and making out with Derric part. Maybe toasting marshmallows or making s'mores or something. But there wasn't any beach fire, there sure as heck weren't any marshmallows, and Derric wanted a beer and I thought why not. One beer. Big deal. Only it was more than one, and it was *all* so stupid. C'n you not take me to Mr. Darrow's till tomorrow?"

Diana evaluated this. "Won't he worry if you're not there when he gets up?"

"He won't check my room. He'll think I'm still in bed."

"And when you get home?"

Becca knew what Diana was asking, so she said, "I'll tell him what happened. He'll find out anyway because of the fire and the fishing shack and all that."

Diana nodded slowly. "Well, the dogs will be happy to see you," she said.

ALTHOUGH BECCA HAD been expecting some sort of lecture from Mrs. Kinsale, she didn't get one. What stood in place of it, though, was a trip into the powder room beneath the stairs in Diana's house. There, Diana stood behind her and told her to have a look in the mirror. She said, "Tell me what you see," and she placed her hands on Becca's shoulders.

What Becca saw was her face robbed of color except where her copious mascara and eyeliner had created deep pits beneath her eyes. Her hair was a matted and tangled mess, her glasses were smudged, and dried vomit graced the front of her T-shirt. She got the point. "Yuck," she said.

"I find that sometimes simple vanity is the cure." Diana indicated the mirror. "This is Becca King drunk."

That said, Diana showed her to the guest room upstairs. Despite how she felt about everything that had happened that night, Becca still felt a thrill at being admitted to this part of the house. She vowed to herself that she would be the perfect guest. She would leave the bedroom in pristine condition and she would clean the bathroom after she used it.

Using it was what Diana suggested: a shower, a hair wash, and then a good night's sleep. They would talk more in the morning. She left Becca in the hallway and went to her own room at the back of the house. The door clicked softly closed behind her.

THE MORNING BROUGHT a raging headache to Becca, along with a roiling stomach. She woke with the golden light of autumn coming in the window, and had she not felt so wretched, she would have enjoyed being where she was. Like the rest of Diana's house, the guest room was colorful and comfortable, with a bed that was like being cradled in security. There was a window seat with pillows on it, and there was an armchair in a corner of the room with a throw that picked up the colors of the walls. It was all exactly as Becca had imagined it might be, and she wanted to get up and go to the window seat and look out at the day . . . only she was totally sick to her stomach.

She heard noise from downstairs: soft music and movement in the kitchen. She went to the bedroom door and eased it open. The fragrance of coffee and bacon would have been wonderful had it not made her wish to throw up.

She did what she could to make herself look like her normal self. She had no makeup with her, so she rooted around the bathroom vanity, but there was nothing to use. She was left with doing something with her hair and her glasses and cleaning up her T-shirt as best she could.

As she descended the stairs, the breakfast smells got stronger and her stomach got queasier. Bright light was pouring in through the kitchen windows and she stopped at the doorway and squinted. She said, "Thanks for letting me stay, Mrs. Kinsale," and Diana turned from the stove where she was frying bacon.

Becca was surprised at the sight of her friend. Diana's face was terribly swollen and beneath her eyes were great big puffs of flesh, as if air had been injected beneath them. It came to her that she'd never seen Diana Kinsale upon rising, and Diana put her hand to her face, laughed awkwardly, and said, "We're a pair, aren't we? I must look the same way you feel. It goes away eventually."

It was a moment when Becca longed for a whisper from Diana because her voice, which was usually so calm, seemed somewhat anxious. Then Diana added, "It's the one thing I'm vain about.

This"—with a gesture at her face—"every morning. Sit, my dear. I expect you don't want breakfast yet, but coffee may help."

Becca made her way to the table, a nook with benches not unlike what you'd find in an old-fashioned diner. There were two places set, and Diana had been at one of them already, for a half-drunk cup of coffee stood there, along with a cotton napkin that lay unfolded next to a plate. Becca hesitated before sliding onto the bench. It wasn't an uneasy stomach that stopped her, though. It was the sight of that incriminating edition of the *South Whidbey Record* inside of which was her old picture. The island newspaper lay next to her own plate, neatly folded. It was exactly like an unspoken accusation.

Becca said nothing. Neither did Diana. Instead, the older woman brought Becca a cup of coffee and a piece of unbuttered toast, and she said, "Start with this. You don't feel like eating, but that's part of the cure. The jam's homemade and a thin coating of it might help things go down. We'll work our way from there."

Becca looked bleakly at the toast. The thought of putting it into her mouth made her want to bolt from the kitchen, but she broke off a piece and used the jam as directed. Because of the threatening presence of that newspaper, anything less than cooperation at this point seemed like something that would put her at risk.

Diana joined her with a plate of bacon and a bowl of soft-boiled eggs. There were egg cups on the table, but Becca didn't know how you were supposed to use them. Even if she *had* known, a yolk that was runny and yellow and oozy . . . She knew she couldn't manage to get that down.

Diana didn't seem bothered by this. She ate quietly. Becca nibbled her toast. Between them was the great unspoken of the newspaper with Laurel's picture on the front and Becca's own inside. It was an invitation to speak, and Becca knew this. It was also an invitation to trust completely.

What made the situation worse for Becca was that this moment did not comprise the first time Mrs. Kinsale had extended a hand to her, asking her to take it and to believe that she would not be betrayed. But so far in the year that she'd known this aging and yet ageless woman, Becca had only been able to trust her so far. Risking more than that meant risking the return of Jeff Corrie to her life.

Diana was the one who finally broke the silence, but she didn't do it until she was finished eating and until the quiet between them had gone on long enough to underscore how unnatural it was. Then she said something that Becca did not expect her to say, waiting as she was for the moment that Diana asked her about the girl whose picture was inside the paper.

Instead of doing that, she said quietly, "You were sent to this island, Becca. Have you realized that yet?" For a moment she looked away, toward the window where the sky was an ever-brightening blue. She looked back at Becca and went on. "I ask because things are quickening."

Becca frowned. "I don't get—"

"You'll have to investigate the word. Quickening. And how it applies." She brought the newspaper to her side of the table. She unfolded it and placed her fingers on Laurel's picture. She said, "I've found in my life that nothing really happens by chance. Not this, not anything. Not last night and not tomorrow. And certainly not your presence on Whidbey. Have you never wondered why I picked you up that first night when I saw you with your bike on the side of Bob Galbreath Road?"

Becca's lips felt dry and she picked up her coffee and took a sip. She said, "I thought it was 'cause that's just who you are."

"Perhaps there's some truth in that. But I'd taken the dogs over town, which I never do. And they'd given me some trouble when I tried to get them back into the truck, which *they* never do. And so my trip was delayed far longer than it should have been. Which put me on the road far later than I would have been. And truth to tell, Becca, I don't stop for strangers and since it was dark when I came upon you, I had no idea if you were young or old or male or female or harmless or frightening or intent upon murdering me where I stood."

Becca smiled. "You knew I wouldn't—"

"That's not the point. The point is chance and the fact that it doesn't exist at the deepest level of things. I've been waiting for you to see that. But time is getting short and although my heart tells me you *will* understand at some point, my mind is beginning to argue with my heart. So I've spoken, and I hope you're able to hear me."

For you are the one. Five simple words and they came to her with a diamond's perfection. They comprised all that Diana was willing to let Becca hear of her thoughts in that moment. But the fact of what had just occurred so blatantly prompted Becca to take a leap of faith.

"The one for *what*?" she asked Diana Kinsale.

Diana extended her hand across the table. "Thank you for that," she said.

TWENTY-FOUR

Hayley wasn't put on restriction after the Maxwelton party. There wasn't much point since she hardly had anything going on from which she could actually *be* restricted. So the only restriction turned out to be what they were going to tell her father. Hayley wasn't surprised when *nothing* turned out to be the answer to that.

Her mom had made this clear the moment Hayley had climbed into the truck in front of the small brown church. Then she'd cried all the way back to Smugglers Cove Farm and Flowers, and all Hayley had been able to say to her was "I'm sorry. I didn't know, Mom."

Then they rode in a silence broken only by Julie Cartwright's occasional stifled sob. By the time they arrived home, Hayley could not have felt more wretched.

Brooke met them in the kitchen. All she said was, "Nice going, Hayley," to which her mother said, "Where's your father? If you've wakened him, Brooke, I swear—"

"Hey," Brooke broke in angrily. "He's still in bed and lucky for you he didn't hear the phone ring and get the news about his precious Hayley." She went to the refrigerator and jerked its door open.

Hayley glanced at her mother and saw that Julie had a stiffness to her that usually suggested she was trying to get herself under control. Julie said, "I was harsh with you, Brooke. I'm on edge. I'm sorry. Go to bed."

"I want some milk. My stomach hurts and—"

"You heard me. Go to bed."

"And *you* heard me. I want some milk." Brooke grabbed a carton, and she took a large glass from a cupboard. She poured milk to the top, taking all that was left.

"You put that back right now and go upstairs," her mother said.

"And you go suck an egg."

"Brooke," Hayley said.

"And you shut *up*," Brooke snapped, and then said to her mother, "*All's* I'm doing is having some milk and *you're* acting like this is some kind of crime. What about Hayley? What's she got to do that you'll finally—"

"Julie? What's going on?"

It was Hayley's father. All of them became statues.

"Julie? Julie! I need to pee."

"This is so stupid, you're stupid, he's stupid," Brooke shot at her mother. "He needs to sleep down here now. He can't climb the stairs and he's going to fall and wow I bet that's what you're waiting for. 'Cause if he falls and breaks his neck—"

Julie advanced on Brooke. She grabbed the glass of milk and

threw it into the sink. The glass shattered and the milk shot upward. Brooke's eyes filled with tears.

"Julie!" their dad cried.

"You go to bed this instant," Julie hissed at Brooke. To Hayley she said, "You stay here because I'm not finished with you."

Brooke took off but she was sobbing as she pounded up the stairs. A door slammed and Cassidy cried out, startled from sleep. And Hayley's dad continued to call for his wife.

Julie left the kitchen with a fierce look at Hayley. Hayley went to the sink and dismally began to clean up the broken glass and the milk. Above, she heard her mother's voice trying to be comforting as she helped her husband to the bathroom.

Hayley felt tears claw at her throat. She knew that she'd caused trouble for her family, but she hadn't intended to do so. On the other hand, she also knew that if she hadn't intended to cause trouble, she shouldn't have gone to the party in the first place.

She'd talked to Isis for just a few seconds before the other girl and her brother were strong-armed out of the church by their furious grandmother. Isis had been in a state of panic. She'd grabbed Hayley by the arm and said, "I had no clue so many people would show up. I didn't tell *anyone* except the kids we invited, and how many were there? Like ten or something? But Aidan knew, and I bet he told because that would be *just* like him. God, I'm so sorry because now I bet your mom won't even let us be friends. Only . . . please don't tell her it was my idea. We can say we heard about it at school. God, I need a hit of nicotine . . ." And she'd started fumbling in her purse for her electronic cigarette but before she could manage to root it out, Nancy Howard was there and she barked, "Get yourself out to the truck."

Now, Hayley sat at the table in the kitchen and waited for the consequences coming her way. But when they arrived, they weren't what she was expecting.

Some ten minutes after she'd gone up to help Hayley's dad, Julie Cartwright was back downstairs. She strode over to the phone and just when Hayley thought she intended to make a call despite the hour, instead she took from beneath the slim Whidbey phone directory a couple of sheets of notebook paper with her own handwriting covering them.

These she thrust at Hayley. "We're not talking any further about this thing at Maxwelton. You're heading in the wrong direction, and that stops now. This is the essay that goes with your college applications." She nodded at the papers. "Put it into your own words. Get it typed up and printed or whatever the format is supposed to be. You have an appointment with Ms. Primavera at the high school on Monday and I'll be there. Are we clear on this?"

They were, Hayley told her.

TWENTY-FIVE

Julie Cartwright was as good as her word. At the appointed hour for their meeting with Tatiana Primavera, she came through the doors to the high school's administration offices. The determined expression on her face told Hayley that they were going to get to the bottom of why, in her senior year, she'd apparently developed a new personality that prominently featured lack of cooperation.

Hayley was waiting for her, sitting on a decrepit chair of phony leather splitting at the seams. She rose. Wordlessly, she and her mom gravitated to the reception desk, where the student aide in charge made the call to Ms. Primavera. There was virtually no wait for the counselor. Within seconds, Tatiana Primavera teetered toward them on the faux Jimmy Choo heels she favored for her footwear at school.

She took them back to her office, where the meeting began with the ceremonious handing over of Hayley's senior essay. Tatiana was thrilled to receive this. She leaned back in her chair, said, "Excellent," as she began to read it. She frowned, however, at the midway point. She glanced up at Hayley, then at her mom, before reading to the end and pursing her lips thoughtfully.

"Well," she said, "as a start it's touching some of the bases. But it doesn't actually reflect . . ." She paused as if considering a way to put things.

Hayley waited. Her mom sat in silence. She held her handbag on her lap with her hands folded over the top of it and her feet planted squarely on the floor. Hayley could see that Tatiana Primavera's birdlike glances between them indicated that she was picking up on their tension.

"Let me put it this way," Tatiana finally said. "Considering the classes you've taken and the grades you have, the essay actually looks a bit . . . Did you write this yourself, Hayley?"

Hayley said nothing, but she felt her mom's eyeballs boring holes into her head. Julie Cartwright said, "Can I . . . ?" and extended her hand. Hayley waited for her to read the essay and to see that all she had done was copy her mother's own work word for word. When she read, Julie Cartwright said, "Is this supposed to tell me . . ." and then she switched gears. "She thinks she's not going to college," she said to Tatiana Primavera. She tossed the essay on the counselor's desk.

Tatiana Primavera frowned at Hayley. "Is there a reason you don't want to go to college?"

Hayley waited for what she knew wasn't going to come in answer: her mother telling the counselor that the family needed Hayley at home to help run the farm. She had overheard her mom on the phone talking to a woman on the island who had a housecleaning business. "What about three days a week?" Julie

Cartwright had asked, and Hayley knew darn well that she wasn't asking to have someone come over to clean *their* place.

"Hayley?" the counselor probed.

"I'll go to the Skagit Valley classes offered on the island. And I'll get a job."

"Jobs are scarce on Whidbey. And even if they weren't—"

"I c'n clean houses," Hayley said. She tossed a meaningful look at her mother.

Tatiana Primavera cast another glance between them. She said carefully, "Do we have a mother-daughter conflict going on here? It might help our discussion to get whatever issues there are between you out in the open."

"There isn't an issue," Julie Cartwright said.

Oh right, Hayley thought. There was just no issue her mom would talk about.

Tatiana nodded doubtfully and went on once again to talk about Hayley's grades and the classes she'd taken. She'd never received less than an A in anything, and her classes were tough. She had honors classes wherever possible; she was in her fourth year of foreign language; she was taking AP statistics. She was poised for the Ivy League. Or if she didn't want to travel far from home, there were places like University of Washington, Evergreen, Seattle U, University of Puget Sound . . . But, really, with her grades, she needed to consider Yale, Harvard, Princeton, Stanford.

"I don't want to—"

"D'you have catalogues for those places?" Julie Cartwright cut in. "We've looked through Brown's and Reed's, but if there are others . . . ? And what else should she be doing?"

"You're signed up for the SAT, yes?" Tatiana asked. "Then, you need to work on this essay. It needs to be good, Hayley, and as it stands right now—"

"She'll be working on it," Julie said. "She's had a bit of trouble getting organized this year, but she's back on track. Aren't you, Hayley?"

Hayley said nothing, merely studying the floor and then finally looking up and giving a shrug.

Tatiana said, "Yes, I see," rather slowly, and the way she said it told Hayley she was unconvinced. But she swung her chair around to her bookshelves and she fingered through the college catalogues there. She said, "You'll find information online, too, Hayley. Let's talk again next week and see if you've made any decisions."

"That's an excellent idea," Julie Cartwright declared.

THEY SAID LITTLE to each other on the way home. Julie announced, "Not a word to your father" and "I know what you're trying to do, Hayley." To the first remark, Hayley puffed out a laugh between her lips and turned her face to the window. To the second she said nothing at all.

When they pulled up at the farmhouse, a car that neither Hayley nor her mom recognized was sitting in front of it. Hayley thought at once that something bad had happened, and she knew her mom was thinking the same thing. Julie slammed on the brakes of the old SUV and practically threw herself out of the vehicle. Hayley was following when the front door opened and Parker Natalia came out onto the porch.

Hayley's dad was right behind him, laboring along with his walker. Parker held the screen door open for him and gave Hayley a casual wave that made him look like a regular visitor. Julie Cartwright murmured, "Who on earth . . . ?" and then Brooke came out of the house as well. She announced, "He's here for *Hayley*," in a way that made Hayley grow hot in the face. She quickly introduced Parker to her mom. He shook her hand, flashed his bright smile, and told them both that Bill Cartwright had invited him to wait. He had been driving along Smugglers Cove Road up to the state park for a hike when he saw the chicken barn with SMUGGLERS COVE FARM AND FLOWERS painted on its side. He'd remembered that was where Hayley lived, so he'd decided to stop by and say hi.

Bill Cartwright said, "Parker's been keeping me entertained with tales of his misspent youth. Brooke too. Eh, Brooke?"

"Oh right. What*ever*," Brooke said. She slinked back into the house.

There was an awkward silence. Under different circumstances, the correct move would have been to keep Parker Natalia away from her father since no one on the island besides family knew exactly what condition he was in other than his doctor and Seth. But Parker himself had preempted that move, so Hayley wasn't sure what to do.

Parker took care of this by saying, "Nice pond up behind the big barn," in a way that suggested a walk to the pond was what he had in mind.

Julie Cartwright said it would be a fine idea for Hayley to take Parker up to it to check it out, especially since it was a completely gorgeous autumn day, and *her* way of speaking suggested that Hayley get Parker out of her father's company.

Hayley wanted to say, "As *if*, Mom," because obviously Parker had eyes and could see that her dad was ill. But instead she said, "Right," and told Parker to follow her.

They walked past the barn in silence until Parker commented that the farm was awesome. Hayley said it was mostly work. Parker said still, it had to be nice to have so much land. There was nothing like this in Nelson. Nelson climbed steeply up from Lake Kootenay on its way into the mountains. No one had space to spread out anywhere.

"Just into the forest with the moose and the grizzlies," he said with a smile.

She smiled in turn. He seemed encouraged by this because then he started to talk for real. He began by saying, "Listen, Hayley, I've got caught up in something and I'm not sure how it happened."

Hayley thought he meant something illegal, and she couldn't figure out why he'd talk to her about it. But then he went on, and things got clear.

He said, "Isis Martin called me one night and asked if I wanted to listen to some music at that pub in Langley. She billed this place as an English pub and asked if I wanted to see it. I said sure because I wasn't doing anything, so we went."

They'd reached the pond. Hayley figured there was no point in indicating its various beauties, which were limited. The perfect blue sky and some dazzling cumulous clouds were reflected in the water, but what did it matter since seeing the pond had obviously just been an excuse?

Parker was continuing. "I don't think I gave her any ideas that night, but before I knew it, we were more or less a couple."

Hayley cast a look his way and said, "Except you sort of did."

"Did what?"

"Give her an idea." When he looked blank, she continued with, "At the Djangofest concert at the high school? At intermission?"

At this, he looked extremely flustered. He colored deeply. He swallowed. "What about intermission?"

"You went outside? So did she? She followed you out and you guys—"

"I don't remember that."

Hayley thought that was hardly a credible answer, sort of like a criminal saying "I don't recall" in court as a way of not lying directly about something. She said, "Well, she came back pretty much glowing and she said . . ." Hayley suddenly didn't want to go on as she remembered what Isis had said and why Isis had followed the Canadian in the first place.

He said, "What? Because what *I* remember is that I went outside to have a smoke. I always get nervous before I play."

She shot him a look that said *like I almost believe you.* But then what did it matter what she believed? She said, "Look. Isis was sure you're gay—"

"I'm not—"

"—so she went outside to prove it. When she came back in, she laughed and said she was way wrong. I assumed you and her . . . Course, maybe she saw you with someone else, but what does it matter anyway?"

He said, "Me and someone else? No way. Anyway . . . this is gonna sound all . . . I dunno . . . but maybe she decided she wanted to hook up with me later and she was laying her claim in advance to keep *you* from . . . whatever."

Hayley saw that he was going even redder in the face, and she had to admit that she found his embarrassment rather endearing. She found him appealing. And who wouldn't, with his glossy hair curling around his head, his dynamite smile, and his air of being just a little dangerous compared to the boys on Whidbey Island?

He ran his hand back through that beautiful hair and he said, "Look, I need to say this. When I got introduced to you, I sort of . . . This is *really* awkward."

He seemed to be waiting for Hayley to say something, but what it was she was supposed to say, she didn't know.

He went on. "I looked at her Facebook page. She's got something like twenty pictures of her and me. Whenever I see her, she's got her iPhone and she's taking pictures and the next thing I know, there I am on her page. I don't get why she's doing this because I haven't exactly—"

"I think it might be Brady," Hayley said, deciding to put Parker out of his misery. She explained the breakup Isis had gone through with her boyfriend in Palo Alto. "She doesn't want to look dumped. But then, who does?"

He looked enormously relieved. He said, "Oh. That's better." Then he gazed at her with his deep brown eyes warm and said meaningfully, "I bet you've never been dumped, Hayley."

It was Hayley's turn to color, and she felt from the heat on her face that she was going as red as a birthday balloon. "Everyone's been dumped."

"I don't think so." He gazed away from her to the pond for a moment and seemed to be gathering his thoughts. He turned back to her and said in a rush, "I want a chance."

"To dump me?"

He laughed. "Boy, I said that wrong. I meant a chance to go out with you. I felt something when I met you and . . . well . . . I think you felt it too. What d'you say?"

Hayley wasn't unaware of the compliment Parker Natalia was paying her. It was twofold. There was the compliment spoken by the attraction of a dazzling young man to her. There was also the compliment of his honesty about the attraction. The second of the two—that honesty—was seriously compelling.

"I say okay," she told him with a smile.

TWENTY-SIX

S eth decided to do a little checking on Parker Natalia once Hayley told him that the Canadian had tracked her down on the farm. On his way to do a hike or something at South Whidbey State Park, the young man had claimed. But when Hayley included the information that Parker had also wanted her advice about getting clear of Isis Martin, Seth had his doubts. Something definitely didn't feel right about that one. Parker hadn't exactly been fighting Isis off with a whip and a chair.

If Parker was setting Hayley up for something, Seth wanted to protect her from the dude. That was what he told himself when he made the phone call to a number in Canada associated with BC Django 21. It turned out the number belonged to the bass player, a guy called David Wilkie.

Seth used music as his excuse, and it was helpful that David Wilkie had been in the audience at South Whidbey High School when Triple Threat had played. So he'd seen Parker Natalia playing with the group, and he wasn't suspicious when Seth asked him about the fiddler. Seth said that Triple Threat was thinking of taking Parker on permanently. He said he was calling to see if the Canadian was reliable.

David's answer was forthright but his tone was not. He said, "Oh he's reliable, all right."

"Meaning what?" Seth asked.

"Meaning he'll turn up for rehearsals and he'll turn up for gigs. He's a great fiddler. Well, you heard that yourself."

"And?" Seth said. "He says you guys dumped him for another fiddler. So if he was reliable and great and all that . . . ?"

"Hey, look. I don't want to bad-mouth the dude. Just watch him, okay?"

"Why?"

"Because sometimes he's trouble. I don't want to say more. Maybe he's changed. Just watch him."

That set off all kinds of alarms. Seth wanted to know what David Wilkie meant. So he tried to probe, but all he learned was that BC Django 21 played regular gigs in Nelson, in nearby Castlegar, in Trail, and as far away as Kelowna, Kamloops, and Vernon. They were building a real following in B.C., and they would've liked to include Parker but "things didn't go that way." Plus . . . well, he started messing around with their mandolin player's little sister and "Really, dude, that's all I want to say." Then he added ominously, "Look at it this way. He's one hell of a musician and there's no question about it. But the deal is this: You're probably setting yourself up for trouble in more ways than one if you make him part of your group. That's all."

That, Seth decided, was more than enough.

TWENTY-SEVEN

"Restriction." Derric said this to the lunch table in general as they compared notes on the fallout from the Maxwelton party. "A month and 'you're lucky it's not longer but your mom thinks a month' . . . blah blah blah." He unwrapped a ham sandwich and tossed the plastic into the center of the table.

Jenn McDaniels said, "That's harsh. But it's definitely better than having your mom read the story of Sodom and Gomorrah to you. Twice, by the way. Like any day now I'm gonna turn into a pillar of salt. Ha. She should be so lucky." She took a bite of her PBJ sandwich and said to Squat, "What about you?"

"I'm becoming my brother," Squat informed them. He grabbed a carrot stick out of Jenn's meager supply and used it to pretend he was smoking a joint. "Bunch of crying. Bunch more of 'I'm a failure as a mother.'"

"Harsher," Jenn said.

"An appointment with Ms. Tatiana and my mom," Hayley said.

"Harshest of all!" Jenn said, and then to Becca, "Bet *you* faced tea and cookies at Mrs. Kinsale's, didn't you?"

Becca said, "As if," and everyone began to give her a bad time until she went on with, "Okay, okay. But it was waffles," as a way to keep them at a distance from the conversation she'd had with Diana Kinsale in the aftermath of the Maxwelton party.

She needn't have worried. Isis Martin took up the reins of the conversation. They were at their regular lunch table, and from what Becca could hear around them in the New Commons, the Maxwelton party along with the fire was *the* topic of conversation. This wasn't surprising since so many of the kids sitting nearby had showed up at the party. And that, it turned out, was what Isis Martin wanted to talk about.

"I didn't tell *anyone* about that party," she declared. "And you'd think I committed some major crime against humanity. Grandam was spitting bullets the whole next day. She called my mom and went on and on. You'd think we'd murdered someone."

There was a moment of silence. Hayley was the one to say, "Someone did die, Isis."

Isis covered her mouth with her hand. Then she said, "I didn't mean . . . But the fire started *after* we were rounded up. It was just a coincidence that someone was camping in that shack. Even Grandam said that and she was ready to accuse us of everything she could think of."

"Do they know who he was?" Becca turned to Derric, who'd be the most likely person to know, considering his dad's job.

"Turned out to be a longtime druggie from Oak Harbor," he told them. "He assaulted both his parents 'bout three months ago, then took off, and the cops've been looking for him ever since."

"Loser," Jenn said.

"He didn't deserve to die," Hayley said quietly.

"I'm not saying he deserved it," Jenn said. "I'm just saying he was a loser. He lit an illegal fire inside that place."

"But so did we," Becca pointed out.

"Our fire wasn't illegal. It was in a fire pit."

"You know what I mean."

They were all quiet again until Isis spoke up, saying, "Guys . . . you haven't told anyone it was my idea, have you? We're all in this together, aren't we? No way did I intend the booze to be there. It was all just something to *do*, you know? Something to do on a Saturday night? It's not like there's any place else to go or anything else to do and I meant that in the best possible way and I wasn't even drunk. Were you?"

They all looked at each other incredulously. Jenn said, "Whatever," and stuffed half of her PBJ into her lunch bag. She said, "I'm outa here," and in very short order, the rest of the kids decided they were, too.

DERRIC'S FOOTSTEPS WERE slow as he and Becca walked to her next class. His arm around her shoulders was heavy. At her classroom door, he drew her to one side and told her what was wrong. "It's worse than restriction. I didn't want to say."

Becca felt a rush of fear. "What?"

"She made me an appointment with a shrink," he told her. "She says it's time they all 'get to the bottom' of what's going on with me. She was all 'you haven't been yourself in months and this is the limit.' She meant the party."

Becca put her hand on his smooth cheek. "I'm sorry," she told him. "But it could . . . It could be a good thing."

"Nope. It couldn't," he replied. "There's not a single way it could be good."

She didn't argue. Instead, she pulled him down to her and kissed him. She thought about loving someone the way she loved this boy and how loving someone sometimes meant letting them find the path they needed to take.

BECCA TOLD HERSELF that just because *she* was going to find out what had happened to Rejoice, it didn't mean she would have to do anything with the information. A phone call to Derric's church in the guise of having to do a report for one of her classes was enough to get her the name of the orphanage that Derric had come from: Children's Hope of Kampala. From there, she had to get her hands on a computer, and this was something she didn't want to do at school.

South Whidbey Commons wasn't a safe place since she didn't want to be seen by one of the many kids who gathered there in the afternoons. So she went to the city library, a cottage-like structure next to the city hall. Some sort of women's reading group was meeting in a room that opened up off the stacks, but that was it as far as users went that afternoon. No one was sitting at the computers, so she logged on and started her search for news of Children's Hope of Kampala and how one might discover the whereabouts of one of its orphans.

What she did discover gave her pause. The orphanage where Derric and his sister had lived had closed its doors. And the closing seemed to be permanent. She was about to follow a link to learn more when she heard, "Art class again?" at her shoulder.

She looked around. There stood Aidan Martin yet again, and his expression was so smug that Becca felt infuriated. She snapped, "What *is* it with you? Every time I'm working on the Internet, you turn up and it's getting creepy. Are you a stalker or something?" She jerked her ear bud from her ear and heard *if she wasn't such a poser.*

Aidan smiled, apparently unoffended by being called a stalker. Becca saw why in a second when he flipped open his chemistry books and pulled a folded piece of paper from it. This he unfolded and placed over the computer's keyboard. It was one of the Have You Seen This Woman flyers.

Becca said nothing although fear shot through her. Aidan put down his backpack and rustled through it till he came up with the front section of a newspaper. She saw that this was the Everett *Herald*, from the closest large town on the mainland. He handed it to her and said, "Page five," and although she knew what she was probably going to find there, she cooperated. Her heart started break dancing.

She saw that the paper, like the *South Whidbey Record*, had the story about Laurel Armstrong and her daughter, Hannah. The paper was running it, just like the *Record*, with the same pictures that the *Record* had used. Not for the first time, Becca felt the walls closing in on her. But she swore she wouldn't give in to this kid and whatever it was that he wanted from her. So she looked at the story and then at him. "So what?" she said.

"Kind of a bizarre coincidence."

"What is? Look, I'm working here, Aidan, so if you have something to say just spit it out instead of creeping around and acting like you're working for the CIA."

"I just recognized the daughter is all." His eyes locked on hers and there was no whisper accompanying what he said, which told her his thoughts and his words were one with each other: perfect truth.

She said, "So? Call the number on the flyer then. 'Cause I don't know why you're announcing to me that you recognize some little kid in the paper."

"That's the coincidence."

"*What* is?"

"It's the same girl you were looking at on the Internet. You remember that, right? The one you were looking at for your art class?" He made air quotes when he said the last two words. He watched her with that smirk on his face.

The smirk replaced her fear with fury. She said, "Coincidences happen, okay? Just like the *coincidence* of you flinging around a burning piece of wood *just* before a shack catches fire and kills someone inside. Got it?"

His expression altered and along with it came *he died and I was pissed but that doesn't mean I meant bad because* . . . which was startling in its clarity. But what was more startling was what accompanied it: less than five seconds of vision of an infant in a facing-backward car seat and a hand giving that infant a bottle. Then the vision was gone and she and Aidan were staring at each other. They held the stare for another five seconds till he turned on his heel and left the library.

Becca remained, but she was frightened. Who was this kid? she wondered. What was he really capable of? And what did it mean that she didn't even have to touch him in order to have a vision?

BECCA NEEDED TO talk with someone about Aidan's continual intrusion into her life. Seth seemed like a godsend. When Becca arrived back at Ralph Darrow's place, she saw that Seth's VW was in the parking area. When she saw him crossing the lawn in front of his grandfather's house, she called out his name.

He was coming from the direction of the forest, Gus bounding along at his side. Gus heard her call and gave a happy yelp. He began to charge toward her in greeting, and he didn't stop when Seth shouted his name. Becca found a stick quickly because she knew the Lab was likely to knock her off her feet with his ecstatic hello. When he got close, she cried, "Gus! Go get it!" and threw the thing high into the hillside that she was descending. Gus followed his nature, which was to follow the stick. Becca continued down to Seth.

"Don't tell Grand," Seth said as Becca joined him. "I swear, Beck. I think he's retarded."

Becca knew he didn't mean his grandfather. "He just gets excited. Watch. He'll bring the stick back."

They waited and Gus proved her correct although, she saw, it was an entirely different stick. When he returned to them with this prize proudly dangling from his jaws, she giggled and added, "More or less." And then to Seth, "Whatcha up to?"

He jerked his head in the direction of the woods. "Just saying hey to Parker," he told her. "He wasn't there, though."

Something in his voice told Becca more was going on than a simple hello. His whisper of *telling Hayley but that would be so lame because she'd think I'm hoping* . . . filled in the blanks. Still, she said, "Oh yeah?" in a way that told Seth he needed to 'fess up.

Seth wrested the stick from Gus and threw it back toward the hillside. He said, "Oh yeah," and matched her tone. He added as if to clue her in on the obvious, "Me and the guys're thinking of asking him to join Triple Threat."

"Can he do that?"

"What d'you mean?"

"Doesn't he have to go back to Canada?" She admitted to herself that she'd been thinking of Parker's return to Canada ever since she'd learned he came from Nelson. For if he went home, maybe he could search for Laurel and somehow put Becca in touch with her mom.

Seth waited for the dog's return. Gus was snuffling around the bushes on the hillside. Seth called his name impatiently. He finally said to Becca, "Yeah. I guess so." He shot her a glance. "Okay. I was checking up on him," he admitted.

"In the tree house?"

"That and other stuff." *Because if that guy meant fires when he said watch out no way do I want Hayley near him.*

Beyond her pleasure at the absolute distinctness of the whisper, Becca knew that Seth might well have discovered something important. She asked him about this.

He told her about a phone call he'd made to the bass player in BC Django 21 and what he'd learned from him. He said, "And don't tell me it was dumb to call because no way am I letting Hayley get involved with some pyro who's gonna mess with her mind. She could end up following him to Canada and wrecking her life."

Becca knew he was lying to himself, at least in part. Seth wasn't over Hayley no matter what he said. But she also knew there was nothing she could do about this since she'd take the same steps to protect Derric if she had to.

She said, "I get it. Just . . . Why were you checking up on him in the woods?"

"Perfect place for him to torch if that's what he's into. Or to hide his gear. Or . . . I don't know. I just needed to see. 'Cause if he's hiding who he really is, it could mean anything."

The whole idea of hiding gave Becca the opening to talk to Seth about Aidan Martin. She told him her concerns. She kept the information to feeling stalked, to becoming scared, and to worrying about his interest in Hannah Armstrong. She said,

"He's really strange, Seth. He's always there and he's always watching and he keeps turning up . . ."

"Maybe he's hot for you."

"That's not it."

"Bet he never turns up when Derric's there. Does he?"

"No, but—"

"Rest my case, then. Look, some dudes don't have a clue how to approach a girl. They're thinking how hot she is and they want to know her and they're total klutzes."

"That's *not* what's going on. He's more like one of those kids who shoots up a high school."

Seth took this in, gazing down at his sandals. "You think that, you got to tell someone."

"I'm telling you."

"You know what I mean. You got to talk to . . . the principal? Or Derric's dad. He c'n check the kid out."

That was the last thing she needed: putting Aidan Martin and his growing suspicions about her *anywhere* near the under-sheriff of Island County. She said, "Anyone I ask is gonna want to know what he's said, what he's done, and what I've seen. Stuff like that. And what do I say? 'He just creeps me out'? I can't do that. All he's doing is turning up when I don't want him to. And I got to keep him from even thinking about calling that number on the Laurel Armstrong flyer and telling someone that this girl called Becca King must know *something* about the missing lady because she was looking at her on the Internet way before those flyers ever went up all around town."

Seth thought about this and finally said, "If he's holding something over you, then we need to get something to hold over him. He's not gonna say word one about you and Hannah Armstrong and her mom if he knows we know something serious about him. You think there's something serious out there?"

Becca considered Aidan: his actions, his words, his whispers, and her vision. She said, "Yeah. I think there is."

TWENTY-EIGHT

Becca knew her options were limited when it came to finding out something about Aidan Martin. There wasn't word one about him via the Internet, so she wondered if there was something about his daily performance in school that she could hold over him: cheating on a test, plagiarizing a paper, bullying some kid, breaking some rule, whatever. But she didn't know a soul who had a class with him, and he kept to himself whenever there was a chance to mingle with other kids.

She talked this over with Jenn McDaniels. They were in the girls' restroom. Jenn was sneaking a cigarette. Becca had followed her in and she stood before her with her arms crossed, shaking her head. Jenn said, "I know. I'm quitting, like . . . sometime."

Becca said, "You're the one who wants to make the All Island girls' soccer team, not me. So when exactly are tryouts?"

"Not till April. I'm good. I'm giving up next month." And when Jenn checked out Becca's expression, she said, "Okay. Next week. I'm quitting next week. Make you happy?" And when Becca didn't answer, "*Okay*. Tomorrow." Becca shook her head and Jenn sputtered in outrage and strode to one of the stalls and threw her cigarette in the toilet. "Happy now?" she demanded. "You're supposed to be my best friend, not my mom."

"I don't know enough Bible to be your mom."

"Well, you're following me just like her, let me tell you. I didn't even hear you come in." Jenn rustled in her backpack and brought out a small plastic bottle of the mouthwash.

Becca wanted to point out that mouthwash didn't do much to kill the odor that clung to her clothes, but she had bigger fish to fry, so she said, "I wanted to talk to you."

"'Bout what?" Jenn gargled, spit, and then examined herself in the mirror, which was a real rarity for Jenn. She was the least vain girl that Becca had ever met.

"About Aidan Martin," Becca told her. "He keeps turning up whenever I'm alone."

"Like at Mr. Darrow's, you mean?"

"Not yet, but he's been there with his grandmother so he knows I live there. So far, he's just shown up sort of *coincidentally*. When I'm in the library here, when I'm in South Whidbey Commons, when I'm in Langley library . . . He sneaks up on me and watches what I'm doing. And he says stuff."

"Like what?"

Becca needed to be creative but not entirely untruthful. "So far, it's how he says my name and the way he kind of looks me over and I've started thinking . . . Like, what do we really know about this kid? He could be like those creeps who kidnap elementary school kids. We need to find out about him, Jenn. But I looked online and there's nothing. So I'm wondering . . . What's he doing here, anyway? Him and his sister. Why're they living here and not where they used to live, especially since their parents aren't even with them?"

Jenn leaned against the lavatory sink. She said, "We need to look at his records. There might be something in them."

"Like what?"

"Like where he came from. Like a warning from another school or something. Like a sign of trouble he got into somewhere."

"So how're we supposed to look at his records?"

"You and me? We can't," Jenn told her. "But I know someone who can."

THEY ACCOSTED SQUAT Cooper as he came out of his AP Tech class. Jenn linked her arm with his and said, "Just the man we're looking for: my passionate lover since kindergarten."

Squat looked from Jenn to Becca and brushed his rusty hair off his forehead. "Why do I think this means trouble?"

Jenn said, "Come with us, my handsome friend."

Squat said, "Now I know it means trouble," but he allowed himself to be led off to the chemistry lab, where they all ducked inside. He said, "I got a class to get to," but he acquiesced. "What?" he said when Jenn had him backed into a corner. "If this is about senior prom, you sure as hell are planning in advance."

"Har har," Jenn said. "Like I want to put on a dress for anyone? Not hardly. This is about looking into Aidan Martin's school records. He's giving Becca grief and we think he's a nutcase."

"So tell the dean." And to Becca, "He stupid enough to be bullying you or something? One word to Derric and the guy's lights are out."

"We'll get to that," Jenn intervened. "But first we want to know what we're dealing with. All we know, the kid could be coming to school with a weapon. A switchblade, a gun, a bomb. It's not like we've got a security system or guards checking everyone's backpack. We want to know who this kid really is and his records're going to tell us. Now, in the old days, someone'd just pull the fire alarm and when everyone scrammed out of the school, that someone'd sneak into the office and look at Aidan Martin's records while dramatic music was playing and a clock was ticking. Nowadays, we just need someone to hack into the school computer, and I know just the guy who can do it."

Squat held up his hands. "No way, Jenn. I'm already in enough trouble after Maxwelton. I lost my computer privileges and even if I still had them, d'you know how much trouble I'd be in if I got caught hacking into the school district's system . . . even if it *could* be hacked into, which I pretty much doubt?"

"Seems to me," Jenn said, "if someone c'n hack into the Pentagon, someone can sure as hell hack into South Whidbey School District."

"Maybe so, but it ain't gonna be me," Squat told her. And then he said to Becca, "Just tell Derric."

"What?" Jenn clasped her hands beneath her chin, "Like 'Oh

Derric, I'm *so* scared. Puhleez help me.' That what you have in mind? Come on, Squat, help us out here."

"Can't do it," he said. He looked regretful as he turned to Becca. "Sorry," he told her.

JENN WAS NOT a girl who was easily defeated. She said to Becca portentously, "It ain't over till it's over," and they went off to their next classes: Becca to Geometry and Jenn to Biology. Becca thought that Jenn meant she was going to strong-arm Squat in some fashion, but within half an hour, she learned what Jenn intended. The fire alarm went off.

The fact that this wasn't a planned event was evident in the expression on the faces of the teachers as everyone vacated the buildings. This was underscored by the arrival of the fire department engines and the fire chief some five minutes later, as well as the scurrying around of Mr. Vansandt, the school principal, along with the dean. It was fifteen minutes before the all clear was given. It was ninety minutes more before Becca saw Jenn McDaniels once again and was given the A-okay sign and a knowing smile as they passed each other on the way to another class.

Becca could picture exactly what her best friend had done. It had begun with a simple and undeniable female request to visit the lavatory. Instead of the restroom, a dash down the hall to the nearest fire alarm and when the school was vacated, a quick trip to the administration office and the room where the kids' files were kept. No problem with being missing among the kids from her class who were gathered outside the school. Since she'd gone to the restroom, she wouldn't be missed, and even if she was, the teacher would assume she'd joined the students assembled elsewhere.

"Simple is always best, hon," Becca's grandmother had said to her many times. She could only hope that her grandma had been right.

This proved to be the case when she met up with Jenn at their lockers after school. Jenn said to her, "Got the goods," and Becca felt a real surge of triumph till she saw what the goods actually were. Jenn had scored Aidan Martin's transcript. That was all. It held only his grades and the name of the school.

"This is it?" Becca sighed, because she didn't see how transcripts were going to be helpful.

"Check out where they're from," Jenn told her and pointed out the school.

It was called Wolf Canyon Academy, a name that indicated it was private. Becca was about to say, "So what? He went to a private school is all," till she saw the location of the place. It was in Moab, Utah.

Jenn asked the logical question. "What was he doing there? Hasn't Isis been going on about Palo Alto, where they're supposedly from? Seems to me she's either lying about that for some reason or Aidan got himself shipped off to a private school in another state. And what does that suggest to you?"

"He was in trouble," Becca said.

"Bet your ass," Jenn agreed.

TWENTY-NINE

Hayley had been on her way to see Tatiana Primavera. The counselor had sent a call slip for her, and Hayley figured that Tatiana was checking up on her progress on the college application essay. She'd done nothing about creating a new essay, though, and she knew Ms. Primavera was going to be all over her for that. So when the fire alarm went off, she felt she had a reprieve.

Outside the school in the assembly area, she caught sight of Isis Martin. Isis waved at her frantically in a come-over-here gesture. She was hanging at the very back of the kids, but she didn't stay there. As the sound of the fire engine's sirens came closer to the school from Maxwelton Road, she grabbed Hayley's arm and took off toward a line of recycling dumpsters.

Hidden from sight, Isis dug around in her shoulder bag. She brought out a pack of Marlboros and used a Bic lighter to fire one up. Hayley raised her eyebrows and Isis said, "The electronic one went dead. Sorry. I know it's nasty but I need the hit."

"Keep it out of sight if you don't want even more trouble. And just don't blow the smoke on me."

"God, have you always been so good?" Isis inhaled and flicked ash off the end of the cigarette. Truth was, she made it look sexy.

Hayley said, "I got saved by the fire alarm. Ms. Primavera wanted to—"

"This is *all* we need," Isis cut in.

"What is?"

"Another fire." She chewed on a fingernail and then took another hit. She said, "We're in so much trouble, Hayley. Nancy called my mom, and of *course* the last thing Lisa Ann wants is to have to come up here *herself* for any reason. So she tells Nancy to set up some consequences for us that'll 'get our attention.' So me and Aidan? We end up having a meeting with the owners of that house on the beach who, let me tell you, are not happy to come up from Olympia or Tacoma or who the hell knows where they're from in order to meet with us. And Grandam along with those guys arrange what me and Aidan're going to do as penance for invading their property. We're replanting everything that got trampled by the cops and the firemen and all the kids, not to mention we're paying for all the plants. We're cleaning up the trash that's everywhere along with the vomit, thank you very much. We're emptying the fire pit and repairing that stupid chaise lounge that someone broke. And—are you ready for this?—someone took a dump in the hot tub and we get to deal with that as well. *And* we have to wash the windows because they're all disgusting from the smoke. After that, we *might* be let out of jail."

"I c'n help you guys," Hayley offered.

"Oh shit no. I'd love it but if Nancy showed up while me and Aidan are supposed to be working and she found you there working with us . . . ? She'd go nuclear. And Aidan's *got* to talk to the sheriff about the fire in that fishing shack *before* the sheriff talks to him, Hayley. But he won't, and *no one* is listening to me no matter how I go at it."

She took a final hit before she dropped her cigarette and carefully smashed it with her foot. She looked over at the kids gathered in dissolving ranks as the wait for the all clear extended. She said, "There better not be a fire," more to herself than to Hayley, and then she swung around and announced, "I got to tell you something, Hayley, but you have to swear that you won't say anything. If you can't do that, then I won't say but I *need* to say so please, Hayley."

Hayley had never heard Isis sound so desperate. "What?"

"You swear?"

"Okay. Yeah. What's wrong?"

"Aidan likes to start fires."

"What?"

Isis looked around furtively. "He was in a special school. A boarding school for, you know, kids with problems? He was there for two years because he set fires. They were real small at first, just a kid having fun with matches, but they got bigger till a whole apartment building burnt down . . . God, you can't tell *anyone*. But it's why he has to talk to the sheriff before the sheriff finds out about the special school on his own. See, everybody knew he was disturbed. And I keep saying that he has to tell the sheriff about it or my mom needs to call the sheriff or *something* because if someone doesn't tell him, he's going to think that Aidan's hiding something. And Aidan's not hiding anything, I swear it. Only now with this shack and the guy dying inside? Hayley, Aidan *didn't* set that fire. It was an accident."

Isis was tearing at her fingernails with her teeth. She flung her hand down and said, "How disgusting," and she lit another cigarette. She said to Hayley, "Is he around? Do you see him?" and Hayley knew she was talking about Aidan.

Hayley looked among the students, but it was an impossible task. Kids were milling around as the wait for the all clear went on and on, and the fire fighters scurried around the school checking to see if there was indeed a fire. She didn't see Aidan anywhere. But she also didn't smell any smoke, other than from Isis's cigarette.

She said no, that she couldn't see him.

Isis said, "He's cured. Completely or they wouldn't've let him out. That's what they said. But *if* he isn't, I'm in so much more trouble because I was s'posed to watch him only how am I s'posed to watch him one hundred percent of the time. See, I saw him with that stick at the party: how it was on fire and he was playing with it and acting loony but there I was with Parker and all I was thinking was how if him and me hooked up, that'd really fix Brady and he *needs* to be fixed and so does that bitchy Madison Ridgeway because . . . God, my life is so screwed up right now. If I didn't have you, I'd blow my brains out."

Hayley decided then and there that this wasn't the moment

to do what a close girlfriend would do and let Isis know about Parker Natalia's visit to the farm and his declaration about wanting a chance with her. She realized she needed to clear this with Isis because she *was* her friend and because, after all, Isis might truly be interested in Parker. But to lay that on her when Isis was already in such a state about her brother . . . ? She couldn't do it.

THIRTY

When Hayley was sent for a second time that day, during the last ten minutes of the final class period, she assumed that Tatiana Primavera was calling her to the office to have the meeting aborted earlier. But when her Spanish teacher gave her the call slip, she discovered that she was being called not to the administrative offices but to the band room.

Since she was in the jazz band, Hayley figured that something had come up, like a new rehearsal time. When she entered the band room, however, it wasn't to see the jazz band director or the members of the band either. This didn't have a thing to do with jazz, for the gathered kids had all been at the Maxwelton Beach party, and calling them together like this didn't bode well for the next few minutes, especially considering who'd called for them.

Hayley recognized the fire chief from his uniform. He'd taken off his hat, but it was tucked under his arm, and he was talking soberly to Mr. Vansandt. Hayley heard her name called, and she looked around to see Isis waving her over just as she'd done earlier in the day.

When the door closed upon the last student, Mr. Vansandt

went to a music stand that stood in the conductor's position in front of the chairs where the students were sitting. He said gravely, "This won't take long, for those of you worried about missing the bus home. Chief Levitt has asked me to gather you together."

A murmur rose among the kids. Karl Levitt set his hat on the music stand and observed them all. He said, "Here's what you need to know. We'll get to the bottom of this sooner or later, but it's going to be a helluva lot easier on everyone if you guys make it sooner."

The murmur among the kids grew in strength. Across from her, Hayley saw Becca King and Derric Mathieson lean their heads together and begin to talk. Becca, she noted, took her hearing device from her ear, as if she couldn't stand to know the worst.

The worst was what Chief Levitt next said. "This happens sometimes when a fire occurs at night. Till you can get a decent look at the location in the light of day, you just don't know. That's how it was with the fishing shack that burnt down. We didn't know, but now we do."

Isis hissed in a breath. Hayley looked at her. Her blue eyes were stricken.

"It was logical to think at first that the fire was an accident: some doped-up fool not watching out when he was cooking his food or trying to stay warm. But now we know it was something different. The way I see things, someone sitting right here in this room knows that, too. And it's going to go a hell of a lot easier on him if he comes forward."

One of the boys—Hayley couldn't see who it was—called out, "You saying someone set that shack on fire?"

"An astute observation," Karl Levitt acknowledged dryly.

"So does that mean . . . What's that mean?" It was another voice.

"What it means is that we're going to begin with the fire starter and work from there," Karl Levitt told them. "He comes forward, it's one thing. Someone turns him in, it's another. We have to dig him out of you all, it's a third."

"He wants someone to rat," a boy murmured close by. It was one of the jocks, Hayley saw. The kid looked around, probably for a likely suspect he could point out to the fire chief.

The rest of the kids said nothing. And the only other thing the fire chief said was, "You guys think about that, okay? Mr. Vansandt here knows how to get in touch with me. Anything that anyone tells us will remain confidential. For now."

IT WAS THE *for now* that got everyone talking. They broke off into tight little groups once the principal and the fire chief allowed them to leave the band room. Hayley gravitated to her lunch table friends who were near the athletic trophy case. Isis went to talk to her brother. They ducked out of the building together.

Jenn McDaniels was talking when Hayley joined the others. She was, it seemed, trying to pump Derric for information. If there was something to be known about the fire and the demise of the druggie and what it meant, surely Sheriff Mathieson would know it and, through him, Derric would know it, too.

"What're we talking?" Jenn was demanding. "If someone set that fire and there was someone inside that house, is this, like, *murder*? Or what?"

Becca said, "No one could've known that guy was hiding out there. And if someone started a fire and didn't know there was someone in the house . . . That's not murder, is it?"

"Your ass it is," Jenn told her. "Isn't it?" she asked Derric.

"Not first degree, I don't think," he said.

"But if you're committing a crime—like robbing a bank—and someone dies, that makes it murder. First degree."

"If you rob a bank," Squat put in, "you c'n see all the other people there. You know they're there and you rob the bank anyway and you end up shooting someone. This is different."

"No way. You don't get some special . . . special . . . excuse or something," Jenn pointed out.

"Don't know," Derric said. "And my dad's not saying. I only know what you guys know: Someone set the fire, and it wasn't an accident."

"But you can find out more, can't you?" Hayley asked him. "If the sheriff thinks it's murder, your dad'll tell you." If Derric did find out, he'd tell the rest of them and she could let Isis know. And if what Isis had said about Aidan starting fires in California was true . . . that a whole apartment building burned down . . . God, she was going to have to tell someone, wasn't she? Now that they knew the fire had been set and a guy had died as a result.

If she didn't tell . . . if she didn't talk Isis into telling . . . if Isis couldn't convince Aidan to talk to the sheriff . . .

Hayley saw that Becca had fixed her gaze directly on her. It was a grave gaze, as if the other girl was actually reading her thoughts from her expression. Hayley tried to make her face a perfect blank. She needed to think everything through.

"S'pose," Derric said in answer to her question. It was a question that, at this point, Hayley had entirely forgotten. But he was looking at her, and she realized that she'd been the person to ask it: Could Derric find out from his dad what the real situation was?

Jenn said, "Well, you ask me, we need to know. 'Cause there were people at that party who weren't even *from* this school and if someone started that fire, then it could have been one of them." She used her fingers to count off the suspects. "There were those guys that showed up with the booze. They looked like Navy guys from up at the base, didn't they? There were three of them. And then there was Parker, that fiddler from Canada. And two kids who already graduated from here and at least three others from the alternative school."

"If Chief Levitt came here, he probably's talked to those guys too," Squat Cooper said. "He's not gonna just point the finger at us."

"There's those other fires, though," Becca said quietly. She was frowning, as if looking inward. But then her gaze shifted to Hayley and her eyes seemed to bore right into Hayley's soul. "They've been getting bigger and worse since the first one, haven't they?" she asked everyone in general. But Hayley *knew* Becca was asking her, although she couldn't figure out why.

"Cops need to figure out who was at each fire."

Squat looked from one of them to the other and he was the one to put it into words. "We all were, weren't we?" he said to Jenn.

THIRTY-ONE

S eth heard about the change in the Maxwelton fire investigation from a fellow carpenter on the job site north of
Freeland. The guy was one of the island's volunteer fire fighters
and also a neighbor and friend of Karl Levitt. He'd been there to
help douse the fishing shack fire, so the fire chief had passed the
word to him. It wasn't a secret anyway. The last issue of the *South
Whidbey Record* had been all over the developing story.

Seth decided to drive up to Coupeville after work to have a
talk with the undersheriff. For in combination with the warnings
he'd heard from the bass player in BC Django 21, Seth had realized that Parker Natalia had been on the island since before the
very first fire. While Seth told himself he hated to be a snitch, he
also told himself that the cops needed to know that along with
his presence at the Maxwelton Beach party, Parker had been
camping in his car at the fairgrounds when the fire occurred
there. The sheriff would want to check him out.

Of course, Seth also knew there was another reason for his
trekking up to Coupeville to talk to the sheriff, and that reason
was Hayley. He had to protect her, he told himself.

So Seth went to Coupeville, ten miles north of the building site. The undersheriff was in, as it happened. Seth had been hoping that maybe Dave Mathieson wouldn't be there, and he'd've been able just to leave a message along the lines of "Check out a dude called Parker Natalia from Nelson, B.C., because he's been on the island since the fires started." But when he stopped at the reception desk and asked for the undersheriff, he was told to "wait over there, please," and he took himself to a bench and picked up a magazine on golfing, which he pretended to read.

Ten minutes after he got there, Dave Mathieson came out. He said Seth's name and he extended his hand. There had been bad blood between them when Derric had been hurt in the woods the previous year, but that seemed to be forgotten now.

"Good to see you," Dave said to him. "Come on back."

He seemed to know that Seth was there on business, so that made things a little easier. He took Seth through to where the offices were, which was mercifully not where the interview rooms and the holding cells were. Seth had seen those already, up close and way too personal.

Inside his office, Dave indicated a chair for Seth and took the one behind the desk for himself. He leaned back, yawned, said, "Damn long day," and then added, "What's up?"

"I heard about the fire," Seth told him. "The guy that died inside the shack? I work with one of the volunteers, and he told me about it."

Dave said, "I heard you're doing construction now. Good for you, Seth."

Seth thanked him politely. He said that he'd been thinking things over and something had dawned on him once he sorted through the number of fires they'd had on the island since the first one in July.

Dave nodded, but he didn't say anything. He looked interested, though, so Seth went on.

"There's this guy." He leaned forward, his hands between his knees. He tried to sound earnest but also reluctant because he *was* earnest and he *was* reluctant. He said, "I hate to be a snitch, Sheriff Mathieson, but now with that guy dying inside the shack . . . ? When someone eats it because of what someone else has done . . . ?"

"You mean when someone sets a fire and someone else dies," Dave said.

"Yeah. I mean, before it didn't seem . . . Well, aside from the property involved, it wasn't *harmful* except the fire at the fairgrounds and the animals and all that, but now it's a person and . . ."

Seth was sort of hoping Dave Mathieson would bail him out by saying something like, "Ah. You have a detail for us, don't you?" and opening up his cop's notebook or whatever they had. But the undersheriff didn't do this. He just waited and pretty much *forced* Seth to rat out a friend.

So Seth gave him Parker's name, which of course the sheriff already had since he had the names of every person who'd been at the Maxwelton party. But what he didn't have was the "watch out for this guy" and the "he could be trouble" that Seth had heard from the BC Django 21 bass player. What he also didn't have was the information about where Parker had been staying till he moved to the tree house in Ralph Darrow's woods. When Dave Mathieson heard all this from Seth's betraying lips, he made a note of the fact.

He said, "Staying at the fairgrounds? We didn't know that. He was up front about when he'd arrived on the island, but as to where he was staying—"

"You mean you've talked to him already?"

"We're in the process of talking to everyone, asking them to account for where they were every time there was a fire." Dave smiled thinly. "Haven't got to you yet but now that you're here . . . What've you got to say about where *you* were, Seth?"

"Not at the fairgrounds, not the night of *that* fire," Seth told him. "We had a gig in Monroe, me and the Triple Threat guys. And hey, I don't start fires."

"Nobody does," Sheriff Mathieson said. "That's what they keep telling me."

SETH LEFT, THINKING he hadn't done much good despite dropping the word to the sheriff that Parker Natalia had been sleeping in his car at the fairgrounds. As for the rest of the fires and Parker's whereabouts: He'd been at the high school for the fire that had occurred during Djangofest and he'd been at the party at Maxwelton Beach and who knew where else he'd been aside from definitely *on* the island from the very moment the first fire had started in that trash bin over at Bailey's Corner.

Seth drove to his grandfather's house. Sometimes only a gab session with Ralph Darrow would cheer Seth straight when he was feeling rotten. And he was definitely feeling rotten about Parker because he knew the main issue in his mind was really Hayley and not some druggie who'd died when a shack burnt down.

At Ralph Darrow's house the porch lights were on in the fading evening, and through the windows he could see Becca at work in the kitchen. He went inside without knocking, as was his habit. He said, "Hey," to Becca and he looked around. "Where's Grand?" he asked.

"Gone to the tree house to invite Parker for dinner." She saw his expression in reaction to this news and added, "There's a bunch," in reference to the food. "He's gonna want you to stay too."

Seth wondered how he was going to face Parker now that he had ratted him out to the sheriff. He didn't have much time to prepare, though. Within thirty seconds of Becca's invitation to stay for dinner, the tramping of more than two feet on the porch and the sound of voices as the front door opened told him Parker had accepted his grandfather's invitation.

Ralph came into the kitchen first, putting his hand on the back of Seth's neck and saying, "What say, favorite male grandson? I hope Miss Becca has invited you for dinner because she's cooked for an army this evening."

"Still working on getting the proportions right," Becca

said to Seth. She nodded a hi to Parker and thanked him for volunteering to help consume her experiment with beef bourguignon.

"Fancy French name for stew," Ralph told Seth.

"Is not!" Becca protested. "It's made with wine."

"The French," Ralph told her, "make everything with wine. They take a dish from the Ozarks, pour wine all over it, and give it a fancy name. You check that online where every detail of every subject known to man is apparently available."

"Not that one, I bet," Becca said. "You're making it up."

"One of the privileges of age," he told her. "Beers for all? Saving yourself, Miss Becca."

"I'm done with beer anyway," she told him.

"I like a woman who learns her lessons fast," Ralph said.

So Becca must have told him about the party, Seth thought. He sort of wished she hadn't because he knew his grandfather would be disappointed that he had been there. But Ralph said nothing about Maxwelton Beach, the fire, or the death in the shack. Seth didn't bring it up, for fear his face would betray that he'd given the sheriff the word about Parker.

Seth caught Becca looking at him, then at Parker. She quirked her mouth in that way she had, which told him she was curious about what was going on.

Parker made himself useful by setting the table as Ralph dropped into a chair next to a pile of newspapers in their recycling basket. He popped open his beer and directed his gaze from one young person to the next. He said, "Ah, youth," and took a gulp of beer. "To what do I owe the pleasure of this visit?" he asked Seth.

The last thing Seth could tell him was the reason he'd come: to talk things over. So he said, "Checking up on you. Dad wants to know did you have your cholesterol checked again like you were supposed to?"

"Oh damn it all." Ralph looked peeved. "You tell your father to keep his mind on his glass blowing."

"What about the diet?" Seth asked. "Becca keeping it low fat as much as possible?"

"God almighty, Seth . . ."

"I'm watching him," Becca said over her shoulder. "Leastwise, when I'm here, I am. When I'm at school . . . I don't know. Could be he's having Whidbey vanilla and whipped cream for lunch, with chips and guacamole for dessert."

"There're worse ways to die," Ralph noted.

"And there's staying alive," Seth told him.

"On a diet of celery, raw potatoes, and carrots? I'd rather kick off now." Ralph harrumphed and took up one of the newspapers from the pile, his way of saying the subject was finished. Unfortunately, his choice was the paper with the Laurel Armstrong picture on the front of it, and as Seth saw this picture, so did Parker.

"Putting a lot of effort into finding her," Parker noted when Ralph unfolded the paper, opened it, and shook it meaningfully in front of his own face. "I've seen flyers with that same picture on them all over town."

Ralph peered over the top of the paper and then turned it to see the picture. "Laurel Armstrong," he said as he read the name.

Seth glanced warily at Becca. At the stove, her back was to them, but Seth could tell by her stiffened posture that she was listening.

Parker repeated the name and a light went on in his face. "Hey, Becca," he said, "isn't that your cousin up in Nelson?"

THIRTY-TWO

Becca hadn't been wearing the ear bud for the AUD box, and she was grateful for that. Normally, she didn't wear it when she was with Ralph Darrow anyway since his whispers and his words were identical. Now, in the kitchen, she'd been picking up mostly on whispers that seemed to be coming from Seth. They spoke of fire and Coupeville and the sheriff's department and even throughout the light talk about Ralph's diet, those thoughts had been there, popping up like ground squirrels checking the air for intruders. They'd kept popping up until Parker mentioned Laurel Armstrong's name, and that put an end to everything other than *here comes major trouble*, which she herself was thinking right along with Seth.

Ralph was studying the picture of Becca's mom. He was also reading the article. He was one second away from making the jump to page five, where the fifth-grade picture of Hannah Armstrong would smile up at him. Someone had to stop him from doing that, and blessed Seth did so.

He said, "Hey, lemme see that, Grand," and he plucked the paper from his grandfather's hands. "Hmmm." He pretended to study the picture. "You sure this is the same lady that's on those flyers? I seen one at South Whidbey Commons. What d'you think, Beck? This look like your cousin? Only, what'd she be doing on Whidbey Island?"

"I never met her," Becca said, turning her back to them and stirring energetically at the French beef stew. She had cornbread in the oven as well. She opened the door and the fragrance was heady.

Behind her, Parker said, "But that was her name, right? And if you never met her, this *could* be her, huh? How amazing is that? You ask me about her and here she is."

"Check it out, Beck," Seth suggested.

Come on take it Becca told her that Seth had something in mind, so she cooperated although she didn't wish to expose her lying face to Ralph Darrow. But she swung away from the stove and went to Seth. She pretended to study the picture and then said, "C'n I hold on to this?" to all of them in general.

Ralph was examining her in a way she didn't much like. Becca said, "The name's the same. I just wish I knew . . . Gosh, it would be nice to know what she looks like 'cause I could tell the sheriff this Laurel Armstrong he's looking for lives in Nelson."

"Could be you ought to do that anyway," Ralph noted. *Because you surely know something young lady* constituted one of the few times his whispers didn't match his words.

"Yeah," Becca said, and she repeated her request with, "C'n I keep this, Mr. Darrow?"

He nodded and gestured to the pile of *South Whidbey Record*s that lay on the chair seat. "Plenty more where that came from."

They were through for the moment. But the reprieve didn't last.

BOTH PARKER AND Seth left soon after the dishes. Becca went to her room, homework in mind. She was ten minutes into it when a knock on her door told her that Ralph Darrow wanted to speak to her. She said, "It's open, Mr. Darrow," and the door swung inward as she turned from her work. She put on her phony glasses. She wasn't using the ear bud, and she didn't intend to use it now, not with the grave expression on Ralph Darrow's face.

He stood in the doorway in his striped pajamas, his robe, and his slippers, with his long gray hair unbound from its usual rubber band. Becca was glad she hadn't yet washed her face of its hideous amount of Goth eye makeup. She was even more glad of this when *get to the bottom of this* preceded Ralph Darrow into the room.

His words confirmed what Becca's fears were: He'd not for a moment forgotten what Parker Natalia had said about Laurel Armstrong. "So, Miss Becca," Ralph began as he lowered himself to the edge of her bed, the only place to sit aside from the desk chair that Becca herself was occupying. "There anything you want to tell me about this cousin of yours up in Nelson, B.C.?"

He was watching her in that way he had of watching Seth. He'd be making a serious evaluation. She settled on saying, "There's not much to tell, Mr. Darrow."

"How's she related to you?"

"Like I said. She's my cousin."

"Through your mom or your dad?"

This was probably a trap, but Becca had no choice. She didn't know who her father was, and sometimes she wondered if Laurel herself knew, given the many lovers she'd had. So she couldn't risk telling Ralph this supposed cousin was from her father's side of the family lest he then ask questions about her father. She said, "My mom's side," and she hurried on with, "Actually, I think she's my mom's first cousin, which makes her . . . my second cousin or something? Truth is, I only actually *think* her name's Laurel Armstrong. I guess it could be Laura Armstrong. I mean, my mom mentioned her a few times is all. And when Parker told us he was from Nelson . . . the name just popped into my head."

Ralph nodded thoughtfully but his whisper of *road apples* didn't suggest he believed what she'd said. She remembered his long ago words about Darrows walking on the right side of the law, and she knew that one of his primary worries in having her on his property had to do with his deciding to believe her initial story. And yet despite her lies to virtually everyone else, the story she'd told to Ralph Darrow had been the complete truth: She *was* waiting for her mother's return to Whidbey to fetch her; she'd *been* intended to stay with a woman called Carol Quinn who had died unexpectedly the night of Becca's arrival; she was *not* a runaway. The only truths she'd left out were her real name and the name of her mother. And now that name hung between the two of them and if Becca admitted that she'd lied to Ralph Darrow in this one small matter, she had a very good idea what he would do.

She couldn't risk telling him. She also couldn't risk his opening the *South Whidbey Record* that even in this moment lay beneath her geometry book. She couldn't point to the picture of Hannah Armstrong and say, "Okay. This is me. And the guy looking for us is Jeff Corrie," because that would lead to why Jeff Corrie was looking and *that* would lead to what Hannah Armstrong could do, which was hear people's thoughts, which even in this moment she could hear from Ralph Darrow as clear as anything, *what's the truth about this child's mother?* It was the single question Becca herself wanted answered.

Then he asked another, one that Becca and her mom hadn't once considered because they'd assumed she'd be carefully ensconced in Carol Quinn's house, where more subterfuge than simply having an identity for Becca would not be necessary. "What's your mom's name, then?" Ralph Darrow asked her.

Becca refused to give in to the panic that swept toward her. She glanced away, past the old man to the shelf on which sat her few books. The name she came up with was Marilla but she knew better than to go for something so strange, so she said, "Rachel," because of *Anne of Green Gables* from which book the name Marilla itself had come. So had Rachel. Rachel Lynde, Marilla Cuthburt's friend and neighbor. A nosy woman with decided opinions who had, at the end of the day, a very good heart. Just like Ralph. She hoped.

"Rachel King," Ralph said.

"Rachel King," she acknowledged.

"Who left you here to stay with Carol Quinn?"

"They went to school together."

"Who was also married," Ralph pointed out.

"Huh?"

"Carol Quinn was married. Makes me wonder why you didn't stay on with her husband, Miss Becca, once you discovered Carol Quinn had passed."

Because Carol's husband hadn't known she was coming. Because Carol Quinn herself had been sworn to secrecy about Becca's identity. Because the story was going to be that Carol needed help around the house and here was this girl on the island who needed a place to stay and it was all supposed to work so well and so easily . . . except Carol had died of a heart attack and when Becca arrived and told Carol's husband her name, the man hadn't a clue who she was or why she was there.

She said, "It sort of seemed . . . I mean, it was, like, an intrusion, Mr. Darrow. I went to the house and there was the sheriff and an ambulance and it didn't seem right. So I ended up at the Cliff Motel, more or less, till I came here to stay with you."

Runaway and trying to keep out of sight except the fact that she's going to school . . .

Becca seized on this. "You don't have to worry. I know it all sounds like a total made up story, but you got to figure that I wouldn't exactly be going to school if I'd run away from home. First, I wouldn't have the stuff I would need to get myself enrolled. The paperwork? You know? And second"—she gestured to her homework—"I probably wouldn't be trying to figure out geometry. And anyway, to be *totally* honest . . ." She hesitated over this last detail, reluctant to bad-mouth the place that had given her a welcome and shelter.

"Yes?" he prompted. "My being a fellow who likes total honesty, Miss Becca, do go on."

"Well, d'you think I'd've chosen Whidbey Island to run away to? I mean, wouldn't a city be better? Seattle? Portland? It's easy, don't you think, to hide out in a city. It sure as heck isn't easy to hide out here."

Truth to that said he was inclined to believe her. So did the fact that he slapped his hands on his knees and stood. He nodded thoughtfully and then looked around him. He seemed to settle on the shelf where she kept her books. He said, "Okay then, Miss Becca," and he walked to the shelf and studied it. She thought he was looking at *Seeing Beyond Sight,* but to her dismay he picked up her childhood copy of *Anne of Green Gables* instead, the one thing she'd brought with her from her other life.

"Now this is a book I haven't seen in years," he said as Becca prayed fervently that he wouldn't open it. "It was Brenda's favorite. Seth's aunt Brenda, my girl. It was also a book Seth's sister loved. All of those *Anne of* books in the series."

He started to open it, but that couldn't happen since *To my sweet Hannah* was written in Becca's grandmother's hand right in plain sight. So Becca said the first thing that came into her mind, "I got it at Good Cheer," which was the thrift shop in Langley. "I was gonna send it to my pen pal for her birthday. I don't think it matters that it's used, do you?"

Ralph turned the book over in his hands and looked up from it. "Didn't know you had a pen pal, Miss Becca."

"Just started last year."

"Now, that's a nice thing. Where's she writing from?"

Becca said the only place she could think of quickly, "Africa," and then she embellished. "Uganda. Derric set it up 'cause she's from the same orphanage as him. We been writing back and forth only . . ." All at once, Becca saw that Ralph Darrow might prove helpful to the search for Rejoice. She said, "Here's what's sort of strange, Mr. Darrow. She was real good about writing back soon as she got my letters, but then she stopped."

"Got adopted, maybe."

"That's what I thought at first, but then I started to wonder because it always seems like something bad's happening to people in Africa, you know? So I looked up the orphanage online and it's closed down. I don't know where she is or how to find her."

Ralph replaced the book on the shelf. He touched the top of *Seeing Beyond Sight*, but he didn't bring it down. Instead, he said, "Might ask the minister at Derric's church about that one. He's the fellow who got folks interested in that orphanage in the first place. Derric can tell you the fellow's name, can't he?"

"Oh sure. He can. That's a good idea."

It was, in fact, a terrible idea. Bringing Derric into her search for Rejoice when he couldn't even bear to think about his sister was not the way to go. But the minister of Derric's church was a possibility.

She said, "Yeah. I'll talk to him. Do you think—" But then her words drifted because Ralph Darrow was staring at her. His eyes had gone blank and so had his face.

Becca realized that he wasn't studying her but rather looking just above her head. She swung to see if there was someone at the window beneath which her desk sat, but there was no one. It came to her that Ralph was staring at nothing, and nothing at all came from him in the form of whispers.

She said, "Mr. Darrow?" He did not respond. Louder then, "Mr. Darrow? You okay?"

For a moment still he did not answer. Then he blinked and seemed to rouse himself. He said, "Well, goodnight then, Miss Becca. Hope you get through that . . ." He frowned. "It's U.S. History you're working on, isn't that what you said?"

She swallowed. The book was open. The geometry problems were in plain sight. "Yeah," she said. "U.S. History."

"Don't stay up late, then. School in the morning."

THIRTY-THREE

Derric's church was called the Congregation of Christ Jesus, Redeemer. It was located in an autumn-brown meadow at the end of South Lone Lake Road, within seeing distance of the wide and tranquil lake itself and within smelling distance of a thoroughbred ranch. The church was a roughly converted barn, and its congregation consisted of islanders with the skills to turn the barn into a house of God, the intention to reach out to all people in need, and the limited time to do both. People in need came first. Hence, the rough conversion of the barn, which would be icy in winter, steaming on rare hot summer days, and had terrible acoustics throughout the year.

Becca knew she had to go there on a Sunday since she had no idea how else to track down the church minister, who did his ministering on a part-time basis. A phone call to the church gave her a recording with the information she needed: the time of services, the minister's name, and the message that people of all faiths were welcome.

The very next Sunday after her conversation with Ralph Darrow, Becca set off on her road bike with plenty of time to get to the Congregation of Christ Jesus, Redeemer. Although the sun was out, the days were rapidly cooling now, and billowing white clouds scudded across the sky.

She didn't want to be seen at the service, so she pedaled past the place and continued down to the lake. There, she could keep the church in sight. She could also watch some Canada geese who were paddling placidly on the lake's still water. Hidden from sight, she saw Derric and his family arrive, and she watched them enter.

She hated seeing Derric only at school, and she hated not talking to him on the phone. Although he had a smart phone, she did not and thus had no way to text him. His computer privileges were history for now, so all they had were the moments they could snatch out of the school day to be together.

He'd cooperated fully with his mom: He'd gone to the psychologist she'd insisted he see. He wasn't happy about it, but he'd come up with no other way to get himself back into his mother's good graces. He'd spent three sessions so far with the man, but from what he'd told Becca, the only subject that came up between them was the party at the beach, his drinking, the fire, and his mom.

Becca wished he would open up about Rejoice so that he could somehow cope with his betrayal of her. But until he was ready . . . there was nothing she could do to bend him to *her* will. At least, she'd finally learned that.

The church service was over an hour long, accompanied by a lot of singing. There was a lengthy period of silence during which she figured the minister was preaching, and then more singing commenced, after which the service was over.

When people began to leave, Becca crept up to the parking area. She remained out of sight behind a long woodshed, where cords of logs were neatly stacked for heating the barn in the coming winter. From there, she could see the minister greeting his congregation as they left the church. Among them were the Mathiesons, and she fixed her gaze on Derric. He looked so sad. He made her heart hurt.

She waited till the last of the cars drove off. The minister went back into the church. He was probably going to close the place up fairly quickly, Becca thought, so she hurried into the parking area and through the great doors of the barn.

It was very plain inside. There were folding chairs, not pews. There were colorful dahlias in vases on a simple altar decorated with a cross. A lectern stood to one side of the altar, and on the other side was a large wooden stand with a Bible open upon it. Along one wall there were bulletin boards with posters and pictures arranged upon them.

The minister was closing the Bible and scooping it off the stand. He was older than Becca had thought he would be, with hair coming out of his ears, very thick glasses, and old-fashioned hearing aids behind each ear.

He was called James John Wagner, Becca knew. She, however, would call him Reverend.

He set the Bible on the altar and began to straighten the chairs into parallel curves that fanned out neatly from a central aisle.

He hadn't seen Becca, so she said his name. When he looked up, she told him her own and went to help him.

She was surprised when he said, "Derric Mathieson's girl-friend. It's very good to meet you, Becca. You just missed Derric and his family. Or"—with a glance at the door—"did you come with them?"

"Came on my own," she said. "Derric doesn't know." She hoped this was sufficient to clue James John Wagner into the fact that he wasn't intended to mention her to Derric.

Young love's difficulties let her know that it wouldn't take much for her to secure Reverend Wagner's confidence. So she said, "I sort of don't want him to. I don't want him to worry or anything."

Pregnant flashed through the minister's mind, but he seemed to dismiss this with *my trial in life to jump to conclusions.* Since from his thoughts it seemed that jumping to conclusions was something the minister was working to expunge from his life, Becca figured this could prove useful to her purpose.

Reverend Wagner smiled and said, "My lips are sealed, then. Shall we have a seat?" He gestured to the fan of chairs and Becca walked over to one.

He didn't sit next to her but rather he swung one of the chairs around to face her. He kept a respectful distance, so they were knee-to-knee without actually touching each other. He said, "Seems like something might be bothering you if you've shown up to talk to the likes of me."

She said, "Yeah."

"Troubles with Derric?"

She shook her head. "Troubles with the place he came from."

The reverend frowned. His mouth said, "Africa?" while his mind said *parents and times haven't changed when it comes to race have they*. Becca was momentarily confused till she put his thought into the context of his age. He was an old guy—maybe seventy or something?—and he was thinking about the times when races mixing could lead to trouble. She supposed it still could in some places in the country, but as far as she knew, Whidbey Island wasn't one of those places.

She said, "The orphanage? Children's Hope of Kampala? I was writing to a girl there, a pen pal thing. She stopped answering and I didn't know why so I looked online and ended up seeing that the orphanage is closed."

Reverend Wagner said regretfully, "We hope it's closed only for now. The need hasn't gone away. But funding has been a struggle from the first." He smiled sadly and added, "You wouldn't be here to offer yourself as a secret benefactress, would you?"

"I wish," she said. "But d'you know . . . what happened to the kids? I mean, the kids who were left there when the orphanage closed? Did they get sent to another orphanage? See, I know from Derric and his mom that you guys at this church were involved with the place. So I was wondering if maybe you know. 'Cause, basically, I hate to lose touch with my pen pal. I have a book I want to send to her and some pictures and stuff and . . . I guess I got worried when she stopped writing."

Reverend Wagner nodded and said he understood her concern, that he wished more kids would take an interest in the challenges faced in third world countries. Then he asked her the name of her pen pal, which, naturally, he was going to need if he was to find out where the girl had been sent.

Becca knew this put her into deep waters since, of course, she had no clue what surname Rejoice had been given when the orphanage had found her. But since she'd said she was writing to her, she had to tell him something, so she said the girl's name was Rejoice Nyombe, Nyombe being the only African name she'd ever heard.

Naturally, Reverend Wagner said the worst at once. "That was Derric's original last name, wasn't it? Is Rejoice a relative?"

She shook her head. "That's even what *I* asked when Derric set me up with her as a pen pal. But Derric said it's a real common last name in Uganda. He said they could be distant cousins, but he doesn't know."

"Ah," the reverend murmured. "Rather like all the Adamses in America. How old is she?"

"She's about thirteen, I think. She told me she doesn't know for sure."

He looked thoughtful, and he pulled on the lobe of one of his large ears. "Unfortunately, thirteen makes it doubtful that she was adopted," he said. "It's always the smaller children who are easier to place. If you were writing to her at Children's Hope . . . And that *is* where you were writing to her, isn't it?" When Becca nodded, he went on with, "So at the time of its closing, she might have gone from the orphanage into one of the convent schools. Or to work, for that matter. Sometimes when there are too many children . . ." *God forbid* spoke of the reverend's worry regarding this matter, and that whisper did nothing to reassure Becca about where Rejoice was or what might have had happened to her. *To work* suggested child labor, or worse. The "worse" Becca didn't even want to consider.

"I sure wish I knew why she stopped writing to me," Becca said.

"That concern speaks well of you."

"D'you think there's any way that you can find out where she is?"

"I'm not sure," he told her, "as the directors in Kampala have all dispersed."

Becca looked down at her feet. She let her body project the dejection she felt. She said, "I don't know what else to do."

Reverend Wagner reached out and patted her hand. "Let me try to get some information for you," he said. "It may take some time, but I'll give it my best. Shall I tell Derric if I discover anything?"

God no, Becca thought. She said, "I'm living over with Ralph Darrow. D'you think you could call me there? Derric doesn't know that me and Rejoice've stopped writing, and if something bad's happened to her . . . ? It would probably bum him out."

"At Ralph Darrow's, then," the reverend said.

THIRTY-FOUR

Brooke and Cassidy weren't making the chores in the chicken barn any easier for Hayley. Cassidy was stalking the birds in an attempt to pet them, and Brooke was stuffing a piece of white bread loaded with jam into her mouth. This was her second piece of bread and jam, which she'd kept carefully hidden in her fleece.

When Hayley protested about the eating and not helping, Brooke said, "Chill. I'm hungry, okay? I'm not hurting you."

"You're also not helping," Hayley pointed out. "And what's with the food? You're already a tub and—"

"Shut up!" Brooke cried. "I am not and I'm hungry!"

"You can't be hungry. You're always eating. What's going *on* with you?"

"Mind your own business!"

"Fine. Then help me. I've got other stuff to do."

What she had to do was mammoth. She'd rewritten her college essay as required by her mom, but a meeting with Tatiana Primavera had resulted in the requirement that she revise the dumb thing because "it lacks a personal tone, Hayley, and that's going to be essential." Aside from that, she had mountains of homework from every single one of her classes.

And *then* there was the home front. Hayley's mom had begun cleaning houses. This was a three-days-a-week time eater for Julie Cartwright, leaving Hayley with the dinner responsibility as well as maintaining the chicken barn and making sure Brooke did her homework, Cassidy had help with her grade school projects, and their dad was taken care of.

So Hayley was stressed, and right now having Brooke and Cassidy be part of the chicken barn problem instead of the chicken barn solution wasn't helping matters. When Brooke still didn't stir from eating her bread and jam, Hayley finally broke. She said sharply, "Come *on*. You're supposed to be helping and you know it."

"I *hate* chicken shit!"

Cassidy squealed. "Brooke said a bad word!"

Hayley shot Brooke a look. They still had to trundle the manure up to the vegetable beds, so she wasn't about to put up with her sister's lack of cooperation. "Am I gonna have to talk to Mom about you?" she asked Brooke pointedly.

"What*ever*," Brooke answered. "Like she's gonna care? Or even notice that you're talking to her?"

Hayley gritted her teeth. Did *anyone* else have to put up with what she had to put up with? And it wasn't like she didn't have other things on her mind as well. There was the whole fire-setting problem still dangling out there waiting for her to make a decision about it.

At the most recent jazz band practice, she'd talked to Derric. It was the only time she saw him at school without Becca or one of the other kids with him. He'd been looking as glum as she'd been feeling, so she'd asked him how he was loving being on restriction. He'd rolled his eyes and said, "Last time *I'm* getting drunk till I'm twenty-one," and that had taken them to the party at Maxwelton Beach.

Derric had told her where things stood. His father had revealed how the fishing shack fire had started. Rags soaked in paint thinner, shoved into a rotting place where the wood of the shack had come loose from its meager foundation. Add to that some crumpled newspapers and a few fatwood sticks brought along for the purpose, and the rest was history. It wasn't, he said, anything that could even *remotely* be called an accident.

The sheriff's department was looking at every source of paint thinner on the island to see who might have bought some recently. But the problem was that there were a bazillion house painters and artists of various ilks on Whidbey, so finding someone who'd bought paint thinner recently wasn't going to be very helpful.

She had to tell Isis about this, Hayley decided. If Aidan did indeed like to start fires, then he could have brought what he needed with him in a backpack that night of the beach party: paint thinner, rags, newspapers, and fatwood sticks. Or he could have even ducked down there in advance of the party and set the whole thing up. But when Hayley told her friend about the paint thinner part, Isis's reaction was one of relief.

She said, "That's *great*. I mean, it's not great because of what happened to the guy inside the shack but it's great because

Aidan . . . See, he *always* used just matches. Matches and bits of wood and straw and stuff that was easy to get his hands on, and no way would he have changed his . . . well, his style." She seemed to think about all this for a moment. Then she frowned and added, "He's gonna be so righteously mad at me now, though. See, I kept bugging him about talking to the sheriff before the sheriff found out about the school in Utah. It's not like I ever thought he might be the person who started the fire because I *didn't* think that. I only thought he should talk to the sheriff. Problem is that now Grandam thinks something's going on because he and I keep having these . . . well, these tense discussions that we stop whenever she comes too near. So she's still making him run to the beach to de-stress himself or whatever and he's doing it and, okay, maybe I haven't been watching him every second like I'm supposed to but—"

Hayley had stopped listening. The mention of Nancy Howard brought to her mind what Nancy Howard did for a living. She interrupted Isis with, "Isis, maybe there's paint thinner on your grandmother's property."

This stopped Isis in her tracks. "She's a chain saw artist. She doesn't paint. And anyway, Aidan used matches and the other stuff like I said."

"But some of her sculptures end up painted, don't they?" Hayley persisted. "Like when she does a sign for someone? Or when someone wants a painted sculpture? And *if* she paints them she'd have—"

"No!" But Hayley could tell that Isis didn't mean her grandmother had no paint thinner. Rather she meant no to the possibility that her brother had set the fire. "He wouldn't have done that," she told Hayley. "He's cured. They wouldn't've let him out if he wasn't. He might've been troubled at one time and okay let's say he still is troubled now and then, but . . . Hayley, someone else *has* to be into setting the fires."

PART IV

Bayview Farmers' Market

THIRTY-FIVE

When Parker Natalia asked her out for a "surprise" date, Hayley was more than ready for a diversion. Hayley couldn't imagine how anything on Whidbey Island might be a surprise to her, but she agreed to the plan and he gave her the date and the time.

When Parker arrived to pick her up, she was helping her dad get out of the house. He'd insisted on an inspection of what he was jokingly calling "the south forty," and when she'd told him she was worried about how he was going to get back inside the house if she wasn't there, he said, "I haven't been outside in four days, Hayley. I'll manage something and don't you worry."

Parker helped her dad negotiate the steps from the porch onto the front path that led to the driveway. He asked, logically, if they'd thought about building a ramp to take the place of the steps. Just when Hayley was about to say that a ramp would be helpful and that Seth could build it in no time flat, her dad announced that "they'll have to pound me into the ground before you catch me using a ramp, son."

Then he started on his perilous way to the barn. Hayley

watched him, biting down on her lip. Parker, she saw from the corner of her eye, watched her.

HAYLEY FIGURED OUT their destination once Parker made the turn off the highway. He headed briefly south then west on the route that would take them over to a place called Keystone. An old army fort lay in that direction, but so did the ferry that took Whidbey Islanders along the upper edge of Admiralty Bay. Its destination was the Victorian town of Port Townsend, with its old brick-built commercial streets and its gingerbread houses stacked on a cliff above them.

Once off the ferry, their first stop was an old-fashioned diner on the town's main street. A bit out of place in a picturesque nineteenth-century town, Nifty Fifties boasted chrome bar stools, individual juke boxes on Formica tables, bright colors on the walls, neon signs, and a menu heavy on burgers, fries, malts, and milk shakes. They ordered and began to flip through the tunes on their table's juke box. Parker chose Elvis Presley—"Love Me Tender"—and he put in the money. He slid some coins in her direction and told her the next selection would be hers.

Hayley felt herself coming alive in the presence of this young man, so different from the boys she knew from South Whidbey High School. It was, she thought, incredible what a difference a few years out of high school made. Parker was a man instead of a boy, sure of himself, easy to be with, interesting to talk to, *and* interested in what she had to say. And when he brought up something tough, he didn't forge into it like someone driving a snow plow.

He said, fingering his silverware, "I c'n tell how much you and your dad mean to each other. The way you were helping him . . . the way you were worried about him getting back into the house . . . That's great, Hayley, to have that with your dad."

She colored a little. And even that, Parker Natalia took in because he went on with, "I c'n tell the whole subject of your dad is a tough one. Your family doesn't like to talk about it, do they? But if you ever want to talk about it, about your dad, about anything . . . ? I'm your guy. Otherwise I just want you to know I respect whatever you want to say or don't want to say."

Hayley was so used to people—well, Seth, let's face it— trying to get her to talk about her father. She was so used to her family not even wanting to talk about not wanting to talk about her father. She was so used to the entire subject of her father being taboo that she felt a chink in the armor that protected her and prevented her from speaking, and she was able to say to the young Canadian, "He's not going to get any better. He's going to get worse, so things're rough."

Parker reached for her hand. She steeled herself for the advice that would do no good. But instead he said, "I'm real sorry. You shouldn't have to go through bad times."

HAYLEY SAW SETH about thirty seconds later. Of all people to be in Port Townsend on the very day of her date with Parker, there he was. At first she thought he'd somehow followed them, and she felt a surge of irritation. But he walked right by the diner, and he seemed intent on his destination.

Inadvertently, Hayley said, "What the heck . . . ?" when she saw him, and that took Parker's gaze to the window, where he noticed Seth, too.

"Bet I know where he's going," Parker said.

"Why?"

"Because we're going there, too."

After their meal, they walked in the same direction Seth had been taking. Hayley figured their destination had something to do with music if Seth was heading there.

She was right. Parker took them to the end of the main street, near the point where there were no longer shops and trendy boutiques but rather marine businesses overlooking a small harbor. There, a coffeehouse had been fashioned out of part of a warehouse and when Parker opened the door for her, Hayley heard fiddle music of a wild nature that reminded her of gypsies around a campfire dancing.

The source of the music turned out to be a girl. She stood on a makeshift dais, and she was accompanied by a guitarist who wasn't at the moment playing but was rather watching her with a grin on his face. Everyone else had grins as well. It was tough not to smile when someone's music was so uplifting.

The girl herself was intriguing. She had curly dark hair that fell to her waist, a cowboy handkerchief rolled up and used as a headband, cowboy boots with her jeans tucked into them, and a

T-shirt with a hole under its arm. Most remarkable was her eye patch, black like a pirate's and somehow in keeping with the rest of her.

Hayley glanced around and found Seth sitting on the edge of an old sofa. He was, like everyone, enthralled. Parker saw Seth, too, and he murmured in her ear, "He wants her," and at Hayley's startled expression he added, "For Triple Threat. That's why he's here."

"What about you?" she asked. "I thought you were playing with—"

"I can't stay much longer," he told her. "Visitor's visa. I have to get back to B.C."

"Oh." Hayley could hear her own disappointment. He was leaving, she thought. Wasn't that just her luck?

He smiled and brushed some hair off her cheek. "But border crossings are easy enough when you've got a passport," he told her.

WHEN THE GIRL'S set ended and she announced that she was taking a break "so you guys better order lattes or they won't let me come back here," Hayley saw Seth approach the girl. It came to her that this was the very first time that she and Seth had been in the same place without him automatically approaching *her*. She told herself she was glad of this. But still it was strange to see him leap to his feet and dash to the girl before anyone else could get to her.

IT WAS JUST after ten when they got back to the island, early hours for a date to end. Parker pointed this out, asking if Hayley had a curfew.

Hayley said that there wasn't much to do on Whidbey after ten o'clock anyway unless you were old enough to get into a bar or knew of a place where a party was happening or wanted to dope up or drink in the woods. So although she always had a midnight curfew, she rarely was out after eleven.

"What about tonight?" Parker asked her. "I can take you home, but if you don't need to . . . I know of a place."

When he shot her a smile, she thought about how she'd like to put her fingers in his curly hair and she'd like to kiss him and—this was really terrible of her—she'd like to feel him pressing against her. But what she said was, "Sure. Long as I'm home by midnight."

They ended up at Ralph Darrow's house, in the parking area. There Parker grabbed a flashlight from his glove compartment, and he led her down the path toward the bright lights from the house. She could see Seth's grandfather and Becca King in the living room as they passed. Becca was feeding some logs into the huge fireplace. Ralph Darrow was reading in a chair near the window with a bright crown of light falling on his long gray hair.

Then they were on the path through the woods, Parker leading but holding her by the hand. She knew where they were going because she'd been in Seth's tree house a hundred times.

When they reached the clearing where the tree house was built into the branches of the two old hemlocks, Hayley realized she was a little bit nervous. She wondered what Parker expected of her, and she felt unsure of herself.

He seemed to sense this when they got to the steps that led up to the place. He turned to her and said, "It's cool, Hayley." He switched off the flashlight for a minute and in the autumn darkness, she felt him move toward her. "No worries," he said.

He kissed her, and the kiss went on and on. Hayley thought how it was a man's self-assured kiss and not the kiss of a boy. She thought how strong he seemed and how his strength was something she wanted as part of her life. And then she simply stopped thinking at all.

He finally broke off. He said huskily, "You're amazing. You want to go up?" And he indicated the tree house above them.

Hayley said, "Yeah. I do."

They used the flashlight to negotiate the steps. Across the deck they went and then they were inside the tree house, which was warm with a fire that had been banked in the wood stove as if waiting for their arrival.

Parker lit a lantern, but turned it low. Hayley looked around. She was acutely aware of there being no place to sit aside from the cot on which a sleeping bag lay. She swallowed a little nervously. She shot him a smile. He smiled in turn.

"Got some dope," he told her.

"Oh." Hayley wasn't sure how to put it without sounding like the most inexperienced goody-good on the planet. "I haven't exactly . . . I mean, I've never done any dope."

"Not even weed?"

She shook her head. She could feel her face getting hot, and she was glad of the low light so he couldn't see how badly she was blushing. But even if he *could* see, it didn't seem to matter. He said, "There's always a first time for everything, huh?"

He had a stash in a tea tin on the windowsill. He said, "Want to try? You won't turn into a heroin addict. Really," with a smile. He began rolling a joint so expertly that only an idiot would have thought he didn't do this on a regular basis.

He came to her, joint in hand. Hayley thought he was going to hand it over or light it and take a toke, but instead he looked at her and touched her hair and moved it behind her ear in a sweet caress. Then he kissed her in that way he had and again the kiss went on and on.

He finally said, "Want to sit?" and indicated the cot. When she hesitated he said, "I can put that sleeping bag on the floor and we can sit there if you'd be more comfortable. Only . . ." He laughed. "I guess it's *still* a sleeping bag. Maybe I shouldn't have brought you here. I see what it could look like from your perspective."

Hayley said to cover her embarrassment, "No. It's okay. Let's sit," and she was the first to do so. He sat next to her and that was when he lit the joint and took a deep hit of it. He told her he was going to teach her how to smoke weed because it was time she was just a *little* bad. He told her to take the smoke in with a lot of air at first, so that was what she did.

She expected to be instantly high, but she felt nothing. He told her to take another hit and he added, "When it's your first time, sometimes you don't feel anything. Not like you're going to feel your second or third time."

She blushed at this because first time and second time had more than one meaning. He seemed to realize this just as he said it because he declared, "Oh *hell*," and he took the joint from her and he set it on the edge of the wood-burning stove. Then he kissed her, at first gently, and then more deeply, and Hayley realized it was fine with her. When the kiss broke off, he said in a low tone, "Have you ever . . ." and she shook her head. "Then we won't," he told her. "I mean, *I* won't. But you're so beautiful and it's hard not to want you. What I mean is that whenever I see you, I can't help thinking about . . . but I want to be respectful. I know how special you are and how far you're going to go in your life and—"

She put her hand over his mouth. "C'n you stop talking and kiss me?" she said.

He grinned. "That I c'n do," and his kiss sent shivers up and down her spine. They intensified when he kissed her neck. They morphed into sighs she didn't even know she was making as he laid her back on the cot. She felt herself heating up so much that she gripped the rumpled sleeping bag tightly just to keep herself from floating off into space.

That was when her fingers closed over something buried among the rumples of the bag. She glanced at it in some confusion.

It was Isis Martin's electronic cigarette.

THIRTY-SIX

S eth had been able to tell a lot from the way Parker and Hayley were acting around each other in the Port Townsend coffee-house although he'd concluded at first that they were there for the same reason he was. As a fiddler, Parker would probably want to hear the girl play. He was as interested in music as Seth, and this girl was an incredible musician. But then Seth noticed that there was a disturbing air of ownership about the way Parker kept his hand on the back of Hayley's neck. He kept moving his fingers lightly through her hair, and the way he kept glancing at her with his eyes all soft and gooey . . . Seth had wanted to say to him, "Hey, take it to a bedroom or something," because it was pretty darn obvious what he had in mind.

As for the fiddler that Seth had come to hear . . . ? He'd read about her in advance of coming to Port Townsend, so he'd known she was good. But just how good . . . ? He hadn't had a clue.

Her name was Prynne Haring. When he went up to her at the end of her set and introduced himself, she said with a roll of her eyes, "It's Hester Prynne Haring, actually. My mom thought *that* would keep me out of trouble."

Seth hadn't the first clue what she meant, but he went along with it, took a risk, and said, "Bet it didn't work." He was pleased when she laughed. She set her fiddle in its case, and said, "What's your instrument?"

He told her guitar. Then he told her Whidbey Island. Then he told her Triple Threat. For her part, she told him she came from Port Gamble and she added, "Music is, like, my whole life, bro."

He said it was the same for him and would she be willing to come over to Whidbey and listen to Triple Threat and, perhaps, join them for a session or two? He said, "We're looking for a fiddler and the way you play . . . You're really something."

"I'm more bluegrass than what you guys are into," she told him frankly. "Django Reinhardt? Gypsy's cool but I dunno. I'm a lone agent. I like things that way."

He said he knew what she meant but he also figured that once she heard Triple Threat, she'd change her mind. She said she would consider it, and Seth decided to wait till after her gig when he'd do a little more talking to her. After all, one of the things she confessed was that she'd never been to Whidbey Island. He'd talk up its charms and its possibilities, he decided, and he'd use the rest of her gig to figure out what those charms and possibilities were.

Thus, he saw Hayley and Parker leave together, ducking out a few minutes before the end of Prynne's performance. Through the windows he also saw how Parker put his arm around Hayley's shoulders. He saw how their heads moved toward each other in a way that blended Parker's dark hair with Hayley's strawberry blonde. He could tell that Hayley was taken with the guy, and who could blame her since Parker appeared to be laying it on. But she was vulnerable and what she didn't need was heartbreak from some bad news dude in Canada. So he *had* to tell her what he'd heard about Parker. After all, that was what friends were for.

ONCE PRYNNE'S GIG was over, Seth spent some time talking her into a trip to Whidbey. He'd pick her up at the ferry, he'd buy her dinner, he'd show her the sights . . . if she would agree to bring her fiddle. "Keep an open mind, Hester," he told her. "That's all I ask."

She told him she would and she added, "It's definitely Prynne, by the way. I don't use Hester. I have this instead of an *A*, if you know what I mean."

Seth didn't know what she meant by the *A*, but he did know what she meant by *this* because she pointed to the eye patch she wore. He'd figured it was all part of her performance getup. But Prynne said, no. It was real.

"Cancer," she told him. "I was seven. They did this and that and nothing worked so they had to dig out the ol' eyeball. They gave me a glass one that I usually wear. But when I'm playing I like the eye patch. I think it kind of adds something." She shrugged.

"Whatever," he said. "I thought it was cool anyway. I mean . . . not that I don't still think it's cool. You got your glass eyeball under it or what?"

"Nope," she told him. "Just the empty socket. It pretty much creeps people out when they see it. Want to see?"

"Sure," he told her. What the hell.

SETH DECIDED TO talk to Hayley at the end of the next Saturday Bayview market. It would be one of the busier Saturdays there because the selling year was drawing to a close. So people would be crowding it while it lasted.

He had to rehearse with Triple Threat first. He needed the time with them. None of the guys knew he'd gone to see Prynne, and he wanted to prepare them for the idea of having a girl join the group. After they made thorough dopes of themselves by going on about a girl with an eye patch—"What is she, a pirate? Yo ho, yo ho . . ." —they were on board with having her come to jam with them.

Seth arrived at the market as the Cartwrights were disassembling their stall. Brooke, he saw, was looking morose and moon-faced. She was monosyllabic when he asked how she was.

"Fat," she said bitterly. Then she added, "'cording to Hayley. You got any money, Seth?"

Whoa, Seth thought. *That* was totally out of character. He said, "Yeah, sure. But what's—"

"It's only I want a piece of that sweet potato pie. But Mom says if I want something to eat, I can have a carrot. As *if.*"

"Oh. Got it." Seth reached for his wallet.

Hayley, however, apparently saw this because she said to her mother, "She's doing it again. Seth, don't give her any money. She's not supposed to eat any—"

"My stomach needs food!" Brooke protested. "It's empty, and I need to eat."

"You need to *stop* eating. Try looking in a mirror instead."

Harsh, Seth thought. That wasn't like Hayley. He began to say to her, "Hey, is there something—" but their mom interrupted.

"Girls," she said tiredly. She glanced at Seth and went on. "Brooke's fine. And there's plenty to eat here."

"There is not!" Brooke stomped off.

"She's probably going to panhandle," Hayley said. "She's got the worst case of the thirteens in history."

Seth wasn't convinced of this, but pressing on about why Brooke was acting so strange wasn't why he was there. So he said to Hayley, "You want a sandwich from the deli when you're finished here? We c'n eat over by the schoolhouse and I'll drive you home."

Hayley opened her mouth and Seth could tell an excuse for turning him down was about to come out, but her mom had heard his invitation and she said, "You go on, Hayley. You've been working hard and you deserve a break. Let's just get this stuff into the truck." She looked around. "And don't let Brooke catch you or Seth'll be buying her a sandwich, too."

"I c'n do that," Seth said.

"She isn't hungry," Hayley told him. And she gave Seth a look that also told him not to say anything more about her sister.

When they'd finished getting the stall disassembled and the

veggie crates loaded into the truck, Seth and Hayley went into the deli that was a feature of the renovated old commercial buildings of Bayview Corner with their wooden stairs and wooden sidewalks. They ordered their sandwiches. While they waited Hayley told Seth what her mom had meant about "working hard" and "deserving a break." She mentioned her college essay and taking the SAT and being up to her eyeballs in homework. Seth waited for her to mention being up to her eyeballs with Parker, too, but when she didn't, he told her he was glad that she was doing what she was supposed to be doing to head to college next year.

She explained that she was "doing it for now," and when he asked her what that was supposed to mean, she said, "It didn't hurt you not to go to college. Matter of fact, it didn't hurt you not to graduate."

He responded with, "Come on, Hayley. You and me were always playing on two different levels. Can you even picture me going to college? Or even getting out of high school? Not hardly. I'm too dumb—"

"You are *not* dumb," Hayley said hotly.

"There's things I won't ever be able to do good and I'm lucky I even passed the GED and anyway that's not what I want to talk about."

Their sandwiches were handed over to them, and Seth scored two drinks. These they took across the road to an old white schoolhouse from the 1800s, where they found a spot in the sun that would keep them warm despite the cool breeze that had begun to blow.

Seth had already decided how to broach the subject of Parker Natalia. "Surprised to see you and Parker over in Port Townsend," he told her.

He saw her hesitate before she took a bite of her sandwich. When she answered, she talked about Prynne.

"She was really good," she said. "But d'you think she's as good as Parker? Parker thinks she's better than he is, but I don't think so. She *was* good, but Parker . . . ? Doesn't it seem to you that Parker has something special?"

Seth could see how much she enjoyed just saying Parker's name, and this worried him. He said, "She's definitely as good as Parker. She's probably better."

"So why's she not in a group?"

"Sometimes people like to go it alone. She's coming over here to jam with Triple Threat, though. That's why *I* went to hear her."

Hayley didn't miss how he emphasized *I*. She frowned. "What's that supposed to mean?"

"Well . . . why'd you guys go?"

"I went because Parker invited me."

"So why'd he want to go?"

"Because he's a musician." Hayley set her sandwich on its wrapper and said, "Want to tell me what's going on, Seth?"

"Just that I sort of wonder about Parker."

"What's that mean?"

Seth set down his sandwich as well. He looked across the street at the last of the stalls being taken down. People were still standing there chatting as if reluctant to have the market end.

The end of the market meant winter was coming. There were a few more good weeks, but the bad stuff was out there.

He said, "I got something I need to tell you, Hayley. You're not going to like it and you're probably going to be seriously ticked off at me. But I did it for you because the one thing you don't need is someone taking a meat cleaver to your heart."

He'd said this without looking at her, but now he turned. A mixture of suspicion, fear, and anger appeared to be washing across her face. "What?" she said in a voice like scissors making a cut through paper.

So he told her what he'd learned from the bass player in BC Django 21. Watch out for the guy. He's trouble.

"What kind of trouble?" Hayley asked.

"Don't know for sure. There was some kind of deal about him and the mandolin player's sister but the real thing is—"

"Wait a minute." Hayley jumped to her feet. "Are you telling me that you . . . that you just . . . you *believed* this person you don't even know at the other end of a telephone call? You talk to him once and you . . . you just believe whatever he says? 'Watch out for the guy. He's trouble'? For all you know, Seth Darrow, Parker borrowed that guy's car and didn't fill it with gas afterwards and the guy got mad and thought, All right I'll fix you real good, buddy. I'll spread the word so that no one trusts you again."

"Hayl, that's not hardly—"

"You don't want me to be happy, do you?"

He got to his feet as well. He said, "I'm just passing along something that I heard. You c'n do with it what you want. I don't care. But for God's sake, keep your eyes open. Because whatever else you think, people aren't always what they seem to be."

She put her hands on her hips. "And that means what?"

"It means Parker's been on the island for every single one of the fires, Hayley."

"Oh my God. Well, if you think what you're thinking, why don't you just report him to the sheriff?" And then, as if seeing an alteration in Seth's face, she went on. "You did! You reported him! I can't believe it."

"Hayley, come on . . ."

"No! No! Watch out for the guy, he could be trouble and *that* means he sets fires. Well, we *both* know why you're thinking what you're thinking. So, if it comes down to it, report yourself to Sheriff Mathieson, Seth. You've been on the island for every one of the fires, too."

She turned on her heel and stalked off, then. So she didn't hear Seth say, "No. Truth is, I haven't been on the island for all of the fires."

THIRTY-SEVEN

At the far end of the farmers' market stood Bayview Hall, a long, flaking white barn-like building that served the purposes of everything from dance hall to Christmastime marketplace. Behind this structure in a vacant field of beaten-down grasses, an outdoor food court was set up each market Saturday from spring to fall. It was here that Becca was meeting with Jenn McDaniels and Squat Cooper.

Squat, with the money to do so, had purchased a cheeseburger, a Coke, and a bag of chips. Becca and Jenn, without the money to purchase anything, were sharing a chicken salad sandwich provided by Becca and two bottles of tap water provided by Jenn. Squat had already pointed out to them that reusing plastic bottles was going to kill them both because of the breakdown of toxic chemicals that went into the bottles' manufacture. To this, Jenn had countered with, "I don't see you parting with any cash to get us something to save our lives, Studboy."

With a roll of his eyes, Squat went to purchase two bottles of flavored water. Becca remarked that Jenn had manipulated Squat into doing this. To that, Jenn smirked, unrepentant.

Squat came back with the waters and handed them over, saying, "Don't say I didn't ever get you anything."

Jenn eyed them and said, "I dunno, Squatman. I don't see any kettlecorn here. Oh well. Guess these'll have to do," and she scored a handful of his chips. She munched for a moment and then brought up to Becca the reason for their meeting. "Background on Wolf Canyon Academy," she told her. "Me and the Squatman got the goods."

Becca was all ears. She'd been consumed by the possible whereabouts of Derric's sister, Rejoice, waiting anxiously to hear anything at all from Reverend Wagner. To have something else to consider even for a moment was welcome. She said, "What?"

"It's a place for dopers and alkies when their parents are at the end of their rope," Jenn said.

"It's a last stop place, not a first stop place," Squat added. "Heavy addictions and big trouble kids."

"I say it's pills," Jenn went on. "Vicodin, Oxy, Valium, whatever. Aidan's one of your medicine cabinet druggies. This place costs major bucks so the family's got piles of it and *that* means they got piles of prescriptions for whatever ails them because you know how rich people are." Jenn grabbed her lower back and said, "'Oh doctor, doctor, I got a backache . . . C'n you give me something?' So he hands over some Oxy and it ends up getting put in the medicine cabinet and the kids dip into it. If you look at Aidan, it's pretty clear he's not into anything like meth. It's gotta be pills."

Becca nodded. She could see, though, that Squat looked

thoughtful. She'd put in her ear bud and, not being able to pick up his whispers, she said, "What d'you think?"

He was chewing some burger, too well brought up to talk with his mouth full. When he was ready, he said, "Seems to me there's all kinds of addictions. Like maybe he's a klepto or something. Maybe he's a peeping Tom. Hell, maybe he's a perv who went after little kids in his old neighborhood. Maybe he gets a thrill from killing animals."

"Maybe he's into setting fires," Becca said.

They all looked at each other. Jenn was the one to voice what all of them were thinking. "I'm telling the cops."

"'Cept," Squat said, "we don't know for sure he's a pyro. I mean, he could be addicted to other things, too. Like eating. Like gambling. Like . . . whatever."

Becca shook her head. "It's got to be fire," she said. "It's the only thing that really explains—" She stopped herself. She couldn't say more because what she had to say was knowledge that had come from the whispers she'd heard about an apartment fire. She thought for a moment and then finished with, "Maybe that's why he's always lurking around when I get on the Internet."

"He knows something's there, and he's worried you'll find it," Jenn said.

BECCA COULDN'T RISK doing research on the topic of fires and Aidan Martin anywhere that the boy might find her doing so. So she settled on the offices of the *South Whidbey*

Record. She used the excuse of a journalism class she was taking at the high school and an assignment given to the students
involving journalists, methods of research, and resulting stories.
She told this tale to one of the island paper's three reporters who
was in the office at work on a story about an ongoing murder trial
at the Coupeville courthouse. He was on a deadline and consequently harried, but he was willing to give her five minutes
during which he sketched out how she might go about looking
into a suspected arson in Palo Alto, California. Start her search
with finding out the name of the Palo Alto newspaper if there
was one, he told her.

Eventually Becca got to the story she needed. She worked
back through time and found it thirty months earlier, an arson
taking place on Middlefield Road. A fire had completely gutted
an apartment building, rendering homeless the residents of the
twenty-two units. Once she read the story, Becca moved forward
through time to follow whatever was available on the investigation. There was little enough information since arsons were,
apparently, not big enough news to make the front page or even
the inside pages of a newspaper for very long once they occurred.
After the first flurry of excitement, there were occasional references to the ongoing investigation and one big story about a
huge donation from Google that provided housing for all of the
people who'd lost everything in the fire. Becca read and sifted
and searched and finally found what she was looking for in a
very brief paragraph some six weeks after the fire had occurred.
A fourteen-year-old boy had been arrested and charged with the

crime of arson, she discovered. There would be a hearing in juvenile court regarding the matter.

Becca did the math on that. The age was right for Aidan to have been charged with the crime and for some kind of deal to have been struck that sent him for two years into a lockdown with heavy emphasis on dealing with his problem. If, of course, he really did have a problem. And Becca thought that he did.

SHE FELT RELIEVED, mostly because her interpretation of the whisper she'd heard had been correct. There *had* been an apartment fire and it had occurred in Palo Alto, California. What remained for her to work out now was what to do with her information.

Obviously, she needed to discover exactly when Aidan and Isis Martin had arrived on Whidbey. For all Becca knew, they could have arrived at the very beginning of the summer, and if that was the case, Aidan had been there from the time of the small conflagration in the trash can at Bailey's Corner to the storm of flames and smoke that had killed the druggie inside the old fisherman's shack.

The best way to find out how long the Martins had been on the island was the direct approach. But the problem was that the direct approach would reveal her suspicions about him to Aidan should she just ask him. She *could* ask Isis, Becca figured, but the better course was probably to get the information from Hayley Cartwright. She and Isis were tight. Hayley would know when Isis and her brother had first shown up on Whidbey.

Becca had to wait a few days to get Hayley alone. She asked her question directly, but Hayley ended up not knowing for sure. Indeed, Hayley ended up totally flustered by the question, which Becca didn't understand until she eased the ear bud out of her ear and began to pick up Hayley's whispers. They were flying fast and furiously from the other girl's mind. *I don't believe that Parker and Isis . . . If he said he didn't then he didn't and what's the point if I don't decide to trust him . . . Seth always gets in the middle of things . . . This deal with Brooke and what in God's name am I supposed to do about . . .* all said that perhaps Hayley had bigger worries than thinking about the arrival of the Martin siblings. Then on top of Hayley's whispers came some memory pictures so vivid that Becca started and Hayley said, "What's wrong?" And that put an end to their conversation because no way was Becca going to tell her about seeing Parker Natalia's hungry face hovering over someone who had to be Hayley and seeing his hands pulling off Hayley's top and seeing Hayley's hand clenched and then hiding something beneath her leg while that leg was on the cot in the tree house that Becca recognized better than anything. So Becca was left once again wondering how to go at something that ought to be relatively easy but wasn't.

She felt as if there was way too much swimming around in her head. She wondered what the point was of having whispers and memory pictures if she couldn't work out what to do with them.

That idea took her back to what Diana Kinsale had said to her. *Things are quickening.* She'd looked up that word—*quickening*—

in a dictionary at school, and there she'd read its meaning: "to cause to move more rapidly, to hasten." Well, she'd thought, *that* was for sure because information was piling up faster now. But what to do with it . . . ? She needed to work this out.

In her room at Ralph's, she took up the book Diana had given her, *Seeing Beyond Sight.* The writing within it was old fashioned and often so obscure that Becca had done very little reading of it. But now she wondered if there might be something useful in its words, so she opened the book to give it another try.

She discovered soon enough that she should have been looking into *Seeing Beyond Sight* all along. For an entire chapter was devoted to the subject of quickening, and seeing this, Becca began to devour it. Thus she found that there was more than merely the dictionary's definition when it came to *quickening,* for the word also applied to the flashes of vision she'd been having. What she read wasn't exactly a breeze to understand, however: "A verbal exploration and subsequent interpretation of the visions will lead the visionary to propel events forward to a safe, desired, or happy conclusion that might not otherwise occur should the visions not be explored completely and understood with a sharp degree of accuracy. This is what we call a quickening."

Becca set the book down. Verbal exploration? Subsequent interpretation? Propelling events forward? How was she to accomplish any of that?

She was considering this when a knock on her bedroom door was followed by Ralph Darrow's quiet, "You available in there, Miss Becca?" She jumped off the bed and returned the book to its shelf. She opened the door and said, "Just doing homework and thinking about a popcorn break. *Without* butter, by the way."

Ralph was holding a piece of paper, half torn from a pad that Becca recognized as being next to the phone in the kitchen. He said to her, "I got this . . . but truth is I'm damned if I c'n remember how. I think it's for you but it *could* be for Seth. Even for Parker. You make anything of it?"

If I tell Seth . . . dad will . . . chris . . . en . . . prob . . . Sarah going . . . grad . . .

Becca blinked at the nature of Ralph's whispers, broken up like a badly tuned radio station. She wondered if the memory pictures she was beginning to pick up were getting in the way of her ability to hear whispers from people.

She looked at the paper Ralph had handed her. *Broad Valley Grow Skag* was written on it, and there was something very wrong about the handwriting. Becca had seen Ralph's writing before, and it was strong and handsome, the writing of a man who'd taken seriously his grade school penmanship training. This, however, was little more than a scrawl. And she hadn't the slightest idea what it meant.

She said, "Mr. Darrow . . ."

He said quickly, "I thought it best to give it to you, Miss Becca. If I give it to Seth and tell him I can't quite remember how I got it or why, he's liable to tell his dad and his dad is going to tell his sister—that's my girl Brenda—and then you and I . . . ? We do not want to be tangling with Brenda. So . . . d'you want to see what this is all about, then? I guess what I'm saying is could you do that for me?"

He seemed perfectly normal as he spoke. So she said she'd help out and do what she could to interpret the note. But, still, she said, "I'm sorta worried about you, Mr. Darrow. If you can't remember how you got this . . ."

He waved her off. "I'm telling you, Miss Becca, somebody said old age is not for sissies, and every day I'm more convinced of the fact. Now. Did you say something about popcorn?"

"No butter," she told him. "I said that, too."

THIRTY-EIGHT

What the *Broad Valley Grow Skag* message meant didn't concern Becca as much as the fact that Ralph's handwriting was so changed and the other fact that he'd forgotten how he'd even gotten the message in the first place. She did find out that Broad Valley Grow*ers* was near a town called La Conner, which was itself situated in Ska*git* Valley, but when she got their phone number and tried to find out how they related to herself, to Parker Natalia, to Seth Darrow, or to Ralph, she came up empty. The place was a tulip farm and they had "no reason in hell that I c'n see, miss" to be calling Ralph Darrow's home on Whidbey Island.

Becca concluded that someone had been calling *about* Broad Valley Growers, and Jenn McDaniels was the most likely person. Jenn was, after all, hot on the trail of all things related to Aidan Martin and to Wolf Canyon Academy.

When Becca cornered her at her locker at the high school, though, Jenn said no. "Don't know nada about tulip farms anywhere" was how she put it. "But I got more on Aidan anyways, courtesy of the Squatman."

Becca smiled. "How'd you twist his arm this time?"

Jenn shook her head. She opened her backpack to shove in some books and a pack of cigarettes fell out. She glanced up, saw Becca's look of disapproval, shoved the cigarettes back in place, and said, "I'm quitting, I'm quitting. I was only testing to see if you noticed."

"Yeah. Right, Jenn. Way to go. What about Squat, then?"

"He found out when Aidan got to Whidbey."

Becca brightened. "You actually got him to break into the district's computer system?"

"Not hardly. He wasn't going for it no matter what I tried and believe me I tried everything but taking my clothes off 'cause him and me aren't *ever* going there, let me tell you. Nope, he found out using the direct approach."

"Which was?"

"He called their grandma and asked. I was sitting right there when he did it, and I swear that kid made *me* believe he was Mr. Vansandt checking on some dates of enrollment at the school and blah blah blah about how 'the kids' like the island and all that. He talked so smooth that Mrs. Howard never said a thing except 'Lemme just check my calendar for you' and that was that."

"And?" Becca said.

"Aidan showed up three days before the first fire." Jenn slammed her locker shut. "So we got him and we better turn him in before he decides to torch South Whidbey Commons. Do we tell the sheriff or the fire chief?"

It seemed like the logical next step, but Becca felt reluctant to take it. She was aware of something tugging at her. She wasn't entirely sure what it was, but she thought it had to do with the idea of quickening and what she'd read in *Seeing Beyond Sight*. So she said, "But that means he would've gotten to the island and set his first fire in less than a week. Why? If he was in a special school or a lockup or whatever because he set fires, they wouldn't've let him out if he wasn't cured."

"So he convinced the shrinks there that he was cured. But he gets out and the fire itch gets to him and he has to scratch it and—*blam*!"

"But if he does that and he gets caught, he goes right back into Wolf Academy, doesn't he?"

"Maybe that's where he wants to be," Jenn said. "I mean, *look* at Whidbey, Becca. He gets here and he feels like he's in the middle of nowhere with nothing to do and he wants out and that's the fastest way. Only no one thinks at first that it's a pyro at work, so he has to keep upping the fires till someone figures it out. He wanted out of that school or whatever it is, and then he wanted back into that school."

"Why would he want back *into* the school? It's a lockup."

"Maybe there's some babe inside and she was putting out for him and he wants to go back because of her."

Becca thought this didn't seem likely. Something was missing. She didn't know what it was but until she discovered it, she didn't want to pass on information that might prove to be false. She said to Jenn, "Lemme find out if this Broad Valley Growers message means something before we pass along any information, okay?"

Jenn said it was fine by her and then muttered, "Uh-oh. Here comes trouble."

TROUBLE WAS AIDAN Martin himself. He was skulking along the corridor, hugging the wall, skateboard under his arm. He was heading in a direction that would take him to the back of the school where the fire had been on the night of Seth's appearance with Triple Threat. That seemed long ago, but the danger associated with that fire still was out there waiting to be eliminated. With Aidan slinking toward the doors that led directly to the location of that disruptive fire, Becca and Jenn looked at each other and made a decision simultaneously.

Once outside, they kept their distance. Aidan headed in the direction of the forest, which covered the easy rise of acreage just beyond the athletic fields of the school. The rains of autumn having not yet begun, both of the girls knew this could mean trouble if Aidan Martin was truly a pyromaniac.

He passed across the athletic field and disappeared behind a huge cedar with drooping branches that hid him at once. Jenn and Becca broke into a run. Just beyond the cedar was a children's playground filled with woodchips that would catch fire nicely if Aidan had anything with him to help things along.

When they got to the cedar, though, he was nowhere in sight. Jenn said to Becca, "Where the hell . . . ?"

"You two looking for me?" was the answer that told them Aidan knew they'd been on his tail. They swung around. He spoke from next to a half-finished wooden chain-saw sculpture that was being fashioned by someone from the stump of a fallen Douglas fir, and as he talked he fixed his stare on Becca.

She caught *needs to be done to fix her good,* which pretty much chilled her to the bone. She immediately wanted to put some distance between Aidan and them, but she wasn't about to be intimidated by what was in the guy's head.

She walked over to him. So did Jenn. "What're you up to?" Jenn demanded.

He looked her over dismissively. His whisper of *she does girls so obvious* told Becca what he thought about Jenn. She wanted to counter with "As if that matters," but instead she said, "Why're you heading out here?"

He said, "Why d'you want to know?" His gaze went to her breasts and then to her face. For once his whispers told her nothing. Jenn's were claiming that *pin this pig against the wall* was the best way to go, and she put that into action with, "Because of Wolf Canyon Academy, Aidan, and why you were there and what we know about you."

What happened next was unexpected and, to Becca, completely unrelated. Aidan was suddenly replaced in her field of vision by an SUV at the side of a busy highway. She saw a group of people surrounding it. This meant nothing at first until from this group emerged a fireman in gear and another one with a baby in his arms and then a woman crying and all of a sudden a girl—little, maybe six years old?—who was white in the face and clutching a little blue blanket.

As the vision faded, what Becca said burst out of her without her control. "What happened to your little brother, Aidan? Did you burn him up, too?"

Jenn gawped at her. Aidan stared. And then he said the worst thing possible, directing every word of it to Becca. "Lots of people do 'research,' you know." He sketched quotation marks in the air. "You aren't the only one who c'n use the Internet. But in *your* case, Becca . . . ? You don't know jack." Then he turned and sauntered off beneath the trees.

"What's that supposed to mean?" Jenn asked Becca as they watched him.

"It means he's just shooting off his mouth," Becca lied. "In his position, we'd probably do the same thing."

But what Becca knew from their encounter with the boy was pretty simple. Just as she could close in on Aidan Martin, so could Aidan Martin close in on her.

WHEN DERRIC PHONED her that night, she thought at first that Jenn had told him about their run-in with Aidan because what he opened with was, "Becca, you're doing it again," and his voice had that tone it sometimes got when he was trying to control his temper.

She said, "Doing what?" and added, "Hey, babe, are you off restriction?" in reference to his calling her at all.

He said, "I get phone time now. Twenty minutes a night because I've been a good boy and the shrink loves my ass for showing up on time once a week and lying my head off about how coming to the U.S. of A. has made my life complete. I got drunk once and it's no big deal, Doctor Mindpicker, sir. It isn't evidence of anything." And then he added fiercely, "Because it frigging *isn't*."

"Still pretty bad then, huh?" She wished he were there so she could see his face. But over the phone, she had only his voice to go by. And that was never enough when it came to Derric.

"Uh . . . yeah, it's pretty bad, Becca. And nice of you to make it all worse."

"What?"

She was in the kitchen, where Ralph had called her to the phone. There was a message bulletin board on the wall above it, and on this she had tacked a picture of herself and Derric taken in the summer. They were on Double Bluff Beach among masses of driftwood. Derric leaned against an enormous log and she leaned against Derric, his arms around her and his chin resting on her shoulder. She remembered the day and the feeling of his arms. "I love you," he'd murmured into her hair.

The memory was sweet and, caught up within it, she missed what he was saying until she heard one telling word. *Rejoice.*

She said, "What? Derric, what're you saying?"

"Christ, Becca, aren't you even listening?"

"I got distracted."

"Great. Thanks. How 'bout *un*-distracting yourself?"

His tone was surly, but beneath it she could hear an element of fear. Sometimes, she knew, anger was an easier place to go to than acknowledging fear, so instead of being ticked off at him because of the tone, she said, "I'm listening now. What's going on?"

"What's going *on*," he told her, "is Mr. Wagner. What's going *on* is Mr. Wagner telling me how cool and nice and *Christian* it was of me to set my girlfriend up with a pen pal in Uganda. What's going *on* is Mr. Wagner saying her name: Rejoice Nyombe. And the best part of what's going *on* is Mr. Wagner saying all this in front of my parents, Becca. So what the hell are you doing? I only ask, see, because I had to have a special session with Doctor Mindpicker and my mom *and* my dad and what I got to hear is that the orphanage is closed down now and no one knows for sure where the kids got sent but 'really, it's nothing to worry about, Derric, so when we learn anything about Rejoice . . . Honey, is that what's been going on with you?'"

"Oh no," Becca whispered. "Derric, I didn't think Mr. Wagner—"

"Yeah, that's it, Becca. You didn't think. And now aside from trying to hide how totally freaked out I am about what *might* be going on with Rejoice, I get to fend them off when they keep asking all about why her last name is Nyombe like mine was and 'isn't that a coincidence and is she a relative that you've never mentioned and is that why you've written letters to her?' See, it's all about those letters, Becca. It's all about how you messed up my life when—"

"I'm only trying to help you."

"That's what you still don't get. I don't need your help with this.

I don't want your help with this. I don't know how many different ways I c'n come up with to tell you. Only . . . what difference does it make at this point because I'm well and truly screwed."

"Why?"

"Because d'you *think* my mom is gonna let this go? *My* mom, the original delver-for-information?"

She said, "But don't you see how this is a good thing? Because if she can't rest till she has information when she's after information, then she's gonna find out what happened to Rejoice. And for God's sake, you *want* that, don't you? Or is this all about keeping yourself looking good in your parents' eyes? I mean, the hell with Rejoice, really, because Derric can't look bad, which is how he'll look if Mom and Dad find out he never told anyone some little girl was really his sister. Is that what this is?"

He was silent. Becca knew at once that she had gone way too far. She also knew that had they been in the room together where she could have seen his face and heard his whispers and—if she was lucky—pick up a memory vision from him, she would have been far more careful. But, she told herself, he'd pushed her into it. He was blaming her and she would *not* be blamed when all she had been trying to do from the very first was—

He swore, which he *never* did. He did it in a low hard voice. And then he said, "Nice going, Becca," and he hung up on her.

He'd never done that before. She felt sick.

THIRTY-NINE

Hayley was more or less grateful that her fingers had come upon Isis Martin's electronic cigarette that night in the tree house. Had she not come across it in the folds of Parker's sleeping bag, she knew that putting the brakes on what was happening between them would have been impossible. She'd been so hot for him that she could barely think at all, let alone think of what it meant that Isis's cigarette was in the tree house. Her mind was telling her that this was a detail she couldn't exactly overlook. But her body was saying who cares?

It didn't help in slowing things down when Parker removed her sweater and her bra. Less did it help that she'd wanted him to do so. Least of all did it help when he murmured, "This is not like *anything* I've ever felt before . . . Not like this . . ." and this at last gave her an opening.

She managed to gather herself together enough to say in a rush, "Parker, I can't. I'm not on the pill and I don't have condoms or anything."

He moved away from her. He sat up on the edge of the cot and put his head in his hands. At first she thought he was ticked off, thinking that she was a tease or something, but then he said, "You're right. Your first time isn't going to be in here on this crummy cot, which would probably fall apart anyway."

Her body was still clamoring, though. It wanted her to say, "Where then? And when, when, when?" But finally her mind managed to make itself heard. It told her that there were a couple of things she needed to know first, so that was when she brought the electronic cigarette out of the folds of the sleeping bag beneath her leg. She said to him innocently, "Gosh. What's this thing? It looks like a cigarette but it's made of . . . Take a look."

She handed it over to him. She battled with herself because she needed to read him, but at the same time what she wanted to read was the inability to lie.

Parker took it in his hand. He said, "I don't know."

She felt a little blow to her spirits. "I think Isis Martin has one of those."

Not even a pause interrupted the flow because he said, "She does?" and he looked around the tree house and frowned as if Isis might jump out from behind the wood stove.

Hayley said, "Parker . . . are you and Isis . . . ? Has she been here with you?"

His head whipped around. "No way! First Isis and now you? She's never been here. Or at least she's never been here with me. I got no idea if she's been here on her own. It's not like I lock the door or anything." And then he gazed deeply into her eyes and he let his gaze wander over the parts of her body that he'd helped her uncover. He went on with, "If you could feel what I feel when I look at you, the one thing you'd know is that I'm not into Isis Martin at all."

Then he kissed her and she wanted him to kiss her and she wanted more. But he said, "Nope. We're not going there, Hayley," and he helped her get back into her clothes.

She decided to believe him. She decided to trust him. Still, there was the matter of the electronic cigarette, so she held on to it, knowing she would have to do something with it eventually.

THE OPPORTUNITY AROSE sooner than she expected, right in the parking lot of South Whidbey High School. Hayley pulled into a parking space near the tennis courts and before she had a chance to gather her school stuff from off the floor, the passenger door of the farm truck was flung open. Isis Martin climbed inside.

"I thought you'd *never* get here," she cried. "Why're you so late? What's going on? *Why* don't you have a way that I can text you?"

Isis clutched a notebook to her chest and for a moment Hayley thought Isis had something inside that explained her state of desperation. But Isis didn't open it, merely clutched it more fiercely to her as her eyes fixed on Hayley's and she went on. "Brady called. Right when he got to school for swimming practice because *no* way could he call from home. And it's the absolute worst. He wants the ring."

Hayley's thoughts were on Isis's electronic cigarette, so for a moment she had no clue. "Didn't you send it to him right when you bought it?"

"Not *that* ring," Isis said. "His father's ring. He says his dad saw that he wasn't wearing it and he asked him why and did Brady lose it and can't he be trusted with anything and they had a big fight and Brady called me and he wants it back. But I think he's lying. I know he wants it for that skank Madison Ridgeway and that's *exactly* what I told him. So he said, 'What happened, did you lose it or something? I need it back and I need it now.' Like everything's all about *him*, and if I don't do what he says he's going to come up here and I-don't-know-what."

"But you want that, don't you?"

"What?"

"Brady. Coming up here."

"Oh, he's not coming up here. Don't be an idiot. He just wants that ring and I don't have it and that's the point. I looked every-where for it."

"I thought you wore it all the time."

"I *did* at first because I'm just that stupid but I took it off right after me and Parker . . . Oh, I don't even know for sure when I took it off."

Hayley felt icy all at once. "When you and Parker what?" she asked.

"Huh?"

"You said you took the ring off when you and Parker . . . and you left off the rest. So I'm asking: when you and Parker what?"

Isis said, "What the hell? What does it matter? Geez, Hayley, this isn't *about* Parker. Don't you even get what's happening here? Brady wants that ring. If I don't get it back to him, he's—"

Hayley fished in her purse. She brought out the electronic cigarette. She opened her palm and showed it to Isis. "What's the deal with this?" she said. "You either left it there or you put it there, Isis."

Isis stared at the device. Her gaze then went to Hayley's face. "Where?"

"You know exactly what I'm saying." Haley's voice was firm.

"God, I do not believe this!" Isis cried, grabbing the cigarette. "Here I am coming to you for advice and all of a sudden it's all you, you, you. I thought we were *friends*, Hayley. But if you're so insecure that you're going to let some . . . some *Canadian* guy come between us . . . Don't you see what's going on in my life right now, or do you just not care because oh-my-God, Isis might have done it with Parker?"

"Have you been to the tree house with him?"

"Like that's even *important* right now? Brady wasn't s'posed to give that ring to anyone. It's not his, it's his dad's. Only he gave it to me and *don't* you see? I took it off and now it's gone. Can I spell it out any better for you? For all I know, my stupid brother took it and sold it so I can't send it back to Brady and Brady will *never* get back together with me now. And by the way, great, on top of everything, I've just found out that you're so self-involved that I can't even depend on you to help me out. And why? Because I'm doing Parker . . . like that's even important. Hey, why don't you tell the sheriff I'm the person who set the fires, Hayley? Yeah, go ahead and do it. I might as well die because everything in my life turns to shit anyway."

She leaped out of the truck on her final words, and she crashed its door shut behind her.

FORTY

Hayley assumed that her friendship with Isis Martin was over at that point. She was actually a little relieved. Parker had said one thing about what had gone on between himself and Isis: nothing. For her part, Isis had made pointed references to something else altogether. So one of them was lying, and Hayley knew which of them she wanted to believe. But this required a certain distance from Isis. So when she jumped out of the farm truck, a large part of Hayley gave a very great sigh of relief.

Still, she wanted very much to talk to someone about the skirmishes going on in her mind. At some other time she might have talked to her mom, but Julie Cartwright was overburdened enough.

On the day of the final farmers' market, the crowd at Bayview was the largest of the year. The trees edging the market were brilliantly orange and red, with the sun shining brightly upon them and the air that surrounded them was crisp and clear. A slight breeze tossed the colorful pennants that welcomed shoppers to the rectangle of stalls and tables, and it blew the scents of autumn everywhere: hot spiced apple cider, pumpkin pies, apple pies, sweet potato pies. The vegetable growers had brought in the last of the lettuces along with beans, a dazzling variety of squashes, and an inordinate supply of fingerling potatoes. The knitters and the weavers had delivered their scarves and hats and gloves, and business for them was brisk as the weather altered. At the Cartwright booth, Julie was making sure that people were signing up for deliveries of fresh eggs throughout the winter as well as for the farm's root vegetables, which would continue to be harvested till the ground hardened.

Hayley was packing up one of her necklaces for a tourist from Spokane when she saw Seth. He had Gus with him on a leash, and the dog was being obedient for once. The Lab was sitting patiently at Seth's side as he talked to a fellow carpenter. When Seth was ready to move, Gus glided next to him like a dog long used to doing his master's bidding. They were coming toward the Cartwright booth, and Seth caught Hayley looking in his direction. He gave one of his head-jerk nods, and he pulled on his ear gauge in that way he had that told her he was feeling nervous. He came over and gave his usual Seth greeting.

"Hey," he said. "How's it going?"

"Okay. How's it going with you?"

"Okay."

Then they were silent. They looked out at the crowd of people who were laughing, chatting, admiring goods, and petting each other's dogs. A beautiful day and a friendly crowd . . . and Hayley knew Seth was the single person she could talk to about her doubts.

He said, "You guys have a good season?"

"Good enough. But Mom's cleaning houses three days a week now and I'm gonna need to get a decent job. She doesn't get that, of course. She says my job's school—"

"It is," Seth told her. "You started applying—"

"I'll graduate and there's an end to it, Seth."

He said meaningfully, "Hayl . . ." but she shook her head.

They fell back into silence again. Seth shuffled his feet. Gus sighed gustily and rubbed his head against Seth's thigh.

Seth said, "Hey, I shouldn't have told you—" at the exact same moment as Hayley said, "Seth, I need to ask you—"

They laughed at this, a little uneasily. Hayley cocked her head and looked at Seth fondly. "You go first," she told him.

"I shouldn't have said anything about Parker," he told her. "The thing that the guy from BC Django 21 told me? You were right. I mean, here's this guy I don't even know up in Canada and all he says is 'watch out for that dude' and what's the deal with that? He could've just been pissed off that Parker's a better musician or something."

She mulled this over but didn't say anything at first.

He went on. "I c'n see Parker's into you. I guess I just want you to be careful."

Hayley was gratified to hear Seth say all this because there was something she wanted to say to him. She introduced the topic with, "She's good. She's excellent, in fact."

That he knew at once that she was referring to the fiddler told Hayley Seth was indeed intrigued by the girl. He said, "Prynne's coming over to play for the guys. I want her bad. I mean . . . I want her in the group."

"That's her name? Prynne?"

"Her first name's Hester. It's s'posed to mean something, but I don't know what."

"Hester Prynne?" Hayley said. "It's from a novel about a Puritan woman who had sex with a guy and got pregnant and had to wear a big red *A* on her chest for the rest of her life." Seth drew his eyebrows together, which told Hayley he wasn't quite on board with what she meant. "*A* for Adultery. She did it with the preacher and went to jail and when she got out, she had to wear the *A*."

"Harsh," he said.

"Puritans."

"How d'you know that, anyway?"

"Honors English," she told him.

"Got it. Anyways, that's what her parents called her, which is probably why she goes by Prynne."

"You like her, huh?"

He glanced at her. "I really do."

Hayley found that she was glad of this because Seth was, at the end of the day, her friend. He deserved to find someone who was going to love him the way he wanted to be loved and the way she herself had never been able to love him. She hoped it would be Prynne.

He said, "Your turn now," and for a second Hayley thought he meant it was her turn for love, but then she remembered they'd interrupted each other.

She said, "Well, it's this." She glanced around to make sure that no one could overhear them before she went on. "I think I might know who started the fires, Seth. Only . . . I'm not sure and I don't know what to do."

He cocked his head at her. "Who is it?"

"I don't like to say. See, I'm not sure *why* I want to give this person's name to the sheriff. Do you see what I mean?"

"Uh . . . no."

"It's private. What I mean is that why I want to give the name is private. It's something sort of bad that happened between us plus something I know and when I put those two things together it seems like I'm trying to cause trouble for that person instead of just trying to be helpful to the sheriff."

He considered this as he examined her face, and Hayley could tell from the heat in her cheeks that she was blushing. That alone seemed enough to tell him what she would have preferred him not to know. Then he said, "Parker."

She said, "What about him?"

"He's involved in this, huh?"

"Parker didn't start those fires! How c'n you even *say* that? You've just apologized for bad-mouthing him to me and all of a sudden he's back on your list and that's totally unfair because you *know* that . . ." She pretty much ran out of steam because of the way he was looking at her.

He said quietly, "Hayl, I didn't say Parker was involved in the *fires*. You just figured that. So think about it, huh?" He looked around, seemed to want to say more, but gave a mighty sigh instead.

LATE THAT AFTERNOON Hayley was up in her room working on a paper for her honors English class. She was deep into it, and didn't hear the knock on her door. But then a voice said, "Hayley? Your mom said you were up here, but I'm sort of scared to open the door. I'm so sorry for being such a bitch. C'n I come in?"

What Hayley thought was "Oh no." She didn't really want to see Isis.

"Hayley . . . ? Okay. I'll go. Only I wanted you to know how sorry I am."

Hayley sighed, got up from her desk, and went to the door. Isis stood there looking abject. She had a small wrapped gift in her hands, cradled within them the way you would hold a baby bird. Her eyes were bright with tears that began to drip down her cheeks as she said, "I want you to forgive me. I understand if you can't. What I want you to know, though, is that I know how bad I am. But I *also* know that there's no one else in my life like you. I learn more being with you for five minutes than I ever learned being with anyone else. And then I dump on you and I walk away and I know in, like, three minutes that what I just did was wrong and I don't even *know* how to be sorrier than I am. I understand if we can't be friends anymore but I wanted to give you this."

Hayley looked at the package. Its wrapping sparkled in the light that came from a window at the end of the hallway. She stepped back from her bedroom door. Isis stepped inside, saying, "I hope you'll take this. When I saw it, I knew I had to get it for you. Would you be willing to open it?"

Hayley took the package. Isis went to the bed and perched on the edge of it. Hayley went to her desk chair and sat. Slowly, she opened the gift. Inside was a square box like something you'd get from a jewelry store. It held a small piece of porcelain shaped like a fortune cookie. This had hinges on it, so she opened it to see a slip of paper not unlike a fortune. "Someone close to you is very sorry," was neatly printed on it. Hayley knew it was Isis's printing. She looked from this to the other girl's face: her trembling lips, her earnest expression.

"I was throwing dog poop again," Isis said. "It's not like my mom hasn't told me I'm crazy a million times. And so has my dad. And they forgive me when I do, like, what I did to you. . . . But I guess they forgive me because they're my parents and they have to 'cause they're stuck with me." She clasped her hands between her knees, as if she was trying to stop them from reaching out to Hayley in order to beseech her to listen. "So what I mean is that I know you have a choice about forgiving me or not and I'm hoping you say, 'Okay, I forgive you, Isis, 'cause I know you don't really mean what you say only sometimes you just get going and can't stop.'"

Then Isis said nothing more. But she looked so hopeful and so contrite and there *was* the fact that she had apologized and that she knew what she'd done was wrong and that she did not blame Hayley for any of it at all. . . .

Hayley said, "You've got to stop dumping on me like that. It's totally hurtful and—"

Isis jumped up from the bed. She flew to Hayley, dropped to her knees on the floor, and hugged her. "I promise. I'll never . . .

never again. Oh, thank you, Hayley." She dropped her head into Hayley's lap, like an earnest supplicant who finally knew that forgiveness was not given lightly and might not be given at all in the future.

With her face shining with relief and joy, Isis lifted her head and said, "Hayley, I got to tell you something. I'm going to go crazy if I don't. And I think that if I tell, you can help me when I start to go off into the dog poop zone. Only, *if* I tell you . . . No one knows outside of my family and that means even Grandam."

Hayley froze. She thought, She's pregnant. That had to be it and Brady had to be the father.

But when Isis went on, in very short order Hayley discovered that Isis's information had nothing to do with Brady at all. She said, "We went to Lake Shasta every year. A week of camping. And I was about eight years old when this happened and Aidan was seven and Robbie was . . . like two months old maybe? He was fussy 'cause it was time for his bottle and he was in the back seat with us. And it was one of those backwards seats, you know? So Mom knew he needed to eat and she handed the bottle over and Aidan was s'posed to hold it for him, but Aidan wasn't paying attention and it didn't seem like . . . I mean, it was only a baby bottle and kids use baby bottles all the time. Only . . ." She seemed to struggle for a moment before she went on. "See, he choked or he breathed in the milk instead of swallowing it right. Dad pulled over to the side of the road and he tried . . . and Mom tried . . . and then the EMTs were there and *they* tried . . . Only no one could save him, and it was Aidan's fault. My mom started screaming at him on the side of the road and then . . . Hayley, she just stopped screaming, dead. And she never said another word about it. Never. And they cremated him. They cremated Robbie and they didn't even have a funeral and he's not buried anywhere and no one says anything and it's like he never existed at all."

Hayley felt like a statue, immovable. It was so terrible a story that she could feel the pain of it, even at this distance of years from the time it had happened.

Isis went on. "That's when Aidan started the fires. They screamed at him that he was only trouble and he had to stop only how could he stop when they wouldn't ever let him just talk about how bad he felt about what had happened to Robbie? It was a little thing, see. Just give the baby his bottle. Only it went all wrong and they would never say anything, not 'We forgive you, Aidan' or 'We should have found a rest stop because that would have made more sense' or anything. But the thing is that people *need* to talk about the bad stuff in their lives 'cause if they don't, it eats them up inside until they do something."

Hayley wasn't sure what to say other than, "Oh gosh. Isis . . ."

Isis rested back on her heels. She said, "That's why I'm not always too good to be around. But I'll try hard because I don't want to do anything else to mess up our friendship. I know you're dating Parker now, and I'm totally cool with it. Him and me . . . It all had to do with Brady. I knew that, and I knew Parker wasn't right for me and anyway I could tell from the first he was into you. So what I'm saying is it's so good that you two are together. And I really mean that. Okay?"

Hayley studied her face. It was so earnest. She said to Isis, "Okay," and then when Isis made a move to hug her, she added, "But did you guys . . . Did you and Parker . . . ?"

Isis waved her off. "Did we have sex? Hayley, it was no big deal. Get rid of the whole virginity package you've got going on and you'll see for yourself."

FORTY-ONE

"I can see forgetting some kinds of stuff," Becca said, "like where you put your car keys or maybe why you walked into a room. Even a message you're s'posed to give to your mom. But this wasn't like that, Seth. This was forgetting even *taking* the message. It's like he came across a jumbled-up piece of paper and he read it and he can't remember anything about it."

Seth frowned. He was standing in the parking lot used by people who walked onto the ferry when they went over to Port Townsend and he'd been watching that same ferry steadily approaching Whidbey when his cell phone had rung with Becca calling. He considered what she was telling him. "Grand's just getting old," he settled on saying. "I don't get why you're so freaked about it."

"I'm freaked because the message could be important, and you know why."

Seth did know that. He said, "Your mom?"

"What if she didn't go all the way to Nelson? Where is this place La Conner? I mean, they said Skagit Valley but where's that?"

"Up north, just off island," he told her. "But, Beck, why'd your mom be on a tulip farm? What's the place called again?"

"Broad Valley Growers. And I don't know, maybe she didn't need to go all the way to Nelson. Maybe she got . . . like . . . a flat tire? Maybe . . . what about amnesia?"

Seth said, "Beck . . ."

"I know it's dumb but don't you see that—"

What he saw was Prynne. The ferry was docking and she was standing with the other walk-on passengers at the very front of it just behind the chain that held the cars back. He waved, but of course she didn't see him since she'd not ever been to Whidbey Island and she didn't know where to look. He saw that she didn't have her eye patch on and that she didn't look exactly pretty but really, truly interesting with her tangled hair and the long skirt she was wearing. She had on her cowboy boots and a faded denim jacket and a slew of chains that winked in the bright sunlight. It came to him that she was just like him, out of step with most other people, and he liked that about her.

"Seth! Seth!"

He realized that Becca had been going on and he stirred himself to say, "Lemme call this place, Beck. I'll feel them out and see if I can find out something. If I can't get an idea what's going on, we can go up to La Conner. We can check the place out and if your mom's there—"

"No! It could be a trick. Ever since those posters went up everywhere, I've had a feeling like something's going to happen. What if someone's put together who Laurel Armstrong is and who I am? That picture of me in the paper . . . the old one when I was in, like, fifth grade . . . ?"

"It barely looked like you."

"Aidan saw me looking at that picture. So what if he called up with that message? He knows I'm looking into him, too."

Seth saw that the ferry had docked and the passengers were disembarking. He began to stride in the direction they would have to come. He said, "'F that's the case, then maybe he's just trying to freak you out." Seth waved to Prynne and this time she saw him. She had her fiddle case dangling from one hand and she lifted it in a form of hello. He said into the phone, "Look. I gotta go, Beck. But we c'n check out this place if you want to. Try not to worry in the meantime. You got to remember, it could've been a message for Grand or even for Parker and Grand just can't remember."

He ended the call then, and there was Prynne, standing in front of him and looking so . . . so . . . so just like Prynne that he wanted to hug her. He was, he realized, exceptionally glad to see her.

THE GLASS EYE looked totally real. Seth hadn't been prepared for that. He said, dumbly, "Hey that thing looks like . . . like the real thing," and then felt like a fool.

Prynne laughed. "What'd you expect? A doll's eye or something? You want me to pop it out for you?"

He held up his hands in a *whoa* gesture. "No way! You look nice."

"Didn't like the eye patch, huh?" she said companionably as they started to walk toward his VW.

"I didn't mean it that way. The eye patch is cool. I'm, like, more or less into eye patches. Who wouldn't be? Especially when you find out they're real. Know what I mean?"

She stopped walking and observed him. "Are you nervous?" she asked directly. "'Cause it seems to me that I should be the nervous one if I'm playing for you guys."

Seth removed his fedora, fiddled around with it, put it back on his head. He said, "Well, yeah. Guess I am. I dunno. It feels like a first date or something. I don't know why. I'm feeling so . . . like pins and needles are sticking in my feet."

"Oh. It's that guy/girl thing. We got to get the first kiss out of the way. I don't want you to think I'm after you or anything because I'm not. But it's just that sometimes there's this guy/girl tension and I've found that just bringing it out in the open and having a decent kiss more or less defuses it."

"Wow. You're pretty direct."

"Yep. No point in being anything else. You up for it?"

"I'm game, yeah." He kissed her softly.

She shook her head. "Nope. Sorry. Very nice and all that, but it's got to last longer and it's got to be serious, if you know what I mean."

He did. He also liked kissing her.

She said then, "Great. That's out of the way. What a relief. Now. Where do I meet the rest of Triple Threat?"

"Why? D'you have to kiss them, too?"

She laughed. Then she locked her arm with his. "Maybe," she told him. "But I sort of don't think so."

PART V
Skagit Valley

FORTY-TWO

Despite Seth's words, what Becca felt was the approach of something. It was like being on a collision course and what she was going to collide with was Aidan Martin. The boy knew very well that she was gathering information about him. But he was a kid who seemed to understand that the best defense was an aggressive offense, and one thing was certain: He didn't scare.

Becca could imagine him doing to her what she was doing to him: following a few trails. How tough would it actually be, she wondered, for him to follow the trail of one Rebecca Dolores King from San Luis Obispo, California? If he did that, it was only a few short steps to learn that the real Becca King was dead of leukemia in her fourteenth year, and from that he could conclude without much trouble that Rebecca Dolores King's identity was now the property of an altogether different person. Sure, he'd have to do a little digging around, but was there anything about life these days that couldn't be discovered by someone who was even moderately in the know about the Internet?

So on the one hand, the whole deal about Broad Valley Growers in Skagit County could be a way for Aidan to see just how much he could make Becca King run around like a chicken without its head. But on the other hand, it could also be a real piece of information that she needed, not because of Aidan and who he was and what he'd done in his life but because of her own life and how it had developed from the moment she'd told her mom what she'd learned from Jeff Corrie's whispers.

The truth was that Broad Valley Growers might have to do with Jeff Corrie just as easily as it might have to do with her mom. Or it might have to do with not a single thing except Aidan Martin's messing with her mind. But in any case, she needed to find out if there was *anything* dangerous associated with that place: like Jeff Corrie hiding out there and using it as bait to lure her to him. Still, calling Broad Valley Growers again and saying, "Hey, is a guy called Jeff Corrie staying with you?" was not an option. But finding out exactly where Jeff Corrie was at the moment seemed a reasonable one.

Becca went into Langley to do her research although she was determined not to use either the public library or South Whidbey Commons since Aidan Martin had already seen her in both places. But he had not yet tracked her to the Hub.

Derric drove her to town. He'd approached her at school. He'd said, "Damn. I'm sorry, Becca," and she knew he meant that he felt bad about hanging up on her when they'd been talking about Rejoice, his parents, and his psychologist. "The whole thing with you talking to Mr. Wagner at my church . . . ?" he said. "It put me over the edge." He'd run his hand over his smooth dark head as if this motion would settle his mind and soothe out of it the whispers of *because if what happened when that place closed down is bad . . . know it is, know it is and all I ever had to say about her was . . . I know that too . . .* He went on to say, "You know, I just wish . . ." and even that he could not complete.

She'd locked her hand with his and said, "I know." For all he'd ever had to do was to tell someone that the very small girl among the children who'd been taken out of the alley in Kampala was his little sister, and that would have made all the difference.

In town, they parted at the Hub. This was somewhat like South Whidbey Commons, only it was a gathering spot not for teenagers but rather for middle school kids. It sat on one of Langley's cross streets, on the lower floor of a white-steepled Methodist church. Inside the Hub, there were games for the kids to play, a place for homework, and a few computers to share. Time was limited on these computers, but a helpful older lady in an electric lime green track suit told Becca that she could use one of them for a few minutes, but only if she waited her turn.

This involved hanging around for an hour, and when it was finally her turn, she did a Google search on Jeff Corrie. As usual, there were a slew of old entries since Corrie had been "a person of interest" for quite some time. Becca quickly saw, though, that since she'd last checked on what was happening with him, something had occurred to put Jeff back into the headlines of the San Diego paper. A story about *Corrie's Claims Prove True* made her heart leap up to her eyeballs.

As she clicked on the story, what Becca thought was that her mom had returned to San Diego. Maybe she'd decided that the better route was a face-to-face confrontation with him.

Her head was filled with this idea when the story in the paper popped up in front of her. And then her world fell off its axis. For the story in question was about Jeff Corrie's partner, Connor West. And Connor West was one hundred percent alive.

Becca could barely take in what was in front of her on the screen. She made out the words but not the sense of them and certainly not what they implied.

Connor West had been found on a boat. Connor West had been found in Acapulco. Connor West was on his way—escorted by the San Diego police with the full permission of the Mexican authorities—back to California.

Becca stared at the story. There had to be some kind of mistake. It was *not* Connor West. It was only someone who looked like Connor West. Or maybe it was someone who'd taken over Connor West's identity much as she'd taken Rebecca King's. When they got him up to San Diego, they'd do a DNA test or they'd use his fingerprints or they'd just compare his picture to a picture of the real Connor West and then . . . But that was stupid. Of *course* it was Connor. He didn't have an identical twin conveniently hidden away for a moment like this. How dumb to think so! How idiotic! How . . .

Becca found she could barely breathe. She felt as if the room were swimming around her. She heard shouting but it was all in her head and what the shouting pounded inside her skull was *you were wrong you were wrong you were wrong you were WRONG*.

Yet she'd heard Jeff's whisper, as clear as anything, that day in the kitchen in San Diego. *Connor West* and *dead* and . . . Hadn't that been it? Yes, it had. She knew it had. Plus those telling words from Jeff's whispers: *she knows.* He'd locked his eyes on hers the moment he'd had that thought. That thought had followed those about Connor West and death and what *had* those words been? Not the memory of them but the words themselves, every single one of them. She strove to remember but all she could come up with was *dead* and then Connor West had disappeared, gone without a single trace, and how did that happen without a person being murdered and his body disposed of, and her mom had believed her, for there was no reason for Connor to flee. So they'd made a run for it because Jeff was dangerous. He'd used his wife's daughter to help him embezzle money, he'd cheated old people out of their life savings, he was being investigated, he was a liar, he was a con man, he was a killer.

But now that image of Jeff Corrie was shattered right before Becca's eyes. And there was nothing she could do about a single thing that had come about from what she'd assumed when she'd heard Jeff's thoughts. Especially was there nothing she could do to get word to her mom.

FORTY-THREE

Becca burst out of the Hub. She fled across the street and through a parking lot that ran along the back of Second Street. It ended in a slope of lawn where seven of the town's multitude of rabbits were munching their way toward winter. At the top of this slope Cascade Street offered its regular view of the water far below and of the distant mountain range that gave the street its name. But Becca was only dimly aware of any of this because she was desperate to find someone, to unburden herself, to understand, to plan, to . . . *anything*.

She pounded in the direction of the Cliff Motel. It wasn't far, just a few blocks to Sixth and Camano and Derric would be there. She could tell him and ask him and he would know what she could do. Only . . . he didn't know a single thing about the whispers, about Jeff Corrie, about her mom, about anything at all. Debbie Grieder was there, her supposed "Aunt Debbie," but even Debbie didn't know the truth. Seth knew part of it, but he was nowhere nearby. And there was no one else. There was *no one* and what was she doing here on this island by herself without her mom and with her grandma dead and not there to offer the kind of wisdom that had always got her through the bad moments in her life because her grandma, too, had heard people's whispers only she had learned to control them like a radio off and on and on and off and if Becca herself had only been able to do that she would have—

Becca forced herself to stop. She had to slow down her tumbling thoughts. She had to consider her options. She herself had been checking the Internet, right? So what would have prevented her mom from doing the exact same thing from Canada? How else would she know when it was safe to return? They'd thought that safety would be indicated by Jeff Corrie's being put on trial and thrown into jail. But wasn't the current situation the very definition of safety, too? Of course it was. And maybe her mom—

"Becca! Hey, Becca?"

Becca swung around. Hayley Cartwright was in her family's farm truck. She'd pulled to the curb. She had her little sister with her and she was leaning out the window. "You look deranged," she said with a smile. "D'you need a ride?"

Seeing Hayley, Becca came up with the answer.

"C'n you take me to Diana Kinsale's house?"

BECCA COULDN'T BEAR the thought of hearing anyone's whispers. Once she was in the truck, she fished around for the AUD box, for Hayley and Brooke were filling the air with thoughts. One of them was thinking about *what's the point 'cause she won't do anything* and *there's never any money* and *who cares if I die*, which was pretty chilling. The other was thinking *there's still that cigarette* and *I can't just can't* and *if I ask him again* and *who do I trust*. While at one time, Becca would have strained to put this all together and in some kind of context, she couldn't trust herself to do that now. So she shoved the ear bud firmly in place to block out the noise even as *tell the police but can I really do that* soared into the air like the crack of a limb falling from a tree in Ralph Darrow's forest.

It wasn't a terribly long drive to Diana's, just a ride along the undulating route of Sandy Point Road. Where it ended in a sharp curve that headed in the direction of the island highway some miles away, Hayley made the zigzag onto Clyde Street.

Diana's dogs were in their run at the back of her house, and they'd begun barking when Hayley pulled into the driveway. Oscar wasn't among them, for he'd be in the house with Diana, but rather than go up to the door directly, Becca went to the dogs and petted each of their heads. She wished she had something to give them, but she'd come empty-handed. She murmured to them and they quieted down, milling around at the fence and nuzzling her hands.

At the front door, Becca rang the bell. No one came to answer.

What Becca thought at first was that Diana wasn't at home, despite the presence of her truck. But through the panel of glass at the side of her door, she could see Diana's shoulder purse dangling from its regular hook and beneath a bench below that hook, Diana's outdoor shoes were arranged. Her indoor slippers were not in place, so she had to be in the house.

As Becca was thinking this, Oscar came padding to the door from the direction of the sun room. She could see the poodle through the glass, and he saw her as well. He looked directly at her with his knowing eyes. She knew he was trying to tell her something and she knew it couldn't be good.

Becca felt a stirring of alarm. She tried the door. It was unlocked. Totally Whidbey Island, she thought. She went inside and Oscar nudged her in a silent greeting so unlike his pals outside. He led the way to the sun room and there Diana lay on a chaise with a comforter drawn up to her chin, her skin looking yellow, and deep circles beneath her eyes.

For a terrible moment, Becca thought she was dead. She cried out. Diana opened her eyes. She didn't seem the least bit startled to find that Becca was inside her house. Instead she said, "Becca. Hello. You've caught me napping," and she sat up, winced, and rubbed her lower back. "Too much yard work. It's the autumn cleanup. I always tell myself to go at it slowly. Things don't need to be done all at once. But then I get going and can't seem to stop. It's silly at my age." She shot Becca a smile.

Becca returned it hesitantly, which caused Diana to say, "Something's happened. Sit next to me. Here. You're shivering."

Becca sat next to her, and Diana put her arm around Becca's shoulders. Becca felt at once the sensation of calming and lifting. She allowed herself just to *feel* for a moment, as her gaze took in the rest of the sun room. Diana's plants were healthy and thriving in their pots, but her loom bore a patina of dust which spoke of the many weeks that Diana had not done any weaving. That dust seemed to match her yellowed skin, the deep circles beneath her eyes, and the air of exhaustion that emanated from her. Not for the first time, Becca wished that Diana would allow her complete access to her whispers.

"Something *has* happened," Diana said quietly.

For a moment Becca thought that Diana had read *her* thoughts and was going to confess something about herself. But when she went on, Becca saw that Diana's words were another version of Hayley Cartwright's saying "You look deranged." So now was the time to tell the truth, if she could bear to do so.

She said, "I made us leave San Diego, Mrs. Kinsale. I heard his whispers . . . his thoughts, see. I was in the kitchen with him and my mom, and he thought I was using the ear bud. He'd been in my bedroom and I knew he'd been reading my journal so I figured if he was going to do that to me, then I was going to get inside his head. But when I heard what he was thinking . . ." Becca felt the tears rising and the last thing she wanted was to start crying now. She plunged on as fast as she could. "I helped him in his business because my mom told him about how I could more or less hear what people were thinking only you're the only person I never could hear. I still can't hear you except when you want me to, and you know that already, don't you? So I would bring sandwiches and cake and coffee to his office and then I would tell him what the people were thinking, as good as I could. He told me it was to help him guide their investments and I believed him. Only what it really was was that he was skimming money off the top of whatever they made. Him and Connor West his partner. I didn't know that and neither did my mom, only what if he wasn't skimming at all? What I mean is what if *Connor* was doing all the skimming because it was Connor who disappeared. And Jeff's whispers were saying that Connor was dead but how would he ever have known that if *he* hadn't killed him and got rid of his body and if he did that to his friend, what did that mean he was going to do to me and my mom? Because he knew, see, that all I would have to do was not wear the ear bud and I'd figure it all out, which I sort of did anyway. But I couldn't say anything to the police because why would they believe me and what was I s'posed to say anyway? 'I read his whispers, which are just like thoughts only less direct and I have to work out what they mean'? Like, the police were going to believe that? So I told my mom and she knew we had to leave till it was safe and Connor's body was found and Jeff was arrested. But she knew he'd try to follow us, which is why she wanted me to hide out here with her friend Carol Quinn. Only Carol Quinn was dead and my mom was gone and I never could reach her on the cell phone and then the sheriff found the cell phone anyway—"

"Shh," Diana said. "I understand it all now."

Until Diana spoke, Becca was unaware that tears were streaming down her own cheeks and onto her old fleece jacket. She wiped her face on its sleeve but she couldn't stop talking because there was more, and what *more* comprised was the very worst, which she had not yet got to.

She said, "I finally remembered part of what he was thinking when I was coming here. 'Dead isn't always dead these days.'

That's what it was but I couldn't remember at first when I saw that Connor West . . ." She didn't think she could say it but she forced herself to go on. "Mrs. Kinsale, he was never dead at all. See, I thought what Jeff meant was that he could make it look like Connor was still alive so that no one could accuse him of getting rid of Connor. I thought Jeff wanted all the money for himself and soon as the police gave up looking for Connor's body, Jeff would be home free. See if he could make it look like Connor was the person embezzling money and the money was all gone and Connor was gone too and if he was willing to do all that to his best friend, what would he do to us if he found out that I knew it all? So we ran, and now . . . Oh God, Mrs. Kinsale, he's alive just like Jeff Corrie said from the first. I saw it in the San Diego paper. He's been in Mexico. Someone turned him in or someone found him or someone did something only it doesn't really matter because the only thing that matters is that I was wrong. And now my mom . . . My mom . . ."

Becca was hiccupping through sobs at this point and Diana tightened her hold around her shoulders. She said, "Let's be calm for a minute. Say nothing more."

"But I need to tell my mom," Becca said. "If she's in Canada—and maybe she's not even there!—I need to tell her that Jeff didn't do it because Connor's alive. And if that's the case, she c'n come back and we c'n go home."

"Quiet now. Just breathe."

At last Becca had said what she'd come to say and she forced herself to be silent. Her breathing was jerky but slowly it calmed and the warmth from Diana increased in its power over her until all she felt was peace. At last, Diana released her from the embrace. She gentled Becca's hair from her face.

She said, "Things are quickening, Becca. Did you read the book to see what quickening means? Events are hurtling you forward. They always have been, but now the pace of them is faster. And this is a good thing. Come with me."

Diana led Becca outside, through the sunroom door and onto the terrace. This looked out at tiny Hat Island in Saratoga Passage, with its looming trees and its handful of houses. As they stood there quietly, a great bald eagle soared above them and out over the water, its head dipping in a search for food. It found it and dove, a flash of white head and white tail feathers and then upwards again with a fish in its talons.

Diana turned to her. "Nothing happens in the world by mistake. Things feel like mistakes, but there are no mistakes."

"But that was one," Becca said. "What I heard. What I told my mom. Why we ran away from San Diego."

"The reason for the running itself turned out to be incorrect," Diana told her. "But the running itself and your journey to this place? That was never a mistake. The why of it all may not be clear to you yet, but it *will* be clear if you allow it time."

"I asked Parker Natalia about my mom," Becca told her. "He's from Nelson and I asked him about her, like whether he knows her. Only he doesn't. He never heard her name before. And what if that means something happened to her?"

"I think it means very little."

"But it's a small town. His family owns a restaurant there. They know lots of people because it's popular so wouldn't she have gone there? She'd even need a job. But he said—"

"You're Becca King, but you're not Becca King," Diana told her. "Why would she be . . . She's this Laurel Armstrong I've been seeing everywhere, isn't she? On the posters, in the newspaper." When Becca nodded, Diana continued. "So why would she still be Laurel Armstrong up in Nelson? And, honestly, why would Parker Natalia even know her? I've lived here on the edge of Langley for thirty years, Becca, and I don't know everyone. Yet there are only one thousand people in the town itself. Who can possibly know everyone? People come and go. And you must keep in mind that she may not have gone to Nelson at all. She may have changed her mind or discovered another place equally as safe and much closer, just over the Cascades, perhaps. She may have remained close by to watch over you and keep an eye on things. Indeed, she herself may have followed Jeff Corrie's story in the papers."

"So what am I supposed to *do*? Just wait?"

Diana smiled. "You've answered your own question. You've answered life's big question."

Becca felt deflated. She wanted a course to follow and waiting around was no course at all. She had a feeling that Diana Kinsale was about to go all Yoda on her in that maddening way of hers, and she wasn't far wrong.

Diana said, "Here's what I believe: Revelations tend to come to us through everyday matters. Today you've learned something about the nature of what you heard in the past through Jeff Corrie's thoughts. I think you have to take that and sit with it for a while. Sit and wait."

"Wait for *what*?"

"The quickening."

FORTY-FOUR

The problem for Becca was one of application. Diana said that you learn something and then you apply it to life. But how was she supposed to do that when half of what she learned came from whispers and now she knew that she couldn't trust them? So could she trust the memory pictures she was starting to receive? Probably not. Becca realized for the first time that this wasn't some special gift she had. Instead it was a terrific cosmic joke bringing ruin on her life and having the potential to bring ruin on the lives of others.

Becca understood from what had happened with Jeff Corrie and Connor West that every single whisper she daily heard or had ever heard was open to doubt. She'd drawn conclusions about so many things based upon those broken-up thoughts, and now she had to sort back through them and try to work out what to do next since sitting around and being patient and waiting for the truth to come to her like a bolt of lightning out of the sky were not options.

So she couldn't trust the whispers and she couldn't trust the memory pictures she'd begun to receive. She was thus down to trusting one thing only: her instincts. They would have to be good.

SHE AND SETH arranged a time for their trip to Broad Valley Growers. It was outside of La Conner, a town that lay next to the Swinomish Channel, which emptied like a river into Skagit Bay. It was on the mainland to the north of Whidbey and just to the east of another island called Fidalgo. The islands themselves and the mainland were connected by bridges in this northern location. The first of them was some fifty miles from Langley, and Seth said that he was glad to drive Becca up there. So she waited for him on the designated day with her stomach uneasy about what they might find when they got to the tulip farm.

She was inside the house. She'd packed them a lunch and she was standing at the living room window, which looked out onto Ralph Darrow's garden of lawn, rhododendrons, and specimen trees. Ralph was raking beneath these trees, and she'd been watching him. He was moving slowly. He was pausing a lot and looking around, as if unsure of what he was supposed to do next. Then he seemed to remember and he went on raking. Moving as slowly and deliberately as he was, Ralph was going to take days to clear out all the leaves.

As Becca watched, Gus came into view, loping across the lawn from the parking area on the hill. Ralph greeted the dog, wrested a ball from Gus's mouth and threw it in the direction of the pond. At that point, he seemed perfectly normal again. Hands on his hips, he watched the dog run. Then he tilted his wide-brimmed gardening hat back on his head and waved at Seth, who was just coming down the path toward the house.

Becca made sure Ralph's lunch was where he could find it, then she gathered her things and went outside. At once she caught a whisper, which sounded to her like *glass eye* but could have been *pass by*. She didn't know who was thinking it—Seth or his granddad—and she no longer believed what she heard anyway. Plus the whisper itself didn't make sense, so in some irritation she rustled for the AUD box. She clipped this onto the waistband of her jeans and shoved the ear bud into place.

Seth and Ralph were in conversation as she crossed the lawn to them. Gus came charging up from the pond in her direction, clearly delighted to have yet another person to throw his ball. She paused to do this and by the time she reached grandson and grandfather, she could see and hear that things weren't fine between them.

Ralph was saying, "Damn it all, Seth, when someone has three things going on at once and one of them is taking down a phone message while smoke's pouring out of the fireplace because the flue didn't get itself open . . . I think I c'n be forgiven for not getting down every detail."

To this Seth said, "Grand, you're not cheating with food, are you? This cholesterol thing—"

"Now you listen to me," Ralph said stormily. "I've lived well into my seventies without a bunch of damn Darrows watching my every move and this has got to stop." He caught sight of Becca and added, "You have anything at all to do with this current inquisition, Miss Becca? You my personal Mata Hari?"

She said, "Mata Who?" and he replied with, "What in damnation are they teaching in school these days?" But even as he spoke there was something in his eyes that spoke of fear.

Seth said, "Okay, Grand. You made your point. Anyways, me and Becca're going up to La Conner to see what this is all about." He called for Gus and said to Becca, "You ready?"

Ralph said, "You're crazy, the two of you. Whoever called is gonna call back once the message isn't answered the way they want. Why don't you sit tight and wait for that?"

Because we can't, was Becca's thought.

Seth's response was a shrug as he told his grandfather it was a nice day for a drive and Becca hadn't ever seen Skagit Valley anyway. Ralph waved them off with a grumpy, "Kids," and he turned back to his work.

As they climbed the hill path to Seth's car, Seth said to her in a low voice, "I dunno, Beck. I think he's just getting old."

Her reply was, "Maybe, but his handwriting . . ." She set her backpack down. She still had the message that Ralph had written, and she hunted through her backpack to find it. She showed it to Seth because he of all people would be able to see the change in Ralph's writing.

This he did because he looked from the message back to Ralph in the garden. He said to Becca, "Is he taking his blood pressure like he's supposed to?"

"I set the reader out for him every morning but sometimes he says he'll take it later."

"You think he might be stashing junk food somewhere? Chips, cheese, Cheetos? Is he going out for burgers and fries with anyone?"

"If he is, I don't know it. And if he's stashing food, I wouldn't even know where to look. I haven't checked his shop. Or the garden shed. And if he's stashing stuff in the forest, I'd *never* find it."

Seth continued walking, Gus shooting ahead of them up to the car. He said nothing more till they reached the VW and were inside, with Gus panting between them from the back seat. Then Seth said, "I hate to turn Grand over to Dad. He'll come over and give Grand hell, and believe me, you don't want that to happen."

"Well, he knows I'm watching him. He doesn't like it and I don't blame him."

Seth started up the car and put it into reverse. "Maybe we're making a big deal out of nothing. It was only a message. It was only one time. And like he said, he was in a hurry."

Only, Becca thought, Ralph's whispers had changed as well. They were choppy. Individual words were broken up, unlike what they had been before. Of course, at one time this would have meant something serious to her, except now she doubted just about everything. She wasn't sure what else to do, but still she worried about Seth's grandfather, as well as the quickening and whether he was part of it.

The journey to La Conner took quite some time. Seth drove them to the far north end of Whidbey Island, where the water flowed swiftly through a narrow strait called Deception Pass, meeting the Strait of Juan de Fuca one hundred eighty feet below a two-lane bridge. This bridge took them onto Fidalgo Island, and as it was another sun-drenched day, there were tourists aplenty at this spot, posing for pictures on the bridge with some of the myriad islands in the strait as a backdrop.

A larger highway coursed from Fidalgo Island onto the mainland. Here a wide valley opened up. It stretched on forever, occasionally interrupted by a copse of trees, a farmhouse, and a barn but otherwise arranged in neat fields upon which at this time of year nothing appeared to be growing. But Seth told Becca that planting was about to begin. For this was tulip country, brilliantly lit in spring by millions of the flowers that made the landscape look like Holland.

Seth suggested that they eat their lunch before visiting Broad Valley Growers. Becca was in a lather to get to this farm, but she said okay since Seth was doing her a favor in bringing her to this place.

He drove them through the town. La Conner sat right on the river-like channel, looking across at one of the many Indian reservations in the state. This began an area that was thick with forest, reached by a bright orange bridge near which Seth parked. They got out, Gus pitched himself joyously toward the channel's water, and Becca soon discovered why Seth had wanted to pause and have lunch before going on to Broad Valley Growers.

He'd met someone. She was called Prynne, and she was "a majorly excellent" fiddler. He was trying to talk her into joining

Triple Threat. But the way he said this told Becca that something else was going on besides Seth Darrow looking for a fiddler for his gypsy jazz group.

She said, "Seth, how cool! When do I get to meet her?"

He said, "Dunno," but she could tell he was pleased that *she* was pleased. Then he added that the girl wore an eye patch when she was playing the fiddle because she'd had cancer as a child and had lost her eye. She had a glass eye now but she didn't wear it when fiddling, he told her.

Glass eye, Becca thought. That *was* what she'd heard. She felt the first relief she'd experienced since learning she'd misinterpreted Jeff Corrie's whispers that long ago day in San Diego.

They spent a little more time by the river, throwing the ball for Gus because no way was he going to get back into the VW without having had his bit of fun. But then they were on their way, and Becca's insides began fluttering as she understood how much closer they were to solving at least one small mystery.

They'd uncovered the location of Broad Valley Growers without any trouble as it had both a Web site and a Facebook page. So Becca knew the road on which the farm sat, but until they reached the place, what she didn't know was how close it was to the interstate highway. This was the same highway that she and her mother had traveled. It rolled north right up the center of California, and it did much the same in the states of Oregon and Washington till it got to the border of Canada. When Becca saw this, her heart pounded in excitement because she realized how it all might have happened: her mom dropping her off in

Mukilteo to catch the ferry over to Whidbey, her mom returning to the interstate and driving north, her mom getting tired and pulling off the road and finding herself in need of rest or food or someone to help repair her car or *whatever*, but in any case ending up at Broad Valley Growers.

They'd have an Internet connection. She'd have kept watch. She'd now know that Connor West had been found alive and well. She'd be peeved at Becca—okay, all right, and who could blame her—for having misinterpreted Jeff Corrie's whispers. But all would be forgiven and they'd be reunited.

Gus seemed to pick up on Becca's growing excitement. From the back seat, he whined. Seth glanced her way and shot her a smile. "You okay?" he asked her. She nodded.

Broad Valley Growers was enormous. It seemed to be a place that not only grew tulips but, in the season, offered various activities for tourists who came to the area to see the colors. The farm was introduced by an arch over a drive, and this drive led not into a farm yard but rather into a parking lot suitable for fifty cars or more. To one side of this sat the biggest barn Becca had ever seen. Its white paint was fresh, and its tall wide door was partially open, allowing someone's rap music to beat the outside air. Opposite this barn was a similarly painted farmhouse with a wide front porch. This house was shaded by a sugar maple, a blaze of red and orange against the pure blue sky.

They got out when Seth parked, nearer to the house than to the barn. In their wake, Gus leapt to the ground. They'd given him some playtime, but clearly not enough because he began to gambol around the house. He snuffled and barked when he spied a chicken enclosure, and he was shooting toward it when a barking Dalmatian came flying off the porch. This dog was followed by two dachshunds.

A chaos of barking erupted from all four dogs. Seth started shouting, "Gus! No! Come!" and into this a bell began to ring energetically. Becca and Seth swung toward the sound, which turned out to be coming from the front porch. A woman had dashed out of the house and into the noise. It seemed the bell was her attempt to still it.

It worked. Three of the dogs retreated, silenced. Gus continued. Seth strode over to him and grabbed his collar. He said, "Hey, bad dog! When're you gonna listen up?" and then to the woman who'd stopped ringing the bell, "Sorry. He's a doofus, but he wouldn't've hurt these guys." He nodded at the other dogs, particularly at the dachshunds, who'd gone back up onto the porch, where they kept a growling watch on the interlopers.

The woman had a dish towel hanging from the waistband of an apron she wore. They'd interrupted her in the midst of baking something, it seemed, because her hands were dusty with flour. She said, "Can I help you two?" She sounded pleasant, which Becca decided was a good thing. She removed the ear bud just to have a listen to anything that might float by in the air.

What she heard was *odd one never too sure* and *come in all sizes is what Jeff says.* At the *Jeff* part, Becca jumped back as if she'd had a shock from an ungrounded outlet.

She said, "Seth, I don't think so," and she would have retreated at once, but he said, "Huh? What?" and looked confused. He added, "He's okay, Beck," and she figured he was referring to the dog, trying to reassure her about Gus's behavior. There wasn't much she could do to clarify matters.

Seth said to the woman, pointing to himself, "Seth Darrow. This is Becca King."

"Darla Vickland," she replied pleasantly.

"This's gonna sound dumb," Seth told her, "but someone from here called my granddad over on Whidbey. He couldn't remember who it was or what they wanted. So we came to see."

What in God's name and *double doofus on toast* and *Jeff is going to want to know* and *some kind of trick* made Becca put the ear bud back in place. Darla Vickland said in some confusion, "Let me understand. You two have come all the way from Whidbey Island because of a phone message?"

Seth said, "He didn't know who it was for, see. Could have been for Becca here or for this dude called Parker Natalia or it could've been for Grand himself only the point is he can't remember and since it could've been important, especially for Becca . . . I guess this sounds kinda lame, huh?"

Worse and worse, Becca thought. They looked like complete idiots. She burst out with, "Is anyone, like, staying with you? I mean, a boarder or something like that? It might be a lady but it could be a man? Someone who maybe used your phone without you knowing?"

The woman's expression changed. She said, "Oh dear, I wonder if one of those darn kids was playing a prank. Listen, why don't you two come inside and let me get my husband?" She smiled and cocked her head and added, "If you wouldn't mind putting your dog in the car, I've got apple pies freshly baked. Let me just get Jeff because he'd probably like to know about this."

Becca clutched Seth's arm and said, "We need to—"

But Seth cut in with, "Apple pie? Righteous," and without a moment to consider that the farm wife might be anything from an ax murderer to a cannibal, he led Gus toward the VW to put him inside, prefatory to gorging himself on her fresh apple pie. Reluctantly, Becca followed him.

The woman walked in the direction of the barn as Becca said fiercely to Seth, "We gotta get out of here. This is a dead end. Or it's not. And it's probably not. Because she said Jeff. Did you *hear* her say Jeff?"

Seth opened the car door and Gus jumped inside. He riffled through the glove compartment for something, brought out a milk bone, and handed it over to the dog. Gus crunched happily and remained in place because the one thing about the Lab that everyone knew was that Gus would do anything if more food was in the offing, including obeying the command to stay.

Seth shut the door and turned to Becca. He caught the expression on her face because he said, "Beck, chill. There's more than one Jeff on the planet."

"No!" she said. "I got to get out of here. Or I got to hide. Just in case. Because what if it is? And she said a prank. And if he got one of those kids to call because she also said kids and Jeff could talk any kid into anything and—"

"Too late now." Seth was looking past Becca in the direction of the barn. "Here he comes. So. That your stepdad or what?"

Becca was afraid to turn and to see the truth, but there was nothing left but to do it. She slowly swung around, knowing beyond anything that, having made such a royal mess out of things, it would be icing on the cake of all the disasters she'd brought upon herself to find Jeff Corrie striding across the farm yard.

Only . . . it wasn't Jeff Corrie. It was just an ordinary man in jeans and a flannel shirt with a great dome of a shining bald head. And Becca would have noticed more of him and tried to decide if he presented danger to her had he been alone or even accompanied only by his wife. But right behind him came five kids of varying ages, laughing, chattering, goofing with each other and with him. And even these kids Becca might have noticed more closely had not one of them been a girl upon whose face Becca's gaze fell and in whose presence every breath of air whooshed right out of Becca's body.

The girl was tall for her age, which had to be around fourteen years. She wore jeans and a T-shirt and rubber boots. She wore a baseball cap with *Indians* scrolled on it so her face was shadowed but despite this Becca would have known her anywhere. For she was bitter-chocolate dark just like her brother, and if she ever smiled, Becca was sure it would be her brother's smile as well.

"Rejoice," she murmured as everything about the telephone message became clear in an instant.

FORTY-FIVE

Despite Isis's apology to her, despite her terrible story about the death of her baby brother, Hayley remained uneasy. She completely knew why. It all had to do with Parker. So just two nights after Isis had come to the farm, Hayley logged onto her family's computer and had a look at the girl's Facebook page. Isis was—as Hayley had come to learn—the least discreet individual she'd ever known, so whatever was going on between her and Parker was probably going to be there in living color.

It didn't take long for her to see that Isis's tale of her tree house encounter with Parker Natalia had pretty much happened the way she'd claimed. For there were pictures aplenty of Isis and Parker, and among them were shots taken in the tree house. Central to these was one of Parker with his shirt off sitting on the edge of the very same cot onto which he'd so lovingly lowered Hayley. Central to these was also one of Isis and Parker together, positioned in such a way that it wasn't rocket science to figure out that most of their clothes were off. And then there were the pictures from the Maxwelton party with Isis hanging all over him. And there were the pictures of them inside the pub in Langley and standing next to Parker's car.

Of course, all of these pictures predated Hayley's own involvement with Parker, but that wasn't the point. The point was Parker and "watch out for that guy" and what Hayley figured that actually meant.

Okay, all right, she told herself. Now she knew. Maybe Isis didn't care that he was a watch-out-for-that-guy-he-could-be-trouble individual and maybe she was posting pictures of herself with him in order to make Brady jealous down in Palo Alto. But Hayley *did* care about these kinds of things. She cared about who was going to be her first man and she cared about not making a total fool of herself.

AS IT HAPPENED, Parker called that same evening, the first time she'd heard from him in several days. He said, "Hey. I'm sorry to be out of touch. I should've called, but I was waiting to get this—"

"I can't talk right now," she said abruptly.

There was a silence at his end. Then he said, "Is something wrong? Is your dad okay? I've been thinking about you nonstop but every time I start to call something happens."

"I've got a ton of homework to do," she said.

"Oh. Okay. But this will only take a minute because I was wondering if you—"

"I'm totally busy, Parker." She hung up. She understood that this wasn't quite fair of her, but at the moment she truly didn't want to get hooked into the warm mellow sound of his voice.

Five minutes after she hung up, she heard the front door-bell ring. Thirty seconds after that Cassidy burst into her room. "There's a guy talking to Dad in the living room but he wants to talk to *you*," she said. At that same moment, their mom called up the stairs, "Hayley? Parker's got something to give you."

Hayley pushed away from her desk. She felt queasy at the thought of seeing him. But there was no real escape at this point.

She went downstairs. He'd come out of the living room, and he was waiting for her. Thankfully, no one else decided they had to witness her meeting with him, so he was alone. He had a CD in his hand. He extended it to her.

"I was at the end of the driveway when I called," he confessed with a sheepish smile. "I c'n tell you've got a lot going on but I wanted you to have this."

This was BC Django 21's music. When Hayley took the disc from him and looked at the cover, she saw that his was one of the faces on it.

"I'd love to listen to it with you right now," he told her. "But with all that's going on here . . . Maybe tomorrow?"

She looked up from the CD. He seemed to read the wariness on her face, because he said, lowering his voice, "Is everything okay?"

Well, Hayley thought, he'd given her the opening she needed. So she said, "Come here, okay?" and she took him outside and onto the front porch.

He said, "What's wrong?" when she turned to him, crossing

her arms beneath her breasts. It was colder than she thought it would be, and she should have put on a fleece because she shuddered. Considerately, he moved at once to take off his jacket. Somehow that made everything inside her break loose at once.

"I don't like users," was how she put it. "I don't like liars. I don't like having to sort through what someone tells me to figure out which part of it is actually the truth and which part is a lie."

Parker's mouth opened, shut. Then he said, "What're you talking about?"

"Hooking up with women and dumping them. You and Isis, to be exact."

He looked past her, out into the dark fields beyond the house, then back again. "Me and Isis *what*?"

It was the pause that got to her. He'd so obviously used it to decide how to play her. "You and Isis and *sex*," Hayley said baldly. "You were in the tree house with her, you had sex, you used that cot, and you were planning the same for me. Only you found out I'm a virgin and that changed things for you so now—"

He held up his hands. "*What's* going on?"

"You know what's going on," she said. "You and Isis and you and me and you and who-knows-because-it-could-be-anyone."

"Me and Isis? Look, I *told* you that dingbat was hanging around and I said she was acting like . . . like I don't know . . . like we were a couple, like we *are* a couple. But I never gave her any encouragement."

"Oh please," she said. "You were going after me just like you went after her."

"No way. I told you she wasn't in the tree house when you asked me about that cigarette thing she uses. *And* I told you I wasn't interested in her. Jesus, Hayley. What's happening here? I thought you and me—"

"So did I. But you tell one story and the facts tell another."

"What facts? What d'you think? That I'm two-timing you with Isis? Why the hell would I do that?"

"So what're you saying? You and Isis never did it? You never did it in the tree house with her? You never had sex with her and then moved on to me for the same thing?"

"'*Course* not."

"And that's your story?"

"What other is there?"

The one that Isis's pictures told, Hayley thought. But she didn't say it. Instead she handed the CD back to Parker and told him to keep it.

"YOU CAN'T LET this *mean* so much, Hayley." Isis had been waiting outside the door to the band room when Hayley emerged.

"It's no big deal," Hayley told her, although that was a total lie. She'd thought that saying goodbye to Parker would take one concern away from her, but it hadn't worked like that. What *was* she? she wondered. In love with the rat? It was like he'd taken up residence in her brain.

Finding the auditorium doors locked, Isis pulled her over to the girls' restroom and they ducked inside. She checked the stalls, found one engaged, and waited impatiently while a lone girl finished up and departed. Then she turned to Hayley and said, "Let me tell you how it happened."

"I don't care how it happened. I just care that he lied."

"Good grief, Hayley, wouldn't you have lied in the same situation? There he is on your front porch, all hopeful about taking your relationship to the next level. And you bring up me and him having sex. What d'you expect? 'Oh sure, Isis and I did it but it was no big deal compared to how I feel about you.' Would *you* have said that in his position?"

"I hope I would have said something truthful," Hayley said.

Isis fished in her shoulder bag. She brought out her electronic cigarette, saying, "I'm gonna tell you what happened."

"I don't want to hear—"

"If you don't hear, you're going to imagine stuff. We were in the tree house. I don't know why he's saying we weren't except he probably panicked when you brought me up. But we were there and we smoked some weed. We got super loaded and he kissed me and I kissed him back because the one thing that dude knows how to do is kiss. Anyway, before we really thought about it . . . I mean, who really thinks when someone's that hot."

"I don't want to hear—"

"You got to. So we had our clothes off and we were . . . you know . . . just doing it like monkeys or whatever. And okay it was excellent but that *doesn't* matter 'cause the only reason I was doing it in the first place was to get at Brady. I know he looks at my Facebook page because he spends, like, half his life on

Facebook. So I knew he'd see pictures of me with Parker. But it didn't *mean* anything to either of us. It was just sex. I bet he was thinking of you the whole time. He's totally nuts about you and you'd be way so dumb to dump him just because him and me . . . Because like I say, it wasn't *about* him and me. It was just something that happened."

"When?" Hayley asked her. "When were you two in the tree house?"

Isis thought about this. "I asked him if he wanted to go to the pub. That place in Langley on Second Street? I invited him. See? He didn't even ask me out, for God's sake. After, we went back to the tree house and that's when it happened. And, Hayley, this is the part you got to believe, okay? I planned it all."

"What?"

"*You* know. Look, I needed something to happen because of Facebook and the pictures and Brady. I don't think Parker was even gonna, you know, take off my top. *I* had to do it. And okay, he went along with it all. I didn't exactly have to rape him. But what I want you to know is that I was the one—"

Hayley stopped her, but this time it wasn't because of the information. Or rather, it *was* because of the information, just not the particular details Isis was giving. She said to the other girl, "What about the ring?"

"What d'you . . ." Isis's voice drifted off as did, obviously, her thoughts. She put it together and said, "Brady's ring, you mean?"

"Were you wearing it that night? Did you take it off? You wouldn't have wanted some lumpy thing like a ring to get in the way. Or Parker wouldn't have wanted that, so he would have taken it off you, maybe. Isis, what happened to the ring?"

Isis's mouth formed an O. But then she shook her head. She said, "You can't be thinking that Parker kept it. Come on, Hayley. He's way too nice a guy."

"Were you wearing that ring when you left the tree house?"

"Sure. I must've been. Sure. 'Cause didn't I take it off when I got home? I took a shower and I wouldn't't've worn it in the shower so I would've put it . . . Oh, I'm sure I had it, Hayley."

"Like you had that?" Hayley nodded at Isis's electronic cigarette.

"No way, no way," Isis told her. "He didn't keep the ring. 'Cause if I forgot it, why wouldn't he just have given it back to me?" Isis sucked in on her cigarette. Her eyes were cloudy and her expression was grave. "I don't like to think that he could've kept that ring to make things bad for someone," she said.

"We know he's a liar, Isis."

FORTY-SIX

If she'd learned nothing else in her first year on Whidbey Island, Becca had learned not to leap wildly into action the second she thought she'd figured something out. So when she saw the African girl at Broad Valley Growers, Becca set about making certain that the girl was exactly who she thought she was.

She said nothing to Seth. Although he knew that Derric had a sister somewhere—he'd learned that much on the day Derric came out of his coma the previous year—he didn't know the full story. So when Becca saw the girl among the other kids at Broad Valley Growers, she kept her feelings and her conclusions to herself and somehow got them through the awkwardness of explaining their mission to La Conner: She spoke once again of a strange phone call and Seth's grandfather. She added to this a man called Jeff Corrie, and a woman called Laurel Armstrong. Jeff and Darla Vickland were pleasant, but they knew nothing of any of these people. So after a piece of apple pie, Seth and Becca left, Seth still in the dark but Becca feeling more illumined as the hours passed. Still, Becca knew that certainty had to be established. She figured that Reverend Wagner was the way to establish it.

She couldn't buttonhole him at church again. There was too much risk of Derric finding out and, besides, she just couldn't wait. A little research via the phone told her that Reverend Wagner and his wife also ran a hospice on the island. Pinewood Sanctuary was its name, and it stood across the street from a Bible camp, which itself loomed over a sheltered body of island water called Deer Lake. Like the Bible camp's entry, the lane into Pinewood Sanctuary carved deeply into forest. Unlike the Bible camp, the two buildings that comprised it had been constructed in a sunny meadow.

Becca rode her bike to this place. She found Reverend Wagner in the meadow. At its edge he was building a deer blind. Not for hunting, he hastened to tell her, but for watching and photographing the does and fawns at dawn and dusk when they came into the meadow to feed. He was sweating over his labor. He wasn't gifted in carpentry.

Becca used the AUD box to save herself from any distractions. She said to him, "Want me to do something there?" He was struggling to hold a board in place and nail it simultaneously. She went to aid him, and he pounded a nail in. It bent to one side, and Reverend Wagner swore. Then he excused himself with "Terrible example from a man of God," and he pulled the nail out. He suggested that they take a break. "I've reached the point of diminishing returns," was how he put it. He lowered the board to the ground and went to sit on a camp chair. There was another, and he patted its seat for Becca.

She joined him and asked her question. "I'm sort of wondering, Reverend Wagner . . . Did you leave a message with Ralph Darrow about a place called Broad Valley Growers?"

He took a handkerchief from his pocket, removed the baseball cap he was wearing, and wiped down his forehead, his neck, and his balding head. "I did," he said. "After you and I talked, I realized that Children's Hope has three branches in this area: here, in Friday Harbor, and in La Conner, and I got to thinking that someone in one of the other branches might be helpful, considering all the different possibilities for this young lady you're looking for. So I phoned those branches, and there you have it."

"That girl I saw at Broad Valley Growers . . . So she *was* Rejoice."

"Ah. You went out to see her," he noted with a nod. "Adopted when she was five," he added. "The family . . . perhaps you saw them, too? All their kids are adopted from various regions in the world. A real melting pot of youngsters and two of the nicest mom and dads you're ever likely to meet." He glanced at Becca and repeated one point. "Five years old," he said. "That's when she was adopted. Rejoice Ayoka was the name, actually, not Nyombe as things turned out. But she was the only Rejoice, so I assumed . . ." His words were spoken in a meaningful way.

Becca cringed inwardly because she knew he'd worked out that she'd lied to him. Not only had she chosen Nyombe as a surname for Rejoice, but she'd also claimed that Rejoice was her pen pal in Africa, which was hardly likely since she'd been sitting up in La Conner for years.

Reverend Wagner said kindly, "Is there anything you'd like me to help you with, Becca? Or should I continue to assume that all of this is confidential?"

Becca clasped her hands between her knees to keep herself from clasping them at the minister's chest. "C'n you please . . . ? Oh gosh, this is awkward. But c'n you not say anything about Rejoice? C'n you not say anything about me asking about her?"

He regarded her evenly. "This has to do with Derric Mathieson, doesn't it?"

She swallowed. "It's not a bad thing. It's just that . . . Well, it's something Derric's got on his mind and needs to work out and if you say something . . . Or if I say something . . . I think it might be better for him to decide what happens next on his own, if you know what I mean."

He thought about this for a moment before he slowly nodded. "I think I do."

"*Thank* you."

"Welcome. Now . . . is there anything else I can help you with? Besides this situation with Rejoice?"

There certainly was, Becca thought at once. There was plenty he could help her with. Or at least there was plenty that she needed *someone* to help her with. But Reverend Wagner was not the person who could find her mom.

Reverend Wagner had his gaze fixed on her face. He seemed to watch a playing out of her emotions there, as careful as she was trying to be to keep them at bay. He said, "You know, Becca, it's not a bad thing to rely on other people occasionally. I think you've just seen that with this circumstance involving Rejoice. Now, I know—having three of my own, all grown up now—that most kids like to rely only on themselves. But sometimes putting your faith elsewhere . . . ? That can work, too."

REVEREND WAGNER'S WORDS hadn't fallen on deaf ears. But there wasn't much anyone could do for Becca when it came to Jeff Corrie. On the other hand, there *was* something that someone could do that might make a difference when it came to Becca's mom. That person was Parker Natalia.

The evening after she'd been to talk to Reverend Wagner, she spoke to the Canadian as she and he did the dishes. She kept the water running and her voice low. Ralph was in the living room and although he was banging around with the fire tools and logs as he built his nightly blaze, there was always a chance he'd overhear.

She said to Parker, "I got to ask a favor. D'you remember my cousin Laurel in Nelson?"

He was wiping a plate and he looked like someone whose mind was a million miles away. Becca picked up *like that's all I think about* from him, along with *maybe it's true but how unreasonable . . . Jesus how much more screwed . . . great going asshole . . . another bright idea only now there's no way without . . .* but none of it made sense to her. She forged ahead. She repeated, "D'you remember my cousin Laurel in Nelson?"

Parker roused himself. "Don't know her, though."

"Yeah. But here's what I'm wondering. You guys have a newspaper up there, right?"

"Sure." He dried a plate and put it on the stack he'd already done.

"I want to put an ad inside it."

"For your cousin?"

"Just her name really big and Seth's phone number." She couldn't risk Ralph's, not only because her mom might call and Ralph might forget all about it but also because Becca had already lied to him about Laurel Armstrong. But Seth could be relied upon to pass along a message from Becca to Laurel and from Laurel to Becca. It would be brief enough anyway. "Come back to Whidbey," to which Laurel could then say, "Be there next week." Or "in two days" or better yet "tomorrow." But in any case, she'd get the message and she'd return and Becca could then tell her about Connor West and about having been wrong about Jeff Corrie.

"See, I can't do the ad because they're gonna want money, right?" Becca said to Parker. "And I've got money to pay for it, but not . . . like . . . a credit card or anything. But I bet you've got a credit card. So if you arrange for the ad and give them the credit card number or whatever and then I c'n pay you . . ."

He nodded but she could tell he wasn't really listening. She could also tell his spirits were low. She could almost feel the weight of his heart.

She said to him, "What's going on, Parker?"

"With me? I blew it."

"What?"

"Everything."

She looked at him, and she breathed in deeply. There were a jumble of words comprising his whispers and then a flash of memory from him that she caught onto just before it faded from sight: Isis pulling a sweater over her head and reaching around to unfasten her bra and a hand—Parker's?—reaching for a bright gold chain that hung between her full breasts. The hand closed around that chain and then . . . nothing. Becca found herself staring at Parker, and he was staring at her. She could feel her cheeks burning with what she'd seen.

She said, "Is this . . . well . . . Isis, maybe?"

Instead of answering directly, he said, "You and Hayley are friends, right?"

"We talk and stuff and usually we have lunch at the same table, but she's more Seth's friend. And Seth's more my friend. If you know what I mean."

He didn't seem to care one way or the other. All that appeared to matter was the "talking to her" part. He said, "Could you talk to her for me? If I wrote her a note, could you give it to her? She's not talking to me now and I don't blame her because I did something righteously stupid because I didn't think about that freaking iPhone not to mention Facebook and it just seemed easier to deny . . ." He looked so pathetic that Becca had to feel some sympathy for him. From what she could work out from his memory pictures and his words, he'd done the deed with Isis but then lied to Hayley.

She said, "You're seriously dumb, Parker."

"She came *on* to me. It's not like I wanted—"

"So you fought her off. *Not.*"

"Jesus. Why are women so . . . Look, I know I blew it. I just didn't expect to get accused. I went to see Hayley just to give her a CD and before I knew it, we were talking about Isis and I could tell she was pissed and I didn't know how to handle it. I know I was wrong. I want to apologize and make things right. All's I'm asking is for you to give her that message. You don't need to talk her into—"

A sharp knock on the front door interrupted Parker's words. It was followed at once by someone ringing the door bell. From the living room, Ralph said, "Tarnation. All right," and grumbled his way over to see who it was.

Dave Mathieson entered. He nodded at Ralph and then his gaze shifted to the kitchen doorway. He saw Becca. He saw Parker standing behind her. He said, "Parker Natalia, right? Let's you and me go somewhere to talk."

FORTY-SEVEN

Parker left with the undersheriff, and he didn't return to the house that night. Becca hadn't the first clue where he and Dave Mathieson had gone, but the fact that the undersheriff had shown up in the first place did not make anything look good for Parker. She figured she should worry about this, but her larger worry was getting a message to Laurel, and Parker had been her last best bet to do that.

She had to wait for another chance with him. In the meantime, she decided that she would fulfill his request that she speak to Hayley.

The problem was finding a time to talk to Hayley when Isis wasn't hanging around her. The only stretch of time that Hayley was without the other girl consisted of the moments that she spent on the reception desk in the administration wing of the high school.

Becca buttonholed her there. To do this, she had to cut a class, but there didn't seem to be any help for that. She removed her ear bud in order to be guided by Hayley's whispers.

Hayley looked very pale. She was fair-skinned anyway, but now she seemed drained. Becca approached her, and Hayley raised her head from some homework. She smiled wanly. Becca said, "You busy?"

"Statistics," Hayley told her and gestured at some sort of graph she was in the midst of creating. "This and the phones," she added. "It's pretty quiet right now. Makes me want to take a nap." *Got to stop this . . . he's always there . . . if Mom won't do something about . . . such a pig . . . impossible* constituted what was in her head.

Becca frowned. It seemed to her that all the progress she'd made with whispers was gone now, defeated by the knowledge of how she'd misinterpreted Jeff Corrie's. She wasn't sure how to get anything back or even if she should make the attempt at all. She said, "Parker asked me—"

No no no no.

That was clear enough, Becca thought. "—to talk to you," she concluded.

"Well, you've just talked to me, so consider your obligation fulfilled," Hayley told her tartly.

Becca squirmed. She didn't like to play the go-between, and she sure didn't like the reason that Parker had made this request of her. But she was in it now, so she decided to plunge onward. She couldn't exactly make things worse between them. She said, "It's just that he feels really bad about what happened and he wanted me to—"

"D'you *know* what happened?" Hayley tossed to one side of the desk the colored pencil she'd been using on the graph. "Did he tell you? Because if he did, the whole idea that he'd ask you to tell me *anything* is outrageous, okay?"

"He knows he blew it. He just wants a chance to talk to you."

"To lie about something else is what you mean. Well, I don't want to listen. You didn't answer anyway. Do you *know* what he did?"

Becca felt hot around the neckline of her sweater. She said, "Isis."

"Right. Parker and Isis and then he lied. I'm not putting up with liars, Becca. You c'n tell him that."

"He's just hoping that you'll give him a chance. Just to *talk* is all. I think he wants to say sorry."

"Great. He's sorry. Tell him you told me, I listened, and the end is the end however he wants to color it. Look, you have Derric. You c'n be sure of him. That's what I want, too. To be sure of someone. Parker's not that person. He's a liar, it's too bad, and there's an end to it."

Becca gave fleeting thought to the whole idea of being sure. Nothing, she knew, was ever for sure. She said, "It's just that sometimes people . . . Things happen and they don't really intend them to or they're sorry they did or they weren't thinking straight. And when that happens—"

"When what happens?" another voice said.

Becca swung around although she knew who was talking. Isis Martin was there, carrying with her an enormous placard reading BATHROOM PASS. She carelessly tossed this onto one of the chairs in reception and came over to the desk, which she hung upon and said, "What's going on?"

"Parker wants to talk to me," Hayley told her. "He sent Becca to ask."

Isis glanced Becca's way, her cool blue eyes appraising. Becca thought she was about to warn Hayley off, but Isis surprised her by saying, "You should talk to him. You *know* it was nothing, him and me." And to Becca, "Where is he? Outside?"

"I think he's with the sheriff," Becca said.

"*What?*" This from Isis.

"The sheriff came for him last night and said they needed to talk and they went somewhere together. He usually comes to the house for breakfast—to Mr. Darrow's house?—but he didn't today."

"He probably took off for Canada," Hayley said. "He probably got deported."

"I don't think it had to do with making him go back to Canada," Becca said. "The sheriff didn't tell him to get his stuff."

Isis turned to Hayley. "The sheriff's got to be asking him about the fires. What else is there?"

The ring . . . but what would that have to do with . . . know about him anyway? . . . he would have talked to the Canadian police and if he found out something . . . did he plan . . . he would have known that cigarette was . . . so if he had the ring . . . lies lies lies on top of lies . . .

The whispers came from them both in great cloudy swirls that turned Becca around and inside out. The only thing she could understand from it all was that Parker had something to do with a ring, which had something to do with Isis or Hayley. How this related to everything else was something that she still didn't know.

FORTY-EIGHT

Isis found Hayley at the local food bank later on that afternoon. Using it represented how far her family had fallen into financial trouble, and for Isis to know this was almost too much to bear. But as if out of nowhere, the girl materialized at the side of Hayley's cart, giving no clue as to how she'd managed to track her down. And Hayley didn't have time to ask.

"Aidan's missing," Isis told her. "I was gonna tell you when you were at the reception desk, but that girl . . . Becca . . ." She chewed her lip.

"*Missing*? How? When?"

"He was there at Grandam's two nights ago, at dinner. He went off the next morning. He hasn't been back. I told Grandam he was staying with a friend, but she's not stupid and I have to find him. God, Hayley, things're bad."

"What's going on?"

She looked around, as if for listeners. "Mom and Dad are coming up here."

"Why?"

"The sheriff . . . It was only a matter of time till he got all of the information. He's been checking every single kid who was at that party, and he looked into me and Aidan and he found out about Wolf Canyon Academy. He called Mom and Dad because the people at Wolf Canyon wouldn't've told him why Aidan was there. Mom and Dad wanted to know why he was calling, course, and he told them some fire setting. They freaked. They called up here and they talked to me and I didn't know what to tell them except that there *were* some fires only I swore Aidan wasn't involved. But I told him they called and they were coming up here as soon as they could work it out. Hayley, I told him and told him he should've talked to the sheriff himself and let him know about everything because of how it would look if he let the sheriff find out on his own. But he *wouldn't* and now he's gone."

"God, Isis. Then he must have—"

"No way. He's cured. But what he thinks is that they'll take him back. Mom and Dad."

"To Wolf Canyon?"

"So he ran." Isis's eyes got bright with tears. "I have to find him. Will you help me? He's hiding somewhere. But if I don't find him fast, I'm scared he might actually . . . you know . . . do something. . . ."

"Is he on foot?"

"He's got a bike. One of those two at Grandam's."

"Then he can't be far."

ISIS BELIEVED IT would be some place close to her grandmother's house. When Hayley suggested that they check his bedroom first for any kind of clue where he might be, Isis panicked.

They *couldn't* go to her grandam's house. Grandam was always there. And if she saw them in Aidan's room, she would ask questions and she *couldn't* ask questions because she had to think—

Hayley said, "But with Aidan missing . . . and since he sets fires—"

"He's cured!" Isis insisted. "But we *got* to find him."

It seemed to them both that the only logical place for Aidan to have gone was back down to Maxwelton Beach, to one of the vacant houses. Thus, they began their search not far from the turnoff to Nancy Howard's house, and they crept along, looking for something unkempt, something deserted, or something not too different from that old fishing shack next to where they'd held their party. But they found nothing. Wherever he'd gone, Aidan was not at Maxwelton Beach.

Swede Hill Road suggested itself next, since it broke to the east and climbed to the south toward Scatchet Head, immense with forest, beach, and bluff. But by the time they'd made their decision that that was the next direction to try, darkness had fallen and Hayley had to get home. The next part of the search would have to wait, she told Isis.

HAYLEY DECIDED THAT while Isis might be fine with keeping her grandmother in the dark, she herself could not keep silent about Aidan Martin's disappearance, considering how much stress he was under with his parents on their way. Still, it felt horrible to name him directly to the undersheriff. So she looked for a halfway point between saying nothing and telling Dave Mathieson that Aidan was missing and trouble might well be on the horizon. When she reached the traffic light at Bayview Corner, she knew what to do. The main offices of the fire department were right on her route.

At the fire station, there was no receptionist, and the offices Hayley looked into were empty. She was about to give up on the whole idea of talking to Chief Levitt when she heard his voice. She found him at the end of a corridor, adding something to a bulletin board with photos of fire scenes on it.

Whoever he was talking to was on his cell phone, which he had balanced against his shoulder. He was saying, "Yeah . . . yeah . . . I got that on record . . ." and when he saw Hayley hanging back, he ended the call and said, "Help you, hon?"

Hayley nearly lost her courage, but she reminded herself that someone had died in the last of the fires. So she stammered, "It's about . . . I have some information?"

Karl Levitt's eyes narrowed. "Come on into my office. You are . . . ?"

Hayley gave him her name. She hated doing so but at the moment she didn't think to withhold it. Still, she said quickly once she'd told him, "Only . . . can you not tell Sheriff Mathieson that what I'm gonna tell you came from me? It's just that what I know was told to me in confidence. If it gets out that I told you and you told him and . . . Can you please keep my name out of it?"

He pointed to a seat in front of his desk. She looked around nervously. The room was functional and messy, with bulletin boards filled with pictures of every spot a fire had occurred from the summer till now.

Karl Levitt said kindly, "Why don't you give me your information?"

"C'n you promise me . . . ?"

"Can't do that. If this has something to do with the fires, and I figure it does since you showed up here, then this whole thing'll come to a trial eventually. Somebody's been killed, and that means we've got a different kettle of fish. But I *can* tell you I'll hold back your name for a while." When Hayley didn't reply at first but rather twisted her hands in her lap, he added, "This is a serious business we're looking at, Hayley. I bet you know that or you wouldn't be here."

"I just hate to—"

"Tell on someone. But here you are, so you must know what's right."

This was true. So Hayley screwed up her courage and told Karl Levitt everything about Aidan Martin that she knew, the entire story from the death of his baby brother to the fires he'd lit in Palo Alto to his incarceration at Wolf Canyon Academy to his present disappearance in advance of his parents' arrival. At the end of it all, she said, "Isis says he's freaked out. He figures they're coming to take him back to the school in Utah and he doesn't want to go. So he's panicked and when he's stressed . . . that's when he sets fires."

Karl Levitt nodded. He'd been taking notes. Hayley asked, "Do you . . . Will you tell the sheriff he's disappeared?"

"Oh yeah," he said. "Got to do that straight off." He stood and ushered her to the door, a hand on her shoulder. He gave it a squeeze. "You did the right thing," he told her kindly. "Even if it doesn't feel so right at the moment."

HAYLEY ONLY PRETENDED to leave. She had a feeling that the very next thing on the fire chief's agenda was going to be a phone call to Dave Mathieson, and that was what happened. So she set off down the corridor, but then tiptoed back to his office.

"Got some information from one of the kids down here, Dave," was what she heard him saying after the preliminary social niceties of hi, how's the wife, and going hunting this year? After that, it was all about Aidan Martin. Isis was mentioned and so were Nancy Howard, the Martin kids' parents, Wolf Canyon Academy, and Aidan's history: the exact how and why of the fire setting. The sheriff seemed to know much of this already, from what Hayley could tell, but then Karl Levitt went on to Aidan's disappearance, and to this Sheriff Mathieson seemed to respond at length.

Then the fire chief made an electrifying comment that rooted Hayley right to the spot. He said, "Since that ring at the scene was from Palo Alto and the Davenport kid handed it over to the girl—this Isis?—there's too many coincidences at this point, Dave."

IT WAS ALMOST dark when Hayley got home. The search for Aidan followed by the Karl Levitt talk had taken far longer than she had anticipated. She was feeling wretched about everything, especially since the fire chief's remark about the ring pointed to horrors to come. Those horrors were what she was thinking about when she got home and found the house completely dark.

Where the hell was Brooke? was what she thought. She was supposed to be working on dinner. She had let Hayley down another time. It was as if she was determined to make everyone's life a misery.

Hayley stormed out of the truck. She hurtled toward the back door. She only got as far as the steps, though, when she found her father. Bill Cartwright was lying unmoving at the bottom of them, a dark and crumpled form in the shadows.

Hayley cried, "Dad!"

He stirred and she thanked God silently that he wasn't dead. She grabbed his arm to help him up, but dropped it quickly when he shrieked in agony. She jumped nearly a foot at the sound of such pain. She shouted, "Brooke! Cassie! Brooke! Brooke!" and she flew into the house and up the stairs for help.

On her bed, Brooke was wearing headphones and listening to music and in a fury, Hayley grabbed them off her head. She shrieked, "Dad's outside! Do you even know that? You selfish little bitch! What in God's name is the matter with you? Get off this bed and out of this room!"

Brooke started to cry. But Hayley's words got her off the bed and out of the room. Hayley grabbed a blanket and followed her down the stairs. In the living room, she saw, Cassidy was watching a video of Cinderella. Nice try, she thought bitterly. As *if.*

Back outside, Bill Cartwright had managed to work himself onto his side. "Why'd you go out?" Brooke shouted at him. "Why won't you just *stay* in the house? What's wrong with you?"

"Shut up!" Hayley screamed at her. She used the blanket to cover her father's body. She said to him, "We got to get you to . . . I'll call 9-1-1."

"No ambulance," he said. "It's my arm is all. Girls, it's okay. Just a fall. If you c'n help me up . . ."

"Where's your walker?" Brooke demanded. "What've you done with your walker? Why won't you use your stupid walker?" She began sobbing, and Hayley wanted to swat her as hard as she could.

She said to Brooke, "Get Cassidy. Get in the truck." And when Brooke looked confused, "Just *do* it, Brooke."

"Why? What're we—"

"We're taking him to the hospital. Now *get* the hell going."

FORTY-NINE

Seth and Prynne found themselves establishing a routine. Two times a week, they had been meeting. He would either go to Port Townsend, where she'd pick him up at the ferry, or she would come over to Whidbey, where he would do the same. When she came to Whidbey, often it was to rehearse with Triple Threat. She fit into the group seamlessly. But what Seth liked best about Prynne was that she *got* him. He'd never felt so completely able to be himself with anyone.

He was at that stage where he wanted to show her off to his entire world. This was one of the reasons he took her to Smugglers Cove Farm and Flowers. He wanted her to meet Hayley and Hayley to meet her. He wanted to share the joy of being what he knew at heart he was: in love with Hester Prynne Haring.

"Someone I want you to meet, if that's okay," was how he told Prynne where they were heading when he turned west on Smugglers Cove Road after he met her at the ferry. This would take them through both forest and farmland, ultimately cutting a course through the old growth state park that lay midway between two arrowheads of land: Lagoon Point and Bush Point with their expansive views of Admiralty Inlet and the northern snow-topped Olympic Peninsula that rose beyond it.

Prynne cast him a curious look, but what she said was, "I like meeting your friends. You've got good friends. That says a lot about you." She smiled and pointed to her eye patch. "You want I should go with Mr. Glass Eye? I got him with me."

"Nope," he told her.

They enjoyed the ride in companionable silence, which was something else Seth loved about Prynne. She was as happy quiet as she was talking. She didn't say much else till they got to Smugglers Cove Farm and Flowers. Seth signaled for the turn into the rutted drive, and Prynne looked around. "Super nice farm," she said.

He was about to drive on by the chicken barn when he saw that the doors were open. He knew that Hayley and her sisters were responsible for the chickens, so he pulled over.

Hayley, he saw when he entered with Prynne, was by herself. She was shoveling chicken droppings. She had on rubber boots, and a baggy sweatshirt overhung her jeans. Her glasses had slipped to the end of her nose, and her face was shiny with perspiration.

"Need some help?" he called.

She looked up. "Help from Brooke would be nice, but that's not happening."

"Got another shovel?"

"No way, Seth. It's disgusting in here." She came to join them. She said, "You're Hester Prynne Haring," to Prynne. "That's a very cool name, except when people ask where the *A* is."

"It's why I go by Prynne. The joke only goes so far."

"I hear you," Hayley said.

"We c'n help do something," Prynne told her. "Really."

"Yuck. No. I'm surprised you can even stand the smell."

"Well, it's organic."

"It definitely has that going."

The two girls laughed and Seth beamed at them. Hayley asked what they were up to. It was a lovely day despite the growing crisp cold of mid-autumn, and she said she wouldn't have minded spending some time outside herself. Seth said he didn't know what the heck they were going to do. "Hang," was how he put it. "See what's up," was Prynne's response.

"Got your fiddle with you?" Hayley asked. "'Cause I'd—"

Parker Natalia strode into the barn. He had a stormy look about him that Seth didn't much like, but he seemed to master it as he came in their direction. Seth and Prynne said hi. Hayley said nothing, but Seth could see that her face got stony.

"C'n I talk to you?" Parker said to Hayley. And he added with a glance at Seth, "Alone?"

Seth glanced between them. He felt Prynne take his hand. She said, "We'll take off, I guess. Hayley, if you get into Langley today, we might be playing at the Commons. Right, Seth?"

"Uh . . . right." Seth felt a gentle tug from Prynne, and she was leading him back the way they'd come. Behind him, he heard Parker say, "We've got some things to work out," and Hayley's reply of, "I don't think so."

Seth heard Parker swear and his antennae went up. Once they were outside, he said to Prynne, "You wait here, okay?" and he nodded at the barbed wire fence that ran along the field at the side of the chicken barn.

She said, "You sure? It looked sort of personal."

"That's what I'm afraid of."

When Seth got back to the barn door, he could hear them arguing, Hayley saying to Parker, "Oh please. The cigarette was right there in the sleeping bag and you might want to check her Facebook page sometime."

"*That's* what this is all about? I do one stupid thing with that loopy blonde—who came on to me like you wouldn't believe— and that's it."

"This isn't about what you did with Isis. This is about the fact that you lied. I don't care what you did with Isis, Parker. I don't care about where or how many times or anything else. I don't like liars and I don't want liars in my life."

"So you freaking called the *sheriff* on me? You had me dragged up to Coupeville and—"

"I didn't call the sheriff!"

"Oh sure, Hayley. If not you, then—"

Seth entered the barn. "It was me," he said. "And I didn't call him. I went to see him."

Parker swung around. His face was dark with anger. He said, "*What* the—"

"I told him he should look at you because of how long you've been on the island. From before the first fire, okay? Hayley didn't do anything at all except maybe care about you when she shouldn't have, from the sounds of it."

Parker stared at Seth. Then he turned to Hayley. He shook his head at both of them. "Jesus, I am *out* of here." He strode from the barn.

Hayley and Seth looked at each other. Hayley's cheeks were bright. She was still holding the shovel she'd been using when he and Prynne had entered the barn, and now she leaned her head against the handle.

He knew what she was feeling. He just didn't know what to do about it. So he said, "Man, I'm sorry, Hayl. I guess I blew it for you."

She shook her head but she didn't look up. "He blew it for himself." And then in a much lower voice, "I am so totally tired."

Seth went to her and put a hand on her shoulder. He said, "Lemme help you here."

"No. You take care of Prynne." She looked up. "Thanks for bringing her by, Seth. Things are right with you guys. Don't mess it up."

He nodded, but still he felt the tug of an old loyalty to her that he would always feel. He vowed to himself that he would do something somehow to make things better for Hayley.

Outside, Prynne was at the fence, hands on top of one of the posts and looking out into a field that rose on a slight but steady incline toward the great forest at the back of the property beyond the pond. When Seth joined her, she said, "Dude, this is one fine place. How come they're not doing something with it? Horses, sheep, cows, goats. Crops. It'd be great for crops."

Seth wasn't sure how to put things, so he settled on saying,

"Hayley's dad's in a bad way. So the rest of 'em—Hayley, her mom, and her little sisters—they're trying to keep things going, but it's hard. Everything went to hell in the last couple years." He sighed. "I wish I knew how to help 'em."

Prynne looked thoughtfully out at the field once again. Seth could tell she was considering something. But she didn't say what was on her mind. Instead, she shot him a look from beneath her eyebrows and said, "She's your ex, isn't she?"

Seth didn't say anything for a moment, but he felt the sour stomach of dread. He hadn't meant wrong in bringing Prynne to meet Hayley, but all of a sudden he could see how this side trip to Smugglers Cove Farm and Flowers might be interpreted. Still, remembering what was at the core of Hayley's dispute with Parker, he wasn't about to say anything less than the truth. He said, "She hasn't been for a while. My girlfriend. I mean she hasn't been my girlfriend for a while."

Prynne smiled. "Not a problem. I guess it's okay for you to want me to meet her. But you got to tell me these things in advance, okay? I don't like to be blindsided." And she added with a grin, "Especially since I'm already blind-sided."

She pointed to her eye patch and then she laughed. Seth grabbed her by the shoulders and kissed her soundly.

THEY WERE ON their way to Langley when they saw Brooke Cartwright, just outside of the town of Freeland. She was sitting at the side of the highway atop a large sack. Not far away was the biggest farmers' supply store on the island, so it was clear where she'd been if not what she was doing on the side of the road.

Seth said, "What the heck?" and pulled over. He stopped the car just beyond her.

Prynne said, "Who's that?" and he said, "Hayley's sister," as he got out and called, "Brooke! What're you doing here?"

Brooke slowly turned her head in his direction. Seth approached her. Behind him, he heard Prynne getting out of the car as well. He said to Brooke, "Whatcha doing? You waiting for your mom?"

Brooke shook her head. She seemed even more down-in-the-dumps than she'd been at any time in the past month. She said, "Waiting for the bus. I got chicken feed."

"How come Hayley didn't bring you? She was working in the barn. We were just there."

"Hayley's mad at me. She said no way was she driving me any-wheres. And anyway, I didn't *know.* It's not like I do things on purpose."

Seth glanced at Prynne for some kind of girl translation. Prynne shrugged. Seth said, "Well, get up off that bag. Me and Prynne c'n take you home."

"Hayley'll only get madder at me."

The poor kid sounded so disconsolate, that Seth extended his hand to her, said, "I ain't taking no for an answer," and when she took his hand and allowed herself to be drawn to her feet, he gave her an around-the-shoulders hug. To his surprise she started to cry.

"Hey, hey, hey!" Seth said. "*What's* going on?"

"D . . . d . . . dad," she sobbed. "He broke his arm. Hayley says it was 'cause I didn't pay attention when I was supposed to. We had to take him to the hospital and there's no insurance and I didn't . . ." She sobbed till she hiccupped.

Prynne touched the girl's shoulder, saying, "*'Course* you didn't and I bet she knows that. She was probably just ticked off and she said the first thing that came into her head."

"N . . . n . . . no. She hates me and it was my fault and everyone's mad and I try to be good. But she says *I* only think about myself and it's not true but when I eat stuff that I'm not s'posed to eat it's only only 'cause—"

"Whoa, it's okay," Seth said. He picked up the chicken feed and said, "You come with us, Brooke."

They urged her to the car and popped her inside. On the way to the farm, they got the story from Brooke, at least as far as Bill Cartwright went. Brooke gave the tale out in fits and starts, but when Seth began to make the turn into the farm, she begged him to let her out so that she could walk the rest of the way. He tried to tell her that Hayley wouldn't freak out if she knew that he'd given her a ride home, but Brooke wasn't convinced, and he finally relented.

She got out, and Seth put the bag of chicken feed into her arms. To him, it looked way too heavy for her to carry up to the chicken barn, but she was relentless. So he let her go, but he watched her progress. She stumbled once and he stopped himself from going to help her. All along, he wondered what the hell he could do.

Prynne got out of the car and they stood there together.

Halfway to the barn, Brooke paused, lowered the sack, sat down on it, and doubled over.

"She crying again?" Seth asked his girlfriend.

"I think something's wrong with her, Seth," Prynne said. "I think it's something bad and she doesn't want her family to know."

FIFTY

Becca's decision to tell Derric about his sister had to do with fairness. He had a right to the information.

She thought at first that she'd tell him on the phone. In that way she wouldn't be able to ease her way into his whispers. But that seemed totally spineless to her. So she waited till they were more or less alone together, but in a situation in which he would be able to see quite clearly that she had no intention of talking him into anything.

There was one special time of day that this could happen: early morning in the weight room at the school. There, Derric not only trained but also worked on strengthening the leg he'd broken so badly the previous year.

As it happened, only one other boy was there when Becca arrived, one of the football players who wore ear buds and an iPod hooked onto his shorts as he grunted through barbell training. Derric was doing bench presses. He didn't have a spotter, which was dumb, but Becca wasn't about to argue with him about that.

She went over to him and looked down at his face. She felt

what she always felt looking at him for the first time any day of the week: a warmth that spread all over her body. She thought what she always thought as well: How did I get so lucky? Her grandmother would have told her it was all about chemistry. You had it with some people. You didn't have it with others. From day one, Becca had had it with Derric. She still didn't know why.

She said, "Looking good, guy. How's it going? How's the leg?"

He shot her a smile. "How'd you get here so early?"

"Bike and bus and bike."

"You should've called me. I could've picked you up. We even could've stopped on the way. You know." He grinned. "Five minutes or something. Or ten. Or an hour."

"That wouldn't exactly be the way to get your leg in shape."

He replaced the weights on the rack above him, sat up, and swung his legs around. He reached for a towel and wiped himself down. He said, "Maybe not my leg. But my lips would have gotten a workout."

She laughed and sat down next to him. There was no way to go at things but directly. She said quietly, "Derric, listen. I've found Rejoice. She's on a farm in La Conner. It's called Broad Valley Growers, and she's been there for years. Since she was maybe four or five. She was adopted by a family, just like you were, only they've got—I don't know—maybe five kids? Six? But she's there and it's Rejoice. I saw her myself."

He was absolutely still. Becca wasn't sure what he was feeling or thinking and she was mightily tempted to jerk the AUD box's ear bud out of her ear so she could discover what was going on with him. But she held true to her purpose and did not do so, allowing him the privacy of his own thoughts.

He said, "How . . ."

She told him. She talked about the phone message that Ralph Darrow had given her, about Ralph Darrow's not even remembering for whom the message was meant, about setting off with Seth to try to find out if someone was trying to get in touch with her or with Parker or with Seth himself, about wondering if this had anything at all to do with the fires on the island for some reason, about discovering that no one at Broad Valley Growers knew a thing about a message at all. This wasn't the entire truth of the matter, but she couldn't bring herself to tell him more: about Laurel, about Jeff Corrie and Connor West, about the mess she herself had created back in San Diego. Telling him about Rejoice was enough.

"She came out of the barn with the rest of the kids," Becca said to him. "Derric, I could *tell* it was Rejoice. She looks just like a girl version of you."

Still, he didn't say a word. She thought that, perhaps, he was struggling to control his fury. Once again she'd intruded, he might have thought. But she *hadn't* this time, not really, and she wanted to bring this up. Still, she didn't do so. Instead she said, "So when I saw her, I went to Reverend Wagner." She saw his face alter, a hardening of his jaw, and she said, "I didn't say much to him other than to find out if he was the person who'd called and left the message with Mr. Darrow. He said yes." She told him the rest of what Reverend Wagner had revealed to her about how he'd traced Rejoice through the other branches of Children's Hope.

"I didn't ask too much about it 'cause it seemed to me that the most important part of everything was that Rejoice was adopted a long time ago." She waited for him to reply and when still he said nothing, she said, "Anyway." And then when the silence went on, "I just wanted you to know. And Reverend Wagner? He's not going to say anything about anything. I made him promise. But the thing is . . ." Derric shot her a look from beneath his eyebrows and Becca could read in that look his expectation of what she was about to say. He thought—and who could blame him after all the ways in which she'd blundered around in his life—that she was about to start preaching about all the wonderful things he could now do regarding his sister. But she said to him, "I just wanted you not to have to worry about her anymore, like where she is and if something bad happened to her because nothing bad did."

He nodded. He swallowed. She could hear it was tough for him to do so. She said, "Hey," and he looked at her then. She was struck to the quick by the expression on his face and in his eyes, which were all of a sudden liquid with tears. "The thing is this. I love you. I've got your back. Now and always."

She had the phone number of Broad Valley Growers with her. She had the mailing address as well. But she suddenly knew that this wasn't the moment to press either upon this boy. She understood that he was meant to find his own way and that he would.

BECCA WAS WORKING on a spaghetti and meatballs dinner when Seth arrived. Ralph was puttering in his shop, repairing a lamp that one of his multitudinous lady friends had brought to him. This particular lady friend was one of the island's many artists, a swarthy glass blower in serious overalls. She'd earlier tramped across Ralph's porch yelling, "Darrow! I need you to lookit this lamp. Get your butt out here 'cause I stepped in horseshit up my place and you don't want me treading inside your house, believe you me."

Ralph had been sitting at the kitchen table opening the day's mail. He murmured, "I swear. That Kathy Broadvent has always spoken pure poetry," and he'd gone outside to engage in a loud and arm waving conversation with the woman.

When Seth arrived, he asked about Parker, saying he wanted to talk to him and asking was he coming to dinner. Becca hadn't seen him but as his car was up in the parking area, she figured he was in the tree house. He'd be there for dinner, probably, she told Seth. She added the information about Dave Mathieson showing up to talk to him.

As things turned out, Seth knew all about that. He revealed that he was the person who'd given Dave Mathieson the information that had led him to speak to Parker in the first place. It all had to do with when Parker had arrived on Whidbey, Seth said, which was in advance of the first fire. He concluded with "So, well . . . I guess I told the undersheriff that. Like, about when Parker got here." *Maybe dumb, maybe not,* he added mentally.

Becca eyed him. "You 'guess' you told the undersheriff?"

"Okay. I *did* tell him. It seemed like it was the right thing to do once I figured out how long he'd been here. Only, you know, my motives weren't exactly pure. So then he thought that Hayley told the sheriff." *Do what's right . . . Prynne would want . . .*

Becca ignored this bit. She wanted, in fact, to ignore whispers altogether, so she wrestled with the AUD box. She turned the unit on and put the ear bud in place. "It's Isis," she told him.

"What's Isis?"

"She's why he thought Hayley told the sheriff." She sketched out the details: Isis, Parker, the tree house, the lies. "Sex," she concluded. "Parker and Isis doing the deed."

"So he did it with Isis and lied to Hayley?"

"Looks that way. Hayley said she was finished with him and he wants another chance and he asked me to talk to her."

"Heavy," Seth said. "Damn. Makes me wonder . . ."

"What?"

"What else might he lie about, Beck?"

As if ready to answer that question himself, Parker entered the house. He shed his jacket. He came toward the kitchen and then saw Seth. He seemed to hesitate. He locked eyes with Seth, and Becca saw that Seth was the one to look away once they gave each other that guy greeting of jerking their heads in a nod.

She said, "Hey," to Parker. She added, "You hungry? We got tons of food tonight," in a pleasant voice that tried to encourage conversation. "It's Italian, so you got to promise not to compare it to your family's restaurant."

Parker said, "Yeah," but that was it.

There was a long and uncomfortable silence during which a scratching upon the front door indicated Seth had brought Gus with him. Parker went to open it and the Lab bounded in, oblivious to any tension that existed in the room.

Seth finally broke the silence. "Look, man, I'm sorry if you got hassled by the sheriff. You got to see that the situation's serious. Someone's dead and someone else is responsible—"

"Conveniently not you," Parker cut in acidly.

"I was over town for two of the fires. But that's not the point 'cause this whole thing stopped being a prank back in August when the fairgrounds fire was set, and you and I both know you were parked in that campgrounds at the fair since when . . . July? So what was I supposed to do? Pretend I never knew that?"

"And since I was there in July, that makes me an arsonist?"

His words were angry and Becca intervened. "They took everyone's name that night at Maxwelton Beach, Parker. Everybody's being checked out."

Parker said, "It doesn't seem that way to me. But what the hell." He went to the table and sat. He played with the silverware at his place. Becca could see that he was upset. He said to her, "You talk to Hayley?"

She quirked her mouth regretfully. "I tried."

He said, "Whatever," and he blew out a breath. "Well, the sheriff and I more or less reached an 'understanding.'" He made quotation marks in the air. "I'm outa here. 'Cause despite what Hayley appears to think, the cops think otherwise."

"You're clear?" Seth said. "Good."

Parker's expression indicated he believed Seth's declaration pretty much the same way he believed anyone *but* Jesus could walk on water. He said, "The only thing that saved me turned out to be that I've never been to California in my life. This is, apparently, some big deal to the sheriff."

"California?" Becca said. "What's that got to do . . . ?" But her words drifted off as she began to see what California might have to do with everything. She turned back to the stove and stirred the sauce.

Parker said, "I was also invited to leave the U.S. of A. as the sheriff had a look at the ol' passport and saw I've more or less overstayed my welcome. So . . ." He regarded them both. "It's been great knowing you. All of you."

Seth said, "You can't blame Hayley."

"Whatever. She doesn't want to listen. I tried to call her again but all she wants to talk about now is some damn ring, like I proposed to someone and she wants to know who."

Becca's senses went on the alert. "Ring?"

"Did I keep a ring, did I find a ring, did Isis give me a ring, where was the ring, who's got the ring." Parker waved his arm to dismiss the subject.

"Sounds like it's a big deal," Seth put in.

"Maybe to her but not to me," Parker announced.

PART VI
Maxwelton Beach 2

FIFTY-ONE

Becca knew it wasn't rocket science to figure out that a ring was probably important in the fire investigation. She'd already picked up all sorts of variations on "the ring" in Hayley's whispers and Isis's whispers.

She wanted to talk to Squat and Jenn about it. She found the chance she needed when her English 10 class broke into groups so that the students could evaluate each other's essays. They'd had to write on the topic of femininity in Shakespeare's *Macbeth*. "Like there *is* any femininity in *Macbeth*?" Squat scoffed in an aside. "Witches and the She-Wolf of Scotland? Puhleez." But as was typical for Squat, he'd written a great essay. Becca and Jenn made short work of informing him that it was perfect before Becca told them about the ring.

She lowered her voice and made a pretense of marking Jenn's essay—"Hey! Go easy on that!" Jenn protested—as they talked.

"A ring keeps coming up," she said. "Hayley, Isis, Parker . . . Everyone's into it."

Squat went right to the fires. "What about a signature on a crime scene? Like a bomber who makes a bomb the same way every time." He considered this and added, "Is it a signet ring? The kind they used to seal up letters with? They poured wax on the letters and smooshed the ring into the wax and that's how you knew the letter was from the person it said it was from."

Jenn looked at him askance. "So the arsonist is leaving his mark? Like a *Z* for Zorro? Why'd he want to do that?"

"To get caught. They always want to get caught."

"If it has to do with the fires," Becca said, "doesn't it make more sense that it's a clue that the arsonist doesn't even know got left there? Like the ring got dropped somehow and the investigators found it."

"How did it get dropped? It was too big and fell off someone's finger?" Jenn asked.

"Or," Becca said, "the person in question wasn't wearing it at all."

"I don't get what you mean."

"I mean it was *put* there. On purpose. It was *taken* there, like, in someone's pocket. To make someone else look guilty when it got found at the crime scene."

"Great. So how d'we figure who had a ring?"

"I'm not sure. But I think . . . 'cause I think I remember . . ." But what Becca remembered was something she couldn't speak about: Parker's memory pictures. A ring could have been what he'd been reaching for on the chain around Isis's neck. And if Isis had left it behind in the tree house, that put the ring into *Parker's* possession. And if *that* was the case . . .

She hated to think ill of the young Canadian. But even more she hated the idea that someone had died because of a fire. Truth to tell, she didn't really want to point an accusing finger at anyone. But then she thought of the whispers—the very *fact* of the whispers in her life—and she thought of the quickening and above all she thought of Diana Kinsale and what Diana might have told her to do.

She said, "We need to know if there's really and truly a ring in evidence."

Jenn said, "Great. How d'we do that?"

"We don't," Becca said.

"Then who . . . ?"

"Derric."

FIFTY-TWO

Hayley had to tell Isis about the ring. That meant she also had to tell Isis about betraying Aidan to the fire chief. She didn't want to do either, but what choice did she have? There was too much at stake.

She asked Isis to meet her in the band room during lunch. She looked frightened, and Hayley couldn't blame her. The call for privacy had signaled something was up.

Hayley told her about talking to Karl Levitt. She steeled herself for an Isis reaction: the accusation of betrayal that she figured she deserved. Before it could come, though, she gave her the news about Brady's ring, about Karl Levitt and the undersheriff talking about it on the phone. She ended with, "It was there, Isis. Brady's ring was there."

"Where?" Isis asked.

"At the fishing shack, at the fire. The undersheriff has it and he traced it—"

"How?"

"I don't know. It says it's from a university, doesn't it? Are there initials inside? If there are, some ring company would have done the engraving. How hard could it be to trace back from the university to the engraver to the initials to who ordered that ring with those initials? *Are* there initials?"

"BAD3," she said.

"Bad three? Huh?"

"Bradley Anthony Davenport the third," Isis whispered. "Brady—my Brady—he's actually Bradley. Bradley Anthony Davenport the fourth. But it *has* to be . . ." Her voice faded off.

"What?"

"Hayley, I can't remember a thing about that ring. The only thing I can think of is that I must have left it in the tree house that night. Parker found it after I left and he knew it was mine and he figured he could . . . He didn't want to be with me. But I kept coming on to him and he didn't know how else to get rid of me."

Hayley said, "You know that's not how it happened. You know Aidan took that ring. He left it at the shack when he set the fire to make it look like you—"

"That's not true! He's my brother! And now everything's ruined because the sheriff knows. He called Grandam last night and then *she* called my parents and she asked questions and they had to tell her and now she knows too and she went berserk because of what it could all have meant with her not knowing and having all this . . . this *stuff* lying around all the time, stuff he could've set fire to." Pathetically, Isis began to cry. She paced hopelessly back and forth.

Hayley stared at her dumbly. "Isis, I don't get . . . Your grandma didn't know what?"

"The fires. Aidan. She never knew."

"Oh my God. Are you saying that she never knew that Aidan started fires? How could she not *know*? He's her grandson!"

"Because it all happened so far away. My mom didn't tell her. And she doesn't follow what's going on in Palo Alto. She *hates* California. She doesn't want to know what's happening there."

"But didn't she wonder why he went to that special school in Utah?"

"They told her it was all about Robbie. And it *was*. Aidan was grieving so bad and he never stopped grieving and . . . Maybe they told her he was into drugs in Palo Alto or he was drinking or something but they never said fires. It's all so stupid."

"What is?"

"That they don't want people to know. So I'm up here with him and I'm s'posed to cover for him and I can't *do* it anymore and I want to go home." She wept bitterly at that point, and it wasn't the controlled weeping from before but rather something that looked more like she was going to head right into extended hysterics. She cried, "He's the only brother I have left. I have to find him, Hayley."

"But you also have to see that Aidan's the only one who—"

"No!" Isis advanced on her. "You listen to me. I *must* have had that ring on that night. I thought I stopped wearing it earlier but I must not have done that. I *must* have kept it on and worn it the night of the party and when Parker and I were making out . . . We were on the beach over by some driftwood and okay so things got carried away but I must've lost it then. That's what happened." Her face was alight. "And Parker took it *then*! He took the ring and he left it at the fire and—"

"You're trying to talk yourself into something you know isn't true," Hayley told her, and for the first time she felt close to tears herself. "Look at the facts. I know you want Aidan to be okay but he isn't okay and he's probably on his way to do God only knows what right now. No one is safe unless he gets found."

Isis looked wild-eyed. "Then we have to find him." She jumped to her feet and ran out of the room.

FIFTY-THREE

Becca found Derric having his regular once-a-week Big Brother afternoon with Josh Grieder at the Cliff Motel. They were in the living room behind the motel office, in the midst of constructing a serious *Tyrannosaurus rex* from Legos.

Josh, always generous with his Derric time when it came to Becca's intruding on it, said that sure, Becca could borrow Derric. But *only* for five minutes 'cause they had serious work to do.

Derric rubbed Josh's head and went with Becca back through the office and outside to stand beneath the porch's overhang. It had begun to rain. The weather was bringing winter now. The days were shorter, colder, and wetter.

"We need to go to Coupeville," Becca told him.

"Say what?"

"We need to go to your dad's office. We've got to get into the evidence files on the fire at Maxwelton Beach."

Derric took her arm and led her along the line of rooms, and all the way to the end of the porch, which looked out onto Camano Street and the community arts center on the other side. "Spill," he said.

Becca told him that it was looking like a ring was involved in the Maxwelton fire. "I keep hearing about it," was how she put it. "Hayley and Isis? They're, like, all over the subject, Derric."

"You think one of *them* set the fires? Not exactly Hayley's style, Becca. That leaves Isis. But why?"

"Don't know. Hayley keeps saying she's got some hot boyfriend in Palo Alto. Maybe she wants Aidan sent back to Utah so she can go home to him."

"Or maybe Aidan's doing it to get *her* carted off to jail."

"Or maybe Parker's doing it 'cause him and Isis hooked up and he doesn't know how else to get rid of her. Point is, though, that we need to see *if* there's a ring in evidence in the first place, so we need to go to Coupeville."

"I could just ask my dad if—"

"Your dad's not going to tell you anything till the case is solved. And maybe not even then 'cause there'll be a trial, right? So we need to go to his office, and then we need to get to the files. I don't have a clue how we c'n do this but we have to try. The question is: C'n we do it soon?"

"Oh, it's way easier than that," Derric told her.

Josh came outside. He put his hands on his hips the way his grandmother did when she was miffed. He said, "Hey, you guys! Five minutes is five minutes!"

"Coming, bro," Derric said. "Let me kiss my girl."

"Yuck! I don't want to see *that*." Josh ducked back inside.

Derric smiled and turned back to Becca. He said, "I'll call Mom. You're coming to dinner. Dad always logs on to his work after dinner. He says it helps to recap the day. We'll do something that'll get him out of his study—"

"Like what? Set a fire?" Becca asked sardonically.

"Like I'll figure it out. But when we do it, you be ready. You'll go into his study and read the file and then you'll know. It'll work, trust me. There are certain distractions that he can't resist. I just have to choose the best one."

THE BEST TURNED out to be Mexican Train dominoes. Derric sweetened the pot of his suggestion that they have a tournament of five rounds after dinner by declaring that if Dave's was the lowest score at the end of those rounds, Derric would detail one of the family's two cars. Dave's reaction was to rub his hands together, say, "Boy oh boy. You set it up and give a yell when it's ready," after which he disappeared into his study, just as Derric had declared he would.

"Mom and I do the dishes," Derric had told Becca, "and that's when he reviews his cases. He'll leave the computer on and he'll still be logged in. The rest is gonna be up to you."

Becca thought she could manage it. She'd never played Mexican Train dominoes, but it was easy enough to learn. She and Derric set the game up in a location as far as possible from Dave's office. This was in the sun room at the back of the house.

Becca discovered that Derric knew his dad pretty well. Dave Mathieson was a take-no-prisoners player. So was Derric, and Rhonda wasn't far behind. A lot of laughter, joking, yelling, and arguing about the rules accompanied each round. And each round was long enough that Becca could see it wasn't going to take much effort to find an appropriate moment to fade out of the room and into Dave's study at the far end of the house.

She declared herself hopeless at the game when they got to the third round. She said, "What's my score, Derric?"

He looked at the sheet of paper on which he'd been tallying the numbers. He winced. "Babe, you're in a class all your own. It's two hundred twenty-four."

"Yikes. I better watch a round to see what I'm doing wrong."

"Just about everything," Dave advised her. "You sit with me if you want to see the master at work."

Sitting with Dave was what Becca did. They were well into the fourth round when she excused herself for a call of nature. The competition among them was intense enough that she felt fairly certain she would have all the time she needed to see what was on Dave's computer.

As Derric had said it would be, the laptop that Dave carried with him in the sheriff's car was on his desk. It was still switched on and bringing it out of sleep mode was all it took.

It opened to an entire list of files rather than merely the one that Becca wished to see. She scanned them as fast as she could and finally found the file when she saw the title *Maxwelton Beach.* But when she opened it, she discovered that it was far larger than she'd expected it to be. All of the interviews had been recorded. All of the photographs of the scene had been included. There was nothing that bore the telling title of *Evidence* or *Clues* that she could see. She clicked on the photographs.

There were two hundred and fifty-four. No way did she have time to look at them all. She murmured, "Damn, damn, damn," and ran her gaze over the thumbnails of them as fast as she dared.

"Hey! Beckster!" Dave Mathieson called from the sun room. "You fall in or something? I'm having a very good game and if you want to learn—"

"He's bullshitting you, Becca," Derric cut in. "Take your time while I clean his clock."

Becca rose from Dave's study chair and listened hard at the door. The game seemed to be resuming. She went back to his desk. She went back to the pictures.

She heard Rhonda say, "You better check, sweetie. She might be sick."

And from Dave, "Is this a setup, you two? I'm destroying you and—"

"Don't be silly. Your turn, Derric. I'll check."

Damn damn double damn, Becca thought. She heard the scrape of a chair. She heard Rhonda call her name. She heard Derric call his mom back. But she knew she had only an instant or two left.

She scrolled desperately. She gazed. She felt on the edge of panic. All of them were talking loudly in the sun room now and she didn't have time to wonder how Derric was going to keep his mom and dad where they were because she was so frantic to—

She *found* it. A wheelbarrow had been upended next to the

woodpile across from the fisherman's shack. The first photo of it showed its entirety. The second showed its handles against a moldy pile of wood. A third gave Becca information she could use. It showed only the single wheel of the wheelbarrow and in front of this wheel lay, unmistakably, a man's large ring.

DERRIC DROVE HER home. She told him exactly where the ring had been. "It was pretty much out in the open," she said. "In the *open*, Derric, like it was no mistake. It has to have been planted."

"I dunno, babe. It was a man's ring? You sure?"

"It looked like . . . I think it was maybe from a college 'cause it was so big."

"But that doesn't necessarily mean that someone planted it there, does it?"

"Not someone. It can't be just someone. It has to be Aidan or Parker."

He continued with his thought. "You said it was near the woodpile, right? Next to a wheelbarrow, yes?" He glanced at her and she nodded. He said, "So if someone planted it, wouldn't that person have put it closer to where the fire started? 'Cause with it at a distance from the fire, it could mean anything."

"Which means . . . what?" She answered her own question. "That a ring by a wheelbarrow doesn't prove a thing." She slumped back against the Forester's seat. She went on with, "We're nowhere, I guess. Unless . . ." And there it was again, that image she'd seen of Parker Natalia reaching for something that hung from a chain around Isis's neck. So quickly had it come and gone as a mental picture that Becca might have forgotten it altogether at some point had Hayley and Isis not been so caught up in whispers about a ring. "Derric," she said, "what if there's something else?"

"Where?" They were heading up East Harbor Road, driving along the huge boot-shaped body of water that was Holmes Harbor. This would take them into the town of Freeland. They'd double back on the highway from there to get to Ralph Darrow's place. Traffic was light, but the rain was insistent.

"At the fire scene," Becca told him. "What if there's a broken chain as well?"

"In the evidence, you mean?"

"Just think about it. If you're wearing a chain with something on it and the chain breaks—"

"The ring falls off," he finished, seeing where she was heading.

"Sure. And you don't know the chain even broke 'cause you're in a hurry—"

"To start a fire and clear out of there."

"But that chain might get caught up in your clothes. And if what's on the chain is heavy enough—"

"It falls to the ground but the chain goes nowhere."

"Not at first. It would take a while. Maybe way after the ring got lost. And even then, you wouldn't notice what's going on with a dumb chain 'cause there are cops everywhere and people are yelling and other people are trying to run . . ."

"Which means that if there *is* a chain, it's either in a different picture from the ring—"

"Or it's still out there somewhere. See what I mean?"

"Not only good looking and sexy as hell, but you're a frigging genius," he told her.

"We need to see if there's a chain," was what she told him.

FIFTY-FOUR

It was Seth's idea to use the metal detector. While he tracked one down, Becca brought Jenn and Squat into the plan to search for the chain Isis Martin had been wearing on the night of the party. Typical of Squat Cooper, he had a grid system for conducting a search developed within minutes.

The military town of Oak Harbor at the north end of the island proved to be the location of the nearest metal detector. When he'd targeted it, Seth went up to rent it, and the plan was put into place. They didn't have a pile of hours prior to darkness falling, so everyone needed to bring a flashlight, Squat told them.

At Maxwelton Beach, they left their cars at the baseball diamond that defined Dave Mackie Park, and they picked their way to the party house via the beach. The scene of the fire having been thoroughly investigated by the sheriff's department, that property was no longer sealed off with police tape, so they climbed through the shrubbery and began their search.

Seth used the metal detector. The rest walked their assigned grids, taking the landscape inch by inch. The metal detector went crazy with all the trash that was on the property: everything from tin cans to rusty nails to discarded tools and keys. But other than that, it was mostly garbage.

They moved from there to the party property, being careful all the while to watch for anyone who might be observing them, with one hand on the phone ready to dial the cops. But as on the fateful night, there were no signs of life in the house where they'd partied and none in the nearest property to it, so they managed to search without being accosted by an understandably suspicious neighbor. When they were finished, they met out in front. No one had come up with a thing aside from beer bottle tops, a rusty political button from an ancient election, half a pair of scissors, two empty tuna cans, three bottle openers, and another button—less rusty—celebrating the Maxwelton Fourth of July parade that was a special feature of this part of the island.

They gathered in a circle. The weather had turned. It was very cold, and rain was threatening. They huddled into their fleeces and hoodies to figure out what it meant that there was no chain to be found.

"We don't know for sure she was even wearing a chain in the first place, do we?" Seth offered this. He leaned against the metal detector and pulled his fedora more firmly down on his head against the chill.

Becca said, "Not exactly. Only . . ." They all looked at her expectantly, but how could she tell them what she'd seen of Parker and Isis in her mind? She couldn't, so she said instead, "It's the only thing that'll help us out. If she had a chain on that night and if it was mostly under her clothes—"

"She wears a chain at school," Squat put in. "I've seen it."

"You? When?" Jenn asked.

"She shows a lot of . . . you know . . . like . . . chest," Squat said. "And this chain, it sort of goes down between her boobs and . . . You know." He ignored their hoots of laughter and said, "Come *on.* You've seen it. I bet if we looked at Facebook right now—"

"Yeah, there's been a chain," Derric admitted. And then to Becca, "Hey, I'm a guy."

"What*ever,*" she responded.

Jenn said, "So if this *alleged* chain broke and fell off her at some point, wouldn't she have noticed when she got home? And wouldn't she have sneaked back to look for it?"

"Not if she didn't know where she lost it," Becca told her. But she had to add silently, And not if Parker removed it from her at some point back in the tree house and hung on to it as well.

Derric snapped his fingers at this and said, "We're forgetting the march."

Becca picked up on his thought. "Oh my God. Yes. To the church. What is it, a mile?"

"Which means Isis could've lost the chain along the way," Seth said.

WITH THE METAL detector, Seth was the one who finally found the chain. They had all spread out across the road, which, thankfully, was narrow enough that the five of them comprised a sufficient number to handle its width. The difficult part was the road's shoulders, which were thick with weeds and the last of the summer grasses, now dying in preparation for winter. As the kids inched along, the metal detector signaled substances of interest time and again. It was only when they were about one hundred yards from the intersection where the church stood that the detector signaled the real thing.

By that time, it was dark and they'd been conducting their search by flashlight. The metal detector beeped and Becca went to Seth as usual and shone her flashlight onto the area of interest. This time something glittered in a rut made by the tires of a car, and that something was Isis Martin's chain.

"We got it!" Becca called out.

"Don't touch it!" This from Squat. "You're never supposed to touch evidence."

They gathered around, looking down at the chain. After a few minutes of discussion, they settled on calling Derric's dad and hoping he wasn't all the way up in Coupeville. If he was in his office there, they would have one hell of a wait for him in the cold and the darkness.

Derric had his cell phone out and was calling his father when Squat came up with the next plan. Since they were going to have to wait for Dave Mathieson to show up, it made sense for Seth and Derric to go back to Dave Mackie Park—some distance back down Maxwelton Road—and bring their cars up while the rest of them "guarded the evidence," as he put it. At least that way they wouldn't have to hike back down there once whatever was going to go down with Isis Martin went down with Isis Martin.

"Like her getting carted off to jail," Jenn said.

This sounded sensible once they learned that, while Dave Mathieson wasn't still up in Coupeville, he was at the café at Greenbank Farm, a repurposed group of agricultural buildings sitting on an expanse of acreage that had been saved from developers some time in the past. Now it was a place of community gatherings, with a café that offered the best pies on the island. Dave had been purchasing one of those pies on Rhonda's orders, but he'd "get down to Maxwelton and see what you kids've found ASAP," he told Derric.

That meant the wait that they'd anticipated, so Seth and Derric started the hike back to the Dave Mackie Park for their cars. Squat, Jenn, and Becca found places to sit just off the road. It was going to be at least a thirty-minute wait, so they huddled together to stay warm. At least when Derric and Seth brought the cars up from the beach, they could wait inside them. For now, there was no shelter but their hoodies and each other. And, of course, it began to rain.

This time, it was no misty island precipitation but instead a real downpour. Jenn swore, Becca groaned, and Squat manfully put his arms around both of them. The wind came up. It creaked through the fir trees that climbed the hillside on the west side of the road. From the alders and maples, it blew leaves which quickly became sodden, forming a slick mat on the surface of the road where pools of rainwater were going to make each curve trickier to negotiate.

"This is just great," Jenn groused.

"Hey, it's romantic," Squat told her. "The dark, the wind, the rain, two damsels in distress."

"Puh-leez." She sighed.

"I guess that means you don't want me to nuzzle your neck?"

"Like I want a potato peeler up my butt."

"That's totally gross," he told her.

"I believe you've caught my point, little man."

Becca had been using the AUD box during the search, the better to concentrate on what she was doing without picking up whispers from her friends. But now she took the ear bud from her ear and disengaged it from the box itself. She removed the whole little unit from the waistband of her jeans and tucked it into the pocket of her jacket.

"See?" Squat said. "You've grossed out Becca, too. She doesn't want to hear another foul image emanating from your mouth."

But the truth was that Becca had decided on a period of practice while they waited. With Jenn and Squat, who was thinking what would be clear. Potentially, their whispers would be complete.

Jenn and Squat continued their verbal sparring while Becca listened in on their whispers. Squat's were about sex. A guy, sixteen years old, what else would you expect, Becca concluded. Jenn's were about soccer: the captain of their team, a senior girl called Cynthia Richardson, the locker room, showers, Cynthia's body, and . . . Becca glanced at her friend in the darkness, seeing only her profile in the dim light that came from a driveway nearby. It came to her that Jenn was thinking about sex as well, although she shifted from that to her ultra-religious mother and what was going to befall her—Jenn—when she finally told the truth.

Life was complicated, Becca thought. She wanted to tell Jenn that everything would all work out because it usually did. Only . . . she wasn't sure that was really the case.

Car lights came from the direction of the beach. The three of them rose in the pouring rain. Jenn stepped into the road and so did the others. Jokingly, they spread out to form a blockade that Seth and Derric would have to obey.

Except it turned out that there was only one car, not two. And the car was neither Seth's VW nor Derric's Forester. It was a Nissan sedan, and given no choice in the matter, it had to slow and then stop. The driver lowered the window, and Isis Martin's voice called out brightly, "Hey! What're you guys doing here?" She sounded friendly enough but her whispers cursed *god damn little bitches*, which unnerved Becca for a moment. Then she caught . . . *happening . . . Mom and Dad? . . . no I won't not again . . . that place* and it came to her that Isis wasn't alone in the car. Aidan had to be with her although he wasn't in sight.

Becca took a chance and called out, "Why's Aidan hiding? Where're you guys going?"

"Excuse me?" Isis looked around innocently. "Aidan's not—"

"He's in the back seat or he's in the trunk or he's just ducked down, Isis," Becca told her.

"And it doesn't matter 'cause the game's over, hot mama," Jenn put in. "We called the sheriff and you're about to be toast." Then she called out, "Hey, Aidan, if you're in there? It's olly-olly-ox-in-free for you. Big sister here set the fire at the shack and probably all the others, too. We know it, she knows it, and the sheriff's about to know it too 'cause we got the evidence and he's on his way to get it."

Becca winced at the flurry of whispers that came at her then because Isis was swearing at Jenn but so was Squat. She would have sworn at Jenn, too, if she hadn't been trying to maintain enough cool among them to keep Isis from taking off in the rain. As it was now, Isis gunned her car's motor as next to her Aidan rose in the passenger's seat and said, "What the *hell*?" to no one in particular.

Just then, the lights of two other cars approached from the direction of the beach. That, at last, would be Seth and Derric. Isis appeared to see them in her rear view mirror because she gunned the engine another time and said, "Get out of the road, you guys."

"Like, where d'you think you're actually going?" Jenn demanded. "This is an island, dummy. And the sheriff's coming."

"Get out of the freaking *way*," Isis cried.

Aidan said to her, "You God damn told me . . ." but instead of finishing, he leaped out of the car. "What the hell, Isis? *You* . . . Because all this time . . . And with Mom and Dad . . . and you were just waiting . . ." He pounded his fist against the rooftop of the car.

"Get back in," Isis ordered.

"Don't do it, man," Squat said.

"Shut your mouth!" Isis screamed.

And the rain fell harder.

Seth and Derric pulled their cars up behind her. Derric got out. He said, "What's going on?"

"What's going on is Isis trying to get her brother arrested and sent to jail or back to his school or whatever so that she can go back to her frigging stupid Palo Alto and run for homecoming queen," Jenn said. "Only what she doesn't know because she's so stupid is—"

Isis floored the accelerator. Squat grabbed Jenn and pulled her to him. Becca jumped out of the way. Isis shot through them like a projectile from a cannon. Without a word, Derric ran back to his car.

BECCA TORE AFTER him. Seth, stepping out of his VW, shouted, "What the hell's going—" as Jenn and Squat stormed him, yelling, "Go, go, go!" They climbed inside as Squat cried out, "We got to be able to tell the sheriff—" He slammed the door closed and cut off the rest of his words.

Aidan, looking stunned, remained on the side of the road, just out of the cones of illumination cast by the headlights of the two cars. He cried out, "You can't—" but the rest of his words were also cut off once Becca crashed her car door closed. Derric hit the gas and they shot after Isis with Seth's VW coming up behind them.

Isis, they saw, was screaming along Maxwelton Road. Ahead

of them she careered through the intersection where the old wooden church stood among the trees. She made a sharp and sudden left onto a road called Sills. Her car slid but she righted it. She hit the gas and sent up a spray of water.

"Damn," Derric said. "She's completely nuts. Where's she going?"

Like most roads on Whidbey, Sills was unlit. It dug deeply into the forest like a landscape scar. In the pouring rain, the cedars were dropping massive amounts of foliage onto the pavement. Alders bent forward, shedding leaves. Douglas firs got whipped by sudden gusts of wind.

The falling rain reflected the Forester's headlights right into the windshield. Ahead of them, they could see the taillights of Isis's car, but not much else. Derric said, "Babe, I'm thinking this isn't—" but that's all he got out when it happened.

The road curved but Isis had not slowed. On the slick pavement, she slid. She overcorrected. She spun the car. It shot off the road at tremendous speed. It smashed head-on into a telephone pole. It burst into flames.

Derric stamped on the brakes. His car also went into a slide as well. Becca felt him instinctively reach out his right arm to keep her safe. He knew enough about skidding to release the brakes as behind him Seth honked frantically as if in warning.

They came to a stop. Seth, Jenn, and Squat were already out of the VW and hurtling toward the fiery mass of metal that was Isis's car.

"Get her out!" Derric yelled.

Flames shot up the telephone pole, and the rain was not enough to douse them. The car itself was completely engulfed. Squat was the one who shouted, "No way can you get her! Keep back!"

"Oh my God!" This was from Jenn. She turned to Becca and covered her face.

"It's bad," from Seth.

"Nine-one-one," from Squat.

And the air was filled with the *whoosh* of flames and the anguished whispers of terrified kids as they all fell back and away, and shakily Derric punched the numbers into his cell phone to bring them help.

FIFTY-FIVE

At Smugglers Cove Farm and Flowers, Seth sat in his VW for a couple of minutes. He'd never been at the scene of someone's death before. The fire chief had told them that she'd probably been killed right when her car hit the telephone pole, so she hadn't even known she was trapped. But that was very small consolation.

The fire trucks had arrived within ten minutes, but it had seemed like an hour. As people who lived in the forest along Sills Road rushed down their unpaved driveways to see what the commotion was, the volunteer firemen doused the flames. Derric's dad had shown up, and an ambulance had come. Through it all Seth asked himself if he could have done anything different.

There were lots of if onlys in his head. If only they hadn't been at Maxwelton looking for the chain. If only Jenn, Squat, and Becca hadn't been blocking the road. If only they'd just let Isis pass by, no matter where she was going. If only he and Derric hadn't decided to chase after her.

Now, he had to tell Hayley. Isis Martin had been her friend, and Seth knew he couldn't put Hayley in the position of discovering what had occurred when she got to school the next day. So he heaved open the car door and trudged up the path to the farmhouse's front door. It was long after dinner but the lights were still on and he found the family in the living room playing Clue. Hayley wasn't with them—too much homework—but she came downstairs when her mom called up for her.

When Seth asked if he could talk to her, she looked concerned. She could tell from his tone, he figured. She said, "What's wrong? Your grandpa's okay, isn't he?"

"Grand's cool," Seth told her. "This's something different."

He jerked his head toward the front of the house. Hayley followed him onto the porch. She shivered but he figured it wasn't exactly from the cold. When they were at the far end of the porch overlooking the fields and the chicken barn below, he told her. He gave it all to her as he'd learned it from Becca, Derric, Squat, and Jenn, and then from a freaked-out and sobbing Aidan Martin. He didn't know how much she already knew, how much Isis had told her, or what Isis had claimed. So he started with Aidan and Wolf Canyon Academy and when she told him she knew all about that and why Aidan had been sent there, he skipped to the ring. This, it turned out, she knew about, too. So he told her about Becca's conclusions that they needed to search for a chain that might have held a ring and might have been broken during the Maxwelton party.

"We found it. Then Isis showed up," he said. "Jenn more or less mouthed off at her and Aidan jumped out of the car."

"*Aidan* was there?" Hayley said.

"Sure. Why?"

She told him about Isis's claim that her brother had run away in advance of their parents coming up to get him. She ended with, "But d'you think he was there all the time? At home?"

"She might've just wanted you to *think* he'd run away. To get you on her side even more. 'Cause that would make him look guilty, wouldn't it? Only thing we can't figure out for sure is why."

"Why what?" Hayley moved to the porch railing and was staring out into the darkness, the light from the house touching only her hair.

"Why Isis did all this in the first place. Geez, does she . . . Did she hate him or something?"

"Aidan?" Hayley turned back to him. Seth saw that her face was drawn and weary.

"Why else would she want him to go down for a bunch of fires anyway?"

"Because she wanted to go back to Palo Alto," Hayley said. "He'd messed up her entire senior year. He'd caused her boyfriend to break up with her. Her parents made her come up here to make sure he was cured but she wanted to go home. What better way . . . ?" Hayley covered her mouth with her fingertips.

Seth wasn't sure what to do. He got the impression from Hayley's reactions and from what she said that Isis had pretty much hooked Hayley like a fish and reeled her in. He felt bad about this, but it wasn't Hayley's fault. She was just a nice person who tried to be friends with some girl who didn't know what friendship was.

IT WAS THE idea of doing something about lies that prompted him to seek out Brooke Cartwright. The next day he finished work early, so he took off for Langley. He intercepted the girl outside of the middle school.

He was standing next to his car and he had Gus with him. Brooke smiled when she saw the golden Lab. Seth said to her, "We got an appointment. Get in," and he was relieved when Brooke assumed it had to do with the dog.

She wasn't happy when he pulled into the Langley clinic's parking lot, on Second Street in the village. She was even less happy when he came around to her side of the car, opened her door, and said, "Gus, you stay." She crossed her arms and narrowed her eyes. She accused him of kidnapping her, to which he said, "Right, kid. It's my new career. Come with me and don't make me carry you 'cause believe me I'll be happy to if that's gonna be what it takes."

"I don't want—"

"This is on me and no one's gonna know. Unless someone has to know. Got it?"

"But—"

"Nope." He put his arm around her shoulders and he gave her a squeeze. "I know you're scared. I know you don't want to cause trouble at home. But you got to trust me. We're gonna work everything out."

"Nothing works out."

"This will."

Seth had phoned the clinic, so Rhonda Mathieson was expecting them. She saw Brooke and said, "Here you are! Come with me, young lady," and she took the girl with her.

That was when Seth called Hayley. She started to protest. He said, "I'm paying, Hayley. There's something wrong besides her just being thirteen years old. Brooke knows it, but she doesn't want to say because of your dad and all the troubles and no insurance and no money and, geez, Hayl. You know all this. So I'm getting Mrs. Mathieson to look her over. If something's wrong with her we c'n at least all sit down and figure out what to do. Which we can't as long as you guys keep mum about everything going on in your lives."

He thought she'd hung up on him when there was only silence that greeted his remarks. But then he heard a little gasp which he knew was a stifled sob which he also knew would humiliate Hayley. He said, "It'll be cool, Hayl. And I'll bring her home," but only the second part could he be sure of.

FIFTY-SIX

Hayley had heard the expression "her heart in her mouth," but she'd never really thought about what it meant until she watched her mother on the phone with Rhonda Mathieson. When Seth had called her with the announcement about Brooke, she'd been furious with him at first. But she'd also assumed that Seth would have already returned Brooke to the farm when she herself arrived home. When Brooke hadn't shown up by the time her mom got back from her house cleaning day, Hayley was actually sick to her stomach with dread.

She didn't have the first clue what to tell her mom, but that didn't matter as things turned out because not ten minutes after Julie Cartwright arrived and before she wondered anything at all about Brooke, Rhonda Mathieson called. Hayley was the one to answer the phone. When she handed it over to her mom, she felt anxiety grip her like a cold fist.

When Julie replaced the receiver in its cradle, she stood there looking at it. Her shoulders were drooping.

Hayley said to her, "What is it?"

"Rhonda thinks Brooke has a bleeding ulcer. She'll need some tests at the hospital and an appointment with a gastro . . . a gastro-whatever-it-is."

Hayley lowered herself to one of the kitchen chairs. She murmured more to herself than to her mom, "But why didn't she . . . why wouldn't she . . . No wonder."

"Yes. No wonder," Julie Cartwright said.

RHONDA MATHIESON DROVE Brooke home. She brought her personally, rather than let Seth return her because Brooke was "making things a little tough for herself," as Rhonda put it.

Brooke ran up the stairs when she came into the house. Rhonda watched her go. Julie went to Rhonda. She took Rhonda's arms above the elbow in a half-hug kind of gesture, and said, "I don't know what to say."

Rhonda patted her hand. "Is there some place we can sit? Is Bill here, by the way? He might want to—"

"I haven't told him yet." Julie Cartwright indicated the living room and its ancient sofa. "It's all a bit difficult right now."

Hayley was watching all this from the doorway to the kitchen, and she found that she wanted to yell and punch the wall. A *bit* difficult? she wanted to shout at her mom. But instead she offered Rhonda Mathieson the only thing they had to offer anyone, which was a cup of tea or instant coffee or water. Rhonda smiled at her, said she wanted not a thing but thanks so much, and she went to the sofa. She sat and waited for Hayley's mom to do the same. To make sure her mom did just that, Hayley went into the living room and planted herself in the rocking chair that her father could no longer use.

Rhonda patted the sofa next to her, an indication of where she wanted Julie to sit. When Hayley's mom had done this, Rhonda gave them the news. First of all, she said, Brooke was extremely upset about having Seth Darrow cart her to the clinic, so Rhonda hadn't told her much because she didn't want to increase the girl's distress. Besides, at this point, only tests were going to be able to pinpoint the exact nature of the problem. But her symptoms suggested a bleeding ulcer, so this was a medical emergency.

"It's an ulcer that's gone untreated," Rhonda explained. "If it isn't dealt with very soon, it can penetrate the lining of the stomach. That permits undigested food and stomach acids to enter the abdominal cavity." Rhonda placed her hand on her own stomach as if in demonstration. "When that happens, the problem becomes acute."

Julie clutched her hands in her lap. "She's been different for months. But I told myself it was her age. Thirteen and you know how difficult children get when they reach adolescence and I thought . . . She kept eating and eating." Julie cleared her throat. Hayley knew very well that her mom didn't want to cry in front of Rhonda Mathieson. After a moment, Julie said, "She never said a word. I've completely failed her."

Hastily Rhonda covered Julie's clutched hands with her own. "Brooke didn't *want* you to know. She herself doesn't know the extent of the problem because I'm not entirely sure. As I said, only tests can tell us, but the eating indicates . . . It would actually have made her stomach feel better to have food in it."

"What kind of tests?" Hayley asked.

"It's called an endoscopy. This'll show the surgeon—"

"Surgery?" Julie's voice wavered.

Rhonda scooted over and put her arm around Julie's shoulder. She waited a moment to explain further: a plastic tube down into Brooke's stomach would contain a probe; the probe would show if there was a bleeding ulcer; the surgeon would use electricity or heat or clips to stop the bleeding, a medical glue would minimize the chance of an occurrence of more bleeding in the future. But there could also be the need for abdominal surgery if the bleeding couldn't be stopped in this way.

"But," Rhonda added quickly when Julie's expression showed horror, "this is at the absolute furthest extreme. The important point is that we need to be proactive. I'd like to set up an appointment for tomorrow. She could go to the emergency room in Coupeville right now, but I think we're okay waiting till the morning."

"No frigging way!"

They swung to where Brooke was standing. She'd come back down the stairs. She was completely white faced.

"I won't," she announced.

"Sweetheart," Rhonda said carefully. "There isn't an option here. If we don't—"

"I said I won't and I *won't*."

Julie rose and went toward her. She said, "You needed to tell me. Brookie, this is dangerous, and I don't understand why—"

"It doesn't matter!" Brooke shouted.

Julie stopped in her tracks. "How on earth can you say—"

"You can't make me. I *won't*," she shrieked. She turned and fled, crying, "Just let me die!"

Rhonda said nothing. Hayley felt tears coming. Thirteen years old, she thought. And then she said to herself that enough was enough.

"Mrs. Mathieson." Hayley didn't know if she could but she knew she had to. Rhonda turned to her, and her face was perplexed but open and willing to listen. Hayley hoped she was also willing to do more. "My dad," she began.

"Don't," Julie said.

Hayley went on. "My dad has ALS, Mrs. Mathieson. Lou Gehrig's disease? ALS. He's going to die. Our family doesn't have medical insurance. And we need help."

THERE WAS NO further discussion over what to do. The Cartwrights would do what had to be done. As to how to pay for it all in a situation in which the family was holding life together with glue and shoe laces and far too much pride . . . ? Rhonda said to them that there were ways. For goodness sakes, Rhonda said, even if the government rejected their obvious need—which was highly unlikely—this was South Whidbey, a place where people helped each other, where fund-raisers were a weekly occurrence, and where—"for God's sake, Julie," she said—there was an organization long established to help people with their medical bills. It was time for action for the Cartwright family and, like it or not, it was time to face facts.

When the phone rang later in the day, Hayley assumed it would be her mother letting them all know what was happening with Brooke. But it turned out that the caller was Parker Natalia, who said when he heard Hayley's voice, "Don't hang up on me, Hayley. I've got a message for Becca, is all."

She wanted to ask him why he didn't call Ralph Darrow's house if he had a message for Becca. Better yet, why didn't he just walk over to the house from the woods? But it turned out that he was in Canada, back in Nelson, where he'd been since two days after Isis Martin had fatally crashed her car. "The sheriff more or less invited me to leave," he told her. "I shouldn't have outstayed my visa."

Hayley didn't know what to say to him. He'd phoned once, after Isis had been killed, but she hadn't returned his call. She'd been drawn to him, true. Chances were she would still be drawn to him if she saw him. But she didn't really want to be drawn to Parker Natalia right now. So she'd avoided him.

Now, she couldn't. So she said, "Sure. I'll give her the message."

It was simple enough. He'd asked around: his friends, his relatives, his old band mates. No one knew Becca's cousin. "Tell her that doesn't mean she's not up here," he said. "Nelson's small. But it's a hell of a lot bigger than Langley. So I c'n keep asking around. I'll do the ad in the paper for her, too. Could you tell her that, Hayley?"

"I'll tell her."

And then it seemed there was nothing more to say, but when she was about to wish him well, he said, "Look. I've talked to

Seth. He let me know what's going on with your family. Your dad, your sister. The whole thing. And listen, Hayley, I just want to say I'm sorry. I added to your mess, and I didn't mean to do that. Maybe sometime you'll be able to . . . I don't know exactly. Maybe we can see each other again. Sometime. Not now, I know. But sometime."

She said, "It's okay. I think we both got used by Isis. It's not your fault."

"Except for the lying, which was totally my fault. I should've been straight with you. I panicked thinking that if you knew that I'd hooked up with Isis first, it would wreck things between you and me."

Hayley understood. But she wasn't really ready for what Parker Natalia had to offer. With him, it would only be a matter of time, and she didn't really need to have her consciousness clouded at the moment. She said, "I'm applying to colleges. Well, universities, really."

"Good going," he said and he sounded as if he meant it.

"I'm hoping for a place with a good environmental science program."

"Excellent," he said. "You go for it, Hayley."

That was it. They parted, if not as friends exactly, then as a man and woman in better understanding of who each of them was.

And that, Hayley decided, was pretty much all you could expect of life: understanding who you were and what made you tick and coming close to understanding others as well.

FIFTY-SEVEN

Becca told herself that, while it had been Laurel's plan to go to Nelson, she could have found another place along the way that seemed equally safe to her. If that was the case, any day Laurel could return to Whidbey ready to whisk Becca into a brave new world that she'd created for them both. Only . . . Becca had to admit that that possibility didn't make a lot of sense.

Nelson had been her intended destination, and there had been a rock solid reason for Laurel's choosing it. Laurel hadn't revealed that reason, but she was there, all right. She just was no longer Laurel. And if she didn't read the Nelson paper, how would she know that Becca was trying to reach her?

Becca wasn't sure what to do next aside from checking up on Jeff Corrie. She found that Connor West's return had triggered all sorts of stories in the San Diego paper. Jeff was "cooperating fully" according to the paper, and this meant on the receiving end of his cooperation were the San Diego police, the IRS, the FBI, and anyone else who wanted to ask him questions about his investment firm. Before, he'd lawyered up because he believed that he was being railroaded with respect to Connor's disappearance. Now that Connor had been found and returned to San Diego, the situation was different and "If you look at the lifestyles of these two men," his lawyer intoned, "you can see who bears most of the responsibility for what occurred at Corrie West Investments. Mr. Corrie has, however, voluntarily put his house on the market and has done the same with his second home in Mammoth Mountain Resort. He's sold his Porsche and he has placed all his stocks, bonds, and mutual funds in an escrow account. He is intent upon making financial amends in every way possible."

What Jeff was really doing, Becca thought with a cynical smile, was trying to keep himself out of prison. The one pleasant consideration in the midst of all that was happening was that Jeff Corrie was going to be very busy in San Diego for quite a while.

As for Becca herself? She knew that she was back to waiting.

ONE STRETCH OF waiting came to an end once the case was closed on all the arsons. Derric told her that he was ready to see Rejoice. His whispers indicated that Isis's death and her attempt to involve her brother in a string of arsons had shaken him deeply. Brothers and sisters were supposed to love each other, his whispers seemed to be saying. Becca only hoped that she was interpreting those whispers correctly this time.

She said, "That's great."

As if she sounded too enthusiastic, he held up his hands and said, "I only want to *see* her, though."

"Sure. See her." She'd been carrying around the address and phone number of Broad Valley Growers since the day she'd got it. She dropped her backpack to the floor near her school locker, and she dumped it out and went through everything till she found it inside her geometry textbook. She handed it over and said, "Here you go," and she pressed her lips together to keep herself from asking when, where, and how he was going to do whatever it was he was going to do.

He glanced at it, folded it, and put it into his wallet. He engaged her eyes in that way he had and said, "I don't need you to protect me or anything but I want you to be there when I see her."

Becca felt a rush of pleasure. "Sure thing," she told him. "Just tell me when you want to go."

He said, to her surprise, "Saturday?"

"I'll make that work," she told him.

"I MIGHT HURL," was how Derric described his state as they approached Broad Valley Growers at two o'clock on Saturday. They'd not phoned in advance because Derric had said he didn't have the nerve. He said that they would take their chances. If she was there, she was there. If not, they'd come back.

The place was gussied up for Thanksgiving, less than a week away. When they parked the car and got out, it was to see the porch decked out in autumn finery, gourds of every shape and color tumbling down the steps. A large sign reading PIE ORDERS BEING TAKEN was out by the road. The scent of them was in the air, along with hot apple cider that seemed to be floating from the trees.

As before, dogs shot out of the house. They were followed soon after by Darla Vickland. She remembered Becca by face but not by name. She said, "Hello, Whidbey Island girl. I saw you drive up." She regarded Derric in a friendly fashion with her expression bright and curious.

Becca and Derric had agreed that Becca would do the initial talking. So she said, "It's Becca King? I was here with Seth Darrow and his dog?"

"Gus," Darla said. "That's pretty bad. I remember the dog's name but not yours."

Becca smiled. "It's hard to forget Gus. Anyways, when we were here, I couldn't help noticing that all your kids were . . ." She paused because she wasn't sure how to put it.

Darla did it for her. "A real mixed bag, huh? We go to church, we look like the United Nations. And I got a feeling I know where you're heading." She nodded at Derric and said to him, "What part of Africa?"

"Uganda," he told her, as well as his first name. "Kampala."

Her eyes widened. "You don't say," was her comment.

Derric went on. "Becca told me there's a girl here who's from Africa too. You know, this sounds sort of strange I bet, but where I am out on Whidbey . . . the south part of the island . . . there's not a heck of a lot of Africans."

"It's mostly Wonder Bread," was how Becca put it. "So when I saw your daughter . . ."

"You're talking about our girl Rejoice," Darla said. "She's from

Kampala too. She came to us through a group at our church."

"I thought it'd be nice for Derric to meet her," Becca said.

Darla shot Derric a look. "She's too young to date. My girls don't step out with a young man before they're sixteen. I'm old-fashioned that way, but I don't believe in buying trouble."

Derric said hastily, "I don't want to date her. Me and Becca? We're . . . well, we're together."

"For a year," Becca added.

Darla smiled at this. "I suppose I c'n let you look in on our Rejoice without worrying too much, then."

"Is she here?" Becca asked.

"Just now, as it happens," Darla said and nodded the way they had come. "Eye appointments this morning in La Conner for the whole crew of them. But they're just back."

Derric and Becca swung around. A clunky old van was pulling into the farm yard. It stopped with a jerk, and while the engine was coughing, the door slid open.

Becca felt Derric take her hand. She looked at him and squeezed his fingers. She turned back to the van. The kids had tumbled out, talking and laughing. Rejoice was there among them. She wore a scarf like a turban on her head. She also had on those strange plastic sun shields that eye doctors give their patients when they've had their pupils dilated. Her brothers and sisters were wearing them as well. So was their dad. This, it seemed, was the source of their joking.

They came toward the house, but then Rejoice fell back. She paused for a moment, staring at Becca and Derric. Mostly at Derric, Becca decided. And Derric stared right back.

Becca heard him murmur so that only she could hear. "I have a sister."

"You sure do."

THEY STOPPED IN Coupeville on their way home. The little Victorian town was awash with lights, its colorful houses and commercial buildings like Christmas packages against a landscape that fell to the oblong shadow of Penn Cove, where oysters and mussels gave the town its reputation. No one was there at this time of day, aside from inside the restaurants. Like Langley, Coupeville rolled up its sidewalks just after five in the afternoon. What life remained in the town was behind closed doors in its B & Bs, its single old bar called Toby's, and its eateries.

The town's pier stretched out into the cove, and near this pier Derric parked the Forester. They walked the pier's length, moving from one pool of light to the next as birds settled for the night and a sharp breeze blew at them over the water, bringing the scent of brine. Across the cove, lights blinked from the houses. A fire had been lit somewhere, and its scent was sharp in the air.

They were heading for the café at the pier's end. Neither of them was ready to go home yet. Becca had left Ralph Darrow a meal to heat up in the microwave, and Derric's mom and dad knew he had a date. They had hours before them and they wanted to talk about what had occurred at Broad Valley Growers.

After pausing in surprise at the sight of someone who, like

her, was clearly from Africa, Rejoice had smiled and had come toward them in something of a rush. She passed her siblings and strode up to Derric. "The saxophone boy!" she cried. "You were in the band. You had the biggest smile ever. We loved to climb all over you. 'Specially Kianga and I. And you let us. You never pushed us away. Only . . . I can't remember your name."

"Derric," he said. "I remember you too."

She laughed joyously. "Oh my God, this is so cool!" And then she took note of Becca, saying, "You were here with that dog. And the guy with the ear gauges."

"Becca King," Becca said. "When I saw you, I could tell you were from Africa and I thought Derric'd like to meet you."

"The coolest *ever*," Rejoice exclaimed. "Mom, did you know . . . ?"

Darla Vickland shook her head. "These two just showed up."

Her husband said, "This calls for pie, I think."

One of the other kids said, "Dad says everything calls for pie."

They all laughed. Darla invited Derric and Becca into the house, and Rejoice locked arms with the boy she didn't know was her brother. She said, "Wow. I hope Kianga shows up some-day too."

Now, on the end of the pier in Coupeville, Derric and Becca entered the café. They hadn't talked much on the drive. There was a lot to say, but Becca knew it could wait. They ordered burg-ers, sweet potato fries, and Cokes when the waitress came. When she went to get their drinks, Derric looked long at Becca.

He said to her, "You feel closer to me than I ever expected anyone to be."

"That's a good thing, isn't it?"

"It's good. And I want this—what we have—never to end. Problem is that I screw up a lot."

"We'll both screw up now and then, don't you think?"

"I want there to be no secrets between us, Becca. Not after today. If it hadn't been for you and everything you've tried to do and tried to make *me* do, I'd never have found her. But I did, only because of you."

He looked so earnest. He was so loving. Becca thought how good it would be for him to know everything about her from A to Z. Only, how could she tell him the A to Z when it began with whispers, when it coursed through the major screwup of her life, and when she had no idea where her story was likely to end? What else would she discover about herself? The whispers had been in place for years. The memory pictures were something new. And then there was the quickening. How could she explain that?

So she said, "Stuff just unfolds, don't you think? And we need to be there—like, to be present—for the unfolding."

Derric nodded. Still, he gazed at her. She had the feeling he was looking into her soul, and she wished like anything she wasn't using the AUD box. But a promise to herself was a promise to herself, and she'd promised herself that Derric would have the privacy he needed to sort through his thoughts.

He said, "I got to tell you something. It's about Courtney Baker. You know. When we were together last year? When you and I were broken up?"

Becca said, "You don't need to tell me. And anyway, I think I already know."

He was silent. He looked beyond her, to the windows through which the town lights made a string like a necklace along the main street at the land end of the pier. He seemed to be getting his courage up about something and Becca wanted to tell him that enough had been said. But then he went on with, "I just wish it'd been you. It was s'posed to be you but I was too dumb to know it at the time."

"It'll be me eventually."

He turned back to her. "When?"

"I guess when I'm not so scared that it'll change things between us." She thought of her mom, of her many stepfathers, of what Laurel's passion for men and her need to be taken care of by a man had done to their lives. "'Cause that's what sex does," she continued. "It changes things, Derric."

"It doesn't have to."

"How can it not? Nothing stays the same, and this . . . you and me and sex . . . It's something important. At least, that's how I want it to be. Not like you and me in the backseat of the Forester or whatever. And not like you and me unprepared for the consequences. But you and me making a decision. We decide. I get on the pill. We act like rational human beings who want to take the next step."

He thought about this. For a moment Becca thought he was going to say that he couldn't wait, that for God's sake he was seventeen and did she have any idea what it meant to be seventeen and male? But he surprised her. He said, "It was only one time with Courtney. After we did it, I felt . . . It was like being empty. Nothing was planned. We'd gone to this Bible group and I figured we were going to talk about *not* doing it. Only, I wanted to do it anyway and I guess she did too. But after . . . We broke up a couple of days later. She thought it was because I'd gotten what I wanted, but that wasn't it at all."

Becca found that his words didn't hurt as much as she'd expected them to. She nodded and was only thankful that he didn't feel it was necessary for her to talk at that point.

Then he said, "I guess you're right. It does change things." Then he smiled that Derric smile of his, the same one his sister, Rejoice, had smiled when she'd first seen the saxophone boy standing in her family's farm yard. "You know, you're pretty smart for a girl," he said. "I'd like to hang with you for a while if that's okay."

It definitely was.

THE PROPERTY LIGHTS were on when Derric and Becca drove up the incline of Ralph Darrow's driveway. The trail lights were also on as they wended their way around the hillock. But the house below the hillock was dark, and Becca would have thought that Ralph was not at home except his truck was in its regular place and the hour suggested he had probably already gone to bed. On the porch, she kissed Derric fondly and went inside the house with a wave goodbye.

If Ralph was asleep, she didn't want to take the chance of waking him up, so Becca didn't turn on any lights. She knew the place well enough to find her way to her room and besides, there was still a glow in the fireplace where embers told her that Ralph was probably at home. She began to cross the room toward the hall that would take her to the back of the house. But she stumbled against Ralph's armchair.

He was sitting in it in absolute silence. She gave a cry of surprise, but then she saw that he was asleep. It was a deep sleep if she hadn't awakened him, but she didn't want to leave him there till morning because she knew what a grump he'd be if he woke up all stiff. So she reached for the light next to his chair to rouse him. She put her hand on his shoulder and said his name and when the light fell on his face, she saw that something was very wrong.

His eyes were open halfway. His face was gray. One side of it pulled down in what looked like a sneer.

She said, "Mr. Darrow? Grand?" He did not respond.

She saw then that he had the receiver of the cordless phone in his hand. He'd had his dinner by the fire because his empty plate was by his chair on the floor, but there was nothing else. No book, no game of chess set up, no magazine, nothing. Just the phone in his hand and she grabbed it from him.

She saw from the screen that he'd dialed nine and one and that's all. And she understood he'd been trying to call for help.

She cried out once, but then she made the emergency call. When that was done, she immediately called Seth.

FIFTY-EIGHT

Seth came out of the hospital and looked around. He saw Prynne sitting on a bench beneath a sugar maple on one side of the parking lot, and he walked over to her. She stood when he reached her.

His throat hurt, so tight it was with everything he'd been holding in. The last thing he wanted to do was to cry, so he concentrated on Prynne. "Aren't you cold? Why'd you come outside?"

"Better energy out here," she said to him. "I wanted to send him whatever I could. What's happening?"

"Dad's calling everyone. My sister, my aunt, all my great-uncles. Nieces, nephews, you name 'em. They're coming."

Prynne gazed up at his face. "But he was breathing, right? Becca said he was breathing. She said his eyes were open. She said . . . Oh Seth, I'm sorry. It's a stroke, right?"

Seth nodded. He went to sit on the bench and he stared at the ground. "I don't want him to die," he said.

Prynne dropped beside him. She put her arm around him and roughly kissed the side of his head. "He *won't*. What happens next?"

"They said the next twenty-four hours will tell them a lot. If he makes it, he'll . . . God, it'll kill him to go into rehab. Or . . . What if he can't live at home anymore? Prynne, he's lived there for more'n forty years. If they make him leave, it'll kill his spirit. It'll—"

"You're getting ahead of yourself," Prynne said. "Maybe this whole situation is something you guys need to take one hour at a time. D'you think?"

He met her earnest gaze. "Yeah. I think."

SETH PICKED UP his sister at the Whidbey-SeaTac Shuttle late the next morning. She'd managed to get the first flight out of San Jose. Prynne was with him still, and he introduced them but Sarah hardly noticed that Prynne was a female and probably Seth's girlfriend because her mind was completely on their grandfather. He was holding on, Seth told her.

"Everyone's at the house," he said.

He meant his parents' place. It was larger than Ralph's and large was needed because Seth and Sarah's aunt Brenda had arrived on the scene, and Aunt Brenda required space to spread out the fullness of her response to her father's condition. This response so far involved a lot of shouting and insisting that "plans" had to be made at once. The great uncles were all there, Ralph's four brothers along with their wives. Along with Seth's mom and dad, the house was teeming with people.

All of them had opinions about what should happen next, but

Brenda was insisting that "as the oldest child of the patient in question," her opinion on the matter held sway. She'd been arguing vociferously for permanent assisted living. They needed to sell Ralph Darrow's property in order to maintain his life in a way that was comfortable, she said.

"You're out of your mind," was how Seth's dad greeted this. Ralph Darrow's brothers joined him in this opinion. "It's too soon to be making decisions like that."

That point didn't deter Brenda, who spoke of gaining conservatorship over her father. Nor did Brenda deter Seth's dad, who suggested that they have a look inside Ralph's safe deposit box at the bank in Freeland, to which he—and not Brenda—was a signatory. That enflamed Brenda, so she began to talk of attorneys. Seth's father said no one had *ever* been able to talk to his sister, and he'd stormed outside.

Seth and Prynne had left at that juncture to pick up Sarah. He didn't particularly want to go back.

Sarah said, "Take me to Grand's."

This was fine by Seth. He wanted to see how Becca was doing. She'd wanted to go to the hospital with the family on the previous night, but Seth had told her to stay at Ralph's and to watch Gus, if she would. He didn't know how long he'd be at the hospital, so he couldn't take the dog.

When they got to Ralph Darrow's place, Gus came charging up from the garden. Becca had been keeping an eye on him from the porch along with Derric Mathieson. They rose from two of the chairs and came to the front steps.

Poor Becca looked like someone who hadn't slept in days. She was still wearing what she'd had on the previous night, and her hair was uncombed and standing up at weird angles. She said, "How is he? What's . . . ?" but didn't seem to want to go on. She was wearing her hearing device and she pulled it from her ear in what looked like a gesture of frustration but then she shuddered for some reason and put it back in.

Seth introduced her and Derric to his sister. Then he said, "He's the same. I guess it's okay because he didn't . . . you know."

Becca said, "I should've been here. I was supposed to be here. I mean, he knew we were going to La Conner and I'd left him dinner and he'd heated it like I told him to and he'd eaten it because I saw the dish on the floor next to his chair. But if I'd been home—"

"You could've been in your room studying," Seth said. "You could've gone to bed. You could've been sitting on the front porch with Derric. Sure, if you'd been in the living room with him you could've grabbed the phone and made the call but what were the chances of that, Beck? Don't blame yourself."

"What's going to happen?" Becca directed the question to all of them in general, but Seth was the one to answer.

"Right now they're all fighting. My dad, my aunt, Grand's brothers. What to do next and everyone wants something different."

"So what's gonna happen?"

"Nothing for now. No way's my dad letting Aunt Brenda sell this place and—"

"*Sell* it?"

"That's what she wants to do."

"But no one even knows what's going to happen to him right now," Derric pointed out.

"Which is why," Sarah said presciently, "there's going to be one hell of a fight in the Darrow clan."

SETH RAN INTO Hayley that afternoon. He and Prynne were just coming out of the hospital, having left Sarah at Ralph Darrow's bedside. Like Seth's, Sarah's position was simple. No one was sending Ralph Darrow anywhere.

At first, Seth thought Hayley was also there because of his grandfather. But it turned out she was there because of Brooke, who was inside and being taken care of. Hayley explained what was going on. Then, with a glance at Prynne, who was listening sympathetically, she said, "Thanks, Seth. For taking her to the clinic."

He said, "It's cool. She just didn't want anyone to know she was feeling rotten. And you guys have so much going on. How were you s'posed to figure the whole thing out?"

Hayley didn't look unburdened. She said, "I guess," in a quiet voice that made Prynne say gently, "But what else, Hayley?"

Hayley gave a shaky smile. She brought her fingers to her lips, and behind them she said, "Brooke knew there's no medical insurance. Derric's mom says there's a group on the island to help people with medical bills, but that's a drop in the bucket at this point unless we do something like . . . Medicaid . . . Welfare. Dad should be on disability, but he's been so stubborn. Like getting on disability will be admitting . . . You know."

Seth wanted to say that he could help her, but he knew he couldn't, for the problem was vaster than Brooke's bleeding ulcer and Hayley's dad's condition. There was also the farm.

Hayley said, as if reading this on his face, "We're going to have to sell. It'll kill my dad. The farm was his great-grandparents' place. But there's no choice. There's just not enough money. I thought if I didn't go to college—"

"You can't do that, Hayley."

"—it might make a difference, but it really won't. Nothing will."

Prynne put her hand on Hayley's arm. She said, "I was talking to Seth about getting through one hour at a time for now. Maybe that's what you guys need to do."

"There aren't enough hours," Hayley replied.

ON THEIR WAY back from the hospital, it had been the plan to take Prynne to the ferry so that she could go home to Port Gamble. But instead she asked if Seth would mind taking her to Smugglers Cove Farm and Flowers instead. She said, "I've been tossing an idea around about that place, Seth. I think there's a simple solution. Not an easy one, but a simple one."

So he took her there. But she didn't have him drive her all the way up to the house. Instead she asked him to stop by the chicken barn. At first he thought she was going to make a suggestion about the chickens or perhaps the barn. But instead, when Prynne got out of the car, she walked to the east of the barn. There she looked out into the fields. They were, as they had been for the last twenty-four months or so, lying fallow. They were useless at the moment, good for nothing but weeds.

That, it turned out, was Prynne's point exactly. "Nothing grows better than weeds," she said.

At first Seth thought she was totally nuts. They were supposed to support themselves growing weeds?

Prynne smiled as if she read his expression. "It's legal now. And there's a huge need for THC. Every day they discover another use for it, Seth. It won't be easy because unless the law changes, it's going to take greenhouses and they'll have to get the state government involved to make sure everything's on the up and up. But the exposure here? They must get at least twelve hours of sun six or eight months of the year. So how tough do you think it's going to be, finding people who're gonna be willing to invest in the biggest cash crop this state is poised to produce?"

"Not *weeds*," Seth said. "You're talking about weed."

"Now that it's completely legal in the state, someone's going to grow it. Why shouldn't it be the Cartwrights?"

He looked out at the fields. He could picture them with their future greenhouses, greenhouses that he would help build. With the state's approval and marijuana now legal and medical marijuana in high demand . . . Prynne was right. Someone was going to grow it. Why shouldn't it be the Cartwright family?

He turned and grabbed her by her shoulders. He kissed her soundly. "I think I got luckier than I've ever been in my entire life when I went to Port Townsend to hear you play the fiddle," he said.

"I don't exactly disagree," she told him. She stepped into his arms and kissed him back.

7/15, 1/17, 12/17